The Old Rugged Double Cross

Jonathan Thomas Stratman

~ For Vernelle ~

The characters in this book are fictitious, and any
resemblance to actual persons is coincidental.

CHAPTER 1

I stood at the bar in the Bide-A-While tavern, sipping a Coke when I first met the brother of my good friend William Stoltz. In fact, it was William who introduced us. "My brother, Vadim." Vah-deem, as William pronounced it.

I spent my previous visit to the Bide-A-While trying, with marginal success, to save a gunshot victim bleeding out on the floor. This was better.

It was late afternoon—quitting time—though in a town with no industry, nobody really worked fixed hours. There were maybe twenty people in the place, six of them women—counting Alice, the bartender—gathered in couples and small groups, drinking, smoking, and talking too loudly, to be heard over the jukebox. Only one sat alone, an old stinky trapper who came in to nurse his beer-a-day in exchange for sweeping the place out.

There was nobody dressed up in here. It was after breakup, late spring, so no parkas or mukluks. The men and women wore chinos or denim pants, sturdy shoes or work boots, a jacket or a flannel shirt, with a felt hat or tied kerchief around the hair, as was appropriate. Most were smoking—cigarettes, cigars, even a pipe or two—and the silvery air swirled and danced.

Two years earlier I had come to the small Alaska town of Chandalar—near Nenana and about eighty miles south of Fairbanks—as mission priest. I'd buried victims of gunshot, freezing, drowning, moose, and the train. One actually died of old age. And I'd been thrown off a sternwheeler, jumped off a very high bridge, and shot at several times.

1

But I'd worked hard to not be *cheechako*—a greenhorn—had made friends and even fallen in love again. Evie and I planned to marry in late summer. This confuses people when they learn I'm an Episcopal priest. But unlike Roman Catholics, we marry.

So, it had been a very difficult two years, but looking down the polished mahogany bar at friends, friends of friends, and now William's brother visiting from our so-called Cold War enemy, Soviet Russia, I couldn't think of a single place I'd rather be.

The Bide-A-While wasn't a big place. The varnished knotty-pine walls, now dulled by time and cigarette smoke, were decorated with various beer posters. A lit Schlitz clock permanently indicated five o'clock, quitting time, or "beer o'clock," as they like to say around here. I asked Alice why they didn't throw it away. She made a face, pulled back to look at me and cocked her head, like I'd suggested we run up Main Street naked together.

"Customers like the light," she said. "Besides, it's right twice a day!"

The bar ran down much of one side of the room, with two small high windows on the other side. A back door led to a storeroom down a short hall with two tiny bathrooms—what the British call "water closets," appropriate because neither of these was any bigger than a closet and you certainly couldn't get a bath there.

At one end of the room, set in its own space like an altar, stood the large, colorfully lit Wurlitzer jukebox, just at that moment pounding out *Rock Around the Clock*, by Bill Haley and His Comets. I felt the bass line vibrating up from the floor through my shoes and I knew that people passing on the street wouldn't hear the other instruments, just the bass.

Vadim raised his stubby brown bottle to toast the group and took a long drink. Seeming to like American beer, it was more like he tipped his head back and poured it down his open throat. He stood as tall as William, about six-two. I guessed half-brother, because except for height, they had no physical traits in common. William, blue eyed to Vadim's brown. William, with his deceptively thin, wiry frame to Vadim's serious bulk—solid as a slab of hanging moose meat. William, with pale complexion, and quiet, next to nut-brown Vadim and his snorts, laughs, and outrageous mugging.

Earlier in the year, I had guessed something about William: that he was more than the school custodian he claimed to be, and in fact more than the Russian spy we had previously thought him to be. He had layers like an onion, and finally at the bottom—as far as we knew—he actually turned out to be an agent for the U.S. Government. He was loosely assigned to security for the DEW Line RADAR station currently being constructed just south of here, at the small railroad settlement of Clear.

Of his brother's visit, William said, "He thinks I am a janitor. He needs to keep thinking that." And then he added, "We do not trust Soviets."

"Even if one of them is your brother?"

William looked at me. "*Especially* if one is your brother."

"He has long dreamed of visiting me here... seeing Alaska," William explained to the knot of us, his friends. It was Evie and me, along with Andy Silas—my first Chandalar friend—and Andy's soon-to-be-bride, Rosie Jimmy. "I cannot imagine what strings he must pull to get out of Russia now," William confided. "He says he will be

3

here about six weeks and wants very badly to pan gold and strike it rich."

"Find gold!" Vadim toasted with his bottle of Olympia. "Go back to Mother Russia a *big* shoot!"

"Shot," said William.

And then there was Alice. When Vadim glimpsed Alice Young, William's steady companion and the Bide-A-While bartender, it stopped him cold and I swear I saw him lick his lips. He set down his beer, placed both hands on the mahogany bar top, and stopped talking mid-sentence. He just stared.

To be sure, Alice was something to stare at. Though only about five-four, a thin-framed strawberry blond, Alice had—and celebrated—a pair of disproportionately sized breasts, forced up and nearly out of the scooped neck of her jade-green dress. As she moved back and forth behind the bar, bending, stooping, lifting, serving, her breasts shifted and shimmied with a hypnotic rhythm all their own. Evie says it's just Alice's 'push-em up' bra. Maybe.

In Alaska, where men easily outnumber women, and any sensible woman did anything possible to cover up, Alice Young enjoyed being the exception. Probably as a result, her business was booming. I'd heard that men nearly as big as Vadim came in with a date and left alone, "cross-eyed, stammering and drooling." We didn't get many women that outrageous this far north.

If William noticed his brother's reaction—and William didn't usually miss much—he didn't let on. I'd wonder about that later.

4

CHAPTER 2

By the end of my first two weeks in Chandalar, I could already identify people from 'outside'—the Lower Forty-eight. We'd had an influx of newcomers lately, what with the buildup at the Clear RADAR station, and I was looking at four of them now. On a Saturday morning in late May, with Evie expected to show up for breakfast—brunch—since she liked to sleep in, I'd walked the few blocks to the general store for eggs.

They had at least one of everything, under a high decorative ceiling of pressed tin. The air hung sweet with old scents of kitchen spices, rubber tires, wax on the polished wood floors, gun oil, and mothballs. Just walking to the egg cooler in the back, an assortment of treasures caught my eye, different each time I came in. I noticed stateside Wonder Bread, varied sizes of beaver traps, an array of Buck knives, railroad pocket watches, cans of matzo balls, corn, peas—all kinds of beans—and a small display of guitar strings.

The four outsiders were ahead of me in line, obviously together. Gary, the checker, only works at one speed so I had time to study them while I waited. They all wore a handgun—three on the hip and one in a shoulder holster. They carried long knives, in sheaths on belts or boots, and each carried a small pack. They wore Filson, the good stuff, the water-resistant hats and jackets, and all with the 'new' sheen still on. So, they had probably gone to Filson in Seattle, just to make this trip. Gary rang up their carton of Luckys and a six pack of Olympia, the stubbies.

"That's four dollars," he said.

One of them dug deep in his trouser pocket for a wad of cash, peeling off four ones, which he placed on the counter.

"Where you fellas from?" asked Gary.

"Fairbanks," said the man. He was taller than me by a good six inches. In fact, they all stood about six-two. A matched set. This one had an unfortunate pair of ears, mounted like sugar-bowl handles low on the sides of his head, with lobes as big as my thumb.

"No," said Gary, "I mean, where you *from*? From the States, right?"

"Fairbanks!" said Big Ears more forcefully, and they all stepped back a little and looked around, like other store patrons might be closing in on them. The place was empty except for me, standing with my egg carton. Big Ears snatched up the cigarettes and beer, gave Gary a hard look, and the four headed out.

Gary looked my way and our eyes met. I said what I knew he was thinking. "Not Fairbanks." He nodded, picked up the bills and waved them in my direction.

"Paper one-dollar bills," he said. "Damn lying cheechakos. Just the eggs?"

"Yep." I handed him a silver dollar—there were darn few paper dollars in circulation in Interior Alaska—and he gave me a quarter back. Paper one-dollar bills were a giveaway that the bearer had just arrived from somewhere, but not Alaska.

"Seventy-five cents?" I asked him. "For a dozen eggs?"

He laughed. "Could sell 'em to you cheaper, but you'd have to pick 'em up in Seattle."

"Funny," I said. "See you Sunday."

6

"Don't start without me." He laughed again, having never darkened the church door.

Walking back, skirting big puddles and even wading in places, I wondered about the four big *cheechakos*. Alaska's storied 'last frontier' image drew greenhorns like them by the Jeepload. They'd come up to hunt in season—though this wasn't hunting season—to pan for gold, or just to irritate the locals and the wild animals.

Only last summer, a woman with a tour group laid herself down in the woods for a nap, like she was in some city park somewhere. She didn't wake up until a black bear sank its teeth into her thigh. I'd be glad when it got melted and dry enough, to even think about lying down for a nap, not that I'd do it around here.

The record books will show that ice on the Tanana River broke up at Nenana on May 5, with nearly three hundred thousand dollars riding on the exact day, hour, and minute. In just about thirty minutes, winter swept away, along with the river ice—and spring, 1957, came flowing right in behind it. As sometimes happens, an ice dam downstream quickly caused the river to back up, flooding both Nenana and our town, nearby Chandalar, with calf-deep muddy water.

For me, the best part about this breakup was not being caught out on the ice when it started to move. Last year, the river ice tried hard to go out beneath me as I walked across. And it very nearly succeeded. The memory still ran deep and dark in my dreams.

Kids love this still-chilly flood time, building rafts, poling around town in 'borrowed' canoes—splashing, falling in a lot. For adults, it meant trying to get things done while wading around wearing knee or hip boots, sometimes through boot-sucking mud. It meant circling humped-up islands of dirty plow snow, boiling drinking water from our shallow wells, and staring longingly at seed catalogs, knowing that friends and relatives in the States already had their gardens in, up, and greening. My garden looked like an estuary.

But as the river ice swept away, grass, new leaves and sprouts of greenery, came rushing in behind, some plants even pushing up through snow like spring just couldn't wait.

Turning my corner, I saw a couple walking, talking, just passing through the intersection one block distant, one of them very tall and one quite small. They were wading the muddy streets as we all did, the town's only sidewalks extending no farther than Main Street. I could see them clearly, Vadim and Alice Young, strolling, talking, heads down, intent. *Why not?* I knew William had been called to Fairbanks. What were they supposed to do by themselves? Sit in their bedrooms and read? And yet something about it bothered me.

Evie showed up at eleven with Andy. She kissed me. "Aw, get a room, you guys," said Andy, shielding his eyes from our debauchery as he made a beeline, squeezing around us in my small kitchen to get to the coffee. "This better be the good stuff!"

The good stuff would be the special-order coffee he imported from a roaster he'd found in Italy on a recent trip. A sniper in Italy during the European war, Andy came back to Alaska with a positive passion for anything Italian—especially coffee. He'd since opened his own Italian restaurant in Fairbanks, Central Alaska's first, was doing well and he certainly looked happy.

Rosie played a big part in that happiness. The waitress owner of Chandalar's own Coffee Cup Café had been in love with Andy since before forever. Okay, since they were orphan children together at the old mission school just outside of town. She always thought that when the two of them grew up Andy would discover how he really felt about her and they'd get married, settle and raise a family. It was all good except for one tiny sticking point.

Turns out, and almost everybody in Chandalar knew this but Rosie, Andy is homosexual, what he calls 'gay.' Somehow in the end it hadn't mattered. Just about two months ago they'd walked into my office, settled themselves in the customer chairs, and announced that they planned to be married, start a life together, even have a child. Would they work it out? I thought so.

"He won't change," I told her at the time, and she turned to look at him.

"I don't want him to."

I snapped back into the moment as Andy poured a steaming mug of the 'good stuff' for each of us. He drank his black while Evie and I adulterated ours with a bit of sugar and evaporated milk from a Carnation can.

He sipped and sighed. "Ahhh."

Evie agreed. "Nothing tastes as good as the first sip of good coffee."

I felt the outsider in me watching them, as from a distance. Here in an Alaskan village, where people had to subsist on what they could hunt or grow, and so many people had so little, small treats and even small gestures of kindness loomed large.

"I brought bacon!" I came out of my reverie to see Andy waving the package at me.

"Real bacon?" I needn't have asked. It obviously was. It was just that none of us, even Andy who now lived in the metropolis of Fairbanks, had eaten much but moose meat for a long time. And now *bacon*. "Life is good," I told them, turning the knob on the propane range, striking a wooden kitchen match, and adjusting the yellow flame.

From the front door of the cabin came what I thought of as a medium knock—not the pounding emergency knock that meant someone had been shot, stabbed, or run over by the train. Nor was it the shy, skittery, I-really-don't-want-to-bother-you knock that I was sometimes not even sure I heard so much as sensed.

"I better get that." I turned the cast iron skillet handle toward Evie, who reached for it, only to be eased aside as Andy stepped in to cook. Always a good thing.

I found one of my occasional parishioners standing in my wanigan, poised to knock again. Arnold Gustafson wore rugged black dungarees with tall, red-rubber work boots on his feet. His heavy wool work shirt—red and black checked—revealed a waffled, white undershirt with a tuft of gray chest hair visible at the base of his throat. He had about a week of salt and pepper whiskers and wore a red felt hunting hat tipped back on his head. Hard of hearing, he tended to shout.

"Father," he roared at me without preamble, "I need your help."

It turned out someone he lived with—Jack—had disappeared. It sounded serious so I showed him into my office and got him settled in the customer chair.

"Has this happened... has he disappeared like this before?"

"Huh?" I repeated the question. He showed his teeth and sucked in a breath, noisily, while considering, then nodded. "Yes, sir, he has. But not for quite a while, and not for so long. And not without giving me some kind of warning he was headed out."

The smell of bacon frying came wafting in at my study door. Arnold raised his nose to sniff, like a husky. I saw him swallow. I knew he was salivating, because I was.

I yanked myself back into the moment. "That would be upsetting," I agreed. I drew a yellow lined tablet from my center desk drawer and a sharpened pencil from the Mason jar on my desk. "I guess I'd better get some details. Who is Jack?"

He cupped his hand behind his ear. "Huh? I guess I'd say Jack is... he's family." He sniffed the air again. I did too. It was hard not to.

"So, the last name is the same, Gustafson?" I shouted.

"Oh, yes."

"And..."

Evie appeared in my study doorframe.

"Sorry to interrupt, Father," she said, not so likely to call me Hardy or just 'hey you,' with a parishioner present. She met my eyes. "Your breakfast is ready."

Arnold and I simultaneously drew in deep breaths of the bacon aroma.

"I... um." I said to Evie, but was reluctant to leave my parishioner at this critical-seeming moment, even if there was bacon. "Mr. Gustafson has lost someone," I explained to her, "a family member, Jack. I think I should do this. You two go ahead."

She cocked her head to one side and turned to Arnold. She smiled at him, that disarming smile that I had begun to suspect launched ships and broke hearts, sometimes both at once.

"Arnie," she said a bit louder, "I need to talk with Father for just a minute."

"Sure." He rose graciously, waving me out of the office, wiping his lips on his sleeve. Now he was drooling.

11

Out in the hall Evie put an arm around my shoulder as she tipped her face close. "Breakfast is on the table," she explained quietly, patiently. "It's hot. You know how Andy is about eating his food while it's hot."

"But…" I protested, a little surprised at her callous attitude.

She smiled at me, kissed me, and leaned even closer, whispering gently, "Hardy, Jack is his *dog*."

I went back into my office, beckoned to Arnold to follow, and we all three headed to the kitchen, where there was extra bacon—I knew there would be—and we shared it with Arnold while he shouted to us about Whiskey Jack, his missing husky.

CHAPTER 3

Early on Monday, Andy and I drove the pickup to Arnold's small log cabin on the south side of Chandalar, where the trail leaves the road, doglegging—within twenty feet of where he sleeps—before heading up and over the railroad tracks. Spotting the truck from his window, Arnold met us in the yard. He approached hopefully, his eyes flicking to the pickup bed.

"Did you find 'im?"

"We been asking around," Andy assured him. "Everybody knows him but nobody's seen him. Thought we'd take a look out here."

Andy gestured at the trail and raised his voice. "Anybody been out on this?"

"Huh?" shouted Arnold. And then, "Nah, not since breakup. Ain't seen a soul. Nobody comes this way when it's warm."

We followed the trail, now a soggy mess, up and over the railroad tracks and off into muskeg, willow shoots and stunted black spruce. It didn't look like much now, but in winter was an established and still much-used dogsled route, part of the Old Mail Trail before airplanes took over postal delivery in the late '30s. With a good layer of snow and the ground frozen solid, this trail would beckon like an open highway.

It headed due south toward the Clear RADAR installation. Stretching from Greenland, across Canada and Alaska to the Bering Sea, these Distant Early Warning RADAR stations—and schoolchildren's 'duck and cover' drills—were all that stood between us and nuclear annihilation at the hands of the Soviets. Or so it seemed.

I fell in behind Andy, Arnold tailing me. "What are we looking for?" I asked.

"I dunno. A dead dog, maybe. Not unusual for a wandering dog to get caught in a rabbit snare or steel trap. Bait smells as good to them as any. Or maybe he caught the scent of a wolf in heat... went to join the party. Doesn't usually turn out so good for a town dog."

We splashed on for maybe twenty minutes before Andy raised his hand and we stopped. Both Arnold and I stretched to peer around him. "See something?"

"Yeah, sorta... but not a dog." He beckoned us up and pointed at the ground. "See that?" I didn't. I saw a trail surface lined with water and mud and interspersed with patches of green. "That!" He pointed again. "Not a dog track."

"Somebody's been through here," shouted Arnold, in my ear. "I never seen 'em!"

Andy tapped my arm. "This." He pointed with a boot toe at a patch of green. "Nothin' straight in the Bush."

I looked more closely and saw an impression in the green, with just a bit of it carrying over into the mud: the imprint of something square-edged and hard.

"Oh, yeah." Andy bent to look into a puddle. "Boot track left in the mud under water. Somebody *has* been through here, walkin' careful." He looked at me. "See it?"

"Just barely."

"Yeah," he said. "That's the odd part. Why hide footprints on a trail nobody uses this time of year? Who would do that?"

Arnold looked up to meet Andy's eyes. "Huh?" Andy said it again.

"Dognappers!" shouted Arnold.

* * *

14

On Tuesday morning, newcomers Victor Huxton and his wife, Linda turned up at my door.

"Call me Vic," he said. Come fall, he would teach a sixth-and-seventh-grade split at the Chandalar Public School where Evie taught. Linda planned to substitute. Most teachers arrived a week or so before Labor Day, but the Huxtons had decided to come north in the spring, to get to know parents and students and to experience an Alaskan summer before the cold set in.

They were both tall, fit, blond, and blue-eyed. They could easily have passed for brother and sister. He wore his hair in a crew cut and smoked a straight-stemmed pipe. She had a husky, sexy voice that made her easy to listen to. She wore hair to her shoulders and a pair of horn-rimmed eyeglasses, the kind that look like tortoise shell with round lenses. A bit old-fashioned, she probably thought they made her look more like a teacher and not so young.

While they had arrived early, their gear hadn't. Now they were stranded and chilly and temporarily needed more warmer clothing and some household items. The school superintendent sent them here to what we call 'the mission barrel,' used clothing and supplies sent from churches in the South Forty-eight. The Huxtons planned to buy enough to tide them over. Later, they'd bring the stuff back as a contribution when their own goods arrived. I told them we'd lend them what they needed, but they wouldn't hear of it.

"A good cause," they said. I admit I liked them right away.

When he found me fussing with the church's antiquated mimeograph, trying to print out a few half-sheet flyers about Arnold's dog, he rolled up his sleeves and we

15

got inky together while Linda sat on my sofa and caught up on my *Saturday Evening Post* collection, March being the most recent. She held up *The Post* cover for us to see, a slant of sunbeam catching, glittering on a ring she wore. The Norman Rockwell cover was one I'd admired, called "The Rookie," a locker room scene where the new, green kid, bat and glove in hand, meets the older baseball veterans.

She moved the magazine aside to peer around at us. "We're missing baseball season!"

Vic wiped the back of his hand across his forehead, in spite of his best efforts, leaving an ink smear. "Boy, don't I know it!"

I understood how they felt. My first baseball season up here had been long and lonely. It wasn't that we didn't get the games, we just didn't get them live. The radio would play recorded games, so we knew the score well before the first pitch. It takes a lot of the drama out of them.

Together we managed to crank the old beast into life, producing a much better-looking page than I'd seen for a while. I shook his hand—after he washed up—and they took a bunch of the fliers and a few thumbtacks to post on their way back to the teacherage.

"See you Sunday," Vic said, and I'll be darned if they didn't actually show up!

As May became June, I began to think about weddings. I had possibly two of them on the horizon... well, three if I counted my own. But I had two that were my direct responsibility, a nice change from funerals. At the same time, with the river level dropping and the land finally drying out, I could turn my attention fully to summer.

Starting the church tractor, an old Farmall Cub, was first on my list. The last two years, one of the church parishioners had come in and done it for me. Now he— also a teacher—had moved on and I was determined to do it myself. Back in Kentucky I'd stood under my share of shade trees staring at engine blocks. Oh sure, I could change spark plugs and oil, refill the radiator I drained last fall, and put in fresh gas, but that was about the extent of it. So, I was standing staring at the Farmall when Butch Neilson happened by, ready to work—or ready to volunteer—he really didn't seem to care as long as he had something to do.

He had come to Chandalar the year before, to meet a stepmother, nearly his own age, whom he'd never seen or previously even heard of. He and Adele, two lonely people, thought they wanted a son and a mother respectively, but discovered they just wanted each other. They fell in love and soon would marry. With him at about six-four and her at four-ten, they were easy to identify at a distance. And, often as not during the wet season, he would simply snatch her up and wade with her in his arms.

He saw me staring and came to stand alongside and stare too. After a few minutes he said, "Troubles?"

"Won't start. Dead as a doornail."

He peered at it. "There's no battery."

He was right, of course. There was only an empty rectangular tray where the battery should have been. Yes, I felt stupid.

"Could jump it."

"Jump it?"

"Hook it up to your truck. Use the truck battery. Or, you could crank it." He walked around to the crank, which

17

I now noticed protruding from the front of the engine. "You know how to crank one of these?"

"Grab it and turn it, I suppose..." I grabbed the crank, ready to give it a spin.

"Wait!"

"Wait?"

"I know something about these... went to school, actually." He looked a little proud. I knew that 'school' involved a period of time spent in the Ohio Penitentiary system.

"Grab it like this." He cupped the crank in his fingers, with his thumb down under the handle, next to his fingers, rather than up over the top like I'd done. "If you grab it in your fist with your thumb wrapped around—and it kicks back—*bang!* You break your wrist! I seen it happen a bunch."

So, we choked it and set the throttle. Butch grabbed the crank correctly, cranked it easily and, on the third spin, the Farmall coughed into life. We shook hands.

"Want me to plow this here?" he asked. I did. It took him three hours and was well worth the three dollars I paid.

That night at about eleven, I was reading, thinking about turning in when I heard a soft knock on my door. To be honest, my first thought was to wonder where I'd left my pistol, an old, snub-nosed-police .38. It had been a rough year. Sliding that thought aside, I went to answer.

I found Marjorie Snetshan at my door, looking tired and a little drunk. "I'm..." she said. I pulled the door wide.

"Come in."

She came in and I helped her out of her coat and offered her hot tea.

"Yes, that would be nice." She reeked of cigarettes and beer and wobbled as she walked. I went to put on the

18

teakettle and found her still standing in the same place when I got back. She was a small, dark woman, probably in her early forties, shoulder-length black hair with gray strands just starting. She looked at the world through sad eyes and wire-framed glasses, like it had disappointed her, left her with only enough energy to drink and go to a warm place when someone invited her. Tonight no one had.

She thanked me when I handed her the tea mug, still standing there, looking uncertain. I smiled at her. "Would you like to sit down?"

"I stink," she said earnestly. "I didn't notice until I got here."

"I have a bathtub," I told her. "Would you like a bath?"

"I... don't even know when I had a bath last," she said. And I went to draw it for her, showing her into the bathroom.

Bolder, I said, "Toss your clothes out and I'll wash them." She apparently didn't find anything strange about that and in a minute or two, her clothing lay in a small pile in my hallway. A very small pile because she didn't have any underwear, or didn't want to toss them out.

"Is this everything?"

"Yes. I lost some of them."

I stuffed my terry-cloth robe in through the bathroom door and told her to take her time. I started the wash, checking her pockets, which were empty, and throwing in her coat for good measure. Then I went across the street to the "mission barrel" to find fresh clothing, including new underpants, that might fit her. I had no clue about bra size so brought several.

Returning, I called through the door. "How are you doing?"

19

"I'm very clean now," she said.

"Hair too?" I sounded to myself like the parent of a small child.

"I found shampoo," she assured me.

Later, drinking her tea, smelling good, wrapped in my robe, she told me there was nobody left in the bar when it closed. Some bartenders would allow her to sleep in back but apparently not this one. Normally in the summer, she could find a shed or open car to just crawl into, but something scared her and she didn't want to be out alone.

"What scared you?"

"Something. Like somebody was following me, or watching me, or something."

"Did you see anyone?"

"No... I... just felt them."

We sat together for a while, me reading a little and her wrapped in the too-large bathrobe sipping her tea.

"I never came home with a priest before. I was almost afraid to knock."

"It's okay, I'm glad you did. I hope you won't mind sleeping on that sofa. I've slept on it myself. It's pretty comfortable." I found her a flannel pajama top, which on her would be most of a nightshirt.

"Oka-ay," she said, drawing the word out and up until it was almost a question. "I could... sleep with you."

"Thank you, that's very kind. But you'll be fine here."

She looked at me, something not adding up. "Do you like to sleep with women... or men?"

"Women, definitely."

She spread her arms wide and struck an expression, one eyebrow raised, as if to say, Well, *I'm* a woman! By then it was after midnight. I fetched her a blanket and felt the odd parental urge to tuck her in, but resisted. When she got herself settled, I gave her a pat on the arm and turned off the light. "You'll be safe here," I told her. "Good night."

She woke me, just after two, standing small and naked by my bed, washed blue in moonlight, feet together, hands clasped. She'd been crying and tracks of tears shone silver beneath each eye. Around her neck she wore a gold locket, and a small cross, silver with enameled flowers at the top, each on its own chain. In the moonlight the cross almost seemed to glow. Instead of a poor, sad woman who drank too much and slept with—I guess—anyone who asked her, she looked heavenly, like an angel in a classic painting.

"Something scared me," she whispered. "Can I sleep with you?"

"You can't sleep *with* me," I told her.

"Oh," she said, and seemed to shrink a little. I admit, I thought first of what people might say. I thought of Evie, thought of any parishioner who might have seen her arrive, thought of how I'd explain this to the bishop—not that he would ever be likely to ask. And finally, I thought of Jesus… what would he do? *Love his neighbor.*

I flipped back the blanket, leaving the sheet in place. "But you can sleep here *next* to me, if you'd like. You'll be warm… and you won't be afraid because I'm right here."

She smiled, nothing so much as relieved, and climbed into bed, pulling the cover over herself, snuggling down next to me, actually wriggling like a child.

"I'm warm now," she told me, and was sleeping in seconds.

In the morning when I woke, she had already gone— I hoped to the Coffee Cup for breakfast, with the money I'd left in her clean pants pocket. I prayed my morning

21

prayer for her, that somehow she'd be safe and warm and happy, but I was pretty sure she wouldn't be. I knew—thought I knew—we'd find her body in a snow bank some winter morning, or someplace she crawled when there was no safe place left.

CHAPTER 4

An early knock at the door as I was up and making coffee—'from the red can'—turned out to be William, back from Fairbanks... or wherever. I thought fleetingly of Marjorie. If she had still been here, what kind of impression might that have made? Oh, well.

Filling the perk pot basket, I waved a greeting. "Alice?"

"She must work this morning," he told me, selecting a white coffee mug with Nenana Ice Classic, 1954 printed on it in sky blue. We had just got coffee perked and poured, and set ourselves up on the tippy stools, when the door 'knocked' again and Evie arrived.

"Hello?" she called, in a voice that made me think of singing. Coming down the short hallway she said, "I smell coffee. Hope you made some for me." We did of course, so there was no danger. I put my lips up and she kissed them, also patting William and kissing the top of his head.

I watched her select a mug and pour coffee. She stood about five-seven, tall among local women, with big brown eyes, high cheekbones and shiny black hair, a little curly. Today she wore denim girl jeans, a white blouse under a pink cotton sweater and 'fashionable' black rubber knee boots.

In short order, she took her place on a tippy stool next to me, and we both looked at William.

He looked back. "What!"

"You've been out in the world," I said. "Tell us something. We want news."

He sipped his coffee. "I have not been very far out. I did hear that they think the flu pandemic has ended."

"I'm not sure I knew there was one," I told him.

"Oh, yes. More than fifty thousand people in the United States have died… a strain of flu that started with birds in Asia."

Evie and I exchanged a glance and she shrugged. "Yikes! Good to know it's over."

"Can you tell us what you've been working on?" I asked.

He made a face, shaking his head. "Not much. Not classified. You know that my main assignment now relates to security at the Clear installation. As though Soviets would come all the way to Alaska to spy on RADAR technology that will most likely be obsolete by the time it is completed!" He sniffed. "But someone has reported *strange* persons doing *strange* things down there, and I must investigate. And all this while my brother is here.

"What 'strange things' are they supposed to be doing there?" I asked him, imagining men in trench coats loitering in the snowdrifts outside the gates or—since the thaw—strolling and splashing around in the muskeg.

He pulled a face shrug. "Just being there is strange. Lately, there are quite a few new workers that I do not recognize. Rough bunch," he added. And the conversation shifted.

"Marjorie Snetshan stayed here last night," I told them when the conversation lagged. I managed to say it casually. Why mention it? Because there are no secrets in the village.

Evie sipped her coffee then turned slowly to meet my eyes, wearing an indecipherable half smile. "Oh," she said, in an exaggerated way, "that's interesting. Tell us where she slept."

"She started out on the sofa."

"And ended up…"

24

"Well," I said, having more trouble with this than I expected, "ended up sleeping in bed with me." She raised her eyebrows. "But on top of the sheet. She was crying and said she was scared."

Evie lowered her face but maintained eye contact while kind of wrinkling her forehead. "Yes, I know," she said. "Marjorie stopped by this morning after she left here. She wanted me to know that 'nothing happened.' Not that I was worried." And she patted my thigh under the table. "Oh, Hardy," she said, as she often does. "But don't make it a habit."

She grew thoughtful. "Marjorie has always been like this... she will sleep—have sex—with anyone. She's so kind and pliable, but somehow attracts the worst kind of man. Instead of the man being grateful, she gets beat up, abused, ends up in Fairbanks in the hospital." She took another sip. "She's already lived longer than I thought she would."

"What would you think," I asked the two of them, "about her living here?"

"Here?!" Evie looked around, now alarmed.

"Well, not *here* here. I was thinking we could wall off a small space for her at the back of the Quonset hut. There's an oil heater, and she could use the plumbing in the parish hall. So, she'd always have a safe place she could go."

Evie considered. "I think it's a pretty good idea." And William agreed.

What started out later as a work party of mostly me, clearing the back of the Quonset hut, turned into a group effort when others arrived. Vic and Linda Huxton showed up spontaneously, along with Butch, Oliver Sam—who builds all our coffins in addition to other church carpentry—and Evie came back around after several hours of homework for her college courses. Together we moved mission barrel supplies forward, clearing space for a bed, small table, and a wardrobe that we stocked with clothing, approximately her size.

At one point I said to Evie, "Those bras are too big."

"How do you know?"

"Never mind."

And we finished the cleanup by taking a pickup load of old seersucker garments—and other completely useless junk—to the dump.

Oliver and Vic took my pickup to the Standard Oil dock to scrounge two-by-fours from among the surplus wood used to ship and store fuel barrels. Before we finished, the two had much of a wall and door opening framed. Watching Vic swing a hammer, I marveled at how quickly a guy can fit in to a new place if he wants to. I imagined a future with more energetic, helping people arriving, participating in our lives here. Later, balanced on the tippy stools with coffee mugs in hand, I toasted all the helpers. "Here's to you!" It felt right.

* * *

Early on Friday, Arnold Gustafson showed up at my door. "Jack's back!" he greeted me, shouting and leading a tall, good-looking husky in through my door. "His collar's gone. Hated to lose that one. Sewed his name on it myself. Hard sewing through that webbing stuff. Now I'll have to do it all over again. Oh, well!"

This was my first clear look at Jack. He was mostly black in the form of a saddle up and over his back, with his legs and feet, and his big bushy husky tale a mix of silver and white. His most prominent feature was bright blue eyes set in a black 'Lone Ranger' mask on an intelligent

26

silver face. I knelt in front of the dog to look him over and he immediately raised and extended a paw for a 'shake,' not something working huskies usually knew.

"Yes, sir, he's a smart one," shouted Arnold. I invited him for coffee, telling him to bring Jack. "Don't mind if I do." He dropped his end of the dog's leash at the door. Jack picked it up and followed along behind, settling himself to keep an eye on Arnold from a kitchen corner.

"Smartest dog I ever knew," vowed Arnold. In a town with hundreds of working dogs, many nearly feral, few were ever allowed loose, Jack being the exception. He knew the boundaries of his yard and wouldn't cross them without permission—which is why his disappearance had been so puzzling and upsetting. He was known for walking to the property line and stopping, even leaning out if he wanted to see something or greet admirers, but not going out.

I raised my mug in Jack's direction, praising him. "Pretty impressive." He thumped his tail as if he understood.

"Yes, sir," Arnold roared, "he's one dog in a million!"

* * *

William suggested a trip to Clear in my Ford, to raid the Clear dump for surplus plywood. We would take Vadim.

"Good," I said. "He looks like a hard worker... big and muscular. He can help load our plywood and fight off the bears. William snorted.

"I have not seen him lift anything heavier than a beer bottle, or do anything more strenuous than stare at the barmaid's breasts."

"What about the gold panning?"

27

"It seems he has no talent for it. He is bringing home a very small pouch with no flakes, no color, as if he just scooped it up along the stream, not panning at all! But..." he sighed, "he is having a good time. To be honest, I will be glad when he returns home and stops staring at Alice." It was the most personal statement I'd ever heard him make.

Though he spent his evenings flirting with Alice, Vadim had been spending his days finding streams to pan in for gold. There was no shortage of such streams, though most would be well panned out long ago. He showed up every day or so, considerably scratched and bug bit, and not looking any wealthier.

"Remember," William cautioned, "Vadim does not know of my government work here." I nodded.

When Vadim climbed into the truck, I asked him, "How is it going? Are you rich yet?"

"*Nyet*," he replied. "Soon. Very soon!" William just rolled his eyes. Vadim wasn't the first person to come to Alaska with the expectation of quickly striking it rich.

Having all three of us crowded into the Ford cab was no picnic. Vadim offered to ride in back.

"No need," I told him regretfully. Any space with him in it felt crowded.

Out and back we passed both State Patrol and Army units stationed on the road, smoking and looking bored. They looked us over carefully and waved us past.

Without thinking I asked, "If there is a saboteur out here, can he just drive up on the highway that easily to make trouble?"

"Hah!" said William.

"Saboteur?" Vadim looked around like he might see one.

28

"You're not talking," I said, at the same time realizing I wasn't supposed to be, either.

"Hah!" William said again, emphasizing that he couldn't talk about it, or wouldn't talk about it in front of Vadim. Heck of a spy I'd make!

The installation at Clear, being a government project, contractors apparently thought nothing of throwing away nearly full sheets of the good, three-quarter-inch plywood. I knew a man who had replaced his whole cabin floor with material scrounged here. The only downside being the bears that had taken up residence at the dump, enjoying the easy pickings from the government commissary. "Welfare bears," Andy called them. So, we went armed.

As it turned out, we found no bears—disappointing Vadim—but no less than seventeen nearly full sheets of plywood, well worth the drive. It would be more than enough for the Quonset hut wall. I didn't have an immediate need for the rest but knew that Oliver and others would. After circling the facility on the haul road, we gave Vadim the scenic tour before we gleefully trucked our trophy plywood home.

* * *

Molly Joseph came on Wednesday, small, dark, and quiet, with a thick braid of hair that hung to her waist. She wore jeans, red high-top Keds, and a blue-plaid flannel shirt. In the three years we'd been doing this, it was the first time I could remember her *not* wearing some kind of parka. She was seeking clothing for young Henry who stomped along at her side, seeking mud puddles. She brought back small garments she'd chosen just a month or two earlier.

29

"He's already too big!" We spent about an hour in the Quonset hut where she marveled at progress on the new wall.

"It's a bedroom for Marjorie Snetshan." She nodded, like she already knew this, but pressed her lips together. She started to speak then hesitated.

"It's... too late for that one," she finally said, as I snapped the padlock. I waited to see if she'd say anything more but she just thanked me. I watched as the two went off up the street now greened with birch and cottonwood trees, and fringed with pink fireweed, the bottom flowers on the stalks already starting to bloom.

The town pulled out all the stops for Independence Day. There were all manner of races up the dusty main street, and plenty of pennies, nickels, dimes, and even quarters salted into a vast sawdust pile for kids to race into and sift. I knew that months from now, I'd still see small solitary figures hopefully sifting the sawdust, and I knew that adults—Andy particularly, yes, and now me—would keep throwing pocket change into the pile, stirring it around until snow fell.

After the Fourth, Chandalar residents emptied out like someone pulled a plug. Nearly everybody went to work the fish camps along the Tanana, each camp set up around a fish wheel revolving slowly in the river current, dropping salmon into a wooden box. Cleaned and split to the tail, the fish would hang on racks in the sun to dry or in a wood shelter filled with alder smoke. Kids would swipe at piles of the bright red and orange salmon eggs, clapping them into their mouths as they raced by.

What was left, or *who* was left, were construction workers for the station at Clear. They were all men, many of them big, shaggy, and bearded. They'd been installed in temporary quarters on three battered, dark, hulking railroad cars on a spur just beyond the main street. The workers traveled the twenty miles each way on gray, military-issue school buses. Yes, it would have made sense to quarter them at Clear, where they worked, but here they had the store, several bars, several churches, the movie at the Pioneers Hall on Friday nights, and the chance to 'socialize.' Which actually meant the chance to try to meet women to have quick sex with.

Bar fights were up and incidents of attempted rape, usually by men too drunk to function. There were probably incidents of full-blown rape that simply didn't get reported. Women spoke of being approached or followed, and one had even been propositioned in the store while buying a can of milk for her baby—the baby on her back! They didn't have to try to fit in. They wouldn't be here long. Honestly, the whole thing left us all feeling a bit uneasy.

A couple of the workers turned up in church and were pleasant, but they were exceptions and we didn't see them much. Work at Clear happened on twelve-hour shifts in any season at any temperature, and the workers tended to be big, tough men who had worked all over the world, usually loners.

On the other hand, the saloons were doing what they used to call a 'land-office business,' Alice among them. If there was a day that went by that someone didn't propose—something—to her, I didn't hear about it.

We finished Marjorie's wall about a week later, both sides with shelves installed on the business side to help organize supplies. It was Evie and I, Oliver, Vic, and Andy, taking a holiday from his restaurant and down from Fairbanks by train. The wall felt solid and looked great,

31

very clean and new. It even smelled good, like new wood. I began to imagine Marjorie in this new space, *her* room, and imagine that this might be the beginning of a new and better life. But I couldn't find her that day, or any day for about a week, and no one had seen her.

"Maybe she went out to fish camp," suggested Andy, and I hoped so.

My phone rang just after midnight and was up to five or six rings before I made it into the office to answer it. It was Evie. She spoke quickly in an undertone as if not wanting to be overheard.

"Hardy, I don't want you to think this is one of those silly-woman things…"

"But…?" I encouraged her to continue.

"Would you come down here and walk around my cabin? I heard noises, and it sounded like someone tried to get in. I've heard it before, so I've been sleeping with my door locked. Can you come?"

"I'm on my way."

It took maybe a minute to dress and just two or three minutes to walk and jog to her cabin, the thirty-eight-caliber police special clunking against my thigh in my trousers pocket. I knew it was overkill, but my first two years in Chandalar had left me at least more cautious. Most likely she had someone drunk strolling around her cabin, looking for a place to bed down. Chances were good we'd find him there, sleeping it off. At least in the summer we didn't have to come out in the morning and find them frozen board stiff.

The sun had just set and would rise again about three thirty, but it wasn't dark and wouldn't be. It was that kind of half-light pilots call civil twilight, plenty bright enough to work in the yard or even read outside if you had to. And

32

some people did, not read, but worked in their gardens. Sometimes the kids played basketball. It wasn't unusual to drift off to sleep hearing the *boing, boing* of the ball, the bang and shudder of the backboard, and wake up hearing the same. They'd play all night!

I knocked on her door. "Evie, it's me." She opened it, wearing her foolish face.

"Sorry, Hardy." I gave her a quick squeeze and kissed her lips.

"Glad you called."

Anytime we got together felt like a date, even if we were armed. I had noticed the long-barreled western pistol she held against her thigh.

"This isn't the first time I've felt this way lately, late at night, after I turn my lights out, like somebody was out there, watching me—watching the cabin. But I can't seem to catch them at it."

"That's pretty much what Marjorie said," I told her. "She said, 'Something scared me.'" We began to circle the cabin, a faint trail through low brush. Even walking carefully, we stepped on twigs that snapped and popped.

"This is what I hear. It's not you, is it?"

"Me? Good grief, no! Why would you think that?"

She allowed herself a brief, impish smile. "Sexual tension?"

"Well, that's possible, but..."

"No, I know. I'd just rather it was you, for whatever reason. A girl can hope."

Then I saw it. "Look at this!" I picked up what I'd spotted on the path. "Been doing any electrical repairs?" I asked her.

"How likely is *that!* What did you find?"

33

I held it out to her, most of a brand-new roll of electrical tape.

CHAPTER 5

"Any fresh word on the midnight electrician?" Andy laughed, topping off his coffee.

"None, fortunately," I said.

Evie gave him a faintly menacing look. "Laugh it up, Italian Boy, but it was kind of scary."

He held up both hands, a surrender. "Yeah, I know, sorry. That would be scary." He turned to me. "What about Marjorie?"

I shook my head. "Still no sign. I'm hoping she's in fish camp, safe with others and probably sober." I had eggs frying, with slices of canned Canadian bacon crisping alongside, and slices of Evie's fresh sourdough bread toasting. When the phone rang, I remember we all glanced at each other, like 'What's wrong now?' But with the sun shining and breakfast nearly ready, I actually went to answer without most of my usual trepidation.

"Hardy," I said.

"It's Frank Jacobs." He sounded serious and I knew this was business.

"I'm here in Chandalar," he said. "Got an early call and flew down. Got a body here—male, Caucasian, sixties maybe—I think you know him."

Working my way down a mental list of 'possibles,' I wasn't ready for the name I heard. "Got no identification," he said, "but I think it's Arnold Gustafson. Can you ID?"

"Oh, no!" I said, before noticing Evie standing in the doorway.

She knew the tone. Her face grew serious and she mouthed, "What?"

Jacobs told me where he was, and I found myself nodding, like he could see me. "A half hour, okay?"

35

"Oh, yeah. I'm going to be busy here and Arnold's got nowhere to go."

I guess it's normal, when you hear of a death, to dredge up your last memory. Following Evie back to the kitchen, to eat a now tasteless breakfast, I 'saw' Arnold sitting right here on one of the tippy stools, drinking coffee, laughing, shouting, his faithful dog watching from the corner. And now suddenly he was gone. Just gone, like the sound of snapped fingers. We'd never see him again—at least in this life—or hear him shouting 'Huh?' across the table at us.

Andy and Evie insisted on going with me, and we parked the truck at the trailhead by Arnold's cabin, finding Whisky Jack leaning across his property line, looking anxious, panting, with his long pink tongue hanging.

"Looks thirsty," said Andy. "Yep, water pan's empty and dry." From a Mason jar, he poured water into the pitcher pump in the yard, and in seconds had pumped the dented, enameled steel pan—the bottom half of an old roasting set—with water to the brim. Andy's eyes met mine. "He ain't been watered in a couple of days. Pretty good dog to stay inside his line all this time, thirsty."

The three of us walked, single file, up and over the railroad tracks and off on the trail through the muskeg, now drier and firmer than our last outing. "Does this trail go anywhere," I asked. "I mean in the summer. I know it goes off toward Clear in the winter. But why would…"

"Anybody be out here in summer?" Andy completed my thought.

"We used to come out here to pick berries." Evie looked around. "No berries ready yet. There's an old airfield off to the left, about a half mile. They abandoned it because they needed more space but couldn't get any, with the river on one end and this swamp on the other. That's when they built the new one out of town. But we used to come out here to play, and cut grass for dog bedding. It's just a huge meadow, the willows never came back."

We'd threaded along about a mile when we heard voices. Pushing around another bend in the trail and through a thicket of stunted swamp spruce, we found Marshal Jacobs with another man. They had a wire stretcher basket and a backpack open, with a camera and some medical things.

The marshal stopped his work long enough to shake hands with each of us. He never said much and this was no exception.

"This him?"

It was. He lay on his back, skin pale, yellowed and bloodless, sagged tight over cheekbones forehead and chin. His eyes were still open, glazed, staring at the large blue bowl of sky above him, immense here with the valley wide open for a hundred miles in three directions.

I dropped to one knee, appreciating that movement and conversation stopped around me. This was my job.
"Unto God's gracious mercy and protection we commit you. The Lord bless you and keep you. The Lord make his face to shine upon you and be gracious unto you. The Lord lift up the light of his countenance upon you and give you peace, now and forevermore. Amen."

Without thinking—I'd been a medic in France in the war—I reached down to grab Arnold by the sleeve of his wool shirt, lifting the arm and letting it drop. Jacobs watched me. He raised his eyebrows.

"Warm during the day," I said. "Not too chilly at night. Still a bit of rigor but starting to pass off."

"Don't forget the dry dog pan," added Evie. "If Arnold were around—alive—there'd never be an empty water pan. So… three days?" Jacobs made an approving face.

I nodded. "Yeah, that's what I think. Most of three days."

"That's what we think, too. Good to know about the dog pan."

I bent to look the body over more closely. Seeing an odd bump behind his ear, I lifted the edge of his stocking cap. "Look at this."

Evie bent to look. "Ugh. I hate this." And then she said, "He's wearing a hearing aid. I didn't even know he had one." From behind his ear, a beige plastic case, about the size of my little finger, connected by a short wire to a tiny speaker in his ear.

"So, what killed him?"

The technician looked at the marshal for clearance and got the nod. "Fell and hit his head on a rock." The two paused, staring at us, as if waiting.

We all thought it. Andy said it. "No rocks here."

"Well sure, there has to be." The marshal turned Arnold's head to show us the back of the skull, bloody and caved in. "Not only fell and hit his head, but snapped his neck in the process. See?" He pointed.

Evie hugged herself, as if cold, and I think we probably all shivered.

"So…" I said, but the marshal interrupted.

"Yeah. He was murdered."

CHAPTER 6

No matter what I told him, or what I promised him with a treat, Whiskey Jack wouldn't step out of his yard. He just looked at me, tongue hanging out, panting a little. He wanted to. He *really* wanted to. He apparently had some experience with truck riding and the sight of the open truck door set him to pacing and barking.

We tried taking him by the collar. He just set his feet. We might have picked him up. At probably eighty pounds he was manageable but we couldn't count on how long he would remain amiable. Andy found his leash hanging alongside the cabin door with a spare collar attached. We buckled that on and still no luck. Even Evie, one of the world's great doggy sweet-talkers, was unable to budge him.

"I got an idea." Andy headed into the unlocked cabin and came back with a wad of something whitish. "Dirty t-shirt," he explained, seeing my look.

Smelling the t-shirt, the dog's expression changed, and he quit fidgeting. When Andy said, "Come!" and started toward the truck, the dog followed.

"Keep that t-shirt," I told him.

"I plan to."

With the dog in the pickup bed, face out in the wind, and ears and tongue streaming, we drove the few blocks back to the rectory. Evie slipped an arm through mine.

"The murderer *can't* be someone we know, can it?"

"Well, it probably isn't... but it could be."

Out of the corner of my eye I saw Andy turn his head to look at her. "Which is why I'm glad to go back to Fairbanks. I hope you people are gonna start locking your doors at night, like we do in the big city... as God intended," he had to add.

"I'm locking mine," Evie said. "But I have been."

I made the turn into my driveway. "It doesn't have to be one of us. The town is lousy with strangers." I told them about the four I'd seen buying cigarettes and beer, and how evasive they'd been about where they were from.

"You should have told the marshal," said Evie, as we climbed down from the truck.

"I didn't think of it. I will. But they're just four among many."

I spent the next couple of hours cultivating my large garden. I had no trouble starting the Farmall, managing to hold the crank properly and not break my wrist. Then I got the disc harrow hooked up and dragged it around and around until the roughly ploughed furrows were smooth and ready for string lines and seeds. I wasn't the only one who would be planting here, which is why I broke up so much ground—nearly one hundred feet by two hundred. I was just glad to not have to do it by hand.

About the time I was ready to finish and park the Farmall, Marshal Jacobs showed up at the edge of the patch and waved. I was glad to shut down and lead the way into my cabin to the perk pot.

I measured scoops of coffee from the red can. "Still think it's murder?" I asked.

"Oh, yeah. Sure of it. Deliberate, first degree, not just a falling out. Somebody made tracks out there—took a weapon—there was nothing at hand would have made that kind of dent in Gustafson's skull. And then they did a really good job of covering up or smearing all tracks and traces."

"They?"

"Too many tracks for just one. At least two, maybe three. Impossible to say, after they finished cleaning up."

I told him about the four tall strangers.

He shrugged. "Good to know. Most likely coincidence. Fact is, your town is full of what we in the law game call 'suspects.' I'll sure be glad when this project is finished and they haul those rail cars out of here." He looked around. "What did you do with the dog?"

"We couldn't leave him at the cabin. Andy has him."

"Andy is going to keep a dog at the restaurant?" He looked skeptical.

"I don't know what he has in mind."

"Do you have a birthday coming up?" he asked.

"Yes. Why?"

"Because I think I know what you'll be getting from Andy."

I looked around. "Oh, I don't have room for a..."

"Sure, you do," he said.

Over coffee, he told me that neighbors had heard the dog barking for most of three days, confirming the window of time we guessed. All the neighbors were several hundred feet away—though some were out of town—so, nobody actually saw anything and nobody went to check. Arnold had gotten so deaf that for the last couple of weeks, the dog would often start barking at night in the yard, and he apparently never knew it.

Before he left, the marshal told me, "There aren't too many reasons people kill—and most victims know their killers. That's one reason this case seems so strange. People kill for sex or money, lover's betrayal, and pent-up-anger, usually aggravated by alcohol. Or just plain bad luck... an accident. Nothing fits."

"Had he been drinking?"

41

"That's for the lab, but I don't think so. I didn't smell it and didn't find evidence of it in the cabin. No bottle out, no glass with residue, nothing. It's just all so... wrong," he said as he left.

It got worse. About suppertime, I answered the door to find a young Athabascan man, about twenty, dressed in the village uniform of flannel shirt and jeans with rubber-bottomed shoe pacs on his feet. He took off his Evinrude cap to reveal black hair cut to a stylish flattop and waxed to perfection. He smoothed back the sides as he spoke. No trouble telling he had come from fish camp. He smelled like wonderful smoked salmon.

"Oliver Sam sent me. Says to tell you Marjorie Snetshan never showed up at the camp."

"At fish camp?" I asked, just to be sure.

"Yeah." And he told me where.

I thanked him and offered him coffee but he declined and headed away, probably out on a short leash to get supplies and get back.

I said it out loud. "Can it get any worse?" That was probably my mistake. Sure, it can always get worse. About eight p.m., my phone rang. Evie had come to dinner, cooked it—moose meat roast—and the two of us were sitting around like old married people, dreaming and planning. Our eyes met and my trepidation about phones reared up like something large and dark that might well tip when I answered, and crush us both. Even so, I lifted the handset. "Hardy."

"Somebody shot your boy, William." It was Marshal Jacobs.

"Oh, no!" I said, trying to sound neutral, this time conscious that Evie had followed me. It didn't work.

She stepped closer. "What? Who?"

42

"How bad," I asked.

"*Who?*" She moved closer still.

"William," I mouthed. Her hand flew to cover her mouth. William was like a favorite uncle to her.

"Not bad," Jacobs continued. "Winged him. Truly just a scratch, but big, painful one. He'll be at St. Joe's overnight. You want to pick him up in the morning?"

"Of course!"

"He'll be loaded up for the pain and need a ride. They say nine, so likely ten."

"We'll be there." I hung up.

"Did I hear right? *William?*"

"You did. Shot... slightly wounded, but okay. As okay as you can be when someone shoots you." I couldn't help shaking my head. "It's like the whole world is going crazy, right here in Chandalar."

I called Alice, who sounded matter of fact. She had already heard—directly from William—as it turned out. I found her at work, jukebox blaring in the background, Johnny Mathis singing, *It's Not for Me to Say*. She had to raise her voice to be heard over Johnny, and what sounded like a pretty good crowd.

"He was out by Clear somewhere. He said it might have been poachers... an accident." As she went to hang up, I heard her say, "Vadim, I'm *not* dancing with you, I'm working." It was good he was able to fight down concern about his brother.

Later I walked Evie home, .38 in my pocket. It was still full daylight, though with the sun lowering, coming in golden from the side. It would have been a beautiful evening except for the day filled with trouble.

43

Along the way, Evie stopped us in the empty road, taking me first by one hand and then the other, turning us to stand with our faces close.

"Tomorrow will be better," she promised, and kissed me on each cheek and then on the lips, slowly. Although I still felt jangled, I did begin to feel like tomorrow was looking up.

In the morning, we caught the small stern-wheel ferry, *Princess of Minto*, at Nenana bound to a small barge with enough square-footage to carry about four cars, or sometimes, one very large truck. Luckily, no trucks in sight. We stood at the rail, smelling the clean cool scent of cottonwoods and water, watching the swirls and whirlpools of it, seeing it all disappear smoothly beneath the bow like it wasn't any big deal, which it wasn't. *A metaphor for life?* I wondered. I promised myself I would remember.

We made it to Fairbanks and to St. Joseph's by nine, waiting until about ten fifteen before they let 'our boy,' William out the door. They insisted on wheel-chairing him to the car, which he didn't like very much but received mildly. I could tell the nurse, a nun, was sweet on him. Women often were. She insisted on helping him into the truck and then kissed him on the cheek before she closed the door.

He just shook his head. "Nuns!"

The bullet had gouged a painful groove across about eight inches of one side of his back, just below the shoulder blade, narrowly missing his spine. "It hurts like... heck," he told us. "The morphine helps."

"Is there anything you need before we leave the city?"

He turned his body cautiously to meet my eyes. "Only coffee—the *good* stuff."

So, we crossed the bridge over the Chena River and made our way to Andy's place—Andrea's—the former saloon now enjoying new life as the first Italian restaurant in the Alaska Interior. To our surprise, the narrow gravel street was already all parked up in front of the restaurant. As far as we knew, they didn't serve breakfast and it was far too early for lunch. We eased William out of the truck and tried to help him along the sidewalk but he shook us off.

"Do not fuss!" he hissed.

We weren't the only ones arriving for coffee. We also found the long, polished mahogany bar completely parked up, as well as a few of the smaller tables. Andy greeted us cheerfully.

"*Buongiorno, buongiorno!*" He attempted to take us to a table by guiding William by the elbow. William shook him off testily.

Andy stepped back to give him a look. "So, *you* get shot and *we* get a pain in the ass!"

"Just give me coffee and no one will be hurt. Remember, I am armed."

Actually, he wasn't. With him all loaded with morphine, the nurse wisely handed his sidearm to me.

Andy took Evie by the elbow, escorting her to the table.

"Why thank you, Andy," she said much too graciously—with a pointed glance in William's direction—and even a small curtsy.

William waved a hand dismissively, and literally collapsed into a chair, groaning as he tweaked his wound, and his eyes kind of wobbled.

"How much morphine did they give you?"

He looked at me blearily. "Not nearly enough."

45

"So, whaddya think?" Andy asked when we were all settled with coffee in front of us and a plate of pressed Italian aniseed cookies.

William sipped his coffee. "It's all delicious!"

"No, I mean who shot you, and why? Do you think you got too close to something out there?"

"I think," said William, taking another sip, "I interrupted a moose poacher. No more than that. And," he went on, "they are already so paranoid at Clear, this might just—how do you say it—put them over the ledge. They see saboteurs behind every tiny tree."

Evie looked thoughtful. "From what I read about it, the Distant Early Warning system is our only real defense against Soviet bombers. Isn't it at least possible that some, presumably Communists, want to make sure it never comes on line?"

William did a face shrug. "That is what they are always saying, Communists this, Communists that." He leaned in and lowered his voice. "It is already operational!"

Evie looked startled. "It's finished?"

Again, the dismissive hand wave. "*Nyet*," he said, "it will not be finished for years, but it *is* running, scanning the skies. So now they are expecting Communist saboteurs every day to arrive."

"Well, I'm *not* expecting them to arrive," Evie declared with feeling.

"Good for you, my dear."

She pressed her lips together. "I think they're already here."

* * *

I was in the office when my phone rang, and answered it first ring, so I didn't have time to work myself into a lather.

"It *was* a poacher." I recognized Marshal Jacob's voice. "This guy called the Highway Patrol from a pay phone near Wasilla to ask if William was okay and to say he was sorry."

I laughed, sounding relieved even to myself. "That's a load off."

"Sure is," said the marshal, "if you believe him."

CHAPTER 7

My new dog arrived, as predicted, with Andy on his next visit. He came with a bowl, a bag of dry food, his leash, and a wadded up, stinky t-shirt, all carried by hand from Fairbanks on the train. He seemed none the worse for wear for having made the trip in the baggage car—the dog, not Andy.

"Can't keep a dog at a restaurant. Health Department's goin' bananas."

"Did you think you could?" I saw a mix of emotions play over his face.

"Well, maybe." It was clear Andy liked Whiskey Jack. "You need to work with him," he encouraged. "Get him used to you. He's a really good dog. In fact, I may need to borrow him back. Turns out, somebody broke into my place… well, okay, opened the door and walked in. But they managed to find my gun vault."

"Uh-oh."

He waved a hand. "Nah, nothing gone that I can tell. Maybe it was kids. I was lucky." He shook his head. "I just hate the thought that some stranger's been walking around in my place."

"So, are you going to start locking up?"

"I'm definitely thinking about it," he said.

After Andy left, Whisky Jack and I sat and stared at each other. I hadn't had a dog since childhood. What did I know about them? Most dogs in Chandalar were working dogs, scarcely socialized, mostly chained when they weren't pulling a sled. A loose dog was an invitation to a dogfight, so didn't happen much. In fact, the only loose dogs in town belonged to the woman who ran the post office, the post mistress, known as Grandma Susie, spiritual grandmother to much of the town. So, in her honor, her street had been renamed with an Athabascan word, *Setsoo*, for 'grandmother.'

The intersection of Setsoo and First Street—my street—was typically congested with her four or five large, well-fed, black or brown Labrador retrievers. They thought nothing of dropping for a nap in the dust, just anywhere and anytime they pleased. In the summer, the largest, a chocolate named Chuck—easily one hundred pounds—even slept out there at night. To make matters worse, the lady rescued a couple of wild herons, who now tame, also inhabited the intersection, roaming around with the dogs. It was lucky more people didn't drive, around here.

"Jack, come!" I told him. But he didn't. He just sat and looked at me. *Job one,* I thought, and we spent about an hour in the driveway, Jack on a long lead. I'd get him out to the end, call him, reel him in, give him a treat and a pet, and then we'd do it again. He thought it was great fun and was a quick learner. By the end of an hour, we didn't need the lead and it only remained for me to wean him from expecting a treat every time.

I also put the leash on him and we walked the property boundaries. He couldn't very well stay in the yard if he didn't know where the yard was. Because it was all going so well, I decided a field trip would be in order. Jack and I walked to the Post Office to pick up my new shipment of window envelopes and letters addressed to Occupant or Current Resident.

At first, we did fine. Jack greeted people mildly, politely. A surprising number of them—the four we met—already knew him by name, liked him and petted him.

Leaving the post office, we walked north on Main Street toward the railroad terminal at the end of the street, with the tracks, the docks, and ultimately the river at its back. There's only one public telephone—outdoors—in Chandalar, located on the street side by the terminal. As we neared, and I hadn't noticed the booth occupied, the folding door opened with a squeak, and a large man squeezed out. I recognized him easily by his over-sized, sugar-bowl-handle ears, even under a red felt hunting hat.

"Good morning," I said, and nodded.

He didn't answer, looked at me without particular interest, and might have passed by. But then he saw—recognized—Whisky Jack. Spinning, he squared off at me and snarled, "I don't like being followed!" Then he reached out to give me a push. It never connected. With a snarl, Whisky Jack, who had been off to one side watering the street, inserted himself between us, teeth bared, formidable. I didn't see it coming.

The big man startled and yanked his hand back, nearly tripped, and his hat fell off. He snatched it back, dusted it on a pant leg and jammed it back on his head. "Maybe I kill that dog the next time I see him."

I must have looked as perplexed as I felt. *Maybe you'll try*, I managed to not say aloud. "Sorry," I said, deciding to take the high road. But he had already turned his back on the two of us and hurried off up the street.

"Good dog!" I scratched the top of Jack's head. Without breaking his gaze, Jack twitched his bushy tail as we watched the man out of sight.

It had been nearly a month since I'd seen the four strangers at the general store. By now I was pretty sure they lived somewhere out of town and weren't laborers from Clear. I hadn't seen them at the Coffee Cup—center of the known universe—or the store, neither of the taverns, and certainly not in church. It's not a big town. Where had they been?

I asked Gary at the store if he remembered the four. He did. And I asked him if he'd seen them. He looked thoughtful.

"Not much. They come in here every couple of days for beer and cigarettes. Never anything more. Oh..." he said, remembering, "and mosquito dope. A couple of them came in here bit to hell." He paused to reconsider his word choice. "Sorry, Father."

I called Andy the next morning and told him about Whisky Jack and the stranger. He laughed.

"Told ya he was a good dog." My other reason for calling was Marjorie Snetshan, still missing.

"We need to find her."

"You're askin' for help?"

"Well, sure."

"I'll be down in the morning."

Chandalar isn't a big area, a corner section of flat land where two rivers meet. We would be looking for old cars, sheds—even larger doghouses—she might have crawled into for shelter. Or she might have simply gotten too drunk and fallen into the river, which might mean we'd never know what happened or where she ended up.

While waiting for Andy, I vowed to do a little more looking around on my own to expand my search horizons beyond town proper. After lunch, with Whisky Jack on his lead, I headed out toward the river, to the place where they moored the big riverboats during the winter, frozen in several feet of ice. Not far ahead of me, a couple turned a corner into view, not noticing me, walking the same direction. It was a very tall man with a shorter woman. It could be Butch and Adele, or it could be who it turned out to be, Vadim out walking with Alice Young.

With Marjorie unaccounted for, it was easy to suspect intrigue or danger in things that might otherwise have seemed normal. Not spying on them, exactly, but certainly keeping an eye on them just in case, Jack and I fell back a bit and tried to be less obvious. Certainly, anyone watching would have thought it was me who was up to something.

Nearing the river, they turned off the main road—hard-packed river sand—onto a rutted side road, little more than a trail. It curved through a thick stand of cottonwood trees, ultimately dead-ending on a sandy bar jutting out into the river. There they stopped to face each other and talk, standing too close for my comfort. I crouched behind a bit of brush and noticed that Jack, apparently also a trained hunting dog, came to lay down beside me.

I watched as Vadim reached out to her, as though he might grab her by the throat. He didn't. He put his hands on her shoulders. *What do we know about him? Nothing!*

I watched as first he tried to kiss her, then did kiss her—though she wasn't helping. I thought about trying to get closer, in the hope of overhearing what they were saying, or reacting quickly if things went badly. Then he reached out a finger and thumb and smoothly—I thought—unbuttoned her top shirt button. She said something, he said something, and then he unbuttoned another. She wasn't helping and, at least at this distance, didn't seem to be encouraging him, but she wasn't backing up, resisting, trying to run, or calling for help, either. And so it went, until her shirt hung open, and he reached in to undo what must have been a front-closing bra.

52

Seeing her bare breasts settle free, exposed, I realized that whatever she was up to was her own business and she didn't need help from me. I was now poised on the knife-edge that separates healthy caution from peeping, and feeling more than awkward—quietly clucking at Jack—I hustled away.

Now I had a new problem: what to tell, or not tell William. Am I a friend if I know what's going on and say nothing? Am I a friend if I know what's going on and tell him? In the moment, walking briskly away, I had no clue. As if in answer, I heard a small branch crack and turned to see William, concealed, seeing them. So, he wasn't back at his cabin, loaded up with painkillers, recovering from a painful gunshot flesh wound. Something Vadim must have thought was a sure thing, to come out on a riverbank and brazenly fondle his brother's girl. Surprise!

William didn't look at me, nor acknowledge that he'd even seen me. But I was pretty sure the branch crack was his way of letting me off the hook. It didn't help much. I walked all the way home lost in my thoughts, only coming back into the moment as I opened my cabin door.

The next day, I was just leaving the rectory with Andy, daypacks on, Whisky Jack on his leash, and weapons ready—as bear repellant—when Vic Huxton came striding up. He looked at us with his straight-stemmed pipe clenched in his teeth, raising his eyebrows, his whole face a question mark.

"Hunting?" Of course, even a greenhorn knew this wasn't hunting season.

"Sort of." Andy filled him in on developments, or non-developments in the Marjorie story.

"I'll go, too." And we drove him back to the teacherage to grab gear.

53

"I think we're lookin' for a body." Andy said what all three of us were thinking.

I was reluctant to give up hope. "You don't think she finally moved in with some old sourdough?"

"That would be nice. But she coulda done that a long time ago. She was always waitin' for one guy—one nice guy—she always said. She wanted a life that was more than a drink and a quick roll, more than a rug and a blanket in front of the fire." Against all odds, and all her life experiences, she still had dreams.

It wasn't a very scientific search. We guessed how far she might have walked late at night after closing time, probably drunk. We checked empty cabins, sheds, even privies, anywhere a person might curl up to stay a bit warm and sheltered. We found nothing. More to the point, we smelled nothing. After two weeks of warm weather, that would be our best clue.

With nearly five hours of trudging around, looking, sniffing... sometimes even calling... we were about to give up. In fact, I'd just suggested heading back to the truck.

"Anything down this way?" Vic pointed at two wheel ruts heading off toward the river. Andy made a face.

"Used to be a watchman cabin out here, back from the A.E.C. days—Alaska Engineering Commission," he added. "They built the railroad. Used to have a hospital here, wood shops, metal shops—everything it takes to build a railroad. That was back in the twenties and thirties. All gone now except the odd shed. Might as well take a look."

We were fifty feet from the frame cabin, still surprisingly intact, when Whisky Jack let out a yowl. He knew, and in about twenty more steps we knew, too. The odor was powerful and unmistakable. Something dead here. We paused outside the door, the sound of flies buzzing already audible.

Andy hesitated, hand on the door. "This ain't gonna be good." It wasn't. Marjorie Snetshan had died here, badly. She was naked, bound cruelly, arranged awkwardly, painfully, bound with carefully, ornately-knotted cotton clothesline. It was as horrible as anything I'd ever seen and, having been a medic in France during the European war, I thought I'd seen just about everything horrible.

We couldn't have stood there a full minute before we all three went back out into the yard, Andy and I wiping away tears and Vic over at the side of the clearing, throwing up.

"At least we found her, and she's accounted for," I would tell Evie later, like somehow that was the end of it. It wasn't. We both knew it wasn't. In spite of all the rope work, her wrists, ankles, and around her mouth had been bound with electrical tape.

So, we knew—we all knew—this was only the beginning.

CHAPTER 8

"Ever seen this?" Frank Jacobs extended an arm, something shiny dangling from his hand. It was a small silver cross, enameled with flowers at the top, on a silver chain. He had flown in from Fairbanks, early, investigating what had now become two murders. We were standing by the perk pot in my kitchen, just ready to pour.

"I have," I said, with no trouble remembering. "I saw it on Marjorie Snetshan the night she asked if she could sleep with me." It was what happened and I figured there was no sense trying to tap dance around it, especially with a marshal.

He raised both eyebrows. "Tell me about it."

So, I told him, and he listened patiently, nothing in his face or voice betraying what he might have actually been thinking.

"Did you have to take her to bed?"

"I didn't *take* her to bed. She came to me afraid and asked to come to bed. In the moment, it seemed... sensible and kind." I had to admit, in the cold light of day, coming from a U.S. Marshal, it seemed less sensible.

"Anybody else know about this?"

"I told Evie and William the next morning. Oh, and Marjorie told Evie as well, just so she'd be clear that 'nothing' happened."

"And nothing did happen?"

"Nothing. She slept on top of the sheet."

"That's good, anyway! I'll do what I can, but you know this whole thing could come out at the inquest or in court... end up in the newspapers."

My stomach felt like I'd swallowed a fistful of lead fishing weights. I must have looked glum.

"Probably won't," he offered. It didn't help.

The marshal and I sat at my kitchen table, sipping silently, lost in our various thoughts, until it occurred to me. "Marjorie wasn't wearing the cross when we found her."

"You sure?"

"Sure, I'm sure. It was the most horrible thing I've ever seen. I think every detail is burned into my brain."

"You sure can't unsee a bad thing," he agreed.

"So where did you find it? Can you tell me?"

"Next to the dish rack at Arnold Gustafson's cabin." He let that sink in. "The only good thing about that—I mean, if he really did kill her—is that with him dead, the danger is over."

"So, do you think the danger is over?"

He shrugged. "No, not really."

* * *

"What?!" Andy gave me a sharp look. "By the sink? No way. I was in there. Besides, wasn't he dead before she was?"

"The coroner says about the same time."

"Hah!" said Andy. "Maybe he killed her and felt so bad about it he went out on the trail and bashed his own brains in."

"That would be hard to prove," I told him.

"Yeah, and harder to do."

We were on our way to the Coffee Cup for lunch, Evie and William supposed to meet us. She was there, at 'our table,' under the dusty moose head, already sipping her coffee. She stood up to put her arms around me and kiss me.

Andy pretended to hide his eyes. "Let's try to keep a lid on that stuff, kids."

William arrived, walking cautiously, favoring his wound, sidestepping rather than turning his body to make it through the light lunchtime crowd.

"Still hurts?" I asked him.

"No," he said, "I just like walking this way."

Rosie, striking a pose with her pad and pencil, looked around. Nice to see all of you. These days, all I see is strangers. Strangers who want to know if we can 'maybe get together later someplace to do something.' I had one want to walk me home last night, to protect me from all the others. He *said*. All these extra people are good for business, but not much else. I'll sure be glad when everybody gets back from fish camp!"

"Yeah, but then it'll be winter again." Andy rose, kissed her on the cheek and headed for the restroom. In spite of herself, she smiled.

"Sure like that guy," she said. "Now who wants what?" It was an easy order. Turned out we all wanted the mooseburgers with cheese and the works.

She had the Philco on and cranked up for news at noon. Patti Page sang us right up to the hour with her new hit, *In Old Cape Cod.* After a jingle for Brylcreem—'a little dab'll do ya'—we heard the headlines.

The news was mostly Chandalar—us, our two murders. Few details were released about either, pending investigation. So far, the authorities hadn't released the part about the local priest 'sleeping' with one of the victims. Beyond that, we heard about a plane crash on takeoff from Bristol Bay, killing six, and the theft of something important—authorities weren't saying what—at the Springfield armory in Massachusetts. We heard that the Clear DEW line site was months ahead of schedule and receiving some kind of award. Of course, courtesy of

William, we knew the site was already up and running for weeks, scanning the western skies for Soviet long-range bombers.

There was an investigation still in progress, having to do with awarding public lands to oil companies and drillers from outside the Territory. The scheme included bilking Native Indian and Eskimo tribes and clandestine wildcat drilling in what could well turn out to be a twentieth-century, old-west-style land grab.

The land grab wasn't news to us, either, since a couple of the perpetrators had locked up Andy and me and attempted to burn us alive. I still had bad dreams about fire.

Later, with lunch finished and the crowd thinning, Rosie came to join us, sliding into a chair next to Andy, her 'intended.' She yawned.

Evie smiled at her. "Up late?"

"Oh, you know, I think there was a drunk wandering around outside my cabin last night. Real late... or real early. I kept hearing noises—thought I even heard someone try the door—but might have been dreaming. I locked up, of course. After what happened to poor Marjorie, it made me pretty nervous. I actually slept with my .357 under the pillow. Even after the noise quit, I was still too jittery to drift off." She yawned again and missed the look I exchanged with Evie.

Andy turned to her abruptly, wrinkling his forehead. "Last night? That happened last night? You sure?"

She looked at him and rolled her eyes. "Of course, I'm sure! I was there, not sleeping, and I'm yawning now."

Now Andy turned to give me a look. She saw it. "Alright, what's goin' on?"

Evie nibbled the last of her dill pickle chip. "The same thing happened to me a few nights ago. I finally called

59

Hardy to come down and look around. Not…" she waved her hand, "that I couldn't have shot him on my own."

"Swell," said Rosie. She turned to Andy. "If you're gonna be around a few days, how about camping with me?"

"Sure," he said, appearing to smile, jiggling his eyebrows suggestively. "Could be fun." But he wasn't smiling and he looked worried. He probably looked like I felt.

* * *

It was a Saturday morning, early, July twenty-seventh. In days it would be August, with little more than a month to first frost and another cycle of unforgiving winter.

"You know what I can't figure…" Andy looked up from his coffee. I waited.

"Why we don't all move to Hawaii?" I offered.

"Or Italy," he added. "Nah. I'm still trying to figger…" He held up an index finger. "One! What Arnold was doing out that trail by himself, carrying no gun, leaving Jack in the yard. And two!" he raised up his middle finger. "Well, I don't know what two was. Anyway, out alone with no weapon, no dog."

"At night." I added. That stopped him.

"How do you know at night?"

I took a sip of coffee to keep him hanging. "Elementary! He doesn't have electricity in the cabin—uses kerosene lanterns."

"Right… so…"

"I saw three. They had all burned dry and the wicks charred after the fuel was gone."

"So, Arnold went out at night. 'Course it wouldn't have been completely dark, since it doesn't get completely dark."

60

"But dark enough inside to have lanterns lit."

Andy set down his coffee mug. "So, he goes out at night with no gun, no dog and leaves the lights on. What does that tell us?"

"I have no idea," I said. But then I did. "He must have heard something. He had his hearing aid in. I think Jack barked and he heard it—for a change—and went out to take a look. But unarmed."

Andy nodded. "So, he didn't hear a bear, or something he thought would be dangerous. He heard—probably voices—something he thought he didn't have to worry about. And somebody killed him for it." He frowned. "You want to tell the marshal?"

"Tell him what?"

Andy nodded again. "Alright, so I get ya. We go out the trail, and see what it was got his curiosity up. Think that's smart?"

I admit I thought a minute about all the trouble we typically got into together. Shot at, nearly burned to death, nearly drowned. "Sure," I said. "Why not!"

* * *

My phone rang after midnight and Jack barked—neither a happy sound.

"It's Alice," her voice shaky. "I'm at home. I can't find William, or… anybody. Can you come over? I think I shot somebody."

"I'm on my way." Threading back though the dim cabin, Jack on my heels, I took a minute to sit on the edge of my bed, thinking about my last episode alone with a woman. Then I went back into my office to call Evie.

"Hardy? What's wrong?" She sounded dazed. I told her and she woke up quickly. "I'll meet you there," she said.

"No, I'll walk by and pick you up. This isn't a good night to be out alone... even with a gun."

The sun was setting before midnight now, and rising about four. I let myself out of the cabin, started to walk away, then turned back to lock the door. It was twilight out, an Alaskan summer night, the temperature in the fifties, quiet except for a distant power plant. I left Jack off the leash and he cavorted and peed as we made our way down the road. Stars were out, though in twilight only the bright ones showed. I could smell the river just over the railroad tracks, cool and dark. And I could smell something in bloom. An owl hooted nearby, and across town one dog barking encouraged another. God was in his heaven, as the poet Browning said, but all was not right with the world. My hand in my jacket pocket gripped the .38. I bet Browning wasn't armed when he wrote that. I knocked once on Evie's door. "It's me!"

Alice met us at the door, smoking nervously under the yellow porch light, the cigarette between two fingers of her left hand and one of William's 1911 Colts in the right. It hung huge in a thin hand extended on a skinny wrist, contrasting with a small silver ring she wore, a relic from her marriage. Wrapped in an oversize terry robe that might also have been William's, she exuded a wispy, sexy, vulnerability that would have been nothing but enticing to a man on the prowl. But what man? Exhaling a silvery stream into the lamplight, she sucked in another lungful, then held it as she talked.

"I heard somebody out here and thought it was... well, honestly, I thought it was Vadim. He's been so... attentive." She exhaled and paused to search the tip of her tongue for a fleck of tobacco. Watching her now, I couldn't help but picture the two of them on the riverbank, her partially undressed.

"But it wasn't him?" I asked.

"No. Not him. Tall but not thick... you know? First, he just walked around the place, not trying to be quiet. Like he wanted me to know he was there. Then he tried the door, but it was locked. Then... look here!" She pulled the door to. "He put his elbow through one of the panes, like to reach in for the lock. I had been sitting up in bed, holding this." She waved the Colt offhandedly. "I turned on the light when I got up then turned on the porch light. By the time I got the door open he was over there," she pointed, "about twenty feet. The gun was cocked. I aimed and shot—low—and I heard a yelp, like I hit him, but it didn't slow him down much. He took off..." She turned, pointing, "toward town." She looked at us and seemed very small. I was glad when Evie reached out to put an arm around her. "Any chance either one of you could stay here tonight? I've got a pretty good sofa."

I could have, but hesitated.

"Sure," said Evie. "I will." She turned to smile at me, as if knowing my thoughts, patting me on the shoulder, then kissing me. "Think you can make your way home alone, big guy?"

"I'll manage," I told her, in my bold, manly voice. "You two lock up... and don't shoot each other."

"You're no fun," said Alice as she closed the door, and I heard the bolt turn.

She was right. I'd seen and couldn't unsee what someone, possibly this monster had done to Marjorie.

It was worth mentioning that the direction Alice pointed, toward town, was also the way to the rail siding and sleeper cars.

Gripping the .38 in my pocket I called Jack and walked home. Alice was right, not a bit fun.

* * *

I'd no more laid my head back on my pillow than the phone rang again.

"Vic's been shot." It was Linda Huxton.

"How bad?"

"Just a scratch, thankfully. He didn't even want me to call you, but..."

"No, it's okay. It's good. I'll be right over."

I found Linda in her bathrobe, and Vic half dressed with his leg propped up, a .22 caliber revolver at hand. Sure enough, he had a nasty flesh wound, a gouge across the side of one calf. It had to hurt.

"I'm a pretty light sleeper," he told me. "Linda can sleep through anything." She nodded dully, looking half asleep now.

"We heard somebody walking around outside," she said, "and Vic got up."

Vic winced. "Yeah, we heard the door knob rattle... somebody trying it. So, I got up, pulled on pants and boots, grabbed this .22, and went outside to look around. Soon as I stepped around the corner, *bang!* I'm nicked. I fired back... three shots at the flash, and heard somebody crashing through the brush. No indication that I'd hit him. And when I went out with the flashlight, no sign of blood.

"It was a good effort," I told him.

By then it was after three. I couldn't see calling out the public health nurse at this hour, for someone who wasn't dying, so I cleaned the wound with hydrogen peroxide and covered it with sterile gauze pads and adhesive tape. "It's gonna hurt in the morning," I said.

64

"Burns like a son-of-a-bitch right now... sorry, Father."

"Sorry, Father!" exclaimed Linda. "So, it's okay to be a garbage mouth in front of your wife." She was kidding, probably trying to ease the tension of a scary evening. We could hear the quaver in her voice and he took her hand.

"Sorry," he said, striving for a meek look. She laughed and turned to me, apologizing for calling me so late. I told them about having been up, about the prowler at Alice Young's. Linda put her fingers to her lips. "Is it always this... dangerous... here?"

"It's usually not dangerous at all. It's usually a safe, quiet, friendly place to live, but..."

"Swell. We had to get here just when the prowler did."

"Well, there you are," I kidded her. "Maybe he followed you."

"Oh, boy," she said.

CHAPTER 9

Riverboat captain, Myles Conway, trailing his wife, Pamela, showed up at my door first thing. I'd met them before. They weren't parishioners, which didn't matter. And we weren't buddies but had always been cordial, but neither smiled now.

"We need marriage counseling," she said, stepping in.

They spent summers here, like geese, arriving after breakup in the spring, flying back south to somewhere in the fall after the freeze. He captained the *Koyukuk*, a large, modern, twin-screw diesel riverboat. He stood a little over six feet, with his brown crewcut worn long, and a thick brown mustache on a perpetually suntanned face. He looked like a handsome cowboy extra in a John Wayne oater—and he knew it.

Plumpish and pale, wearing a perpetually worried look, Pamela was as unlike him as she could be. They didn't even look like they'd date! I supposed the real question was why they married in the first place. Maybe they'd surprise me.

I led them into the office, dragging in an extra chair, which he accepted and plopped into. Right now, she looked like if she smiled her face would break. It wasn't hard to figure out whose idea marriage counseling was.

Many couples who come to talk about their marriage will beat around the bush, as though they're not exactly sure why they came. As though they might just turn to each other and say, 'I dunno, why *did* we come?'

So, I smiled at them encouragingly. "What seems to be the problem?"

He didn't say anything. In fact, he turned his head to gaze out the window. She looked at him for a heartbeat, saw that he intended to say nothing then slid forward to the edge of her chair.

"My husband will fuck anything that doesn't run away."

That wasn't the surprise I'd been hoping for.

He turned from the window. "She knew what I was like when she married me. What's the big deal?" He turned to her and grinned, like this was fun. "That's how I met you."

Usually, I let a married couple speak to each other, until they voice their own solution. Most adults know what they *should* be doing. But only two sentences in, I knew these two wouldn't have a common truth to arrive at if you gave them a flashlight and a map!

"You signed a contract," I said, mostly to him. "You entered an agreement, promising to be involved with only one person. This one. What you were like before is immaterial. You promised to leave all that."

"Aw," he said, "I might have known you'd take her side."

"The question is, why don't *you*?"

She was on the train the next morning and I never saw her again.

Him, I saw entirely too much. Tall, dark, predatory. No longer encumbered with a wife, he spent all time ashore, in any of the river towns along the Tanana or Yukon, trying to score. Although I hadn't seen it myself, I'd heard he could be charming. He would buy a woman a drink and do anything in his power to get her into bed. It seemed that most of the time that approach worked.

Sometimes, he'd single out one woman and spend days with her, like they were teenagers going steady. They'd be the new couple. They'd be everywhere together until he shipped out, and she would 'wait' for him. Hah! When the *Koyukuk* returned, he'd duck her and take up with another. It helped that he was also said to be a very competent fist fighter. I supposed it went with the territory. It's probably more accurate to say he was just bigger, and probably meaner, than most of the locals.

"Wonder how well he dodges bullets," was Andy's question—around here, a good one.

I was at Evie's for coffee one morning fairly early when her phone rang. She answered it and listened for a second before handing it over. "For you."

Surprised, I held the receiver up to my ear. "Hardy," I said.

"Oh," said a man's voice, "and this is Myles... Conway. Sorry I woke you." He laughed, sounding a little drunk. "Didn't realize you were sleeping there." And he hung up before I could tell him I wasn't.

"He's been calling," Evie said. "Wants to 'buy me dinner at the Coffee Cup, or somewhere in Fairbanks, or Anchorage, or Seattle... or maybe just go out for a drink.'" She looked at me. "You don't have to punch him. I can handle this."

"I know you can." I must have been glowering. She smiled at me, full wattage. I felt my face unlock and couldn't help smiling back.

"Couldn't I just punch him a little?"

* * *

Andy showed up in the morning with Vic limping, in tow. I knew they'd arrived. About twenty seconds before Andy knocked, Jack's ears went up and he gave one low, sharp bark. So, I was ready for the knock.

"Good boy!" I told him, and he thumped his tail.

Both Andy and Vic carried light packs and long guns, Andy with his Mauser and Vic with a Remington pump, twelve-gauge duck gun. They both wore hip boots and Andy suggested I dig mine out, too. He had also arranged to borrow a green-painted canvas canoe, which we picked up on the way and loaded with the dog into the back of the Ford.

"We're going to paddle down the trail?" I asked him.

"It's pretty wet out there, 'specially the first part. We'll carry it or drag it, mostly. But there are a few places we'll need to paddle. We can leave it when we get across the swamp."

We parked next to Arnold's cabin, at the trailhead. When I dropped the tailgate, Jack bounded out joyfully, and galloped up to the door doing his full-body puppy wag. It was clear he thought he was coming home to his old master. We let him in, let him sniff around. Of course, he found nothing and after a few minutes turned to me, looked me in the eyes, his tail finally pausing.

"He's not here," I told him. Answering what seemed like the obvious question. "He's gone on. You'll see him again... later. For now, it's just me." He came over and sniffed the back of my hand, gave it a lick and headed around me out the door. Andy and I exchanged a glance.

"Spooky," he said.

With three carrying, paddles tied to our packs, and the canoe weight at about fifty pounds, we started off well. I had questions about how far Vic would make it on his shot leg. He bent his face into a fake smile.

"It'll hurt less when I get warmed up."

Andy grinned at him. "Sure, it will."

With Andy in the lead and Whisky Jack patrolling in circles around us, we headed due south on a bright day that promised to be warm and perfect in every way—except for the clouds of voracious mosquitoes that wanted our blood. Apparently *all* of it.

"They'll thin out as it warms up," Andy assured us.

We all wore felt hunting hats that worked pretty well with the war-surplus Marine mosquito nets intended to be worn over combat helmets. A drawstring cinched it up tightly around the neck. And we all wore gloves, only occasionally showing a bit of wrist, which mosquitoes had little trouble finding.

"Ouch! Damn!" Vic smacked his wrist.

"Don't scratch it! Here, I got some alcohol." Andy dug in his pack for a tiny, repurposed Mapleine syrup bottle he'd filled with rubbing alcohol.

"Thanks!" Vic handed it back and yanked his cuffs down.

Carrying our canoe, we continued south on what might laughingly be called a trail. In places, it had gone dry and firm, making easy passage. We made good time on what amounted to islands, raised hillocks in the muskeg. Other times we waded, usually ankle-to-knee deep. Andy, in the lead, carried a six-foot staff to ferret out the sudden deep holes in the swampy terrain. Occasionally we launched the canoe and paddled shallow lakes or channels as Jack swam or waded along.

Nothing taller than about fifteen feet grew out here, mostly small willows with the occasional stand of stunted black swamp spruce. There was nothing to climb up on to get a look around. So, on we slogged.

After a good deal of wading, Andy raised a hand and turned. "Let's park the canoe here. If I remember right, this is going to be dry for a while." He started to turn away, then turned back. "There should be an old cabin just up here—if it's still standin'. Let's go in quiet."

He bolted a shell into the Mauser, checking the safety. I reached into my pocket to clutch the .38, which I already knew was there because of its weight. What were we expecting? Easy. We were expecting trouble, and it found us.

"Moose," I said. I was raising my hand to point at the great creature—a bull—when a shot rang out. As one, the three of us dove for cover, not that there was much more than tall grass and thin willows to hide behind. Also startled, the moose ducked and jumped sideways, surprisingly agile, then spun and galloped off into the spruce, thudding hoof beats quickly fading in the soft earth.

"Stay down," ordered Andy tersely, and I saw him scanning with the Mauser scope, finger close to the trigger. "Not seein' nothing," he said at last, with no more shots fired. "You guys stay flat." Cautiously he rose, making a target of himself, but there were no more shots. Whoever it was, the one shot had been intended to keep us in place while he fled. It worked.

"Come on... be ready."

Andy led us cautiously around the spruce stand to a small old plank cabin with a rusty corrugated-steel roof. Rough but mostly weather-tight, we found it empty but not dusty. Someone had been using it, sleeping on the cot, sitting on the chair, using the table. Just a bit of warmth remained in the ashes of a tiny iron pot-belly stove, while not a single shred of anything else remained as a clue. Except for one.

"Hey, look here!" Vic held up a light dog chain, clipped to part of an old hasp on the wall. Drawing his

71

gloved hand along the chain revealed its end, a dog collar made from harness webbing. He held it out for inspection. Hand-sewn in the webbing was the name 'JACK.'

I grabbed and unclipped it.

"The missing collar! Jack was held here—and likely escaped."

"Yeah, but why?" Vic glanced out the door, looking nervous. "Are you guys worried about whoever it was coming back?"

"Nah," said Andy. But he stepped to the door and made another sweep with the scope. "He just wanted to get away. All he gets if he comes back is trouble."

Andy turned, studying the cabin more closely. "He had gear stacked here," he said, pointing. "Cases of something. You can make out the outlines in the dust." He wrinkled his forehead, looking thoughtful. "Never seen anybody so clean. Nothing in the stove. No trash. No cigarette butts or coffee grounds. This is... spooky."

"Spooky?" I perched on the edge of the table.

He pulled off his mosquito net and stuffed it in his pocket then removed his hat and scratched his scalp. "He's not a hunter... too tidy, for one thing. I can't imagine he's a gold prospector. Yeah, there's a stream here, but this area was all claimed and panned way back in the nineteen teens. Not like... escaped from jail, or it would be all over the news." He looked around. "And he had a lot of gear, so he's out here for some reason and doesn't wanna be seen."

I put Jack's collar on him and we turned back for town. We'd been out for about four hours, slogged and paddled five or six miles, and had been shot at. So, we'd already put in a pretty good day.

"You know," said Andy as he closed the cabin door, "if we could get up on any kind of hill here, we could see the RADAR towers at Clear."

Vic was over at the side, peeing, and swiveled just the top of his body to look at Andy.

"Yeah, but if they were spies trying to get a look at the towers, wouldn't they just drive out there and cruise around the whole thing like all the other tourists?" He swatted away a mosquito and shook himself off. "Here," he said to the mosquito, sticking out a bare wrist. "Bite this. You can't have that."

We laughed and turned for home. He was right about spies. Why not drive?

* * *

Evie sat up straight on my sofa where she'd been slouched, studying. It was a Friday evening, end of the week, and we were goofing off together. She stretched her arms straight out sideways from her shoulders, making fists, twisting her wrists.

"Want coffee?" She rose and headed for my kitchen and I could hear her clanking around with the perk pot.

"Sure. That would be great." I was reading the new novel by James Agee, *A Death in the Family*. I hadn't known Agee but we went to the same school in Tennessee, what had been called, in his day, St. Andrew's School for Mountain Boys, near Sewanee and the University of the South. Of course, he attended in the early twenties, and I much later. Reading him now, I sensed greatness. He had been most known as a film critic, dying just a couple of years ago at the age of forty-five, mostly from alcohol.

Coffee on, I watched Evie come back from the kitchen. In languid moments, she had a straight-legged way of walking that swung her hips. It was poetry. Instead of returning to her couch, she came over, kissed me, removed my book and settled herself on my lap. It felt so… domestic.

She sighed. "We need to talk." I can't deny my heart rate shot up. In our history, those have seldom been promising words.

"Okay," I said. What choice did I have? She had me pinned.

"I have the chance to take a class I need at the University in Fairbanks, instead of going all the way back to Seattle to the U."

"Wow," I said. This was going better than I hoped.

"*But…*"

Uh-oh! There it was. I mentally cringed.

"I have to be gone all August."

"Oh." That didn't seem so bad. "Well, isn't that a good thing?"

"Yeah." She drew back a little to focus on my face. "Except for the wedding we were planning to have, sometime this month."

"Oh," I said. "That."

"You still want to, right?"

"I'd marry you right this minute."

She kissed me again. "You're sweet."

"And then we could get right up from this chair and go to bed together."

"You're such a *guy*." She laughed, climbed off my lap and went back to the kitchen to pour coffee. "But that *would* be nice," she called back.

"Ever think about not waiting," I asked, when she came around the corner, bearing coffee.

"Constantly." She sipped, then made a face and changed the subject. "I'll be lucky to get back here for Butch and Adele's ceremony."

On Monday morning, we met at her place for coffee and, carrying her small bag, we walked to the depot together, to put her on the morning train north to Fairbanks.

The conductor, a sturdy man with bushy eyebrows, stepped down to the sandy platform and placed his step. "All aboard."

She kissed me, slowly, very nicely. "Something to remember me by." She turned away, then turned back. "Try to stay out of trouble," she said.

"You know me." I did my best to look innocent.

"That's why I said it." I watched her climb up the steps and, from the platform, followed her progress along through the car. Just about the time she found her seat, the engine bell began to clang, then the whistle blew, and the big locomotive lurched into motion. I waved and she blew kisses. It was silly and very nice. And I'd miss her.

But now I had to settle into a routine of life without her. Since he'd been wounded I hadn't seen much of William, and with Evie and Andy in Fairbanks, I was pretty much on my own. I threw myself into all the priest things, visiting the sick, keeping office hours for people who just needed to talk, even showing up at choir practice to add a voice. I had my garden to work in. Potatoes, carrots and peas were up nicely, but so were weeds. So, I weeded. And I helped Oliver put a new roof on his sister's place, lifting the heavy roofing rolls from the pickup bed, then climbing up with the hammer to help nail it all in place. Butch showed up to help just as we were finishing.

I had invited Vic and Linda to come by for morning coffee and one morning they did. I warned them about the tippy stools and we sat sipping and gossiping like old friends, Vic's straight pipe clenched in his teeth as he puffed occasional clouds of really good-smelling smoke.

When I commented, he said, "I smoke this cherry stuff for Linda. It doesn't taste as good as it smells."

"It's a filthy habit," she confided, "but it does actually smell pretty good and it's better than the cigars he used to smoke. I'm used to it now, and even kind of like it. Once when he was gone, I tried it myself. But I try to get him to smoke outside."

"That's harder in the winter," I observed, "when the temp is minus thirty-five." She agreed.

Two nights later, my phone rang and woke me, just after three. Though I thought it might be Evie, it was Alice.

"Father, I'm sorry, but he's here again. He tried the door. I... could you come?"

"I'm on my way."

"I grabbed the .38 and mostly jogged the three blocks or so with Jack at my heels, but to no avail. I made several loops around the small cabin but found no one, and nothing—like a roll of electrical tape—left behind. I knocked.

"It's Hardy." When she opened the door in her robe, Colt in hand, she threw her arms around me and I hoped the safety was on. She drew me in, waited for Jack then closed the door and bolted it.

"I can't find William. He doesn't answer. I suppose he's out of town on some secret thing. I can't even find Vadim, who I usually can't get rid of. I think he's out panning at Snow Creek." She looked at me, blinking back tears. "Do you think Evie would mind coming over again?"

"Evie's in Fairbanks for the month at the U.

"Oh," she said, pressing her lips together, hanging her head. "Okay."

I looked at my watch. "Look," I said, "it's already after three. How about I just camp on your couch here... though I'm pretty sure you've heard the last of him for tonight. Would that be okay?"

She brightened. "Oh, would you?!" She scurried to find a blanket. The couch wasn't bad, but morning felt a little awkward. In the hard light of day, there we were together and it all seemed a little silly. I was glad to pocket my .38, call Jack, and walk home. *Is this a prank? Does someone just like scaring single ladies?* But in light of Marjorie's really tragic death, could we afford to not take it seriously? I didn't think so.

I had to be away for most of a week. I arranged with Andy to take Jack with him, back to Fairbanks. Oliver, in his boat, would haul me around to the nearby fish camps where I would hold communion services and visit anyone who was sick, both for a blessing and a bit of medical evaluation. I carried a bag with most of the things I would be likely to need, including syringes and a vial each of penicillin and tetanus immunoglobulin, courtesy of the public health nurse. Cuts, punctures, and the occasional burn were common in an outdoor camp where everybody lived and played around a campfire and worked with sharp tools.

It was a regularly scheduled trip, had been planned since last spring and I knew people were counting on it. But I had some trepidation about being gone now, with someone prowling and frightening people. I still hadn't

77

seen or heard from William, presumably healed and back on duty. Alice said he was occupied with an ongoing problem at Clear. He wouldn't say what. Vadim was in and out of town, not really reachable, and I wasn't confident yet that the prowler wasn't him! So, I phoned Vic, who agreed to be on call, and to show up if needed. He said he would wake Linda—if he could—to go along. We both felt it was reassuring to have a woman along in the middle of the night.

That all arranged, I cast us off and stepped into Oliver's long Tanana freight boat, piled high with our gear and with supplies he would deliver. We motored away down the broad, muddy river. The week of camp life would be a blur of wood smoke and mosquitos, privies, camp cooking—getting to taste really good smoked salmon right from the smokehouse—a mix of old and new friends, and lots of smiles.

After a week of wonderful communal camping, the rectory cabin felt empty and way too quiet with no little kids dashing around underfoot. With some regret, I bathed away the pungent scent of wood smoke and threw my clothes into the washer. On the other hand, it was good to have running water and a flush toilet, to bathe and wash my clothes. And it was good to sleep in my own bed, instead of on a pad on the hard floor of a canvas-topped shelter, also housing two other men and a boy—one of them a ferocious snorer.

It wasn't long before I had Alice at my door.

"It happened twice," she said. "I called Vic and he came right over with a gun. He said he couldn't wake Linda, so it was just the two of us. Both times he circled the cabin and checked things. The second time, it was nearly four o'clock, so he stayed—slept on the couch." She looked at me. "Is he a little creepy? I mean, when you look at me, you look at my face. When he looks at me… he looks at everything. I was wearing my robe, but I felt like it wasn't enough. He looked at me like I was a present he wanted to unwrap!"

"Vic? Really?" I must have looked as amazed or perplexed as I felt. "I… I don't know. I never got that sense from him."

She nearly laughed. "Well, you wouldn't, would you? You're a man. It was like he couldn't take his eyes off my tits, and they weren't even showing. I was cold and scared and had 'em wrapped up tight."

"But you…"

"Show 'em off? Sure. I get to. It's good for business. But *I* get to decide when that happens. It's my body. And he stands too close, too. He said he couldn't wake Linda. In the end, I wasn't sure if I really did feel safer having him there. Anyway… I'm sure glad you're back."

It's nice to be appreciated, I guess. Later, on the phone, I asked Evie about Vic.

"Creepy? No… never saw that. But I've never been alone with him, especially in my bathrobe in the middle of the night. That's too bad when something scares you and you call for help and then the *help* scares you."

We had a moment of long silence on the phone, hearing just the slight rustle of static on the line, feeling the presence of each other. "I hate to get off," she said finally, "but I have an exam in the morning. I've gotta study."

"Yeah, I know. I love you."

"I love you back." I heard a click as the line closed. "Sigh," I said to my empty office. *Snap out of it, you, it's only a month!* Yes, but a long one.

79

The prowler spent a busy week. He'd circled Butch and Adele's cabin two nights—with Butch away on a job. The second night, tiny Adele, with the house lantern snuffed, sneaked out the door and aimed a blast from the twelve-gauge shotgun, high in the prowler's direction. She said he hadn't been back. I didn't have to wonder why.

But I did wonder how many houses here in town the prowler had staked out? And I couldn't shake the vivid memory of my last glimpse of poor Marjorie. If this was his work, it was nothing but horrible, and I began to want to catch this guy, really, really badly.

CHAPTER 10

"They call it 'ground clutter,'" explained William, as he sipped his coffee. It was just the two of us on a Monday morning and he was explaining DEW Line RADAR to me, what showed up on the screen and what didn't, and what had been keeping him out of town and preoccupied.

"These RADARs cannot really track what they see on the ground. They are aimed out into the sky. But it does not mean they do not catch a glimpse. One fellow out there can already recognize large animals on his screen and knows when, and approximately where, to pick up his moose. Last fall, just from system testing, he was quite successful."

"But these that they saw now *weren't* moose?"

"No. They saw something out there, but not ghost images. RADAR techs sometime refer to them as *angels*—what they call 'blips' that show up on the screen but are revealed to be not anything. In this case, one fellow—the moose hunter—several times has seen movement where there usually is not any, and not supposed to be."

I topped off his coffee. "Are they that nervous out at Clear?"

He took a sip and met my eyes across his coffee mug. "They are, right now. Next week is scheduled a top-secret test Soviet missile launch. At least we believe it is a test. We *hope* it is a test."

"It's top secret, but you know—well, the U.S. Government knows—about it?"

He managed to look modest. "It *is* what we do. So now we need to be especially, how do you say… on our best foot."

"But the Russians, they don't know you're up and running, do they? Clear Station isn't supposed to be operational for a few more months."

He made a face. "I am fairly certain they know we can see them. It is, after all, what *they* do."

The conversation shifted to Vic, and to Alice's unease. "Perhaps I should speak to him?" William spoke mildly, but with a steely glint in his eye. I knew that glint. It could be dangerous.

"No, let me. I recruited him. Besides, it's more like a conversation a priest would have, than a... well...a boyfriend."

"I am a *boyfriend* now?" He made an embarrassed face and went out shaking his head. I didn't ask him about the scene with Alice and Vadim on the sandbar. I knew he was dangerous.

* * *

It was what Myles Conway should have known, a few nights later, when he started his full-court press on Alice at the bar. After several hours of increasingly aggressive behavior, she started calling around, finally reaching William at my house.

"I'm sorry," she told him on the phone. "I even offered to shoot him—showed him the sawed-off! He thinks it's foreplay. Would you come over?"

"Most certainly," William replied, nearly purring. He removed the three handguns he carried, handing only the smallest to me. "Hold this, just in case." The others I stuffed in a kitchen cabinet, next to the sugar.

It took only a few minutes to walk the several blocks to the Bide-A-While, to find Conway just a little drunk and fully involved in his campaign to bed Alice. It didn't bother him at all that he still had his most recent 'steady,'

Judy, the woman he came in with, by his side. I recognized her as a waitress at the Woolworth's counter in Fairbanks. According to Alice, he'd been hustling Judy so aggressively that she walked off her job and gave notice on her apartment. Already planning to move aboard the *Koyukuk*, she'd been picking out curtains for the captain's cabin from the Sears & Roebuck catalog.

"He's just so dreamy," she told Alice.

But by that night, with the honeymoon already at an end, she was a good deal drunker than Myles. "No, I am not interested in a 'threesome,' thank you very much." She was really hoping someone would "kick the shit out of him."

Relieved, Alice turned to look at us, as we walked in and Conway followed her gaze.

"Uh-oh. The boyfriend!" He'd been here before and knew how this played. So, he set down the dregs of his beer and whirled, aiming a good-sized fist at the side of William's head. Thin, quiet, nearly bookish, I could understand that William probably looked like an easy target. He wasn't.

William easily caught the wrist with his right hand, smoothly pulling, allowing Conway's forward motion to draw him off balance. Next, his left hand caught Conway by the throat, spinning him, quickly driving him the five or six feet to the knotty-pine wall, where he made a big *thud*. He seemed to hang there for a long moment before William pitched him out the door and into the street. We watched and waited but he didn't bother trying to get back in.

"Rah, rah, sis-boom-bah!" chanted Judy, a little too drunk to perform a cheer she probably learned in high

83

school, a little too long ago, finally collapsing in a drunken heap. But she smiled as we helped her up.

She'd have to find a ride back to Fairbanks and beg for her job and her apartment, but the evening hadn't been a complete loss.

* * *

There's something that happens in Interior Alaska as soon as July turns. The air is still warm, leaves still green. The sky is still bright and of course it's still light enough most of the night to be out and about. But there's a whisper... autumn... and further out, its big surly brother, winter.

I'll be honest, the notion of heading into another winter makes me a little blue. This would be my third winter here. And the first two nearly killed me.

The Alaska Territory's official flower is the forget-me-not, but it ought to be an amazing, prolific, pink-flowering weed, appropriately called fireweed. It earns its name by being among the first plants to bloom on freshly burned ground. But here in the Interior, it grows furiously everywhere, all summer long. It blooms from the bottom of the blossom cluster, rising. The folklore is that the first frost happens just as the final blossoms open at the top. They were already two-thirds of the way up.

The next time Vic came by without Linda, I told him we needed to talk. His eyebrows rose and he sucked on the straight stem of a new pipe. He looked around nervously when I invited him into my office and closed the door.

"The last time this happened to me," he said, "I had to stay after school. What's this about?"

We were still standing, him taller and me looking up at him when I said, "It's about you and Alice the night you stayed over. It's about you scaring her."

His clay pipe came unclenched from his teeth, fell all the way to the floor, missed the braided rag rug and smashed to smithereens, spreading ashes and a small plug of still-glowing leaf material across the linoleum tiles. "Me and... Alice?" he croaked.

I knew that for a teacher in a small town, any suggestion of sexual impropriety could be a potential career killer. A sudden dash of the mere possibility must have felt like a pail of icy water to the face.

"Sit down," I said. "Let's talk."

"I... I..." he said.

I felt bad for him. "I didn't mean to startle you, but I think you need to know you scared her. And whatever it was you were doing or thinking that night, you need to not do again."

"I guess not." He sat suddenly in my client chair, like his knees had given out, and even sitting, continued to look shaken and couldn't seem to complete a sentence. "To be completely honest, she *is* about the sexiest woman I've ever seen in my life. Even wrapped in a robe. Linda and I don't... well... we... uh... don't, anymore, if you get my drift. And I might have, well... I might have... but I guess I thought Alice and I... we... were both on the same wavelength. I thought... I can see now I was wrong. I feel so embarrassed. I'll have to apologize."

"Don't apologize," I said. "I don't think it will make things better. Just don't let it happen again. As they say, 'Go thou and sin no more.'"

"Oh," he said, "you can count on that!"

I confess I felt a little bad about having to talk to him about this, and about his wounded, slightly shaky look as he left. I thought again about what a really decent guy he was, and how lucky we were to have him here.

* * *

Andy showed up with my dog and his new car. Well, new to him. He had gotten a good deal on a 1953 Chevy, just four years old, a straight six, running strong. Two toned, it had a cream-colored top up around the windows with a sky blue lower body. He paid one hundred fifty dollars for it, put on two new tires, and hit the road for Chandalar. He was like a kid with a new toy, absolutely desperate to drive somewhere.

"Ready for a road trip?" he asked.

"To where?" He had just come south from Fairbanks and I didn't think he'd want to turn around and drive right back.

"Let's keep going south," he suggested. "Cruise down to Clear."

Since there were no other options, except maybe driving in circles around town—what we used to call 'dragging the gut'—we set off. We had all four windows rolled down. In my mirror I could see Jack's face as he rode with his head stuck out, ears blowing back, mouth open, smiling, and his long pink tongue lolling.

We had a nice day for it, bright and warm, with a few flat-bottomed puffy clouds easing slowly out across the flats. We stopped on a little bit of rise to look out. From there it was easy to see how wet this country is. Bright reflecting pools marched out across the plain like a giant passed through here scattering mirrors, deeply blue now, with clouds easing across them as well. Way off in the distance—maybe ten miles yet—we could see the massive RADAR towers, prominent on the flats, taller than anything else for at least a hundred miles.

Andy pulled out the Mauser, taking the end caps off the scope and using it to examine the terrain. In about two

86

minutes, we had the Highway Patrol speeding up, reminding us we couldn't hunt here now, and checking our identifications.

"Not hunting. Just using the scope." Andy went out of his way to smile when he said it.

The cop was taller than both of us, barrel-chested, and not interested in dialogue. He didn't bother smiling. "Use it somewhere else."

Andy looked around. "It's a highway... public right of way. I don't see no signs."

The cop stepped closer.

"We're going," I said, and got Andy by the elbow.

"See that you do." The cop spent another minute practicing his hard look, thumbs tucked in his gun belt, then climbed back into his black and white cruiser. Pulling out, he floored it, spitting gravel and leaving dust to hang in the air long after he'd moved out of sight.

"Asshole!" said Andy, uncharacteristically. "Sorry, Father."

"No," I said, "I think you called it."

I'd seen that Highway Patrolman before, much friendlier. Everything about his demeanor now said he was under some pressure and I couldn't help but wonder what was really going on.

Driving home, we went back to talking about the prowler. He hadn't heard about William and Myles Conway at the bar.

"I miss all the good stuff! Think it's Conway? Think he's the prowler?"

"He could be. He's pretty definite about wanting, and getting sex. Still, I can't imagine him sneaking around cabins in the dark. Can't imagine him torturing and murdering women, either. Not impossible, I guess."

Andy frowned, thinking. "I bet it's someone we *don't* know. Probably living on one of those sleeper cars."

And I told him that's what I thought, too. But how to prove it? One thing led to another and that's when Andy had the idea.

"Hey," he said. "Let's set a trap. It'll be easy. We'll get a bunch of guys and everybody hide in the woods until the prowler shows, then *bam*, we got 'im."

The only problem with his idea, with setting this kind of trap, is that someone needs to agree to be the 'cheese.' At the Bide-A-While, Alice looked up from polishing the already gleaming bar top.

"No way!" Even though her cabin would be surrounded, and she safe, trying to talk her into it seemed wrong so we headed back to my place to do more planning.

"We don't even need anybody in the cabin!" Andy was excited about this. We can put Alice someplace else for the night. She can stay out at William's."

We were sitting in my living room, and I leaned back to put my feet up. "It would be better if someone was there, maybe listening to the radio or moving around. It has to look convincing. Another thing I'm concerned about—if a couple of us are positioned around the cabin and shooting starts—how do we keep from shooting each other?"

Andy nodded, thinking the problem through. "No shooting," he said, at last. "We'll set snares with rope. Each of us will man one and when this creep steps in, we just yank up the rope end!"

"But we still need bait."

Andy grimaced. "Don't say bait."

About then the phone rang and I went into the office to answer. "Hardy," I said.

"It's Alice. I've been thinking about your plan." She said it in a rush like she needed to get it out before she changed her mind. "I'll do it."

"You sure?"

"No," she said, "but I'll do it anyway. Let me know when." And she hung up.

When I went back into the living room, Andy looked up expectantly. "That was the bait," I told him. "She's in."

In the end, five of us surrounded the cabin, hidden in darkness, each manning a rope with a loop laid out on the rough path around Alice's cabin. It was Andy, me, Oliver, Vic, and Butch. We chanced a daylight planning trip, each selecting a spot to hide and wait. It would be a long couple of hours, with no guarantee anybody would show.

On Thursday night, the sun set at about ten thirty. As agreed, we crept into our hiding places in the dark by about eleven thirty. I brought a boat floatation cushion to sit on and made myself moderately comfortable leaning against a birch tree, concealed behind a bush. Only four of us were armed. Since there was no guarantee the prowler would turn up here, Butch didn't want to leave Adele without her twelve-gauge."

There we sat, listening to mosquitoes buzz around us trying to breach our face nets. "No bug dope," Andy had cautioned. "That stuff stinks!" So, we were bait, too.

About one o'clock, I think I'd been dozing when I heard a twig crack. Alice had long since turned in, leaving only her bathroom light on, as was her custom. I could picture her wide awake, fully dressed under a nightie, lying on her bed clutching a .45.

I saw a figure pass between me and the bathroom window. Tall, bulky... definitely a man, face hidden by shadow under a felt hunting hat. Certainly big enough to

89

be Conway! We waited. Sure enough, he went to the door and tried it, then appeared to be heading for one of the windows. When he stopped, right in the middle of Oliver's rope loop, as if considering his next move, Oliver yanked!

The figure startled, teetered, fell, cursed then cursed some more as Oliver hauled him through the brush by his feet. The shooting I expected, feared, didn't happen, though there was a lot of cursing, mostly in Russian.

The five of us fell on him, with difficulty holding down arms and legs, Andy sitting on his chest. Andy produced a flashlight and trained it on our captive's face. He didn't need to. All of us already knew we'd bagged Vadim.

We'd made enough noise that Alice came out cautiously.

"Vadim?!" She looked down at him and bunched her eyebrows in disbelief. "What are *you* doing here?" Then she looked at us. "Come on, guys, it's Vadim. Let him up."

We did so, reluctantly.

"I came for… kissing…" he said, "for love making… as you promised."

Alice looked confused. She looked worse than that with her clothing on under her robe and one skinny wrist stuck out, fist clenching her Colt grip.

"I promised?"

"In your note." He fished in his jacket pocket and came up with a folded sheet of light-blue note paper, obviously torn from a bar pad, with "Bide-A-While, Chandalar, Alaska printed at the top.

The darker blue script, handwriting with a feminine look, was addressed to Vadim and invited him here now, to spend the night—and more.

There was a bit of Scotch tape at the top, now folded over.

"I found this," he explained, "when I got to lodge tonight, tape to my door, to come here now. I change my clothes, shower, shave... I smell good..." he informed us. Not necessary, because he reeked of cheap cologne. We could have easily located him in the dark.

Andy, with a puzzled look on his face, stepped forward.

"Empty your pockets." Vadim did. There wasn't much—no electrical tape—just gum wrappers, lint, and six packaged condoms. Andy looked at him, puzzled. "Six?" Vadim shrugged modestly.

Andy looked around. "Let's call it a night."

While we were all still bunched around Vadim, Alice stepped up and laid her hand flat on his chest. She had to reach up.

"I like you," she told him. "But I don't love you and I don't plan to have sex with you. I'm sorry you got your hopes up, but I didn't write this note and I won't be writing any others. And I especially won't be writing any that promise sex. We can be friends, but that's all. Do you understand?"

He looked around at all of us, glum, and more than a little chagrined. He knew she was telling him in front of witnesses. He shook his head, like he couldn't quite believe what he was hearing, and generally looked sad.

"But you let me feeling your titties," he protested.

She flushed pink instantly, right up her neck to her face, visible even by flashlight.

"I did. That was a big misunderstanding on my part. I'm sorry. We won't be doing that again, either." Now he looked *really* glum. I guessed I would too, in the same situation.

I yawned. "It's past our bedtimes."

We let go of Vadim and watched him walk away, clearly dejected and, I thought, a bit dazed.

"He was set up," said Andy.

I turned to look at him. "We all were."

CHAPTER 11

Morning brought Frank Jacobs early for coffee. "Flew down this morning. Knew you'd be up." He looked at Andy, who had spent the night on my couch. "You, too." With less than four hours of sleep, we weren't very up. The coffee helped. He filled his cup and declined canned milk. "We got zilch on Marjorie's murder."

"You're ahead of us." Andy sat on a tippy stool to pull on his boots. "Well, almost. We did manage to capture a horny Russian."

The marshal looked interested. "Tell me about it." He listened and didn't laugh. "Poor guy," he said of Vadim. "Way up and then way, way down." He looked at me, then at Andy. "But you know what this means."

"It means one of us," I said, "somehow tipped off the real prowler. He knew we'd be there." I thought about it a minute more. "And it means he's playing with us."

"You guys talk about this at the Bide-A-While?" We looked at each other and nodded.

"Probably," Andy said.

"Yep. There's your leak." The marshal looked around. "Got any donuts? A donut right now would go real good with this fine Italian coffee."

Andy did a double take. "I wish!" he said. "A donut in Chandalar? I don't think so."

"No?" The marshal smiled and reached into a canvas pack at his feet. "Well, then, have one of mine." He produced a bag of fresh ones from the bakery in Fairbanks. It was like manna from heaven.

Later, munching and dunking happily, we got back to the prowler, and I said what we were all thinking.

"So, it *could* be someone we know."

The marshal took a bite of donut. "That's a long shot. Fact is, your town is full of strangers. And this guy is likely a pro. He's done this somewhere before. But it could be someone *somebody* in your group knows. It could even be Alice who tipped it, talking about it and overheard."

Andy puffed defensively. "It has to be a stranger. It *can't* be somebody from here. We all *know* everybody we know. I don't believe any of us is a torture murderer."

"Wait a bit." The marshal held up a cautionary hand. "We don't actually know that the prowler is the murderer. Could be related... or not." He was right, of course. Alice, from her work at the Bide-A-While, with her low-cut tops and stunning breast views, was well known and universally admired—by men at least—not just in Chandalar, but for miles around.

"And don't forget," he added, "your prowler could be a woman. You hear about that. Occasionally."

Andy set down his coffee mug. "It's not just Alice being prowled. It's women all over town. He ticked them off on his fingers: Evie, Adele, Linda... maybe more who we don't even know about. The others are not so well known as Alice and not nearly so exposed." He hesitated. "So to speak."

So, there we were. Nowhere. It felt like we had circled all the way back around to square zip. We probably did know something but had no idea what.

* * *

On Monday morning, Molly Joseph came up the dirt road leading Henry, who had already outgrown most of his recent mission barrel clothing. She wore a scarf tied over straight black hair hanging nearly to her waist, a brown plaid jacket, blue jeans and what must have been child-sized, red U.S. Keds high tops.

94

Hard to believe the first time she'd come searching for clothing and supplies, Henry had still been on the inside. Now he walked and talked, cavorted really, through piles of old clothing on the floor like I'd cavorted at his age, through piles of dry oak leaves in the South. I could almost smell them.

Molly brought back a load of clothing and came searching for more, including something like a warm jacket, a parka, really, for Henry. I think we both knew she'd end up making one herself, so she mostly collected garments she could deconstruct. Most of our clothing came from churches in Tennessee, where I'd gone to seminary, and points south. They never sent us used parkas. We did find a tiny, dandy, seersucker blazer, just Henry's size. Molly held it up and giggled, hand over her mouth to hide laughter in the old Native way. I noticed something I never had before, how small and cute she was, with an infectious laugh.

So, we were both laughing when Vic and Linda showed up to sort and fold clothing. I made sure everybody knew each other. They did. Vic and Linda brought back the last of what they'd borrowed, all freshly washed and folded. For once, the folded piles threatened to outnumber the garments in piles on the floors. That wouldn't last.

We worked through the morning and I invited them all to lunch, but Molly said she had to get Henry home for his nap. So, Vic, Linda, and I came back over to the rectory. Linda made coffee while I sliced moose meat and made sandwiches. We talked about not much, laughed a lot, and I was sorry to see them head off up the road later.

I split wood for about an hour, working up a healthy sweat while Whisky Jack lazed alongside, sleeping in the sun. It felt good to use those muscles and I marveled at how much stronger and more muscular I was now than when I arrived. Oh, I'd been in shape before, when I worked my way through seminary as a boxer. I used to travel the Mid-South on weekends to compete at local events we called 'smokers.' They were casual boxing events—yes, always smoky—sponsored by social clubs in towns like Chattanooga, Knoxville, or Memphis. The winner—often me—would take home sixty-to-seventy percent of the purse.

I'd met my late wife, Mary, at one of those events. Knocked down in a bout, I wasn't doing so well, when I saw her face—like an angel's—above me and her lips moving. "Get up!" she said, and I did, won the fight, won the girl and lived happily ever after, until she died suddenly of polio. Thinking my life was pretty much done, I came up here, probably to die, but didn't. I met Andy and Evie, and my heart started beating again. True, I'd lost Mary, but I hadn't lost the shape of her in my heart. It was like a door to a room filled with memory, that I now walked past, but knew was there, and knew I could open.

Of course, after all that, I wasn't in such good physical condition anymore. So, this felt good. I stacked most of my wood, lost in thought, only coming back into the moment as I dropped the last few pieces into place. It was like, in one second, I time-traveled from Sewanee—three years and three thousand miles ago—to Chandalar, and it left me dazed.

* * *

William showed up for coffee the next morning. It had been ten days since I'd seen him. The thin man looked thinner and worn. I looked him over carefully. "What have you been doing?" He just rolled his eyes and reached for a coffee mug.

"They are crazy out there," he said, referring to the RADAR station. He pulled off his wire rims to pinch and massage the bridge of his nose. "They believe they are under attack!"

I laughed. It seemed absurd. "By whom?"

"Well, that is just it. They are not sure. They are seeing shapes at the margins of their screens, screens aimed to the skies. They say they are seeing 'angels.' What they are actually seeing is ghosts!"

It didn't take long for the conversation to slide over to the topic of Vadim—and Alice.

"I saw you out by the river, seeing the two of them."

He nodded. "Yes, I know."

"You let me see you seeing them, so I wouldn't have to worry about whether I should tell you."

He nodded again. "This is so."

"And..." I was moving onto shaky ground here. "Alice, who most likely loves you, allowed herself to be fondled by Vadim because you told her to."

He hung his head, made a face, and looked—for him—a little embarrassed.

"Yes, that is also true. How did you know?"

"Well, for one, you didn't shoot him." He laughed, was silent for a bit, then spoke, staring into the bottom of his coffee mug.

"It was a misunderstanding. I told her to go along with anything he suggested... meaning spy things, *not* meaning she should allow herself to be undressed and fondled. I admit not foreseeing the possibility of fondling." He shrugged. "Yes, I do feel stupid."

We sipped coffee and the kitchen clock ticked. Somewhere out on the block I heard a child squeal and a dog bark. Distantly, a two-stroke chain saw fired up, sputtering at first. I could imagine the cloud of oil-rich smoke and fount of fresh chips as it bit into wood.

"I love my brother," he said finally, "but I do not know him well and cannot afford to trust him just because he is my brother. He is Russian, but more, he is a Soviet, and they are our sworn enemies. Premier Malenkov is nothing but a bit of candy, a 'sweet,' soon to be devoured from within by a man named Nikita Khrushchev, a blunt, hard tool. He is the power behind that throne. Khrushchev has ambitions and one of them is to subdue and subject the United States.

"So, why is my brother here? And why now? I do not know. Is he truly just here for panning gold? It is hard to believe. At a time when more than seventy percent of the United States is *off limits* to visiting Soviets, here—somehow—is my brother!"

He paused, sipped his coffee, holding the cup close enough that steam fogged the bottoms of his lenses. "So, I must watch him… in a way *test* him… or possibly suffer consequences."

It was then I told him about setting a trap for the prowler and catching Vadim. He laughed. Vadim had also told him, confessing—in the process—of his crush on what Vadim called 'William's lady.'

William's eyes met mine. "Vadim is not the prowler." He hesitated. "And he certainly is not a murderer of women. Vadim is a *lover* of women. A great, passionate fool who would cut off his hand before he would harm—especially—someone he is feeling this way about."

"He was set up," I said.

"Indeed."

* * *

Alice brought me a magazine. I'm not a prude. I've been around... the army, college. But I couldn't look at it. It was a much-handled 'bondage' magazine from before the war. We've all seen plenty of lurid, pulp-magazine covers with voluptuous, scantily-clad women tied up and threatened. In this magazine, they were tied up and weren't just threatened. It was all happening in glorious black and white and looked painfully real. Real whips and ropes, real welts, real degradation, and plenty of rough-looking sex. I tossed it into the woodstove and watched it burn, before remembering it might be evidence.

Alice shook her head. "I couldn't look at it, either. I found it in my storeroom, back in a corner on the floor."

I made a face. "Who goes back there?"

"I find all kinds of people back there, doing... things. But since Marjorie died, it's mostly just Ray."

"Ray?"

"He's a trapper. At least that's what he says he is. I haven't seen him trap anything but beers. He trades me one beer a day for sweeping the place out. When it gets real cold out, I let him sit and drink where it's warm as long as he likes. The hard part about it is he stinks so bad.

"He squats in abandoned cabins around here, rarely has much of a fire—so never takes off his clothes—and certainly never bathes.

"Truth... he spends a lot of time staring at me, which a lot of my customers do. There aren't many women around here to stare at, and no exposed skin. So, you know... it's okay. It is what it is. But..." she shivered, "it's one thing to imagine sex with a woman, and another to imagine..."

She didn't finish her sentence. After seeing the magazine, she didn't have to.

99

* * *

The wedding of Butch and Adele Neilson finally happened on the afternoon of the third Saturday in August. With fish camps ending and people drifting back into Chandalar from summer employment on the river or the railroad, we had a full house. Everyone knew them both and liked them.

Best of all, for me at least, Evie came home on a break from her education master classes. In the absence of a degree, they would temporarily certify her for another year of employment as a third-grade teacher in the Chandalar school.

"Welcome home," I told her as she walked into my outstretched arms. I kissed her and then we just stood together for what seemed a long time. I could have stood longer. She felt warm and perfect.

Adele radiated light. She was a beautiful bride—tiny, not more than four feet ten in her parka and wool socks— but today wearing a yellow dress she'd found and loved, from the mission barrel. Months earlier, she'd also discovered a pair of white high-heeled shoes, just her size, with one heel broken off and taped inside for safe-keeping. Butch had managed to glue and nail the shoe back together, but the protruding nail head made her limp a little until Evie pulled Adele aside and put a Band-Aid on her sore foot.

In frequent Chandalar style, the wedding was not without controversy. *Technically*, Adele was marrying her son—well, step-son. And yes, Adele and he already shared a surname, Neilson, because Adele had originally been married to Butch's father, Big Scotty, who died.

When Butch had first arrived, about a year ago, he came as her son. At first that seemed fine, until he found

100

himself falling in love with her and wanting more. So, he'd had to go away and then come anew, bearing a bunch of daisies. I'd been there on the platform as he stepped down from the train, swept her into his arms, literally picked her up. It had taken maybe thirty seconds for her to put aside dreams of motherhood, and here they were.

Dressing Butch for the wedding had not been so easy. Fortunately, we had buried his father's old pinstripe suit on his father. It had a double-breast and looked like something from a George Raft gangster movie. Although maybe it was the two-tone wingtip shoes. There was nothing else in Chandalar, certainly nothing in the mission barrel, and not even anything in Fairbanks big enough to fit Butch. Having a formal suit made just to get married, that he'd never wear again, didn't make a lick of sense. Finally, digging through the Eddie Bauer catalog, they found a Pendleton wool shirt in a double XX size, a soft plaid, with stripes of yellow, black and predominately, a deep, sky blue. He wore that over a brand new, blazingly white t-shirt, with a fresh pair of black Dickies work dungarees and his 'pretty good' pair of Romeos. It was about as close to sartorial splendor as we were likely to get in Chandalar, at least for someone as large as Butch.

We were all there: William with Alice—and Vadim— Andy with Rosie, Evie and me, of course, Oliver, Vic and Linda, Molly Joseph with Henry, and even Marshal Frank Jacobs who flew in specially, plus a full house of congregation and well-wishers. We all spilled out onto the porch and down the steps of the little log church, a bright bouquet of celebration under a deep blue and flawless sky. We then headed across the street to the parish hall for coffee and a Rosie-baked-and-decorated sheet cake the size of Nebraska. Birches along the lane were already going to gold, and pink fireweed had bloomed to the top. It was a soft, balmy evening with the temperature in the high sixties. It all felt wonderful and carefree, and I thought just for a second, it might go on this way forever.

It wouldn't.

CHAPTER 12

Myles Conway stalked Evie. With the *Koyukuk* on the ways for a prop repair, he jumped the train to Fairbanks and managed to track her down at the University. She came out of a seminar on modern education techniques to find him waiting.

"He was sober and absolutely charming," she reported.

He asked her out for drinks and she declined. So, he asked her to dinner and she declined that, too.

"I'm engaged," she told him.

"Where's the ring? No ring, no engagement."

"Sorry," she said.

"Really?" He leaned in.

"No, I was just being polite."

"So, not sorry."

"Not a bit."

He straightened... preened, she recalled, even running his fingers through his thick hair.

"You know you want me. A big guy, good-looking. A guy who knows all the tricks with women. A guy who can really... please you."

"I have one of those," she told him.

"So," he said, out of other options, "how 'bout we just sleep together? I won't tell."

"You bet you won't!"

But he did. Even without actually sleeping with her, he came back to Chandalar and spent his three days ashore telling anyone who'd listen about the remarkable nights he'd spent with Evie, and how I didn't know.

* * *

Alice called me. "He's here and he's lying his ass off about sex with Evie." She hesitated.

"What?"

"He's talking about tying her up... doing... whatever he wanted. It reminded me of..."

"Yes. I'm on my way."

I took the gun. I told myself I wouldn't use it. But if my time in Chandalar had taught me anything, it was to not show up for a gunfight without a gun.

I found him drinking but not drunk. "Well, well," he said, not a bit surprised. It all felt like something from a John Wayne movie.

I didn't confront him, didn't want to give him the excuse or opportunity to just start swinging. So, I slid up on the stool next to him and asked Alice for a ginger ale. When it came, I took a sip. Vernor's, from back in the Midwest, my favorite.

I turned to look at him. "You've been talking about Evie. Lying. I'd like you to stop. I'm asking you nicely, to stop."

"Lying, is it? You're that sure?"

"Absolutely."

"So, you're..." he looked around, checking his audience, "calling me a liar?" I knew this game. I'd played it in junior high.

"Absolutely."

He stood up, satisfied. This was what he wanted. He smiled at the onlookers. Then here came the big, slow fist. I tipped my head to let it drift past. He looked confused. With apparently only one punch in his collection, this usually worked for him. Now he wasn't sure what to do.

Sliding off the stool, I reached out to tap the end of his nose with my index finger. This was his last chance but he

104

wasn't smart enough to take it. His eyes crossed. He didn't block me, couldn't block me. If I had actually punched him, he'd be folding his nose back into place with a lot of blood.

"You can still back out," I told him.

He flushed purple. "So can you," he said, and came at me windmilling, with no guard up. For all his practice, he really wasn't very good at this.

I bent him at the middle with a short sharp jab. He *ooofed* a belch of stale beer breath in my direction, but didn't slow much. There were only six other drinkers in the bar, but this was where legends began. He'd need to make the most of it.

More wild punches, still no guard. I slapped him across his cheek, hard. It made a resounding *thwack* in the room, leaving a red handprint, but on he came.

This wasn't going well for him, and by the look in his wild eyes, he knew it. For all his 'manliness,' he was already way out of breath, huffing, stumbling, and he couldn't keep his hands up for defense.

Since he clearly wasn't going to stop, I slugged him, a left to the jaw that spun his head. He tried to stiff-arm me to the knotty-pine wall but I collapsed his nose to his face with a sickening crack and cascade of blood down his front. He stopped in his tracks, looked down, then sat down suddenly as his knees buckled, rocking, moaning, and bleeding on the barroom floor.

His small but fervent audience applauded me as I massaged my sore fists. I admit I waved to them and went to finish my ginger ale. If Conway hoped to be a 'legend,' now he was, and he would never live it down.

* * *

"You did what?" Evie nearly snarled. This was a whole new side of her and not nearly the 'atta boy' I'd been expecting.

"I... he was lying... about you! He asked for a fight and I gave it to him."

"An idiot spouts off in a bar and you, the priest, go over to brawl with him in public?! What kind of example do you suppose *that* sets for your parishioners? For my students? Am I glad you're tougher? I always knew you were tougher, but that's not the point, is it?"

"Well I..." I said, and gave it up. I saw her point.

"Oh, Hardy," she said, more softly, "what am I going to do with you?"

"Kiss me?" I ventured, without much hope, but she did.

* * *

On the first day of hunting season, William, Andy, Vic, and I went south for moose, instead of downriver— east—as we had done before. This was William's idea. His friend, the one who saw ghosts on RADAR images, insisted we'd find moose there. I was willing to give it a go.

We wore our tall boots but didn't need them. It was drier now, the river quite low. We'd had no rain at all for at least a month. Somewhere upwind, crews were tending a wildfire that gave us bright orange sunsets, and in the sharp, cooler air, a smoky tang.

We parked at the trailhead by Arnold Gustafson's cabin, all wearing gloves, wool jackets, and red hunting hats. I thought about bringing Jack, but in the end, left him with Evie. We didn't need a dog scaring the moose, just in case we actually saw one. We all carried long guns in addition to handguns, Andy with the Mauser, me with my father's old lever-action .30-30, and Vic carrying one of Andy's surplus war rifles, a Springfield .30-06. He'd showed up with a .22, hardly a moose rifle, but Andy insisted he carry a moose gun and offered to lend him one, so we doubled back to Andy's cabin to pull it from his under-floor 'vault.'

Vic looked it all over with interest. "A gun rack and a vault. Think you got enough guns?"

Andy smiled. "How many guns does an Alaskan need?"

Vic made an I-don't-know face.

"Just one more," I told him. Andy laughed.

I'm still not sure what William carried—something European. Long-barreled and long-scoped, it featured an adjustable monopod brace that fit under the stock to steady the shot. One thing about it: I hadn't seen him miss yet.

We weren't planning to be out overnight, so only carried light packs with water and snacks, a bit of emergency gear—flares, first aid—and optimistically, bolts of cheese cloth, long knives and a meat saw, just in case we actually shot something.

We were out at about five, well before sunrise. It was nippy, with the temperature in the middle thirties and a fog laying in low. Dampness amplified the raw chill. There was a light glaze of frost on the railroad tracks, no doubt a harbinger. From the rise of railroad tracks, Andy looked out over the flatland. "Won't be long, this will all be under three or four feet of snow and thirty below."

"Oh, boy!" said William, practicing irony. "I can hardly wait."

"You get used to it though, right?" Vic looked around, hopeful.

"*Sure, you do.*" Andy said it falsely, big, then winked. "Someday."

Vic just grinned. "I'm out of here. Linda lied."

"Somebody lied to somebody," Andy replied. "I'm guessing it wasn't her."

So, bantering quietly, we followed the slight trail out across the flats. The sun, when it rose, cast the whole landscape in a warm yellow glow, making something lovely out of a lowland bog. Here and there, intricate moisture-covered spider webs strung between grass and willows shone like silver.

Andy looked back at me over his shoulder. "Heard your buddy Conway rented the Patterson place. Guess he's staying around for the winter."

"*My* buddy? Swell."

"Not doin' much drinking, though. At least not at the Bide-A-While."

"Not until his nose heals."

We soon passed the place Arnold's body had been discovered. And in another mile or two, the shack where Jack had been kept, empty and dusty again, with its door ajar.

By midmorning, we had made about ten miles— roughly halfway to the area supposedly revealed on the RADAR scopes. We were all cautiously excited. I remember thinking we should be seeing moose. Personally, I liked finding moose closer to the trailhead and the truck.

The land rose a little here but not enough for a viewpoint. We still couldn't see much of anything in any direction except the Alaska Range way off south—and when the fog burned off, a glimpse of Denali.

Passing through a little willow thicket, we flushed a couple of ptarmigan, not yet turning white. On another day, with a shotgun, they might have been tempting. We paused a few seconds, startled by the explosive launch, watching their backs as they flew away.

I turned, took one step, and a bullet exploded a small birch tree at just about my head level. Throwing myself flat, my Winchester out in front of me, I remember thinking that a hunter had mistaken us for a moose. It happened all the time, in spite of such things as bright red hats. But what might have been a random shot or two, quickly became a large-bore firefight, bullets from big guns *zipping* and *spatting* as they passed by or slammed into trees, half-rotten stumps and the ground around us.

"Hide your hats." It was Andy calling out between shots, at half voice. "No sense giving them a target." I quickly snatched mine off and stuffed it beneath me. In one second, I'd been yanked back to France. Tiny, deadly lead slugs flew willy-nilly. My face pressed to the ground, smelling dirt, my heartbeat thundered in my ears. Then silence. As abruptly as the shooting started, it stopped, and we waited several minutes. Nothing.

"These are not moose hunters." William's voice had a casual sound. He said it like he might say, 'It is sunny today,' or 'Please pass the salt.'

"Ya *think?*" Andy, also sounded unreasonably calm. "I wonder if they're gone."

I risked looking up to see him, just in front of me, raise his red hat on a fragment of branch. A shot rang out, the hat spinning away, a dime-sized hole in its crown.

"Nope!" he said. "Still here."

William's voice: "Keep your heads down. Cock your weapons." I didn't want to. But just the same, I levered a

109

shell into the chamber. Whatever came next, I wasn't for it. I wanted to get home to Evie in one piece. I wanted us all to get home in one piece.

"We are pinned down," said William, still very calm, as if hearing my thoughts. "They are not shooting at us by accident. We must consider they intend to harm us."

"I... forgot to load mine." Vic's voice, quavering, sounded clearly terrified. Oddly it made me feel better that not everybody was so matter-of-fact.

"Go ahead and load 'er up now." Andy slipped the caps off his Zeiss scope and squirreled himself around to face the shooters. The movement of the grass and brush around him drew a couple of random shots.

"I... I can't." Vic had just borrowed the gun without taking the time to figure out how it all worked. He must have thought no one would be attacking him before he had time to make sense of it. Of course, being shot at also makes it hard to concentrate. I crawled to him through the grass. With no jaunty pipe in his teeth, and his face paper white, he didn't look so good. In fact, he probably looked like I felt.

I knew the gun. I'd used it before. "Like this." We got him loaded up, including a shell in the chamber.

"We're ready here." For no particular reason, I slithered back to my original spot.

"If you got ear plugs," said Andy, "use 'em now." I had and I did.

"We are going to return fire," said William. "But do not empty your weapon. Three or four rounds will be sufficient." What he didn't say in his professorial tone was that if we emptied our guns, they might come running up to finish us off. But I got his drift.

Facing the wrong direction for shooting, I shifted around for better position. I must have raised my body farther than intended. A shot rang out, and the bullet zipped across my back, cleanly slicing the fabric of my wool coat. It felt better now, roomier, for having been slit open.

"Ouch!"

"Got you?" Andy's voice, with just a touch of panic. He was probably imagining having to tell Evie that he'd taken me out and let me get shot. I'd sound panicky, too.

"No, I'm good. Just a little tailor work on the back of my jacket."

"Swell." He was trying to scan with the scope, without raising his head enough to be a target. It wasn't working. I knew he owned a sniper's periscope, but was pretty sure he hadn't brought it along on a moose hunt. As if this weren't all bad enough, we also had the sun in our eyes. The perfect ambush.

"Okay... can't see anything from down here. We gotta return fire all at the same time, so I can jump up and try to find some raised cover. And we gotta fire without actually getting our asses shot off. Any questions?"

"I have to go to the bathroom."

"Sure, Vic, you go ahead." Andy's eyes met mine. "Don't get shot."

"You, too."

"On three. One. Two. *Three.*"

I didn't get up. I kind of rolled over on my side, not bothering to try to aim, just pointing the rifle, firing, levering in a new shell, and firing again. I did it four times, leaving myself four rounds, and then when I stopped, quickly slid four fresh rounds into the chamber.

As soon as we finished our little volley, we got a volley back. They were set up for shooting and were aiming, so it was close. I took another slug through the padded shoulder of my jacket before I remembered to roll back flat.

In the next silence, I heard one shot fired, and then quickly, another—from our side. And then a faint cry from the other side, sounding like a hit. It was Andy shooting.

"Got one." I rolled around to where I could see him sighting through the scope. "Up ahead," he whispered, "up one hundred yards... spruce thicket... can't see nothing... well, except part of a guy who's now got his own bullet hole.

"Okay," he said after a space, "looks like they're headin' out. I'm for lettin' 'em head."

"Yes," said William. "By all means, allow them to leave."

"Draggin' one."

I rolled over on my back, suddenly feeling both shaky and short of breath, my heart still pounding. I'd been here before, *after* it was all over. It wasn't just me. Vic rolled over and threw up. I didn't blame him.

"Anybody shot?" Andy was still peering through the scope. "Feel around. Sometimes you get hit and don't know it." I felt around.

"No holes, no blood," I reported.

"Not shot," huffed Vic.

"So, who wants to stand up first?" Andy took his eye from the scope to look in William's direction. "How about you, old-timer? But slow. Maybe lead with your hat on a stick."

"Old-timer!" William muttered but slowly raised his red hat on a bit of branch, as we collectively held our breaths. Nothing. No shot rang out. Still, Andy sighted.

"Here I am going." William thrust himself up into the air. I don't know if he was breathing as he did it. I know I wasn't. Again, no shots rang out.

"Okay, now you other guys." Vic and I slowly stood while Andy kept watch through the scope. Still no shots.

Unexpectedly, William began to jog through the brush and bunch grass toward the small clump of short, black spruce. Seeing him, I jumped up to follow then Vic, with Andy still aiming. We made it into the spruce, finding no one, nothing but a spatter pattern of dark red blood on a tree trunk, confirming a bullseye for Andy. And a good thing, too. Otherwise, we'd still be pinned down.

It was then I realized, as I had before in times of trouble, that I'd forgotten to pray. I'd say that to Evie later: "I forgot to pray, again." I remember what she said the last time.

"God won't save you."

I must have looked a bit shocked. "Huh?"

"It's what you said to me. God won't swoop down on his cloud just because you're in trouble."

"I said that?"

"You said God gives us the tools to save ourselves. That *we're* the moving parts." She was right, I did say that... did believe that.

"And my action is my prayer."

"Hardy!" said Andy, harder, and I realized he'd already said it once.

I looked up. "Huh?"

"You here?"

"Only a little." He gave me an 'Andy' look: funny, serious, and a little nutty.

"Ahead or back?" he repeated... apparently.

I looked at the three of them looking at me. "Since they could be set up around the next bend, or the next after that, turning back seems sensible. We could still see a moose on the way home."

"Unanimous then." Andy looked at William, who nodded, and as if on cue, we all stepped for home.

We were much closer to home, maybe a mile from the truck, when I looked off east into a little spruce bog and sure enough, there was our moose. He stood taller and thicker than a horse, with a massive spreading rack. He hadn't seen us—they're nearsighted—and with the breeze in our faces, hadn't smelled us. Munching the green ends off the black spruce, he didn't hear us. I looked at Andy who looked at me.

"You saw 'im. He's yours... first shot anyway."

Still a little shaky after the ambush, I managed to aim, take and release a breath, squeeze the trigger, and drop the huge creature where he stood. Andy jogged closer, firing one more shot with his handgun to make sure the creature couldn't shift and harm us, and to limit its suffering. Then he beckoned us closer.

"Good shot!" He waited until we had all gathered around the moose. "Our elders," he said, "knew the songs to sing to spirits of these hunted creatures." He made a face and shook his head. "But I don't know them. So maybe a prayer to the Creator." He bent to put his palm flat on the moose shoulder. "Thank you, moose," he said.

When we'd each thanked the moose, I said, "Heavenly Father, thank you for sending us home safe today. Thank you for this moose. Thank you for the food

114

and warmth of his meat and hide. Thank you for the strength and wildness his spirit brings to ours. In Jesus' name, amen."

"Amen," the others echoed, and we set about skinning our moose, no easy task, and getting ready to pack out a good share of his nearly two thousand pounds. We, along with many of our parishioners and others, would eat well this winter, thanks to this moose.

I've always enjoyed hunting. As a boy, I'd go out deer hunting in the autumn hardwood forests of Kentucky and Tennessee, carrying this very rifle! But I'd learned that a lot of the magic of hunting dissipated rapidly, after we bagged our quarry and had to skin it out and pack it home. I thought about that now in the mess, stickiness, and pervasive smell of blood. We rolled and tied the hide, cheesecloth-wrapped the huge quarters to carry as flies and insects came from absolutely everywhere to join in.

We'd come out hunting and bagged this fine moose. But we all found it difficult to keep from looking back over our shoulders, to keep from startling or freezing at bird calls or the skitter of other small creatures. Was there someone out there? Were they even now circling? In the end, I was glad to shoulder my moose quarter and stagger off toward the safety of truck and home.

But the larger question: Was someone hunting *us*?

CHAPTER 13

After each year's successful hunt, we hold a big moose-ribs party in my backyard. We bring tables and chairs over from the parish hall, set them up in a long line under the cottonwoods and build a big crackling fire. Andy and Rosie concoct a sticky, tangy, delicious barbecue sauce. They grill the huge ribs over the fire as we drink beer or soda, laugh, talk, and carry on, telling tall tales and hunting 'lies' into the dusk.

We had another big crowd including Adele and Butch just back from their honeymoon at Circle Hot Springs, Oliver, Vic and Linda, and William and Alice with Vadim. Even Frank Jacobs, flying home from somewhere, stopped by.

Sitting with Evie, holding her hand, we watched Molly Joseph trail young Henry, trying to keep him from dashing or falling into the fire. We both looked ahead to the time we'd be married and have one of our own to chase. Meanwhile, we contented ourselves watching our new dog work the crowd for bits of moose meat on discarded bones.

In the cold and dark of the coming winter, I would conjure this scene: firelight and starlight, everybody bundled up in checkerboard or plaid wool or flannel. There were felt hats on mostly-unshaven men with women wearing headscarves. Cigarettes, pipes, and cigars lifted silver smoke skyward as yellow cottonwood leaves came drifting down. Although I'd been to other barbecues in other places, usually warmer, for me this had a distinctly 'Alaska' look and feel to it.

Through the long evening, we all talked and laughed, ate wonderful barbequed moose meat, and dribbled sticky sauce on our shirtfronts. Too soon it was all done for another year. With the fire burned to coals and the tables washed and carried away, the crowd stumbled happily, contentedly, off into darkness as a few of us crowded into my kitchen to wash and dry dishes and try to remember where everything was supposed to go.

"Who *lives* here?" said Rosie, when—for about the third time—I had no idea where something went. I knew in her kitchen, there'd be an exact place for everything.

I shrugged. "I try to be spontaneous." She threw a soggy dishtowel at me.

* * *

"I flew that area you were ambushed... saw nothing, nobody." It was the five of us, Frank, Andy, and me still sitting around holding coffee cups, smelling of wood smoke, with Rosie asleep in a stuffed chair and Evie curled up on the sofa next to me, her head pillowed on my thigh.

"Nobody at all? Not even hunters?"

He shook his head. "Nobody."

Andy leaned in. "Doesn't mean they're not out there."

"It means they don't want to be seen," said Evie, without opening her eyes, apparently not asleep.

The marshal smiled at her. "Bingo," he said. "Clear Base is jittery as hell. Sorry, Father. They're certain they're about to be attacked."

I met his eyes. "Are they?"

He pursed his lips and blew. "Tell me who would want to attack them?"

"That's not a mystery," said Andy. "Russians."

"Commit an act of war on U.S. soil? You think?" I asked him.

"It's only an act of war," said the marshal, "if it can be traced back to them."

* * *

117

There's something about being ambushed and shot at that leaves a mark. In my case, it seemed to have dialed my startle reflex up past ten. As I went about my day, unexpected things—a bird taking off, a leaf blowing, someone waving—kept rushing up in my peripheral vision. And noises kept me ducking: a slammed car door, a branch breaking sharply underfoot, an unexpected tail thump from Jack, and the list went on. I knew I'd settle down eventually, if I didn't give myself a heart attack first.

I keep my .38 on a shelf in my office, concealed behind the collected works of William Shakespeare. The gun was an inadvertent gift my first year in Chandalar from a distraught man who tried to end himself here in my customer chair. I managed to catch his arm in time to save him, but not to save my roof, which leaked through several raining and thawing cycles before I climbed up to replace the splintered shingles. Although I see him fairly frequently—he's gone on to be the dog-mushing bright light of Chandalar—he's never asked for the gun back.

Coming to Alaska, newly ordained, I brought a few vestments, a Bible that had belonged to my father, a book of common prayer, and such. It never occurred to me to bring along, or that I might have semi-regular use for, a pocket gun.

Sliding it off the shelf, I blew off the dust and flipped open the cylinder to check the load. I had five shells in and the hammer on the empty chamber.

Now as I picked up my prayer book and my re-purposed Mapleine bottle of holy oil, I also stuffed the gun in my jacket pocket, calling for Jack to ride along, as I set out on my rounds.

The morning passed quickly. I worked up an appetite visiting the old and the sick, praying over them, talking

118

with them, administering the blessing. It was light, pleasant work. I had no one too old or so sick as to be worrisome, and had finished up the last of it at just about lunchtime.

With Evie at school, on the job in meetings, and getting her classroom set up, I found myself alone for lunch and made for the Coffee Cup, my mouth watering with visions of mooseburger with melted cheese on a bun, fries on the side, and pretty good coffee.

Rosie waved at me across the busy restaurant, as I threaded my way over to the customary seat under the dusty moose head. In seconds, she was headed in my direction, several of the heavy mugs in one hand and the glass coffee pot held high in the other.

Dressed in her pink waitress outfit, with 'Rosie' scripted across one breast, she wore her fashionable white-framed eyeglasses swept back stylishly at the bows. She now had four identical pairs, in addition to the white, she had teal, black, and fire-engine red—though I hadn't seen her wear the red pair to work yet. On her feet she wore bobby sox with black and white saddle shoes, revealing firm, brown calves. Soon it would be mukluks or long underwear worn with the dress as winter came and everybody but Alice covered up.

I added sugar and canned milk to my coffee—yes, coffee from the red can, but not too bad—and sipped it slowly. Set to Fairbanks station KFAR, Pat Boone's *Love Letters in the Sand*, gave way to Elvis' new, *Let Me Be Your Teddy Bear* which took us up to noon and the news.

After a chewing-gum jingle, *Double Good, Doublemint Gum*, the smooth-voiced announcer started in. As promised, the Soviets had successfully test-launched an intercontinental ballistic missile—ICBM—so now, they were officially capable of annihilating vast numbers of people at great distance by rocket. Us.

The very next item had the U.S. exploding a test atomic bomb in Nevada. Was that supposed to make us feel safer? It didn't. It felt like the whole world had 'officially' gone mad.

The weapon stolen from the Springfield Armory was a shoulder-carried pipe kind of thing similar to what we'd had in the war in France. We called them a stovepipe, or bazooka, named after a comedian's horn. It would fire a rocket at a tank without kicking back. There had to be tens of thousands of them, surplus after the war, and I wondered what was so special about this one.

Rosie showed up with the mooseburger and fries during an ad for felt insoles for mukluks and boots. "Don't spend another winter with cold feet! On sale now, two sets for one dollar at the Northern Commercial Company."

Local news featured the continuing trial of two Fairbanks men for tampering with oil leases in the Federal Naval Oil Reserve, and murdering Alaska Eskimo statesman, Joseph Senengatuk. One of them had also tried very hard to kill Andy and me, nearly succeeding several times, but they weren't on trial for that.

Rosie's eyes met mine as she topped off my coffee. "Don't listen to that, it'll spoil your appetite." She was right. "I'd change the channel," she said, "but..."

The 'but' was, there was only one other station, also from Fairbanks, at noon broadcasting the same news off the same wire.

Before walking away, she sat—more like perched—on the edge of the chair and leaned close. "He was back last night... the prowler. I almost called you. It was about one o'clock. He wasn't tryin' to be quiet, either. I thought about shooting him but didn't want to open the door. And then I always worry... that it's some drunk in the wrong place. That's the trouble with nights that get dark. Can't tell who I'd be shooting at." Then she sprang to her feet and was gone.

The mooseburger and fries were very tasty and it would take more than nuclear proliferation and the possibility of annihilation to put me off my food. However, news of the return of the prowler, now absent for several weeks, left me chewing slowly, lost in thought. I might have heard, distantly, the little brass bell over the door. But I didn't snap back into the moment until someone slid into the chair across from me—Marshal Frank Jacobs. He shrugged out of his olive uniform jacket and hung his hat—still the broad-brimmed summer Smokey the Bear campaign hat—on an empty chair.

"Thought I might find you here." He eyed the last of my lunch. "How's that mooseburger?" When I told him, he ordered one for himself, coffee black. He smiled, but not much. "We need to talk." I sat up straighter and turned slightly to focus on him. "Not here," he added. "Back at your place."

Jimmie Rogers came on singing his hit, *Honeycomb*, which I knew I'd be humming through the afternoon. As the marshal chewed, and as we intermittently talked about nothing of consequence, I had a chance to glance around the room. With the lunch crowd drifting away, stubbing out smokes and grabbing a last mouthful of coffee, the noise level fell. Rosie shifted from delivering food and pouring coffee to wiping down tables and chairs, adjusting ketchups and mustards, and generally setting things right. There was a layer of moisture on the bottoms of the plate-glass windows, and the strong good smells of cigarette

121

smoke, grease, and coffee drifted in the air. A shift in the clouds produced sunbeams, illuminating the last of the smoke and silvery dust motes that shivered and danced when the door opened and the breeze blew in.

"Still nobody to be seen out where you fellas got ambushed." The marshal finished chewing his bite before speaking again. "My gut tells me there's something going on out there, so I keep flying over." He took another bite and chewed awhile. "But nothing."

With the room emptying, I caught his eye. "We have most of this place to ourselves. Want to talk here?"

Before answering, he glanced at Rosie wiping tables, her body moving almost imperceptibly to the music. "Nah, it can wait." Something inside me, a tiny alarm bell, began to ring in that moment. His restrained mood and reluctance to discuss... whatever it was... in the presence of Rosie, someone he might even have considered a personal friend, all added up to nothing but trouble.

Even back outside, he was reluctant to say what he had apparently come to say. Which continued to ratchet up my anxiety. It was only when we'd reached the rectory and he'd declined more coffee, patting his belly, saying "Couldn't possibly," that we settled in my office. I watched him struggle to arrange his holster in a way that would be comfortable in my customer chair. We both knew from experience there was no way. Finally, when he'd shoved it out the side, under the chair arm, he turned to me with intent. But before speaking, he pinched a small paper envelope out of a shirt pocket, and from it drew something on a gold chain.

He held it up. "Recognize this?"

I nodded. "I think so. I can't be certain because I only saw it by moonlight—and from several feet away—but it looks like a locket Marjorie Snetshan wore the night she stayed here."

Jacobs smiled grimly. "Bingo!"

"But it wasn't with the body." He shook his head. "So where *did* you find it?" I asked him.

"Well," he said, "that's why I'm here. See, we got an anonymous call about where we might find it. So, I went hunting. Sure enough!" He flipped his wrist, setting the locket to swing on its chain.

"So, where?" I asked again. His eyes met mine.

"This is where it gets a little sticky. The office took an anonymous call, a couple days ago. Caller wanted to know if we were still looking for the killer of 'that Indian bitch, in Chandalar.' Sounded maybe a little drunk. Told us exactly where to find this." He tucked the locket back in its envelope and slid the envelope back into his shirt pocket.

"We found it, stored under the floor with a good supply of firearms and ammunition."

"At Andy's," I said.

"Yep!"

"But you can't think Andy had anything to do with her death?"

"I don't. But when you find evidence in a murder investigation, you got to follow it, got to ask the questions, but..."

"We both know it was the murderer who called in."

"Bingo," he said.

* * *

I told Evie I planned to stake out her place but didn't tell anybody else. It hadn't gone so well the last time. "So, don't shoot me!"

123

"You're no fun," she said. And then, "Be careful. This creep isn't just a peeper. There's a good chance he's also a murderer."

I showed her where I'd be hiding and we agreed if I fired three quick shots that I was in trouble and she should stay inside. She pressed her lips together, clearly not caring much for my plan, but managed to not say anything.

I spent parts of four very dark frosty nights dozing on my boat cushion, leaning against a tree. I would arrive just before midnight and depart just after three, when I figured the prowler either wasn't going to show up or was lurking elsewhere.

On the fourth night at about two o'clock I heard someone come cautiously down the trail toward Evie's cabin. There was no moon, no stars visible through a gauze of mist, and for once no night sounds—of engines, birds, or dog barks. Even the nearest of the town's two power generators had shut down or broken down... again. Just for this moment, it felt and sounded like the whole world paused. And that's when he appeared.

I think he meant to sneak up, so came quietly up the trail. But once at the cabin, feeling safe and probably powerful, he began to make more noise, circling the cabin, not caring if twigs snapped underfoot. He did something else, too, something he'd never done before, and it made the hair rise on the back of my neck. In the glow of her lit bathroom window, I watched him feel his way along the wall to the telephone wire drop. He knew where it was. From my hiding place, I could hear the *snick* of the wire as he clipped it. He'd never done *that* before.

I rose soundlessly, pulling the .38 out of my pocket. Extending my arm, aiming, I thumbed back the hammer, making a soft but audible click. In the silence, he heard it and froze. Still with his back to me, I saw him appear to be raising his hands. What I didn't make out in the darkness was the handgun.

He spun, dropping into a crouch as he fired—wildly, blindly—into the darkness, and I thought he'd never stop. I fired once, with no apparent effect, while throwing myself flat in the low brush, mindful that Evie—inside the cabin—was in my target field. Pressing my cheek tight to frosty ground, smelling dirt and leaf mold, I didn't actually count the number of times he shot, but knew in the end it seemed like twelve or more, so not a revolver. I leapt up when he quit firing, wondering how quickly he could load another magazine. It was then I realized he'd been moving while firing, abruptly sprinting away around the corner of the cabin, headed for Main Street. I gave chase with some confidence, knowing I still had four rounds ready to fire. I ran past the cabin door just as the porch light flicked on and Evie cautiously emerged, clutching her revolver.

She called after me, "Are you alright?"

"I'm good," I shouted back over my shoulder, hoping to stay that way.

The only working streetlight on Main, just by the telephone booth at the railroad terminal, wouldn't help me. We were running a cross-block path through berry bushes and tall grass, leading straight in the direction of the general store, my quarry now a silhouette against the night-lit store windows.

Shooting at him was out of the question, though tempting. I had missed him at twenty feet thanks in part to the Colt's two-inch barrel. I could only imagine how much I'd miss him by at the sixty or eighty feet he had on me now. I imagined store windows shattering and complicated explanations in the morning.

125

He turned left on Main and then left again at the next corner. I'd already begun to suspect I wouldn't catch him. He appeared tall—unusual for around here—and possibly thin, wearing a long, military-style parka shell. He'd been holding back on the uncertain trail, but now, out on smooth road, steadily opened the distance between us. Panting, sweating, I clutched at one slim hope that I might be wearing him down—until just about the time I reached the Setsoo intersection where the postmistress lived. It was there, sprinting full out, I tripped on Chuck, the one-hundred-pound chocolate Lab, sound asleep in the middle of the road.

Chuck yelped as I went airborne, and he scooted up sharply, lumbering for the safety of his porch. For me, flying through the air and darkness seemed to take a long time. I imagined myself wearing a cape, like in a comic book. But that's where the resemblance ended. I was headed nowhere but down.

Hitting the ground hard, sliding in the dust, I know I shouted. The good part? I managed to *not* pull the trigger. I had no trouble imagining that story circulating. 'Did you hear about that crazy Hardy, probably drunk, running around after midnight, shooting?' When it got back to the bishop, and it would, he'd want to talk about it. I wouldn't.

So, I'd lost the prowler. I picked myself up, brushed off the dust and dropped the .38 into my jacket pocket.

"Darn!" I said with feeling. As if in response—and it made me shiver—ahead in darkness, and safely out of reach, I heard him laughing.

CHAPTER 14

"He thinks this is a game!" Evie thudded her mug down on the tabletop with feeling, slopping coffee. She and William had showed up early and we were all in our places on the tippy stools well before sunrise.

She gave the spilled coffee a stern look and climbed off her stool to get a dishrag to wipe it up. I saw her turn to look at my kitchen clock, a black cat clock she had given me, with a tail that wagged, eyes that swiveled, and a pencil-thin Charles Boyer-type mustache. I admit I thought it was a little strange, but she liked it. And now it told her she needed to be on her way.

In short order she finished her coffee, kissed me on the lips and William on the top of his head, gathering her stack of books and supplies for the first day of the school year. It was a Tuesday, the day after Labor Day, September third. "Wish me luck," she said.

"I will, but you don't need it."

"Flatterer!" she said, and went out.

"It is a deadly game," said William, in her vacuum, still pondering the prowler. He had been holding his mug close in both hands, staring at it. He turned to make significant eye contact as small spots of condensation faded from his lenses. "The cutting of the telephone wire makes it so. Makes him not a mere prowler. And of course," he paused, "we now know he is armed and ready to shoot—a lot!"

I could feel myself frowning. "All bad news."

William pursed his lips and pushed them sideways, thoughtfully. "Even though he escaped. You surprised him. You returned fire and you chased him. It *may* be, he will lay low for a time." He took a sip. "But if he killed

Marjorie, he will be back. They say it is a sickness, and he will be compelled to return."

Our conversation turned to problems at Clear RADAR station and another upcoming Soviet missile test scheduled for the following week.

"There is talk," said William, lowering his voice, his eyes shifting from side to side as though, here in my kitchen, we might be overheard or observed. "There is talk," he said again, "received through international espionage channels, of the possibility of sabotage at one of these early warning stations."

"But which," I asked him.

He did a face shrug. "That *is* the question. The belief has always been that a Soviet attack would come in over the North Pole. It is the shortest distance. The truth is it could be any of them. What is worse is that we once thought it would be Soviet bombers coming down, and we tried to prepare for that. But now we believe the attack is much more likely to come in the form of missiles, possibly with nuclear warheads."

"And we can see the missiles with this RADAR?"

"Oh, no," he said. "We can see bombers. No missiles. Which is why, scarcely finished, there is already talk of upgrading the technology. As I said, nearly finished, already obsolete."

He was right. He had said that all along.

"The brass heads at Clear..."

"Hats. Brass hats," I said.

"Brass *hats*," he corrected himself, "out there, are all in a lather. So..." he rose in place, standing over his tippy stool, to tip back the last drops of his coffee, "I must be off to Clear, to keep America safe... from something."

He rose, as if to go, but lingered by the table. "Your wedding? Was set for August? Did you two...?"

"No, nothing like that. Evie had to be in school and we just let the date get by."

He looked at me. "So, is there a new date?"

I hesitated, feeling a little awkward. Feeling oddly, like I had been dropped unexpectedly into a conversation with a relative, perhaps an older uncle, and left wanting."

"She hasn't mentioned another date."

"Have you... mentioned?"

"Well, I... no."

"Hmm," he said, and nothing more. Sliding into his wool jacket, he went out.

I spent the morning writing letters to churches in the States, asking for their still-useful clothing and for cash. Some things like diapers and Vaseline, powdered milk for baby formula, we had to buy new. At lunchtime, I made a fresh pot of coffee—from the red can—and sliced moose meat from a roast for sandwiches. When I first came here, just three years ago, I had to store food in my small, enclosed back porch to keep it cool. It was always either a race to get things eaten before they spoiled, or to figure out how to use them frozen solid. A little more than a year ago, I'd bought myself this fine Amana refrigerator and never tired of just reaching in for what I wanted. I felt so modern!

As I chewed, I fed bits of moose meat to Jack, who always showed up at mealtime, from napping in some other part of the house, usually on or near the floor furnace grate.

I thought about Evie. She hadn't mentioned another wedding date. And I wondered if maybe something had shifted, if she'd changed her mind about marrying me. She hadn't said anything. She hadn't been that keen originally,

129

though she'd warmed up to the idea. But what if she had decided to not marry? Did I want to hear that, to have that conversation, when everything *seemed* to be flowing along so well?

Then I shifted to pondering our prowler. The one clear conclusion I wanted to come to was that he wasn't from around here, wasn't one of us. It helped that he had managed to set up poor horny Vadim to be captured, something easily managed by anyone who spent time at the Bide-A-While. I began to imagine the prowler as someone large and dark, a sexual deviant who lived in one of the battered rail cars, and came out at night ultimately to torture and kill.

After lunch, I put stamps on my stateside letters, whistled up Jack and we set out the several blocks to the post office. It was a gray day, heavily overcast with a lowering sky that looked like snow, though it was about a month early. With daytime temperature still in the mid-thirties, it was also not really cold enough. The birches and alders had gone heavily to yellow, with many leaves already fallen. Occasionally an aspen stood in deep crimson contrast, like a biblical burning bush.

The one-story, green-painted, ramshackle post office stood on a corner facing Main. I was walking down the building's long side, ready to turn the corner when I paused to clip Jack's leash on him. He complained, a drawn-out husky yowl, which said to me he felt more than capable of walking along on his own. He probably was but after our last adventure downtown I didn't want to risk it.

Sure enough, we no more than turned the corner than I literally ran into the man I had come to think of as Big Ears. Head down, he came charging along the planked sidewalk, intent on a letter he had sliced open with a long knife, envelopes and knife in one hand and the letter in the other. He was unshaven, bug bit, and smelled—both of wood smoke and clothing worn too long—which told me something about his recent accommodations. He saw Jack, yanked up short and focused on me. "You!" he snarled, waving the knife in my direction.

That was enough for Jack, who charged him, jerking the leash tight. I had to back up quickly to draw him away. Whatever it was between this stranger and me had gone on long enough and blown way out of proportion. I dropped Jack's leash loop over a snub of bench top and turned with my hands raised slightly, ready to try to defuse whatever he thought was going on. To my relief, I saw him slide the big knife into a belt sheath, and shove his clutch of mail into a jacket pocket.

We made eye contact and I smiled. He didn't. To my surprise, he suddenly spun, showing me his back and—the next thing I knew—the sole of his Redwing boot came rocketing straight for my nose.

Luckily, I boxed in college and through seminary, a welterweight at about 145 pounds. I know, it's not very priest-like, but I was good at it. And while many seminarians survived on low-pay janitorial or other part-time work, Mary and I managed reasonably well on my fight winnings. Yes, it only worked because I usually won.

But I'm a bit older now, out of training and, even with all my wood chopping, out of shape. Reaction time is the first thing that goes. Well, 'wind' is first. I wasn't quick enough to get my face completely out of the way, and felt his boot sole scrape along my cheek. It hurt, but not as much as clean contact with the front of my nose.

I'd never fought feet before! I'd heard of it, but this was my first experience.

"Um..." I said, still determined to try to talk this thing down. He spun again and punched another foot in my direction. I sidestepped and blocked it with a forearm.

The thing about sticking your leg all the way up in the air, no matter how quickly or savagely, is that you open your crotch completely. I had never kicked any opponent in the crotch. I didn't believe in it. But when he spun again and kicked, again head high, I stepped in to catch and lift the raised leg and give him a tap in his 'business' with my toe. I won't say he folded—well he did fold—but he didn't collapse and curl up like I knew he wanted to.

I heard a shout from across the street by the general store, and out of the corner of my eye saw someone running. It all blended with Jack's aggressive barking and attempts to pull himself loose from the bench.

With his face right at my shoulder level, I pondered a quick right jab to the point of his nose but let it go. I still hoped to be the bigger man, even though this guy stood about six inches taller than me.

"Let's talk about this," I said, which is when he went for his revolver, fortunately deep in his jacket in a shoulder holster.

I sidestepped and kicked his right knee joint from behind, folding him to the ground. But he rose like a phoenix, limping, with a handful of gun aimed at my face. I put my hands up, stepped back, and watched him start to squeeze the trigger. I'd seen that posture before. He shoved his hand forward, pulled his head back and set his face, squinted his eyes against the big bang. I threw up my arms to shield my face, as if that would help.

Big Butch arrived—the shouter from across the street—simultaneously shouldering Big Ears aside while yanking the pistol skyward, ripping it right out of his

132

fingers. It discharged into the air with an ear-ringing slam. Judging by the man's roar of pain, the action darn near snapped off his trigger finger. As if that wasn't enough, Butch slapped him openhanded, driving him all the way to the planks.

Neither of us were prepared for what he did next. He rolled and ran. End of story. We stood and watched him, me wondering if this was the prowler I'd chased. He was tall enough and fast enough. Wrong gun, though. The prowler carried a smaller caliber semi-automatic. Butch held a larger-bore revolver, a Smith and Wesson with a six-inch barrel, probably a .44 Magnum. It was the grizzly gun everybody around here talked about but the first I'd seen.

Butch, still holding the pistol by its barrel, turned to me. "I knew you had him, Father. Nasty scrape, though." With a look of concern, he reached over to brush the gouge on my cheek with a work roughened thumb. It felt like he was running a rasp across my face and I had to work to not flinch. "Why are people always tryin' to shoot you," he asked earnestly. Just last winter, he had been all that stood between me and another gunman.

"I..." was all I could say. I had no explanation.

"Here." He held the revolver grip out to me. "Take this thing." I did. I knew he had an aversion to handguns, maybe having something to do with his Ohio prison residency. I took it, snapped out the cylinder and emptied it, dropping the pistol, grip first into my jacket patch pocket with several inches of muzzle sticking out.

Butch eyed me. "Convert or else? Is that the new priest look?"

"Funny."

We shook hands and I retrieved my dog and mailed my letters. Walking all the way back home, shaking with left-over adrenalin, I pondered what there was about me that made a total stranger want to beat me up or shoot me? Was he some new form of aggressive atheist? I hoped not.

* * *

"Kicked him in the balls?" Andy's jaw dropped. "And now you're brawling right on Main Street instead of in the bar! Is that better or worse? And you a priest!" He smiled. "Good for you! That should bring 'em in on Sunday."

On a sunny Thursday morning, we were sitting in my cozy kitchen on the tippy stools, sipping fresh-made coffee—the Italian roast—though poured from a plain old campfire-blackened American perk pot. He looked at it now. "Humph! We gotta get you a French press."

In retrospect, the encounter on Main Street didn't feel like 'Good for me.' It felt like a core failure, the simple triumph of thuggery over two years of seminary and plain knowing better. I said as much.

He grew a little more serious, but not much. "A pistol beats a full hand of high moral intent," he reminded me.

Long hours spent in a restaurant that was going gangbusters had prompted him to take a day or so away, jumping into the new-to-him Chevy for a head-clearing ride to Nenana and on to Chandalar. This would likely be his last trip until after the river froze. Once ice chunks started coming down the Tanana, they'd pull the *Princess of Minto* up on the ways and then we'd be cut off—except for the train—while waiting for river ice to freeze hard enough to drive over.

Andy sipped his coffee and tried changing the subject. "Heard any more from your prowler?"

"No, fortunately."

134

"Well, that's good news." He pondered. "Hey! Do you 'spose this guy is the prowler?"

I walked to the coffee pot to refill my mug. "I thought of that. He's tall enough, and fast enough. And that would explain why he set into me on the street, maybe thinking I'd recognize him from the other night. Of course, I can't. The one thing that makes it not likely, is that this guy was carrying a serious big revolver, and the actual prowler was firing something much smaller and semi-auto. I think he must have shot nine... ten rounds without reloading. And you know how the sounds are different, the big *POW!* as opposed to the tighter sort of *crack! crack! crack!*"

Andy thought that one over. "Maybe he has two guns. Most of the rest of us do. Or maybe he has one for work during the day and another for night, you know, like dress-up."

"Right," I said.

"Yeah, well maybe you scared him off. Maybe we won't see him again. That'd be good."

"It would," I said, "except that William assures me these guys always do it again, whether he comes back here or moves on to somewhere else. He says this kind of behavior is like a compulsion. There's only so long the prowler can go without needing the charge—like a drug fix—of doing it again. The trouble is, he keeps getting more serious and raising the ante. Last time he clipped the phone wire. I don't want to think about what comes next."

"So, this guy you were brawling with on the public street..." I winced. "Well," he said, "it's not like he gave you any choice. You gotta protect yourself. So why do you suppose he's got the big hard-on for you?" He paused. "Sorry, Father."

135

"I'll bet," I said. He laughed. I thought about it for a minute. Why was I involved in an ongoing conflict with someone I didn't even know? "He seems to think I know something about him or what he's doing."

Andy leaned forward, looking thoughtful. "If he's not our prowler, what *is* he up to? Maybe you should know. Maybe *it's your duty* to find out. Since he tried to kick you in the head and then tried to kill you. You gotta admit it would be nice to find out."

Andy was right. And that started us thinking. It wasn't long before we had a plan in place. It was simple. The next time Big Ears came into town, we'd follow him home.

We needed an easy way to know when he'd be back in town. Sitting in the Coffee Cup for days, peering out the window didn't seem like the best idea. Neither did loitering unobtrusively on the sidewalk across from the store or post office. On a Main Street often completely empty, there's no such thing as 'unobtrusive.' We'd start getting questions after the first ten minutes. Eventually we hit on the idea of slipping the word to Gary at the store, to let us know when any of the four strangers came in. I called him.

"No problem," he said. "Heard you dumped that big guy on his ass. Wish I'd been there. But you know, I ain't seen but just him with the big ears for a couple of weeks."

"He's all we need." I hung up the phone.

We knew that whatever Big Ears was involved in, it took him out of town. So, we assembled day packs at my place. We packed food and warm outdoor gear, with guns and ammunition enough for a full day of shadowing a dangerous armed man.

"What do you think?" I asked Andy. "Should we bring Vic in?" Andy hesitated.

136

"He didn't do so good in the ambush," he reminded. "You had to help him load his gun. Might be better off just you and me." He was right. More isn't always better.

Saturday, midmorning, we were playing chess—me losing—when Gary called.

"Yeah, your guy was just in here for beer and cigarettes, heading..." he hesitated, and I knew he would be peering out the store's plate-glass window. "Yeah, into the Post Office."

I thanked him and we quickly scrambled into gear and packs and grabbed guns. Squeezing out the door, we left Jack to yowl his disappointment. We picked up sight of our man just a block from the rectory, headed east on Setsoo, as he threaded the intersection littered with four big reclining Labradors and a couple of strolling herons. The birds shied, but the dogs rose to greet the stranger and, to his credit, he gave each one a pet and a scratch behind the ears.

Andy shook his head. "Can't be all bad."

"Even Hitler liked dogs," I reminded him.

A few steps later he asked, "Did he really?"

I served in France clear through to the armistice, and there had been plenty of talk about Hitler's dogs, his beloved German Shepherd, Muckl, and Blondi, a wolfhound.

"It's a fact," I told him. I didn't tell him that Blondi died when *Der Fuhrer* used her to test his cyanide capsule in case he needed to commit suicide. Hearing that, Andy would want to shoot him again.

We trailed Big Ears east and south over short city blocks to the trailhead next to Arnold Gustafson's old cabin. The cabin looked increasingly forlorn, with

137

windowpanes grown hazy and weeds taking over the front path.

Once we crossed the railroad tracks, hitting the old trail proper, we had to fall back. It wasn't like in the movies, following the quarry along a crowded city street where we could turn suddenly and pretend to study a storefront display. Here, *any* sight of us would be too much and could spook Big Ears, get us shot, or both. So, we moved slowly, cautiously. Andy read trail sign as easily as road signs, commenting.

"Oh, he stopped here." Or, "Took a leak over there." Andy tracked so well and so easily, he might have said, 'Yep, he was whistling here... the *Wiffenpoof Song*.' Or, 'Here, he started thinking about lunch. Probably a baloney sandwich.'

We soon passed the spot where Arnold Gustafson had been killed, passed the cabin where we knew Whiskey Jack had been held and his collar found. In a few more miles we eased uneventfully past the site of our ambush.

"I'm glad to get past here," I said to Andy's back. He just grunted, intent on his trail.

We'd packed moose meat sandwiches and ate while walking. Apparently Big Ears did the same.

"Ah-ha!" Andy sprang at some bit of something he spotted on the path and came up holding a potato chip between thumb and forefinger. I thought for a moment he would pop it in his mouth, but he resisted.

The valley had been frosty when we started, frost on steel at the rail crossing, frost silvering last leaves on berry bushes and tall grass, and ice skimming the occasional puddle. By noon it had all melted and we were opening jackets and stuffing gloves in our pockets.

The terrain continued very flat and boggy, with stands of stunted spruce and willow. We skirted small grassy ponds now gone dry, stepping and occasionally stumbling over small rough hillocks of frost-lifted swamp peat. A partly clear morning with bursts of sunshine and at least the welcome suggestion of warmth, soon blanketed over with sulky gray clouds. In another month, a little lower, these would be snow clouds. I could wait.

Eventually we came to a fork that had Andy pondering briefly before leading us eastward. We hadn't gone far on that track, less than a mile, before he dropped into a couch and beckoned me closer, his voice low.

"I think he's leadin' us."

"Huh?"

"Trail got clearer all of a sudden. Like we're 'sposed to follow it. Or like he wanted to make sure we went this way instead of the other."

"Ambush?"

He thought about it. "Could be."

"Is it time to turn around?"

He thought about that. "If we turn around, we go all the way back to town not knowing nothin'." He looked ahead to the trail. "Let's go a little farther. You hold back—shell in the chamber—a hundred yards or more. Let's make it so he can't shoot both of us at the time so easy."

"Why you in front?" I asked him. "Maybe I should go first, then when they shoot at me, you can nail them."

"Nah," he said. "I got this." And then he added, "Used to do this for a living."

On we went, at a crawl. Turning east helped, as the filtered sun arced southwest and less in our eyes. We were following a ragged footpath now, off the beaten sled track, which even in summer, formed a neat groove just a little wider than a dogsled, in a mostly straight line south across tundra.

On any other day, being out on the trail with Andy, after frost and with mosquitoes all done for the season, would be a picnic. But there's something about walking along, expecting to be shot at that makes it less fun. We'd walk awhile and then we'd both crouch while Andy scanned the land ahead through his scope. Then we'd walk on some more.

Though still quite flat, I noticed the terrain changing, from swampy peat to gravel, slightly higher. Soon we started to see the occasional round rock, shaped smooth by eons of moving water. Then inexplicably, a human-stacked pile of round rocks—a cairn—tented on willow poles by a camouflage net, to be invisible from the air.

Andy beckoned me up, and again we crouched, speaking softly.

"Somebody buried here?" I asked him.

He did a face shrug. "I don't think so." He jerked his thumb. "We got this cairn here." He pointed. "And I'm betting we got a stream over there, and 660 feet over, we got another cairn." He rose and spotted with the scope. "Can't see from here." He turned to face me. "Okay," he said, "I know what they're doin' out here, and why they don't want anybody to know about it."

CHAPTER 15

"It's gold. That's what they're doing!" Andy looked over the top of a coffee mug, held in both hands. It was Saturday morning at my place, with Evie and William also in attendance. Sunlight beamed through the early frost on my kitchen window as, on the radio, Mitch Miller and the gang were whistling their way through *The March on the River Kwai*. Now the tune would be in my head all day.

"Well, it's gold *claims*, at least," Andy continued. "They've either bought up some of the old turn-of-the-century gold claims... or they're jumping 'em. Either way, it works better if no one knows."

I'd already heard his theory on the long walk home. According to Andy, from the center of a gold stream, claim markers would be installed 330 feet out, extending to include a total of thirteen hundred feet of streambed. Apparently, they did gold claims this way from 1898 up until about 1917 when America joined the war on Germany. His theory still didn't make a lot of sense to me.

"This is all such a big secret that he'd shoot me... without provocation... on the street?"

"Yeah," said Andy, "can't really explain that one."

William sipped his coffee and dabbed at his drippy nose. "It is good to know there is some reason for them to be hiding out there, one that does not include an attack. If it's true," he added.

Talk of gold turned the conversation to what luck Vadim might be having as a prospector. "None," said William. "He is the worst gold miner ever. He started out panning but now is digging a shaft in a hillside." He sniffed. "That is one more difference between us. On a holiday, I will sit on the beach in the sun. Vadim will

141

shovel, sweat, attract biting insects, and have a marvelous time."

I spent the morning on winter prep, putting up new plastic on windows, changing the light bulb that provides just enough heat to keep my propane tanks flowing when it gets really cold. Improbably, when it gets down to forty or fifty below, just that much heat keeps it going.

In the afternoon, I visited a couple of the sick people on my prayer list, praying with them briefly, blessing them and anointing them with holy oil.

I joined Evie for dinner at her place. Pasta with red sauce, canned mushrooms, and moose meatballs, served with a 'saucy' little red, a screw-top vintage from early Tuesday. I twisted open the cap and poured into decorative jelly jars while she served. It was all delightful.

We did up the dishes together, standing by the sink with her washing and me drying, both of us feeling sort of goofy happy and domestic. We were playing house, and we knew it. And we both liked it. We sat close on her sofa, side by side, feeling the warmth of each other. The July 6th Saturday Evening Post had finally arrived in the mail, the one with sandlot baseball on the cover. I was paging through it while Evie read Chandler's, *The Big Sleep*, pausing to read in what was supposed to be a Marlowe voice, "Dead men are heavier than broken hearts." We agreed that the man could write.

At about ten o'clock, I kissed her, long and slow. Smiling, I started for home in the frosty air, pausing outside her door just long enough to hear the bolt click.

At ten minutes after one my phone rang, springing me from bed but freezing me in place on my braided rug until I figured out what I was hearing and what it meant. I threaded my way through darkness and objects—like a

142

footstool—left carelessly in the path, to answer on about the fifth ring. It was Linda Huxton, voice low and quivering, in trouble.

"Vic's gone," she said, "to Fairbanks," which I knew. "'I can't not go,' he told me, 'it's a gun show!'"

"What's the matter?"

"He's here, the prowler is..." Just that quickly, the line clicked dead. I slammed down the phone, stumbling back toward my bedroom, kicking the footstool again, making what would be a nasty and painful bruise on my shin.

Yanking on my clothing and boots, grabbing the .38 from beside my bed, I ran out of my house with one arm in my jacket, turning the key to start the engine and letting it warm just about as much time as it took me to get my other arm into the other sleeve. I reversed out of the driveway, tires spitting gravel. Pausing only to check for sleeping dogs in the intersection, I floored it down Setsoo, then a right turn, accelerating the several blocks remaining to the teacherage.

Driving, I thought all the extra thoughts you think... why did Vic go off and leave her alone? She lives in an apartment building with all the other teachers, why didn't she just pound on the wall? Mostly I just hoped I'd make it in time.

Reaching the teacherage, slamming on the brakes, the Ford slid to a stop while I jumped out. Linda must have been watching for me. Her lights came on and I saw her in the window as I jogged across the yard and up onto the low porch. As I reached the door, her yellow porch light snapped on, and I remember thinking it must have been one of those new bug lights.

Hearing her fumble with locks and chain, I turned to scan the yard. The first bullet shattered the glass light shade, somehow missing the bulb. I jumped back, losing my footing, tumbling off the porch. I snapped off only one shot of my own while diving for the ground and darkness. The fusillade ended in the time it took to squeeze a light trigger ten times. Yes, I counted. As before, the sharp *crack* of the sound, without any real *boom* to it, made me think he was firing something like a .22—still potentially deadly.

By the time Linda managed to yank the door open, it was all over. Again, I heard his footsteps running away. Still on the ground, I raised and aimed the .38 into darkness, ultimately not firing, knowing there were other houses within lethal range.

Across the face of the building, I saw lights go on, heard doors unlocking, opening, and in seconds lay encircled by three armed teachers who, at first, must have thought I was the shooter. I put down my gun and raised my hands, lying that way until Linda came out to save me, framing me in a rhomboid of whiter light from her apartment door.

Picking up my gun as they backed off, I dropped it into my pocket wondering, as Andy would put it so eloquently the next day, "how a prowler who sets up a deliberate ambush, can be such a piss-poor shooter?"

Walking back up onto the low porch, I checked myself for bullet holes. As I suspected, I had none. Linda took me by the arm, dragging me into her apartment where she thumped the door shut tight. She snapped a pair of locks and set the security chain, her face paper white.

"Are you okay?" I asked.

"Are you?" she gasped. Her eyes were still round, open too wide, and she was breathing through her mouth, panting, nearly in shock. "When I heard all the shots, I thought you were..." she couldn't say it.

"Dead," I added.

She nodded. "I thought that too." I got her a glass of water from the kitchen sink and settled her on a kitchen chair, noticing my own hand shaking.

She sipped the water, aspirated a little and burst into a fit of coughing. I guess it doesn't help but I patted her on the back, just in case. "I almost got you killed," she said, when she could talk again.

I thought about it a minute. "I think he's teaching me a lesson. I almost got *him* a few nights ago at Evie's. Now this. Fortunately, this guy is a really bad shot."

I sat with her a few minutes, then went to knock on the neighbor's doors on either side of her apartment while their lights were still on. They nodded seriously when I explained that we have a prowler, and that Vic was away. Each of them showed me a weapon, assuring me they'd be ready to use it if there was any more trouble.

"You have armed men on both sides, ready to help," I told her. "If anything troubles you, pound on the walls." I went out, still cautious, walked across the frosty yard to my truck and drove home.

* * *

Two days later, Vadim disappeared, or more precisely, failed to turn up. The phone rang. It was Alice.

"Vadim hasn't come in from the mine. William isn't answering. I'm worried!"

We all knew the claim Vadim had been working. It belonged to an older local man, another of Alice's admirers, who had allowed him to work the claim in exchange for ten percent of anything he could find. So far, a ten-percent share of nothing.

"My father worked that claim back in aught six," the old man told us. Leaning on the bar at the Bide-A-While, he paused to tip back his stubby for a long swallow. Telling tales is dry work. "It panned out, about an ounce of gold flakes in a little leather pouch. I still got it. The real stuff. He never traded it in."

With Andy in Fairbanks, I called Oliver. The two of us, bundled against the frosty air, headed downriver in his long Tanana freight boat, passing sheets of skim ice only a half or three-quarters of an inch thick. It didn't add up to anything, but would soon. They still had the river ferry in service. The Tanana ran west here, making the optical illusion of Tortella Hill, on the other side, look like it ran east.

We didn't say much. Oliver and I shared a history of going out to find dead men. The most recent had been a drowned duck hunter when his canoe flipped. The idea of finding someone like Vadim dead—someone we knew well and had been so alive—made it hard to breathe, let alone talk.

As it turned out, we found something worse than a body—a caved-in mine shaft—and no sign at all of Vadim, dead or alive.

Oliver turned from the wreckage. "Ain't surviving that. Too much sand here. No air pockets. Same thing happened just downriver here in the thirties. Twelve men buried. Never dug them out, either. Sad. Alice gonna take this hard."

"And William," I reminded him.

He nodded. "And William. But William won't say nothing. Alice will."

But first things first. After three years in Chandalar, and too many dead, I knew the blessing by heart. "Unto

146

God's gracious mercy and protection, we commit you. The Lord bless you and keep you. The Lord make his face to shine upon you, and be gracious unto you. The Lord lift up his countenance upon you and give you peace, both now and forevermore. Amen."

"Amen," echoed Oliver.

We circled the camp for maybe an hour, trying to make sense of it, trying to figure out what was the story we'd be telling back in town. I'd phone the marshal, of course, and he'd have a bunch of questions for me, which I typically couldn't answer. So, knowing there'd be a quiz, I tried to bone up now, on site.

An animal had been through, dumping cans and tearing at cartons. A trail of soggy Ritz cracker crumbs led off toward the river. Vadim had been living in a lean-to constructed mostly of beach findings, bleached poles and the odd slab of sawn lumber, topped with a canvas tarp. He'd left the downstream side open, closing the upstream side to block the prevailing breeze, which would be darn cool now, right off the river. His mosquito netting, no longer required, had been rolled up tight and tied.

His guns were here, shells chambered in each. William's guns, actually, a .22 caliber pump rifle and a 12-gauge pump shotgun. Another gun I knew about, a sidearm, wasn't here. It was a 357 Magnum revolver that Vadim bought in the bar and typically carried in a hip holster as bear repellant, now likely buried with him.

We stood staring at the remains of the mine. "We should dig him out."

Oliver looked at me. "Too dangerous. He dug in there and he's dead. No sense us bein' dead, too."

He was right, of course.

Why did I make a last circle around the camp? Two reasons. Because Andy would ask me if I had. It's what he would do. So, I did.

The other reason? Because something about this felt wrong. I looked at Oliver. His knitted eyebrows and lips pressed together told me something. "What do you think?"

He looked at me and didn't say anything, just shook his head. So, it wasn't just me.

I stepped to the perimeter of the camp and walked that circle all the way around. That's how I found the boot print—well, part of a boot print. I found just a bit of a heel print, frosted, still distinct, in a camp where everything else had a weathered, blurred look.

"Hello!" I said. Oliver looked up from poking in the fire pit.

"You found something."

"Maybe." I looked around, but didn't see another print, or any other clue that might support it. "I found a sharp heel print."

His eyebrows went up. "Sharp? Ain't nothing sharp here." He came over to squat and stare at it. "Good find!" He looked up. "We'll make a injun o' you yet."

I had to turn away so he wouldn't see me smiling. That was as close to a gold star as I had gotten lately.

We didn't pack up the camp or take the guns. It was a good bet the marshal would fly in here before sunset to see for himself, or that William would come downstream by boat, maybe in the morning. The chance of someone else showing up was slim, the chance of someone taking something, even slimmer. I paused for one last look, holding the boat rope in my hand, the final thing before I pushed off and stepped in. I noticed Oliver did the same, standing in the stern by the burbling outboard. Marshal

Jacobs would ask me, he always did, "Were there any signs of foul play?"

Probably not, and yet...

* * *

"No!" was all William said when we told him. And then, "He came all this way." Oliver gave him a rough pat on the shoulder, as did I. William took off his wire rims and pinched the bridge of his nose. "He was thirty-five, no thirty-six. Too young to die. But then, who is not?"

On the phone, the marshal's terse voice didn't sound real. It sounded like one of those tinny aliens from outer space in the movies. "Tell me what you saw." Over the wire, it sounded a lot like 'Take me to your leader.'

So, I told him what I'd seen, including the footprint. "There's something you're not telling me," he said at the end.

"Only that... and I know this amounts to nothing... it *felt* wrong."

I could hear him shift gears. On the one hand, he seemed to relax. On the other, I could feel his attention sharpen and his interest pique. "Tell me about it."

"Nothing more to tell. It's just how I felt." I looked across my office to Oliver sitting in my guest chair. "How we both felt," I added. Oliver nodded.

"That's enough for me. I'm on my way," he said, and rang off.

And then there was Alice. The three of us found her behind the bar, wearing her typical scoop neck and a bar apron tied around her waist. She looked from me to William, to Oliver and then back, reading the truth on our faces.

"Oh, no!" she said. "A cave in?!" She clasped both hands in front of her lips. A single tear rolled from each eye, leaving sad trails down her cheeks. No more.

She looked down at her bar sink and went back to washing glasses mindlessly. "How did it happen? Did he suffer?"

"Sandy soil," I told her. "It was probably pretty quick." We both knew it wasn't quick enough. He would have lived a minute or two, surely panicking, breathing and swallowing river sand—suffocating. But we didn't talk about that.

When William walked around behind the bar, to take her in his arms, she quit washing dishes, leaving wet handprints on his jacket, weeping quietly into his chest. "I couldn't love him," she murmured.

"You *did* love him," William said. "You gave him all you could... and more. He could not have had a better friend."

* * *

We met the marshal back at Vadim's camp at about three. To our surprise, he showed up with Andy, who greeted me with a thump on the shoulder, and called me brother, which pleased me. He quickly went from the one footprint Oliver and I had found, to a sketchy trail headed off west. The marshal nodded appreciatively. "Wish I had you along on all my cases."

William was very quiet. He stood in one spot, mid camp, and surveyed the tumbled-in shaft mouth. I had never thought him religious. He seldom came to church. But now he crossed himself in the Russian Orthodox way, middle and first fingers with his thumb to a point, saying in Russian, "Lord," at his forehead, "Jesus Christ," at his

150

stomach, "Son of God," on his right shoulder, and "have mercy upon us," on his left.

Wordlessly he surveyed the lean-to. Then he turned to watch the muddy river swirl past with a rise of yellow-leaved birch and aspen beyond, beneath a sad sky. I saw him shake his head.

"Vadim had such high hopes—about everything! And now this. Our father has been dead many years, but Vadim's mother is yet alive. This will be hard news for her." Then he turned to stare off west, just as the sun eased below clouds and a warm yellow light found his face. "Wherever he has gone," he said, "I am wishing him well... hoping he finds happiness."

It seemed an odd thing to say about a dead man.

CHAPTER 16

Molly Joseph, with young Henry, came to see me. She knocked and when I opened the door, said—as shy parishioners often do—"I..." and then didn't know what else to say. I assumed she needed to talk and invited her in. I waited as she shed her light parka and unwrapped Henry, and then I led them into my office.

She sat in the customer chair, pulling Henry up to sit on her lap. Although the weather had grown chilly, it was neither cold nor snowy enough yet for mukluks, so she still wore her red, high-top Keds with jeans and a red-plaid flannel shirt. She stood only about four feet ten, so her feet dangled, with toes pointing to reach the floor, making her look like a child, too.

She looked up at me, her face grave. "Someone is sneaking on me," she said. "I hear him at night. He walks around and around my cabin but I can't see him. He wants me to know he is there. In the morning, I can find his tracks easily. He wants me to be afraid." She turned her face to the floor. "And I *am* afraid," she whispered.

So that's where the prowler went. I had wondered. We'd gone about two weeks since the ambush at the teacherage, two very quiet weeks, or so it seemed. And now this. He hadn't stopped, hadn't gone away, had simply shifted to a new victim.

"You're not the only one." And I told her about the other women. I think she felt better, but not much. And I felt worse. She was the only one of the group who did not have a telephone.

"Do you have a weapon?" I asked her.

"I have a bird gun, a .410/.22 over-and-under."

152

"Can you shoot it?" She smiled and looked at the floor, which told me of course she could and it was a stupid question. She was so small, so nearly childlike, it was easy to forget she was an adult, a mother—unmarried as far as I knew—and as fully self-sufficient as anyone else around here.

"Sorry," I told her. "Stupid question."

She smiled and put her hand over her mouth, giggling softly. Henry did the same. I later found out she was a crack shot and could bring down a goose with a head shot, using the .22 barrel of her over-and-under, unlike most who used the wider-load shotgun pellets on birds. "I don't like to chew the BBs," she told me.

I watched her ruffle Henry's hair fondly, and without planning to, asked her, "Did you marry?"

She gave a quick smile at the question, then looked down. "I wondered when... if... you would ask." She nodded at Henry.

"No, I didn't ask because of Henry. I asked... because of me. Because of Evie."

"Ahhh." She nodded. "I did not marry. I might have, but he did not love Henry. And," she did a head bob, "he did not ask. He did not... *decide*."

Since we knew the prowler's main targets, or thought we did, a few of us put together a plan to patrol nightly until we caught this guy. It was Vic's idea and I thought a good one. Oliver said he was in, also Butch, William, and Andy when they were here, and even Gary, the checker at the general store. Actually, as word got out, his wife volunteered him.

It wasn't a complicated plan. We were patrolling the homes of the women who had already been prowled. Each of us would head out, armed, on our assigned nights, and walk from house to house, varying the route and the times as much as possible. We reasoned that sooner or later, we had to catch this guy in the act, or at least see something suspicious we could follow up on.

When Frank Jacobs heard of our plan, he was less than enthusiastic. "What's gonna happen," he cautioned, "is something like, one of you heroes gets his night wrong and shoots one of you other heroes."

"Make sure it's really your night," I cautioned the group, "and don't shoot without a clear target."

Like many good plans, it didn't really work. Night after night we had zero sightings as it got more and more cold. We started out in jackets but as October slipped in, switched to parkas. As it happened, I was on patrol the night of the first significant snowfall. I got to see the world as a magical and beautiful place while hunting for someone who might well be a sexual predator and cruel murderer.

One Saturday night I wasn't on patrol and my phone rang at about one fifteen. I was pretty sure I knew what it would be. I had taken to stretching the phone cord as far as it would reach toward my bedroom, resting it on a chair to help cut my response time. Sure enough, I heard Evie's voice, low and stressed.

"Hardy, he's here, he's..." and then the click, as—I was pretty sure—the line was cut. I dressed and ran, only checking the calendar as I flew by... Vic's night to patrol. Of course, it would be easy enough to be patrolling on the other side of town, maybe eight blocks distant. Or it could be something worse, and I ran also fearing what might have happened to Vic.

I made it to Evie's on the run, in about two minute's time, to find her porch light on and the cut phone line—

again—but nothing more. I circled the cabin several times in both directions and then did a wider circle, in case someone had hidden in her little woods, to watch me. I found no one. Nothing. I rapped on her door. "It's me." She came out, this time fully dressed, again clutching her Colt.

"I'm sorry," she said. "He *was* here!"

"There's nothing to be sorry about." I put my arms around her under the porch light and kissed her cheek. "I know he was. Phone lines don't cut themselves." We stood that way together, maybe twenty seconds, and I remember I had just stepped back when someone fired a single shot, very loud.

Evie's eyes met mine. "Shotgun," she said.

"Get inside... lock the door," I told her, turning to dash away.

"Hell, no," she said with feeling, shocking me a little. She banged wide the cabin door to grab her parka, stuffing arms through sleeves and somehow zipping it on the run. Side by side we ran up the snowy road, guns in hands, and I heard her laugh just a little, the mission girl resurfacing. "Sorry, Father," she said.

CHAPTER 17

Two of the prowled women had shotguns, Adele and Molly. Since I knew... believed... Butch to be at home, we ran straight for Molly's.

Though the town had streetlights on every corner, most were out. In the six blocks we jogged, we passed through only two pools of white light, nearly stumbling on Vic, stretched out on the snowy road on a dark corner.

He sat up with his knees bent, groaning, holding his head. "That way!" Sure enough, he pointed toward Molly's.

I looked at Evie, only slightly visible in starlight. "Would you stay with Vic?" I could see her grin at me in the darkness.

"Sure."

Running into Molly's yard, it was obvious we'd missed the prowler again. Her lights were on and through frosty windows, I could see her bustling around doing something. I slowed to a walk and came in cautiously, actually looking for a gunshot victim in her yard. Alas, there was none.

I approached calling, "Molly, it's Father Hardy." I saw her pause, turn to pick up her shotgun and step out. "Are you alright?" She nodded. "What happened?"

"I was sleeping, and woke up to a noise at my door. Sticks breaking. Someone come like a wolf, circling my cabin. She looked at the ground. "I was very afraid."

"I don't blame you." I patted her on the shoulder. "You put sticks out?"

"Yes, to make sure I know when he comes. And I shoveled back the snow." She pinched my parka sleeve between two fingers and drew me in through her cabin door, into the light of a single sixty-watt bulb hanging from a twisted fabric-covered cord. I flipped back my parka hood and she leaned the shotgun securely in the corner of the counter in her tiny kitchen area.

The whole place was about the size of my living room. In the back corner, between the two metal bedsteads, a curtain strung on a wire concealed the indoor 'honey bucket.' She'd lined her cabin walls with layers of newspaper and cardboard for insulation, and decorated with color pictures of Alaska, collected from calendars and *The National Geographic*. Just inside the door stood a small table and two chairs. A pitcher pump mounted next to the sink provided indoor water, and a wood-burning cook stove kept the cabin cozy.

"What happened next?" I asked her.

"Sometimes he just circles. Tonight, he came to my door, rattled the knob, but I already locked it. I have a bar, too." She showed me a four-foot length of two-by-four, shaved slightly to fit under a pair of sturdy u-shaped barn door pulls and screwed firmly into the doorframe. The prowler wouldn't be breaking through that door. The problem in the door was the four windowpanes.

"He broke this one." She pointed to the pane at the bottom left, directly above the doorknob. Then she pointed to the pane at the top left, shot-gunned away. "I broke this one."

"You're going to need a new door," I told her. She smiled a little.

"But not a new me."

She looked so fragile and dear in that moment, I pulled her into my arms and gave her a quick squeeze of relief, and she let me. Then she broke open the breach of her

Savage combination, pulling out the .22 and the .410 cartridges.

"Shouldn't you leave that loaded? He may come again."

She just shook her head and nodded toward baby Henry, somehow sleeping through all the excitement. "Not safe," she said.

She had been cutting squares of cardboard when I arrived, with a long, very sharp hunting knife. As she finished cutting the second square, I tacked the first one over the shot-out pane—higher than she could reach without standing on something—and taped the edges with medical adhesive tape.

"With this?" I asked her. She shrugged.

"All I got."

"It works."

I was taping the second one when I heard Evie's voice. "Hello the house. Hardy?" I stepped out.

"It's okay. We're fixing the door."

I watched as Evie led Vic, who was holding his head and still a bit unsteady, across the yard. Opening the door, I led them into the cabin where Molly took over, gently shoving Vic into a kitchen chair. Pulling back his parka hood, she began to dab at his wound with a cotton ball soaked in hydrogen peroxide.

"I think you saved me," she said to Vic. Eye to eye with her, for once, he smiled shyly, then ducked his head. She took him by the chin and raised his head level to finish the job.

"Look!" She pointed at Vic's wound. "Hit with a board. See the line." I did look and sure enough, through the bruise and damage of the wound, I could see the angled imprint of a sharp edge.

Evie shook her head. "You might have a concussion."

"Feels like it," said Vic. "I've never been walloped so hard. It nearly took me right off my feet. And then I guess my knees let go and I ended up sitting down anyway." He flinched as Molly applied a sterile gauze pad, pressing it into place, taping it with more from the adhesive roll. "Ouch!"

She grinned at him. "All done!" She stepped back, examining her work, and he rose slowly.

I looked up at him. "You were lucky."

He looked at me like I was off my nut. "Lucky? I nearly got my head knocked off!"

"The last two times I spotted this guy, he emptied the whole magazine at me. I counted ten rounds each, so a total of twenty rounds he's aimed in my direction."

"One thing we know," said Vic, as he and I and Evie said our goodnights and headed out the door.

"What's that?"

"The guy is a darn lousy shot."

* * *

William didn't want to believe he'd lost his brother. "I am not certain he has died." He watched as Rosie topped off his heavy mug, setting down the pot to pull a small pad from her apron string and a yellow, gnawed-on pencil stub from behind her ear.

It was lunchtime at the Coffee Cup Café. The place was about three-quarters full, the windows frosty about halfway up, and the air heavy with the homey scent of cigarettes and hot meat on the grill.

We both ordered the moose meat cheeseburgers. "Out of the moose," she said. "It'll have to be beef." That was a letdown. Next to moose meat, the beef was almost flavorless.

We lapsed into comfortable silence as she spun away. Someone called out, "Hey Rosie, where's my lunch?"

"It's cookin'!" she called back.

She had KFAR on the radio. At the top of the news at noon, Russia's launch of what they called Sputnik I, a rocket into space.

"It is more than that," said William, pulling himself from thoughts of Vadim. "The Sputnik is now in orbit around the earth. Not just up and down, blasting some stray dog into space. Now they are there. They are owning space and we are not."

I had to wonder that he—a born Russian—now considered the U.S. 'we' and the Soviets 'they.' It was definitely our gain.

In other headlines, the National Guard was still on patrol in Little Rock, called up by President Eisenhower to enforce school integration. At the Springfield National Armory in Massachusetts, authorities described themselves as "still baffled." They had quit calling the stolen weapon a bazooka, and it was now described as a 'prototype shoulder weapon.' They were offering a $50,000 reward and suggesting the theft had something to do with Communists. The late senator Joe McCarthy would be proud.

"Wow!" I looked at William. "Fifty-thousand dollars! That's about fifteen years of regular wages. I wonder what's the big deal with that?"

"Umm," was all William had to say. Which always made me think he knew something. An ad came on, Japanese women make good wives. Reply to a post office box, enclose one dollar for the list. I could imagine lonely sourdoughs all across the Tanana Valley writing down that post office box and mailing in their dollars, hoping for a match. According to the radio announcer, Japanese women were unfailingly polite, respectful, quiet, and 'willing to serve her man.' I remember thinking, *It's a strange world.* Not long ago, the Japanese were our deadly enemies. Now they wanted to send us their spare women.

Locally, someone had taken a shot at one of the river pilots. Apparently, the *Koyukuk* had been just below Chandalar, moving slowly, pushing a heavy barge upstream. At about fast-walking speed, the boat was an easy target, and someone fired a shot from shore, exploding a cup of hot coffee all over the pilot, Myles Conway. Authorities were mystified. William's eyes met mine.

"I am hearing there are too many suspects to consider. At last, Conway has irritated someone who is a very good shot. I wonder who?" Then he took another sip of his coffee, and just for a moment, smiled.

Meanwhile in New York, the Milwaukee Braves and New York Yankees were headed into game three for the championship, Milwaukee favored. *Oh well.* I'd always been a Yankees guy if the Brooklyn Dodgers weren't playing.

"We could hold a memorial," I suggested. William looked at me and blinked. "For the Yankees, or Captain Conway's coffee cup?"

"For Vadim," I reminded.

"Oh," he said. He held his mug close and blinked both eyes behind the lenses of his wire rims. "Not yet."

* * *

Evie and I, with Whiskey Jack in the pickup bed, went out along the river to the ways for the annual haul-out of the *Princess of Minto* with her car barge. It was October 28th, my third haul-out since coming to Chandalar. For

161

about a week, larger ice chunks had been an increasing impediment, not so much a hazard, like the *Titanic*, as an inconvenience—a busted rudder or a paddle on the paddlewheel.

My first year, impact with a surprise floe left her rudderless, swept away downriver with three cars on her barge and three frantic drivers. To get her back, they had to call the *Taku Chief*, a river tug down from Nenana, to give chase and ultimately haul her off a sandbar.

We bundled up. The temperature had fallen below freezing and the wind off the river hurt, sharp enough to shave. Above, with the humidity low, the hazeless sky arced endlessly, deep and intensely blue, piercingly bright. As we climbed back into the Ford, I waited to turn the key.

"Did you hear? Someone took a shot at Myles Conway."

She turned her brown eyes to mine, dark eyebrows lifting. "Gosh, what a surprise."

"I guess... whoever it was... missed him and hit his coffee cup."

Her forehead furrowed. "You call that a miss? I say that person was aiming at the coffee cup and I call it a pretty darn good shot." And then she looked away, out the windshield at the river, but I saw the smile.

We drove home a little quiet. With the ferry out of service, we were now officially stuck here, not that Chandalar was a bad place to be. It would be most of a month before the river froze hard enough to drive over. Last year I parked the truck on the other side so we could walk across the railroad bridge if we wanted to drive to Fairbanks. This year I hadn't. So, unless we took the train, we had no way out.

The temperature dropped to zero that night. I have a thermometer mounted to a window frame at the front of my house, out of the wind. I could almost watch the red stripe sink. Condensation froze white inside on the windowpanes, on the door hinges, on the latch and knob. Opening the door swept a low cloud of freezing air across the room. When I came in with an armload of wood, Evie watched it sweep in ahead of me.

"Yep," she said, "it's winter."

When I asked if she wanted to stay the night she fell into her version of a Mae West routine. "You mean *stay* the night," she said in a quasi-seductive voice, leaning and looking in the direction of the bedroom. "Or *stay*." She dropped her voice dully on the word and jerked her head at the couch.

I smiled at her. "Your choice."

"That's not fair." She rolled her eyes. "Oh well, I guess it's the couch." She smiled slyly. "But don't be surprised if you see me a little later."

"Don't you be surprised." I got her a blanket. This sexual bantering was getting more and more risky.

I settled her on the sofa, and kissed her goodnight, and kissed her goodnight, and might have kept it up but she said, "Go to bed, Hardy. While you can." And I went, calling Jack, turning out lights on my way.

Jack started his turning-around ritual on the rag rug beside my bed. Tonight he had a hard time finding exactly the right spot, but finally flopped down. I got undressed and crawled in, had no more than settled my head on the pillow when Jack got up—after all that turning around— abandoned me, and went back into the living room to sleep next to the sofa. So much for *man's* best friend.

The next thing I knew, I had been sleeping and Jack woke me with a low growl. I looked around at the room, softly aglow with pale blue moonlight, and listened hard. I didn't hear anything, but thought I had, just before waking. Did I dream it?

I heard Jack get up from his rug in the living room, tap his toenails on the linoleum down the hallway toward my room, and jab at my cheek with his cold nose. "What?" I muttered, wanting very much to roll over and go back to sleep.

There's a dog, Rin Tin Tin, who has his own series on TV, not that I get to see it in Chandalar. When something's wrong, like when his boy, Rusty, has been tied to the railroad tracks, someone just says, 'What's wrong, Rinty?' and Rinty, a big handsome German Shepherd, leads rescuers to Rusty, or spells out the clue with some-kind-of-doggy anagram. 'Rusty's on the railroad tracks,' they cry, and run for their horses and their bugle.

All Jack could do was keep going with the low growl, and perform a sort of agitated tap dance until I crawled out of bed, pulled on my pants and grabbed the .38 from my bedside table. I hoped he hadn't woken Evie. She met me in the hall, long legs bare, apparently wearing nothing but one of my shirts.

She reached out to take my arm, pulling herself close, soft and warm against my side in the cooling house. "He woke you?" I whispered. I called Jack and he came and sat by my leg, leaning.

"No. We woke together. I think someone cut the plastic on your living room window, just above my head, like they thought they might slide the window open."

164

"Not someone from around here." Anybody local would know that none of these windows would open again until they thawed in the spring.

Evie put her face close to mine. "Is the prowler prowling you?"

I shrugged. "Dunno. Why would he?"

The three of us stood that way, close, cooling, listening. I had just whispered, "False alarm?" when someone rattled the doorknob. No knocking, just rattling, trying the lock. So, not a false alarm.

"Stay here."

"Hell, no..." she began, but trailed off. I touched my finger to her lips.

"Stay," I said. I felt as if I were talking to Jack. I started for the living room and the front door, Jack just behind my leg.

Approaching the door from the side, I reached out to flip on the porch light switch, at the same time calling out, "Who's there?" Still from the side, I grabbed the knob as if to open the door. The result was instantaneous. Three shots fired in a tight grouping through the center of the door at belt buckle height. If I'd been standing behind the door when I grabbed the knob, I'd be bleeding out on the floor right now.

Jack went crazy. Without thinking about it, I reached up to twist the bolt, snatched the door open and let him out into the night. He went with a snarl and a fusillade of barking. I heard a shot, then another, and the distant sound of cloth ripping and a curse. Fearful I'd sent my dog out to be murdered, I called out. "Jack... come!" I waited the long seconds until he came bounding back into the wanigan, a shred of cloth in his teeth and no apparent wounds.

I pulled him in the door and drew a great lungful of air, letting it all out in a whoosh of relief. Safe! Somehow, we were all safe.

Evie came out to join me, now all dressed, and we both petted and fussed over Jack who had alerted us, maybe saved us. He jumped and turned and frolicked, liking the attention. He had probably also liked the game, 'chasing strangers in the night,' and would be happy if we'd play it again.

I would be happy if we didn't.

CHAPTER 18

"Darn big bullet holes! Not a .22... not your prowler." That was Andy's summation. He had flown down with the marshal the next morning to examine the bullet holes in my door and provide emotional support. He'd showed up with a package under his arm, wrapped and taped in a grocery bag, comfortably missing Evie who had gotten up early and gone off to get ready for school. He bent down to examine the bullet holes. "Nice grouping," he said, sarcastic then looked up. "Got any coffee?"

"You'll have to make it."

"No problem," he smiled, threading past, heading for the kitchen.

"Umm..." The marshal looked at me. "You've seriously pissed somebody off."

"You think?"

"That's how I'd bet." He hesitated some more. "You must have some idea who'd want to murder you close up, in cold blood."

I thought about that odd phrase, 'in cold blood.' It meant someone not in the heat of passion. It meant a calculated kill by someone who simply wanted me out of the way.

"Just the guy with the big ears," and I told him about the altercation on Main Street."

"Big Butch saved your ass," he said. "Sorry, Father." He laughed. "You probably didn't get the dispatch, but people aren't supposed to be trying to kill other people, especially in the middle of town. You should have called me to come out right then. That's why the U.S. government pays me. This is the second darn shooting in less than a month." He looked at me. "You wouldn't know anything about anyone shooting at Myles Conway?"

"Nope!"

"I heard about your little adventure with Conway in the saloon. If we can find this shooter, we're thinking of giving him a reward. I guess Conway nearly soiled himself."

"You think it's a man?"

That stopped him. "I guess you're right. More likely to be a woman, but what kind of woman shoots like that?"

I just shook my head. I knew a couple of women who could.

Andy appeared. "You two ready for coffee?" As usual, we were. And not only were we having the good Italian roast coffee, but we were having it from my new French press coffee pot.

"Ta da!" Andy threw up his arm grandly, in presentation. He was right. It did taste better. I would miss the delicate and not-so-subtle hint of aluminum.

When we all had coffee and were seated, the marshal looked around. Though seldom at a loss for words, when he looked up and cleared his throat like he had something to say, all that came out was, "Ummm..."

Andy toasted him with a coffee mug. "Well said! Hear, hear."

Jacobs bunched up his face in a grimace. "Shut up over there." Andy pretended to be contrite.

"I know how you guys are. You like to handle things on your own." He looked at me. "You like to solve things. You're getting a reputation for it. But you've got a serious body count going on out here, especially if you add in the two attempts on you." He poked a forefinger in my direction. "So, I'm asking you—telling you—to stay out of this thing. Stay home." He met my eyes. "Stay off the street if necessary. Do everything you can to not get killed by this guy, or your prowler guy—or anybody else— before we can round them up. Let the people who do this do this," he concluded, and took a sip from his coffee mug. It was the most words I'd heard from him at one sitting.

"What did you *think* we were going to do?"

He looked from Andy to me. "I thought you and dead-eye here—maybe with your buddy William—would gun up and go out hunting for trouble. Like you usually do."

"Oh," I said. It was hard to argue. As I thought about it now, he was right.

"So, promise me you'll stay in town and do your best to stay out of trouble."

I admit I rolled my eyes. "Okay, I promise."

"Good!" he said with feeling, and setting his cup down with a firm *clunk*, stood up over his tippy stool to head out.

"You, too?" he said to Andy. "Stay out of trouble?"

Andy raised his hands in mock surrender. "You know *me*."

"Yeah, I do. That's why we're having this talk."

Andy nodded. "Okay. I'll be good."

Headed down the hall I heard Jacobs snort. "Sure, you will. Like usual. You flying back with me, Silas?" he called over his shoulder to Andy.

"Nah, you go on. I'll get the train."

With the river not yet frozen, Jacobs had landed on skis at the airport, just out of town, and borrowed an orange CAA truck for the run in. We heard the truck start, warm up a minute or two, then clunk into gear and drive away. Until he left, we sat silent, sipping our French-

169

pressed, Italian-roasted, Alaska-brewed coffee, pondering his warning.

Andy gave me a heavy-browed mock-serious look. "So, what *are* we going to do?" He nodded to himself. "Maybe some fireside knitting."

I laughed and then he laughed. I knew he was trouble. "We could do what the marshal asked us to. Stay here in town, try to not be a target."

He made his absurd face. "Twice you been nearly killed within these two blocks, firmly *in town*! What's left to do? Take to your bed? I'll be honest with you. It... bugs me, that Big Ears is doing all the shooting and we're the ones who have to stay in, keep our noses clean."

"So, are you suggesting something?"

He set down his mug and nodded. "I'm suggesting we sneak out there onto the flats, find those... claim jumpers, or whatever they are, and give *them* something to stay in about. Maybe a few near misses. Something that says don't come into town and make trouble with us. That's what I'm suggesting." He looked pleased with himself and got up to completely drain the pot, stray grounds and all. "That's what I'm saying."

I reminded him we had troubles of our own in town without having to go out on the flats looking for more. And I filled him in on the prowler incident with Molly Joseph. His face sobered.

"Yeah, that's not good. You know what else... something I thought of?" I shook my head. "I been meaning to tell you this, but I warn you," he held out his free hand, palm down, "it's an odd thought."

"Okay," I said, "warned."

"It's just this. Of all the women bein' prowled... think about 'em. About how they look. Evie... she's Indian, but taller. Alice is white... small, skinny... big breasts."

"Do you have a point?"

"I'm gettin' to it. Linda Huxton is taller and blond, fair skinned, good build.

"Taller than what?"

"*That's* my point! Taller than both Adele and Molly, who are both Indian, with similar skin color, hair color and... well... build."

"Breast size?" I asked.

"Yeah," he said, "that."

"So, you're saying..."

"I'm saying they both could be Marjorie, alike enough to be sisters. I'm sayin' we need to consider he's not after these other women at all.

It was a guess. We both knew it. Based on not much. Still, with Marjorie dead and Molly the most aggressively attacked, it had to be considered.

"Adele's got Big Butch handy," Andy reasoned. And she had a phone, to keep Butch available for jobs. Plus, she turned a big-bore shotgun on the prowler right away. Those were three compelling reasons to want to prowl elsewhere.

But first things first. We spent the balance of the day driving to the abandoned mission school, about a mile above town, where the river cut in, and the riverbank fell away in car-sized chunks. Someday, in-the-not-too-distant future, this would all be gone. The river gives and the river takes away. The old mission had opened as an Episcopal boarding school for Athabascan children in the early century, becoming an orphanage in the late teens and twenties on the heels of the influenza epidemic. Now it sat

171

empty—haunted, many of the locals felt—and I couldn't disagree. Standing in the hallway or on the stairs, on a bitter cold winter day, it wasn't difficult to imagine distant children's voices, laughter... sobs... and I always came out of there chilled to the bone, more than cold.

The three of us, Andy, me, and Jack, went out in the Ford to salvage an exterior door that would fit at Molly's, help warm the place up, and bolt securely now that hers had been wrecked. Luckily we soon found a good, solid one, just the right size, on a small, emptied-out building. It didn't take long to back out the hinge screws and throw it in the truck bed to haul away.

Molly seemed especially quiet and ill at ease when we arrived, her Savage close at hand and, I noticed, loaded. Henry and Jack hit it off and frolicked in the snow as we worked. With the new lockable glassless door solidly in place, she smiled, seemed to relax, and brewed us hot tea with fireweed honey.

Driving back toward town, with Andy literally riding shotgun, a 12-gauge standing vertically between his knees, I saw him out of the corner of my eye as he turned to look at me.

"So, what do you say?"

"About what?"

"Huh! You know what. About going after one of these guys who's after us!"

"Maybe it's the same guy."

"I thought about that," he said, "but no, I don't think so."

"I've seen them both," I reminded, "they're both fast, white, I think, fit... and tall."

Andy stood about five four. "All those tall white guys look alike," he said. "But I don't think it's the same guy.

172

Prowler's carryin' a lightweight, semi-automatic, probably a .22 caliber. No way those were bullet holes from a .22 in your door. Butch took a revolver, a *big* revolver, away from Big Ears. In my mind, that makes Big Ears *not* the prowler."

We'd missed lunch, and I admit I was hungry, so when Andy said, "Cheeseburger," I watched my hands turn the black Bakelite steering wheel toward Main Street and the Coffee Cup. The bell tinkled as we went in and Rosie, Andy's sweetie, stuck out her lips to kiss him as she made a coffee-pot pass through the room. Knowing a good thing when I saw it, I stuck out my cheek and she kissed me, too, doubtless leaving a lipstick imprint. Sure enough, I wiped my cheek with a paper napkin, rewarded with a red smear.

The place was about half full, mostly men, smoking, drinking coffee, and 'telling each other lies,' as Andy says. We took our customary places under the dusty moose head but declined menus, responding to the siren song of the famous Coffee Cup moose cheeseburger and fries, served with a cup of coffee, regrettably from the red can.

Rosie had the Philco dialed to KFAR and Elvis sang us up to the three o'clock news with *Jailhouse Rock*, another huge hit.

"No more truck drivin' for him," said Andy.

In the news, a U.S. Air Force general, Archie J. Old, Jr., had led a squadron of three Boeing B-52 bombers on a flight all the way around the world in forty-five hours, nineteen minutes. Andy snorted. "I remember when you couldn't do it in less than eighty days."

"In Fairbanks, police were calling the *Koyukuk* shooting an act of malicious vandalism—probably teens out on a lark. There were no suspects.

173

Andy smiled, sipped his coffee, and made a bad coffee face. "Hah! Too many suspects. Darn near every woman in the valley. Too bad she missed."

I said, "She didn't. She made her point."

"Who do we know who could make a shot like...?" I looked at him. "Oh! Never mind."

In Seattle, someone had broken into a cargo container on the docks at night, shooting a night watchman. It turned out he had been playing cards with his fellow night watchmen and, just moments before, had drawn what is known—so Andy told me—as the 'death card,' the ace of spades. The watchman laughed about it, then he went out to make his rounds and sure enough, someone shot him dead.

There were no new developments on the Springfield Armory theft. Except that now it had grown to a tripod-mounted, recoilless rocket launcher, sounding quite a bit more dangerous. There was speculation the weapon was making its way to the Far East, probably in the hands of gunrunning Communist sympathizers, headed for Southeast Asia and the tiny country of Vietnam. Communist rebels there had been seeking to overthrow the U.S.-supported government of President Diem, whom *Life Magazine* had already labeled "The Tough Miracle Man of Vietnam."

Andy sipped his coffee and made a face. "Who cares?"

I admit I already had a bad feeling about Vietnam, having met and nearly been killed by a rogue agent from our new government agency operating there, the CIA. He was a psychopath in what sounded like a psychopathic agency.

"It just all feels wrong," I told Andy.

174

"Aw," he said, "it'll blow over."

Vic came in for a Coke. He pulled up a chair and, being tall, got into it by just stepping over the chair back, all accomplished while pulling off his parka. I looked at him. "You're not teaching?"

"Was. They let us out early. Had some kind of furnace snafu. It's colder than a fritter in there. We had the kids all sitting at their desks in their parkas. I saw your sweetie heading home as I came down to check the mail. I heard a Coke calling my name, and here I am."

We talked a bit about Vietnam, and then Vic started asking Andy about beaver trapping, something he wanted to try.

He leaned forward, all eager. "I read about Kit Carson and some of the old-time mountain men trapping beaver. I want to stick my arm down into the ice-cold water to set the trap. Whew! I never could see how they could do that."

"Around here," Andy reminded, "you gotta break through four feet of ice before you can stick your arm in."

That brought him up short. "Forgot about that," he said.

He asked about prowler news and I told him Andy's theory, that the prowler was after Adele or Molly. "I can see that," he said. He sat and thought about it. "Well," he said, "what about Rosie?"

"I think she's too tall," I told him, "with too much figure, like Evie. She doesn't look as much like Marjorie as these other ladies."

Vic raised his eyebrows. "Well, then, we got him!"

"Got him?" asked Andy.

"Sure," said Vic, enthusiastic. "If there's only two women—or one—to guard, it'll be a piece o' cake!"

Maybe, I thought, but without much confidence.

175

CHAPTER 19

It was like Myles Conway fell off the planet. He used to say, "Hey, I'm just here for a good time!" Apparently still here—people said they saw him—but it seemed like the good-time train might have left the station without him. Word was, Conway didn't get out much, just sat in his cabin and drank a lot. Other people had tried that, usually with a bad result.

The one time he saw Evie, he was staggering drunk and said, "I'll get you, bitch," and I wanted to go over and slug him again.

"Nah." She shrugged it off. "He was too drunk to even remember saying it."

Maybe.

The season's first blizzard hit with a huge snow dump and wind gusts up to fifty miles an hour. It would be my night to be out but I not only wouldn't be able to patrol, I wouldn't even be able to walk, with the wind blowing each footstep backward!

Late afternoon, Evie called to say she was walking over. I timed her, and she did, then Andy and Rosie, and finally William and Alice came too. We had a quorum at our first-blizzard-of-the-season party.

We drank coffee, whipped up divine moose meat sandwiches—courtesy of Andy and Rosie—and otherwise stayed close to the fire and enjoyed each other's company. With the storm on the way, I had filled up my back porch with firewood. We didn't even have to go out and crawl through the snowdrifts to bring it in! As the evening wore on, the three women went off to the living room to play canasta and the three men retreated to the tippy stools to talk 'man stuff.'

William had ordered a new hunting rifle, finally buying American—a Winchester Model 70 with the twenty-four-inch barrel, chambered for a .30-06 cartridge. He had also pulled strings to get the American-made 8x Unertl scope, the combination popular among snipers in the Japanese war and in Korea.

Andy made an approving face. "Good choices." Then couldn't resist a dig. "Not too heavy for you, is it? I know you have to screw on that little stick mono-pod to hold up that big heavy rifle you have now."

William waved him away, shaking his head. He looked at me. "Jealousy."

"So, tell me," said Andy. "I bet you know. What's the big deal with this Springfield Armory bazooka?"

The question froze William, frankly shocking both Andy and me. For a long moment, it didn't even look like he breathed. Then he turned his head from right to left, as if checking to see if he could be overheard—in my kitchen.

Finally, he looked up at us, meeting Andy's eyes and then mine. "It is atomic," he said simply. "Nuclear."

Andy's jaw dropped. "Nuclear? That's crazy!"

"It is," agreed William. He took a sip of his cooling coffee and climbed off the stool for a reheat.

I couldn't help shaking my head. "So that's why it's such a big deal." He nodded.

Andy looked up. "And this thing is shoulder mounted?"

"Well," he said, "not really. It is called a Davy Crockett recoilless spigot gun—sometimes a recoilless rifle—but they are not that. It looks like a big bazooka with a four- or six-inch tube. The stolen weapon is a four-inch.

177

The missile itself weighs about fifty pounds and so is usually fired from a tripod. I suppose it could be shoulder-fired but would not be very accurate. But then again, with a weapon that deadly, I am not sure it matters. One of the problems with firing the weapon is not killing the crew. The explosion is not large but radiation kills everything within about a two-mile radius."

"And this thing is headed for Vietnam?" I asked him.

He smiled a tight, unpleasant-looking smile. "No," he said, "that is deliberate misinformation. The fact is, no one seems to know where it is or where it is going."

Evie meandered into the kitchen to fill her coffee mug.

"Are you three talking about something interesting?" She studied our faces and frowned. "Looks like it. Something serious. Come on, spill."

"You're right," I said. "We were talking about women."

She said something like "Humph!" and went back to the living room.

Later, after everyone had gone, I walked Evie home through the waning storm, the two of us holding on to each other as we buffeted down the road center, blazing the only set of tracks through an unbroken field of freshly knee-high snow. The wind had died off just a little but it was bitter cold and snow kept blowing in our eyes.

"So, what were you *really* talking about?" She asked, still having to raise her voice.

She'd heard about the Springfield Armory heist. "Something about stealing a bazooka?"

"Turns out, it's nuclear." She stopped dead in the roadway, snow swirling around her. I couldn't see her face, wrapped up behind a red knitted muffler, but I could see her eyes, and they were startled wide.

"A nuclear bomb? How big?"

"Big enough." But then I told her what William had said. "It's not so much the explosion as the radiation that kills... instantly."

* * *

The storm dumped nearly two feet of fresh snow on the Tanana Valley. As often happens, the next morning was clear, blindingly bright and beautiful. I was out just after sunrise, about nine thirty, with my snow shovel. The plow had already been by, sealing my driveway behind a nearly six-foot wall of snow. For some secret plowman reason, they pushed all the street snow to my side, leaving the uninhabited far side of the road clear. The snow pile stood so tall that when Butch showed up to help shovel, all I could see was the shiny, sweaty top of his nearly shaved head, gleaming in the sun.

There were three of us shoveling, ultimately—Oliver came too—none too many for my sixty-some feet of driveway. But we got it all cleared out in an hour or so. I invited the crew in for coffee but they had miles to shovel before they slept, and headed away.

My telephone was ringing when I made it back indoors. I picked it up. "Hardy." It was William.

"I am wondering if you have seen Alice this morning? She does not answer her phone—the line may be down—and she has not made it to work. She wanted me to stay over with her last night, but I had to be out early. I am calling from Clear."

I'd been out shoveling snow at minus thirty-five degrees, but had not been cold. In fact, I came in sweating. But in that moment, I felt chilled. "Maybe she overslept," I said falsely.

"Alice?"

"Okay, maybe not. I'm sure it's nothing. Give me your number and I'll walk over and check on her and call you back—or she will—when she gets to a working phone."

"Ah," he said, "perfect." He said it in a way that made me realize he didn't believe it, either. Walking over, I imagined the full spectrum of what I might discover. In a way, what I found was worse. I found no sign of Alice at all. And what I did find—the phone line cut, the door ajar, the fire out—gripped like an icy fist on my insides, making it hard to even breathe.

With the door ajar, a stretched triangular drift of snow, eight inches deep in the doorway, penetrated most of six feet across the braided living room rug. Alice wasn't there and hadn't been, probably since William dropped her off the night before. Her bed lay undisturbed, though a nightie had been tossed across it. She had an oil heater, set fairly low because she also liked to keep a wood fire going. Last night, after the fire went out, the oil heater hadn't been able to keep up and a glass of water stood frozen on her kitchen counter, near the door.

So much for Andy's theory about the prowler's choice of women. Leaving all as it was, I jogged a shortcut back to the rectory and the telephone, huffing, slogging, tripping through glittering, powdery snow with some drifts waist high.

On the phone, I heard the sharp intake of William's breath. "It is as I feared. I am coming. Call Andy!" I did.

The telephone line to Fairbanks added a tinny, anxious crackle to the already scary message. Andy picked up on the first ring, as if sensing trouble. "Oh, shit!" he said. And then, "I'm on my way."

When I called Vic, Linda answered. "Oh no!" she said. "Vic's asleep... didn't go in today. He had one of his nights." Then she added, "I didn't. I slept like the dead, as usual. Should I wake him?"

Under the circumstances, sleeping like 'the dead,' slammed me, hitting far too close to home and the moment's deepest fears about Alice. Add to all that, I couldn't stop seeing Marjorie as I'd last seen her. Like the marshal said, you sure can't un-see a bad thing.

But I shook it off. "Let him sleep a bit. Give him an hour." William would be here sooner but I knew it would take at least that long for Andy to make it down on the Fairbanks road. Just after a blizzard there'd be plows out and doubtless slow going at times.

I debated with myself for a few long minutes then called the school office to leave a message for Evie. I managed to somehow not say, "Tell her to call home." She rang back in two minutes and gasped when I told her. I meant to tell her to stay put but was too slow.

"Pick me up," she said, and hung up.

In a little more than an hour, about twenty of us met at the rectory, armed to the teeth, jammed into my living room, faces grim. Frank Jacobs was there. He'd ridden down with Andy. Vic arrived looking bleary. Even his straight-stemmed pipe drooped. "Looks like you were up all night," I told him.

He made a face. "Tell me about it. Fortunately, it doesn't happen often."

Of course, everybody came dressed for the cold—about minus thirty—and the likelihood of being out all night. Most came with light backpacks and snowshoes or skis. It wouldn't be an exaggeration to say that every man and woman, there were three—Evie, Rosie and Adele—in

181

that room, would have paid for the privilege of shooting the prowler, especially if he had now harmed Alice in addition to Marjorie.

William had already divided the area and now assigned searchers. He didn't mince words, and what he said made me want to throw up.

"This is potentially a violent sex crime. Some nakedness, on the part of this prowler is likely... is necessary. So, heated space will be required. Also, even at night, the ability of this monster to transport... a person... in a blizzard, very far... is unlikely."

The marshal spoke up. "Maybe a mile, maximum?"

William nodded. "It looks like he carried her, probably over his shoulder, which limits him. She weighs one hundred pounds and he's walking through snow and drifts. The only places we find tracks are out of the wind and none of them show sled runners. So probably less than a mile. Fire three quick shots if you find..." he hesitated, "anything."

Filing out, Evie's eyes met mine. She looked miserable.

"You're with me," I told her. I had Jack on his leash and she bent to scratch behind his ears.

"Yes," was all she said, softly.

The sun set almost immediately, about three thirty, as if giving up on us. But the long twilight hung on, only fading as stars emerged layer on layer, up and up into the deep black arch of the heavens. The stars shone so small and so impossibly far away, and yet I could read my watch by the soft blue luminous shimmer of starlight reflected off snow.

Andy fell into step with us, walking down the Cat-scraped roadbed. Tied to his pack, his Yukon-style

182

snowshoes, more than four feet long, rattled with each mukluked step.

He managed to make eye contact with Evie. "When we find her, if this goes bad, *don't* go in."

She nodded a little, eyes mostly to the ground.

"Hear me?!"

"Yes!" she said too sharply. Then she waved at him apologetically with her heavy mitt. "Sorry. But you can't think—if it does go wrong—that I won't imagine something as bad as whatever we find. Maybe worse."

"Yeah," he said. "I hear ya."

Neither of us told her that finding Marjorie had been worse than anything we *could* have imagined. Much worse.

The presumption of heat eliminated many woodsheds and small outbuildings. But Chandalar's initial boom and fifty years of bust included building and abandoning many small structures with iron stoves, especially for railroad workers. Cabins that still stood. Even today, itinerant trappers and gold panners in need of shelter might simply squat in a cabin for the summer or the winter before moving on.

It was so dry in this climate that not much rotted. But some cabins had been crushed by the snow load, or torched by kids or occupants who drank, or simply dismantled for the building of other more useful things like privies and dog houses. Since Evie and Andy had grown up here, roaming this whole area, they led the way to many places that might otherwise have been unfindable.

But in the end, there was nothing found and no signal shots fired. Nearing midnight, cold, hungry... depressed... we looped back south of town just as the moon rose three-quarters full, casting long deep-blue moon shadows on the snow-blanketed landscape.

"Where are we?" I asked, by now completely disoriented.

Andy pointed. "Looks different in snow. This here trail is the one that takes us back past the Gustafson place." I had Jack off the leash and sure enough, as we crossed the tracks back into town his ears tipped forward and he barked several times sharply before surging ahead.

It was smoky on the moonlit street. There were three cabins immediately in view, Arnold's and two more. One of them, supposedly rented by Myles Conway. In my mind, he was easily a suspect. But the cabin looked cold and dark, the path untracked. That didn't mean he wasn't the prowler, just that he wasn't here. So, where was he?

Andy first noticed smoke from Arnold's chimney, and then flickering lantern light through the window. At this temperature, warm smoke rose then super-cooled, falling back to creep at ground level.

"Uh-oh, smoke and light... somebody livin' here. Better get your dog."

Jack had rushed up to the cabin, happy to be home, barking and scratching at the door. It was the tracks in the snow that alerted me. It wasn't shoveled out or tramped down, just a few poked-out foot holes through otherwise untroubled snow. And then with my hand on Jack's collar to pull him away, I noticed the door lock—a rusty hasp, which had been there—and a shiny new silver padlock.

I turned to call. "Andy..." and he came on the run, Evie trailing, and saw the padlock. We both knew there was almost no chance it would be lantern-lit inside and locked from the outside.

I began a search for a tool, and spotted just the leaning handle tip of what turned out to be a heavy axe, frozen in place, protruding from a drift of snow. Andy kicked the handle to break the axe loose and then grabbed it before I could. He hit the padlock twice with the blunt side. The lock, probably brittle in the cold, shattered, its pieces falling and sinking in the snow. Our eyes met.

"Gun!" he said, and waited while I pulled off my mitts, grabbed and cocked the .38 in my gloved hand. "Ready?"

He turned the knob and we crashed the door open.

CHAPTER 20

It takes a long time to warm up a cabin that started out in the minus thirties. Every object in the room is *that* cold, and continues to radiate cold long after air in the room has warmed. The prowler likely built up a big fire and restoked it as he left, very early in the morning. But it had now burned down to the last glowing embers, leaving the cabin temperature probably in the low forties. Not near warm enough.

We found Alice arranged on the table top in the same painful, sacrificial posture as Marjorie, her back bent with legs spread. Her wrists, ankles, and a gag had all been taped in place with shiny, black electrical tape. She'd also been ritually tied and knotted with cotton clothesline around her neck, arms, and even her exposed breasts.

Bare breasted but not naked, the prowler had grabbed her flannel shirt at the top and yanked, spraying hard buttons around the room like small white teeth. We kept stepping on them. He'd knifed her bra at the center, leaving the halves in place.

She was conscious, eyes open—no tears but lots of blinking—and she shivered uncontrollably, a likely mixture of adrenaline and early hypothermia. Evie's eyes met mine.

"Fire the shots," I told her. Andy had already pulled his hunting knife to cut her loose, and I pulled off my parka, stripping to my skin to put my warmed undershirt, flannel shirt, and wool sweater on her as fast as I could.

Andy helped her off the table and she tried to stand on her own, but couldn't. Her knees buckled and she said her feet and legs were all pins and needles.

"Hold me up," she said, and I did. Pulling her close against me, warming her with my own body heat and supporting her, easing her in the direction of Andy's quickly built-up crackling fire. I wrapped both of us together inside my parka, against my skin for maximum warmth.

"Signal again," I directed. Evie stepped outside to fire off another three rounds. She came back in and set down her rifle.

"I'm going for the truck." I could tell she was planning to jog the distance back to the rectory.

"Wait!" I handed her my .38. Our eyes met and I managed to not tell her to be careful. She knew that.

Within about fifteen minutes we had most of the search party collected in the cabin. Among the last to arrive was William, with Frank Jacobs right behind. The two had been searching the farthest afield. I yanked my head at William and he came, unzipping his long down parka to take Alice from me and fold her inside.

From her secure position, held tightly against him, Alice looked around.

"I... I knew... y-y-you'd f-f-find me." Our eyes met.

"Can you tell us... anything?" She shook her head.

"I felt like I'd seen him before, like I know him, actually," she said, teeth chattering. "Tall, thin... It's confusing because I've probably seen every man in the Valley at least once. All the drinkers, anyway," she added. "He had a knit mask over his head—a balaclava—and he talked in a fake, gravelly voice."

William looked down at the top of her head. "What was he wearing?"

She closed her eyes, searching her memory. "I knew you'd ask. So that's what I thought about instead of

187

...being raped and killed. He wore a long army parka. Khakis. Army boots... the big white bunny ones. He had..." her eyes shifted from side to side, and she couldn't help lowering her voice. "He... exposed himself, and demanded that I look at him. He has a much smaller penis than... anybody," she finished weakly.

I heard the Ford slide into place outside and the horn honk. I knew Evie would have the heat all the way up and the fan set to 'hurricane.'

"Let's get her to the nurse."

"I can feel my feet now," chattered Alice. "I can walk." No matter. William tipped her into his arms with ease and carried her to the truck. I heard the doors slam, heard it shift and drive away. By now, most of the searchers had drifted off, happy to go home to warm mugs of something, a place by the stove, and the satisfaction of having found Alice alive. Everybody loves a happy ending.

Then the cabin door opened and in came Evie. She'd stayed behind. I was glad to see her. I zipped up my parka, the lining now cold against my bare flesh, and I shivered.

"I thought you'd gone."

"I wanted to stay with you." She kissed me impulsively, and handed back the .38. "Could she tell you anything?"

"No... well... not much."

"Which is it?"

"She described him pretty well, but..."

"Nothing you can use to find him."

"No, nothing."

She cocked her head. "But she told you *something*."

I took a breath. "We've always wondered if the prowler was from somewhere else—from Nenana,

Fairbanks, or maybe Clear." I looked around at the cold cabin. "Let's get out of here." She nodded. There were two kerosene lanterns lit, now burned low on fuel. We each blew one out, pulled open the door and headed out into moonlight.

"She thought she knew him," I said. "He's definitely from here."

* * *

Too jittery to sleep, we gathered at the rectory. Evie and me, Andy, Rosie, and Frank Jacobs settled on tippy stools. Andy had insisted we use the already beloved French press, and we were now just waiting for coffee to reach its exact instant of perfection. Rosie confided, "He's getting more and more silly about coffee," and no one argued. But no one complained, either.

Standing over the coffee pot, Andy grinned and waved his empty mug. "Yeah, like this will settle us down."

"I could drink the pot and still be tired enough to sleep," I said. "It's been a big day."

"We were lucky today," Rosie said. But when no one agreed she looked around. "Weren't we?"

"Maybe." Jacobs held his empty mug in both hands and peered in at the bottom. I hoped I'd gotten it clean.
"We got her back alive, mostly unharmed. Though she's going to have some bad dreams for a while." He waved a hand at Rosie. "No, you're right. There's no way we weren't lucky. But..."

"It wasn't luck." I held out my mug for coffee as Andy bottomed the French press plunger and signaled a pour. "The prowler was... playing with us."

Rosie tilted her head, raised one eyebrow and looked perplexed.

189

The marshal took a first sip and sighed, a satisfied, Andy-like sigh. Rosie eyed him. "Don't *you* start that stuff!"

He sat up straighter on his stool. "No ma'am," he said. He took another sip and sighed again. "The prowler didn't want Alice, wasn't really interested in her. Which is why he didn't finish stripping her, why we got her back alive... why we found her before she froze. He knew—somehow—that we had started believing he was only interested in native women who looked like Marjorie. Which *is* what we believe, and he just confirmed it. So, he set this thing up to make us think something else." He looked around. "And I suggest, we let him think he was successful. We tell *no one!* No matter how much we think we trust them. Because somehow, this guy knows everything we're doing and thinking. He's probably not one of us, but he's close. He has a pipeline. We don't want him to think he has to grab somebody else to make his point."

I admit I shivered. Maybe we all did. Tonight we'd come closer than I wanted, to losing someone else. I could still see Alice's wild eyes when Andy and I broke in at the cabin door. Tied up as she was, she had no way to be sure it *was* us. It's a good bet she thought it was the prowler returning, to finish what he started.

* * *

It took a few days for the search and rescue to fall away from the tips of our tongues. We were chugging through November, with a heavy snow accumulation and river ice already more than two feet thick. Meanwhile back in the states, lawns were still green, leaves were turning but mostly still on the trees. Baseball had finished, but football played on with the Baltimore Colts vying for top of their heap.

Several more times I mentioned a memorial for Vadim and several times William politely rejected the notion.

"We will wait. But thank you."

On a Friday morning, the week before Thanksgiving, I delivered a parishioner to the morning train. He'd had tuberculosis as a young man and now needed to turn up twice yearly to be tested. He didn't mind a whit because to him it meant a paid trip to Fairbanks on the train and an overnight at the locally ritzy Traveler's Inn. He planned a visit to the bakery, and would return with a shopping bag filled with one or two of everything. And he'd always see a movie. This time it was *Gunfight at the O.K. Corral*, with Burt Lancaster and Kirk Douglas, though I suspected Rhonda Fleming was the real draw. It was safe to say he had a soft spot for busty redheads.

We waited together on the snowy platform, which wasn't a platform at all. For some reason I didn't get, the railroad hauled in sand—not river silt—but real beach sand, shipped in from somewhere. In the summer, kids on bikes would come shooting in off the street only to bog down completely.

But it was all frozen now, easy walking on a hard pack of about six inches of snow. I suppose it would have been easy biking, too, had anyone been crazy enough to want to bike at thirty below.

With the bell clanging, brakes hissing and squealing, the big diesel *thrumming*, the huge blue-and-gold engine came rolling in. The brakeman leaned down to drop lightly with his steel step in hand, smiling, even doffing his brakeman cap before the train came to a complete stop. He reminded me of Fred Astaire in a railroad uniform.

I always enjoy the bit of carnival atmosphere involved with meeting the train. There was the excitement of people arriving or departing, as well as just the opportunity to participate without actually having to pack up and go anywhere.

Two ladies came down the short stair, gripping the handrail and taking the brakeman's hand. Searching the crowd for familiar faces, their own faces lit up with the happiness of just being home—that best place on earth.

But the third passenger wasn't smiling, wasn't 'home,' and didn't appear to be meeting anyone. Stepping out into the frigid air, he pulled a fur-trimmed, flapped hat down over his big ears. Then he attempted to snap the hat flaps below his chin, with one hand, head down, while descending from the car. There was no trouble spotting him. At six feet-whatever, he was a full foot taller than anybody on the platform.

Once on the platform, he looked up, eyes scanning the crowd, starting on his left and rotating right, toward me. Closer, closer. I dropped my heavy mitt on its tether. Jamming my hand deep into my parka pocket, I gripped the .38, pulling it up, thumb on the hammer. Starting to cock it, and roughly shouldering my parishioner out of the line of fire, I hoped desperately to be ready with my pistol before the big-eared man could find his.

And then... his eyes flicked right past me and kept going. There was no flash of recognition, no desperate attempt to get to a firearm, and certainly no terrible instant of aiming and reverberation of a really big pistol in this relatively small space. He walked past. It wasn't the OK Corral.

I thumbed down the hammer, apologized for jostling my friend, and got him boarded. Then I climbed into the Ford and drove home, all the way wondering what the heck just happened.

Later, on the phone, Andy said, "Nah, he just didn't see you."

"But he did see me. He looked right at me, right through me, and then just... walked right by."

Andy snorted. "That's crazy. Last time he saw you he tried to kick your face off *and* shoot you. How could he not recognize you now?"

I didn't know. Didn't have a clue. I hung up wondering, and walked around wondering until I forgot to, several days later.

* * *

Alice hadn't worked for three full days after her ordeal, and for a time it was whispered around, somewhat frantically, that she had her bags packed. Nobody blamed her.

But on that fourth day, at four when her shift was scheduled to begin, she came in the bar's back door, hung up her parka, donned her apron, and then emerged through the hanging curtain, head down, to her accustomed spot behind the bar.

The place was filled, to capacity. Every chair was occupied and most of the standing room as well. Everybody held a drink, mostly unsipped. Miners, trappers, storekeepers, the depot agents, teachers, the nurse, the priest (me) and his friends, all burst into applause and cheers. And then we toasted her and drank.

Alice looked up, looked around, nothing less than stunned, and her mouth fell open. Tears ran down her cheeks as, for the first time since the ordeal, she began to cry, to sob. William, and those of us who knew her well, hugged her. Some of the old sourdoughs were too shy to do more than give her a roughish pat on the arm, but it was all heartfelt and made me teary, too.

Alaskans are warm caring people, but they usually keep their love under wraps, tucked away safe and warm. That evening love came out and made its way through the crowded, warm, smoky room.

* * *

Andy laughed, though it wasn't really funny. "So, the only solid piece of I.D. we got on this guy is his small pee-pee? That's not helpful... is it?" It was about a week later and we'd met for lunch at the Coffee Cup.

William pressed his lips together. "What would you propose," he enquired stiffly, "that we should consult the national... small *pee-pee* registry?" He shook his head and raised his mug in Rosie's direction. She headed our way with the pot.

She was wearing the white, sweptwing glasses with the pink waitress uniform, *Rosie* scripted over her left breast in red stitching. She had calf-high mukluks on her feet and waffled long johns visible on her legs. She usually pulled the long johns up out of sight, so as not to spoil her 'look.' But not today. The temperature had dropped overnight to the low minus forties. Every time the door opened, an icy cloud roiled across the floor, seeking something as silly as a bare leg. There were none to be found.

I'd already seen Alice this morning. Even Alice showed up for work in a turtleneck, doubtless disappointing her legions of fans.

We'd all ordered the cheeseburgers and they arrived sided with great golden wedges of fries—Matanuska

Valley potatoes—Rosie informed us. Andy reviewed his plate, sighed happily, and Rosie patted him on the top of his head. Then she put her arm around him and gave him a squeeze. He looked up at her and smiled, genuinely fond, genuinely happy. I took a bite of my burger. It was only the beef, but I didn't care.

"Did you ever find your claim jumpers?" Andy asked William, around a mouthful of burger.

William dabbed at his lips with the paper napkin. "There is still no sign. The army sent scouts through the area. They found the camouflage nets, claim posts, and cairns you described, but nobody." He smiled. "It may be the first time in Alaska that people were actually happy to find evidence of claim jumping."

Andy looked up. "And not saboteurs."

"Exactly."

CHAPTER 21

The day before Thanksgiving it snowed again, hard. The radio forecaster predicted a full foot of accumulation. Fortunately, it just whispered down softly and piled up, preferable to our last wind-driven storm, snow smoothly sculpted into huge drifts and eaves-high cornices that completely blocked doors and windows. After the last big storm, Butch had gone around town helping to dig people out of their homes where they were trapped.

With the restaurant closed for Thanksgiving, Andy came home on the train to Chandalar and was in the process of organizing a Thanksgiving extravaganza at my house. It would be for the 'usual known suspects:' Evie and me, Andy and Rosie, William and Alice, Butch and Adele, Oliver, Vic and Linda—also Molly and young Henry, who otherwise would have to be thankful alone. There were so many of us that we had to bring a bigger table over from the parish hall and set it up in my living room, shoving other furniture aside.

Today we were in my kitchen, prepping. We had the radio on and young crooner Andy Williams, apparently without any of the other Williams Brothers, was singing his new hit, *Butterfly*. I knew I'd have the refrain, 'I'm crazy about you, you butterfly,' in my head for days.

I was chopping hazel nuts for 'Andy's Famous Stuffing,' which he'd never actually made before but had already named. And, as was his tradition, he'd brought a massive goose that he shot himself. Unlike others who used a shotgun for such hunting, Andy would bring down a flying bird with a .22, usually a bullet to the head, so bits of steel shot were never on Andy's menu.

"We had a big meeting at Clear," William confided. The tough spy sat at my kitchen table, wearing a white kitchen apron trimmed with a fine blue line, as he crunched up bits of stale bread. "They praised us—Security—for figuring out the station was *not* under attack."

Andy looked at him. "That's good, huh?"

"Only if it is true."

"You think it's not?" I asked.

He paused to consider. "I will give you my most... *technical* answer." He almost smiled. "Try to keep up."

"Okay." Andy leaned forward, ready to accept the challenge.

"It feels wrong," said William.

"That's it? That's your technical answer?" Andy looked concerned and shook his head. "Go with your gut, I always say."

It was true. He did always say that. I'd heard him. The bad part... he was usually right.

"So, what's next?" I asked.

William looked up at us, then pulled off his spectacles to polish them on his apron hem. "According to the Army and the highway patrol, nothing is next. They have all but cleared out, and happy to go. It is Thanksgiving. They want to be home. And deep snow and cold temperatures are not for them."

Andy used a wooden kitchen match to light the propane, then loaded sticks of butter, four of them, into a sauce pan to melt. "But really," he asked, "what could go wrong out there? It's only one of a string of RADAR stations in the Far North, stuck out in a godforsaken wasteland of not much, right now under about five feet of snow. It's not exactly ground zero on the world stage now, is it?"

William looked at him and shrugged. "And that is exactly how we should like it to remain."

That evening, we all gathered for dinner and it was wonderful. It is the custom among Anglicans and Episcopalians to say grace before a meal. But I've come to like the Quaker tradition of taking each other's hands around the table, and for just a moment, being silently thankful... for the meal, for everything.

I certainly felt thankful. I had come to Chandalar alone, friendless, with a broken heart. My beloved wife had died quite suddenly, leaving me alone with a lifetime of dreams and plans.

In this moment, I held Evie's hand on my left and Andy's hand on my right, and the connection continued all the way around the table, encompassing people I loved, who loved me. To say I felt thankful would be the understatement of a lifetime. I squeezed the hands I held and made a quiet kissing sound in Evie's direction, as had become my custom.

"That's not for me, is it?" asked Andy.

"In your dreams," I told him. And to the group, "I'm thankful. Let's eat!"

* * *

The prowler just disappeared. It helped that the weather wasn't at all conducive to prowling. Record cold kept people close to home, windows sheeted over with frost. Record snow had some people shoveling their roofs! And record winds produced drifts ten and twelve feet high in places, wind-sculpted in beautiful but odd ways around trees, cars, and cabins. To get up on the roof, there was no ladder necessary, they just walked up the crusted snow drift to the top.

Snowshoeing became a daily occurrence just to make my rounds. I'd park the truck on a stretch of plowed-out road, scale the mountain of thrown snow, snowshoe to the parishioner's cabin, and then remove the snowshoes, sometimes stepping down two or three feet off the snow pack to get in the door. Admittedly that didn't happen much. The church paid Butch his desired wage, one dollar an hour, to dig those people out, and he did, smiling all the while. He loved to work.

Andy stayed in Chandalar, occasionally with me. He busied himself with odds and ends of things he'd let go while getting the restaurant established in Fairbanks. Now that it was doing well, and he could count on Tony, his head cook, Andy could afford to take time off to do things like installing plastic on the insides of his cabin windows and cleaning all his guns.

It was like old times having him around. Every morning just about seven, I'd hear the knock on my front door and in he'd come. With school not starting until nine, and some days cancelled for snow or extreme cold, Evie would show up as well, and William—usually without Alice, who worked late and liked to sleep late.

"So, this big-ears guy looked right at you and didn't try to kick you in the face or shoot you?" Andy shook his head. "Maybe he reformed." We were in our usual places on the tippy stools drinking coffee, except for Evie who had decided to fry eggs. She switched on the radio. The tubes warmed up and sound filled the small kitchen as Mitch Miller and the gang performed their up-tempo, cheery version of *The Yellow Rose of Texas*. As the song ended and she reached to turn the volume down, we heard the little xylophone melody that signaled a weather report.

Andy waved his arm at her. "Leave that up for a minute. I want to find out if it's gonna be windy and snowy. I think it will be." She did and it would be. We expected four more days of high wind and heavy snow, plus temperatures exceeding minus fifty.

"Drat!" Evie turned the radio down.

"Drat?" echoed William.

"They close school when it dips below minus fifty," which he well knew, having been custodian there until just this year. The superintendent still didn't know what to make of his custodian moving directly to a job at the top of security at Clear.

At minus fifty, they couldn't heat the school, plus the school board worried about kids going back and forth at that temperature. However, when they cancelled school, it wasn't unusual to see the kids playing outside, sledding and building sometimes massive snow forts.

"But I don't get," said Andy, back on his original theme, "why he didn't shoot you... or kick you."

"Are you disappointed?"

"Nah, 'course not. I just don't get it."

I didn't, either. "He just didn't recognize me."

"No dog," said William.

"Huh?" Andy made a face.

"There was no dog!" William said again. He sipped his coffee and accepted a plate with egg and toast from Evie. "Thank you, my dear." She smiled and made a small curtsy.

Andy took his plate, then froze with it in front of him, lost in thought. She waited expectantly for his gracious 'thank you.' He was either oblivious or not going to give her the satisfaction. She flicked the side of his head with her middle finger. He looked up startled and turned to William. "What'd you mean, 'no dog'?"

"We have been wrong about this," William continued. "It is the dog he recognizes, not the man." He forked his fried egg onto a piece of buttered toast and took a bite, chewing happily. Turning to me he smiled.

"He does not even know who you are."

* * *

In spite of our resolve to stay indoors near the stove and maybe catch up on some reading, a call from Maxine, the public health nurse soon rousted us out into the cold. One of our older parishioners, Elsie Lucas, wasn't thriving and needed to get to Fairbanks on the train. Maxine would ride with her, but needed help getting her to the station. I quickly double-checked to make sure I'd plugged in the Ford's head-bolt heater. Otherwise, at this temperature with the oil thickened and sludge-like, we wouldn't be driving anywhere. Fortunately, it was plugged in and the truck started easily.

Elsie's cabin stood nearly a mile out of town beyond the railroad loop, but short of the old mission school in what was historically the Native village. Butch went out early to prepare, shoveling some forty feet of pathway through up to three feet of snow. At about nine forty-five we showed up in a well-warmed pickup truck to deliver them to the train station, to catch the ten-ten north.

The sun had just risen in a clear sky and the blinding light flowed in around us like molten gold but, absolutely heatless. There was no denying it was a beautiful day, and bitterly cold.

With Elsie, Maxine, and me in the cab, Andy rode in the exposed pickup bed. I could only imagine the wind-chill temperature. He sat with his back to the cab, head

201

down, conserving body heat. Fortunately, we didn't have far to go. Deep in his parka hood, with a muffler wrapped around the lower part of his face, only his eyes showed.

"You drive," I'd told him.

"Nah," he said, "somebody's gonna be cold. Might as well be me." Then he gave me a nudge with his elbow. "I'm the tough one."

Later, back at the rectory the three of us, Evie, Andy, and me—never far from the woodstove—spent the early part of the afternoon catching up on all the *Saturday Evening Post* magazines we hadn't had time to read. When the phone rang, with Evie close, she picked it up. "Father Hardy's phone," she said, then "Oh, hi! Yes, it's me. No... I haven't moved in. I just happened to be standing near the phone."

By now, thinking one of the parishioners—or the bishop—thought I'd moved in my girlfriend, I hurried to take the line, only to find that Evie refused to give up the phone. "I'm talking here," she whispered, covering the mouthpiece. Then her face grew serious. "Uh-oh." She handed me the handset voluntarily. "It's Frank Jacobs."

Relieved, I took the phone. My relief didn't last.

"Got another dead one for you... a stiff, I should say. Really stiff."

"Who is it?"

"No clue. Apparently not one of yours. California driver's license... bogus, I should mention. Clear security picked him up. They're saying... Caucasian, about six feet, blond and blue, maybe thirty. Just came up here to die, I guess."

"And he froze?"

"Yeah, but that was just a bit after somebody shot him. Looks like he might have been trying to walk out for help.

But yeah, he froze after that." I think Jacobs finally heard himself, regretting his tone, because he paused. "Sorry, Father, it's been a long day. I got two more, one of them a kid, who actually did freeze—drunk—out north of here along the Steese Highway. I..." He hesitated a beat, regrouping.

"No, I get it," I told him.

"Say... I'm still in Fairbanks. Plane won't start for a while. *Somebody* didn't leave it plugged in, thank you very much." I sensed him looking around, probably glaring at someone in his office. "So, I'm not going to get down there today. But I'll come tomorrow, probably midday. I was hoping you could get out there and secure the body—get somebody to help you—maybe drop it in your meat shed. Don't worry about clues. Everything is either snow covered or blown away by now."

"Sure," I told him, "I can do that." We finished up the conversation and I hung up, turning to find Evie standing close, looking worried. She had handed over the phone as soon as she heard 'corpse,' without hearing whose corpse.

"It's not one of ours. He's carrying a false ID so nobody knows who this guy is. Just another frozen guy with a bullet hole, found out on the Clear road."

"Oh," she said. "That's going to set William off again. I've never seen him so spooky. He's sure something bad is going to happen out there on his watch. He finally relaxed when he thought it was just claim jumpers."

"*Just* claim jumpers," echoed Andy. "As if nobody ever got shot for *that* around here!"

Evie's eyes met mine. "Yes, but if this man *was* shot for claim jumping, it's better for William."

Andy didn't look up from his article about whether England still needed a queen. "But not for the dead guy," he said.

Andy and I picked up the dead man, blessed him, and transported him, not to the meat shed, which had recently burned to the ground—very nearly with us in it—but to the Quonset hut. In fact, we set him on a couple of wide boards and sawhorses in the back part, in what was to have been Marjorie's room. Dead men in the warm are often hard to handle, like big mattresses that always have inadequate handles. Frozen dead men are much easier, even the big ones.

Andy reached to finger the dead man's parka ruff. "Great parka! That's not coyote or dog ruff. That's real wolverine."

It was hard to examine the wolverine ruff without also seeing the frozen-open, glazed blue eyes of the corpse. Although dressed warmly, I couldn't help a shiver as I covered him with a sheet.

"Feels colder in here than outside," Andy said. "Do you wanna hang out with this frozen guy or get back to the fire?"

"Fire, definitely," I told him. We headed for the door and forgot about the parka for a time.

CHAPTER 22

It was on a visit to Fairbanks that I next saw the parka. It was sitting on a chair in Frank Jacob's office, in a shopping bag from the Northern Commercial Company. Even stuffed in the bag, I recognized it immediately because of the wolverine ruff. We had been talking about the dead man.

"Still no ID," he said. "The trail is colder than last summer's salmon."

Jacobs was sitting behind his big steel desk, the top almost completely cleared, as usual. On impulse I asked him, pointing at the sack. "What's going to happen to his gear... to that parka?"

He looked at me a long moment. "No next of kin. We usually throw the clothes away."

"Throw away? You're kidding."

"Not kidding." He flicked a lonely fountain pen on his desktop, watching it spin in place like a propeller. "People don't usually want stuff with bloodstains and a bullet hole."

"I do."

"Well then," he looked up at me, "it's yours."

Later, back in Chandalar, back in the quiet and frosty seclusion of the Quonset hut, surrounded by heaps and mounds of probable dead people's clothing, I pulled the parka out of its NC bag and began to go through the pockets.

It's a habit, even though I knew this particular garment had come from the coroner with its pockets well checked. But in my three years in Chandalar, I had often found things, small treasures in abandoned garments, enough to encourage me to always check. I've found pocket change aplenty. A few old receipts and shopping lists—occasionally folding money—once, several twenties! But usually it's just paperclips, pocket lint, or nothing.

Today, in the parka pocket of a murdered man, the first thing I found was a hole, not at the bottom of the pocket, in the obvious place, but higher on the side. Finding the hole made me feel around below the pocket, down in the parka lining. Sure enough, I felt coins, maybe quarters, and something else. It was metal by the feel of it, about one inch by two inches, slightly curved with a rough edge.

I slowly worked all the objects back up through the parka lining toward the pocket and then retrieved three quarters plus an embossed metal plate back through the hole. There was print on the plate that I couldn't read, so took myself closer to the frosty window and diminishing daylight.

I read it, then read it again to be certain. And then I read it again. Although I knew it had to be a mistake, it kept reading the same: Manufactured by Springfield Armory, Springfield Massachusetts, August 1954. Then there came a twelve-digit serial number followed by 'Property of the U.S. Army.'

Suddenly, I had a pretty good idea where the missing mystery weapon could be, and it gave me a very bad feeling.

* * *

I couldn't connect with William or with Alice, who frequently knew where to find William. I tried the marshal, who was out, tried the office at Clear that William frequently used. No one answered. Even Andy didn't pick up his restaurant phone.

206

Finally, I dug in my wallet for the *secret* number. "When nothing else works, call this number." William had given me this nearly two years earlier and I'd carried it ever since and never dialed it. Nothing ever seemed dire enough to take the chance—whatever chance I could possibly be taking just by calling a telephone number.

I'd never actually even seen a number like this one. First came a one, then *ten more* digits! Like I might be placing a call to the moon. Even in Fairbanks it only took four numbers to dial locally, and seven to call anywhere in the U.S. Now I was preparing to place a call with ten digits. Even that seemed a little scary.

I picked up the handset and dialed zero.

"Operator."

"I need to place a long-distance call."

"That number please." I gave it to her. "That's *not* a phone number.

"It is."

"I'm afraid you'll have to try back later with the *correct* number."

"Operator?"

"Yes."

"Please place the call." She hesitated a long moment, waiting for me to relent. The more we waited, the more I wondered why she couldn't just *try* the number. I began to wonder if the phone company docked her pay for frivolous phone numbers.

"Please?"

She let out a long breath. I could tell she was being very patient with me, and that I was really asking a lot from her. Too much, really. "Very well, sir." I admit I smiled. "But it won't work!" I heard her dial it.

207

It rang half of once. A voice said, "Yes." It wasn't a question, nor was it really a statement. It was as non-committal a *yes* as could possibly be had. Then he said, "I have this, Operator," and we both heard the click as she hung up.

I swallowed hard. "This is Father Hardy, calling from Chandalar." Then realizing I probably wasn't talking to someone in Alaska, I added, "Chandalar, Alaska."

"Yes," said the voice again, in the same tone.

"I need to leave a message for William Stoltz. I need him to call me as quickly as possible."

I thought the voice might say yes again, but he didn't. I heard something—tapping—a typewriter, very fast. "Are you in immediate danger?" asked the voice.

"No, I'm fine, but I've discovered information."

"Yes," said the voice again, maybe slightly rushed, as if not wanting to hear more. Like something he could be shot for. "Stay by your phone. He will call." The line clicked dead.

I looked at my watch, at the hour, minute, and second, and began to think about spies communicating. I imagined my message being transferred through dead letter drops, secret ciphers, men on park benches trading newspapers, and finally, by a beautiful dark-haired spy—she looked a lot like Evie—in a trench coat.

My phone rang. I glanced at my Timex. It had been forty-five seconds. I picked up the handset.

"Yes."

"Are you in danger?" It was William's voice, sounding close, concerned, reassuring.

"No, I'm good... safe... but I found something you need to see."

"Something...?"

"Something national. I'm pretty sure... I'm certain. You need to see this." He hesitated. I could imagine him looking at his own watch, calculating.

"I will be there..." again the hesitation. "Today," he said. "Tonight. Lock your door, don't go out."

That caught me by surprise. "I..." I started to say, then, "Okay."

Again, the line clicked dead.

I locked my doors, feeling immediately jittery, and dropped my .38 into my pants pocket. What had changed? Nothing! So why did I suddenly feel this way? I made a circuit of the tiny log-cabin rectory, even checking my windows, though I knew they were frozen shut. I stopped to load my father's old .30-30 deer rifle, propping it in a corner, midway between back door and front—kitchen and living room—just in case. And then I began to wait.

Why does waiting feel worse than just hanging around taking it easy? Why does food suddenly have less taste and magazine articles become too lengthy and difficult to stay interested in? I don't know why, but I do know it happens. That afternoon it happened to me.

Nearing suppertime someone knocked at my front door. I froze. Since I still had small pieces of frosty wood glued and screwed over the last set of bullet holes, I approached the door with considerable caution.

"Who's there?"

"Har-deee, it's Evie!" she said, like I should know this. "And it's really cold out here." And then less boisterously, "Who were you expecting?"

I swung open the door, pulled her in, quickly closed the door and locked it. She threw back her parka hood, unwrapped her muffler and looked at me like my team might be missing one of its huskies.

I gave her the quick version and watched as the same thing appeared to happen to her. "Ohhh," she said, one hand rising to her throat as she peered from side to side, even appearing to shrink a bit. But that moment passed.

"Hah!" she cried, clearly shifting gears while unzipping her parka and opening the closet door. "Buck up, Hardy." She came and wrapped her arms around me, kissed me, nuzzled my ear, and in a very romantic voice asked, "What's for dinner?"

"Dinner?"

"You invited me, remember?"

I did remember, though I admit I'd lost sight of it.

She grabbed me by each shoulder to peer deeply into my eyes. I always imagined, looking into hers, that I could fall in and keep falling and not mind a bit.

"This isn't the old bachelor trick, is it? Invite a girl to dinner and then let her cook it?"

"I... I... no!" I admit she caught me off guard. I turned, and turned her, toward the kitchen. "I know exactly what to cook," I said. I didn't really, but knew I would by the time we reached the kitchen.

We had breakfast for dinner, which I claimed was my plan all along. But a can of Canadian bacon turned out to be the only meat not frozen, and that settled it. I often wished there would be a way to quickly thaw things. That would be wonderful. What were the chances?

So, we had eggs, the Canadian bacon, and hotcakes with butter and 'real' Mapleine-flavored syrup that I mixed up myself with a cup of sugar. Since I knew breakfast to be Evie's favorite meal anyway, the day was saved.

After dinner, dishes all washed and dried and still no sign of William, we sat very close—okay, snuggled—on the sofa and I brought her up to date on my day.

210

She made a scary face. "The nuclear mystery weapon? No wonder you were acting weird."

"I wasn't acting weird. I was being cautious. As William told me to be." I looked at my watch, wondering again when he might appear.

I showed her the metal plate. We even looked at it through a magnifying glass. It had been riveted to something, and looked like it had been cut loose by filing off the rivet heads. Which is why a few raised, rough, metal splinters remained. Chances were good the plate had chewed its own way through the pocket.

But the more we talked about it, the more I became convinced that I'd probably 'cried wolf'... with agents from the Federal Government. Even now they might be swearing out a warrant for unauthorized use of some super-secret government telephone connection, and for wasting their time.

Evie held it in both hands. "Do you know how many weapons must come out of Springfield," she asked, "probably wearing one of these tags? I mean, it's the *national* armory! Like rifles, even. Andy has one, a Springfield .30-06. So, we hear on the radio there's a Springfield weapon missing, some kind of scary one, and immediately assume it's been delivered here to East Left Elbow, Alaska, for some nefarious purpose. What are the chances?"

She was right. And the more I thought about it, the crazier it got. As the minutes ticked by, anxiety began to bleed out of my cells as my earlier behavior, and the secret phone call came to appear nearly comical. In fact, we were both laughing about it when we heard the knock.

Rising from the sofa, still laughing, ready to feel foolish when William told us this came from something like a 1946 Daisy BB gun. Nevertheless, I found myself reaching into my pocket for the .38 to reassure myself it was there, even though I could feel its weight as I walked.

Again, I approached the door cautiously, the door patches reminding me to stand at the side.

"Who's there?"

"William." I let him in.

When he had his parka off and 'hung' on my front room sofa, and we'd poured coffee and settled ourselves back near the woodstove, I pulled out the metal plate, handing it to him.

"I'm afraid I've probably wasted your time." He shrugged, held the plate up to lamplight and examined it through his bifocals. "When I found it, I thought it was... well, the nuclear bazooka." He smiled that benign sort of kindly smile I imagined he'd perfected to keep people from knowing he was dangerous. He unbuttoned the top button of his blue wool cardigan, tweezered a slip of paper between two fingers from his shirt pocket, and moved his lips as he read the numbers off silently, his expression unchanged. He pointed at the tag, at the serial number. "This little sequence," he said, "tells us it is..."

"A BB gun," I said, and laughed.

"Tells us it is nuclear," he said.

CHAPTER 23

William smiled his faint smile. "You have made everything better... and everything worse." Then he asked to use my telephone and excused himself. I could hear him in my office, reciting that same long number to the operator. "Yes, it *is* a telephone number," I heard him say, which made me feel better.

Evie squeezed my hand. "Want coffee?" I just nodded, still a bit dazed by developments. "You're like... a national hero," she said, climbing off the sofa to head for the kitchen. "No wonder I love you." I admit her words gave me a warm feeling, as did the view of the back of her in motion.

"Better *and* worse?" I asked William when he returned. He dropped into my easy chair with a long sigh.

"First, a bit of news," he said. "The dead man has been identified."

"A secret agent? Soldier of fortune? Soviet infiltrator?"

He waved me off. "An American from California. His name is... was... Steven James."

"Sniper?" I had run out of guesses.

"A minerals geologist."

"With a false ID?"

He shook his head. "Perhaps they are clannish."

"Perhaps," I said, thinking it through, "they *are* claim jumping and it's better if nobody can get a handle on who they really are, or what they really are up to."

"That makes sense," William agreed. "But it does not explain who shot him, or why." Evie arrived with coffee.

"So how better and how worse?" I pressed him when we had all settled.

He sipped. "Better, because every agent in the free world... no, every agent *everywhere* has been searching for this weapon. Federal agents almost had it in Seattle, and you know how that turned out."

I nodded. "Someone killed the security guard. But why worse?"

"Because now we have reason to believe the weapon is at hand."

"Here, close to the RADAR station, you mean? Is that worse? At least now you have an idea where to look." He shook his head and his expression shifted, such that I actually braced myself for whatever he was about to say.

"I can tell you this now, as you will hear it anyway on the radio in the morning. It appears the weapon is also close to the one technology station on the planet to be visited by President Eisenhower... next Thursday."

"Thursday?" I asked. "You mean like in a week... seven days... Thursday?" He nodded.

"Can't you call him off?"

"The President? Call off the President? That would be above my pay grade. And... it is now a matter of pride with him—with all of Washington D.C.—showing the Soviets who is superior after Sputnik. He is determined."

"Okay," I said. "You're right. That is worse. Much worse."

* * *

The next morning, Saturday, well before sunrise, my phone rang. Standing almost next to it, I didn't have time to get anxious about it, I just picked it up. "Hardy."

"I'm calling for William Stoltz. Is he there?"

By now William's status as a government agent wasn't much of a secret. "Call him at his office at Clear Station." I told him. "Do you have the number?"

"I do," said the voice. "This *is* Clear Station. We were expecting him yesterday. He never showed."

* * *

I called Alice first. He was frequently with her when he was otherwise out of contact. I found her at work, upbeat, cheery. "Not here," she said. "Did you try Clear?"

"They called me. Did he say anything about needing to be anywhere else?"

"No," she said, in a much smaller, tighter voice. "He went off to work, pretty much like normal... said I might not see him for a couple of days. Oh..." she said, "he took the new Winchester!"

Without a plan, I dialed Andy at the restaurant in Fairbanks. Tony answered, told me Andy was taking a few days off and I might see him. Sure enough, I hung up the phone in time to hear a car door *clunk* from my driveway and in he came.

"Uh-oh," was all he said. And then, "I'll get my gear." He turned around and was gone.

I started thinking about who else to call. I thought of Vic first. He was able bodied but not quick and not much of a sneaker. Oliver was good in the woods, also a good shot, but older and heavier. With the temperature still in the minus forties, I wasn't sure he'd be up for this kind of hunting party.

On a hunch, I called Frank Jacobs. I guess I was thinking that he and William might be up to something together, especially with the President's arrival now just four days away.

"That's not good," he said. "Let me check around. Maybe the Highway Patrol knows something. But listen to me. Stay out of this. I know he's your buddy and all, and know you and Andy will expect to go out hunting for your

215

friend. But if he's right, if that Davy Crockett thing *is* out there, then the farther away you are, the better. Do you hear me?" he asked, with a certain amount of menace.

"Of course." I slipped the .38 into my pocket, replaced the handset and went to check my pack. There's something about even approaching my pack or any of my outdoor gear that draws Jack from his favored spot by the furnace grate. I had no more reached out to touch it than I heard his doggy nails click-clicking down the hallway, and saw his 'I'm ready' smile and the little dance he did when he was excited to get going. Then unexpectedly, he barked.

In the next second I heard a quick knock, a cheery hello, and footsteps. Jack raced off to greet and in short order I found myself face to face with Evie, come for coffee.

She looked at me, quickly taking stock. I was already wearing high mukluks and half my trail gear, counting out ammo, with pack and rifle at hand. She came and kissed me, then stood back and cocked her head to give me her suspicious look.

"What's up? It's nearly minus forty out there. It's colder than a witch's... well, you know." She looked at me another beat. "Something's wrong and you were about to go off without telling me. Am I right?" She was, of course. I gave her the short version and told her Andy was on his way.

"I'll get my stuff," was all she said. She turned to go then turned back. "Andy will say 'just leave her.' I know how he is. But if you *do* leave me, I promise to hunt you both down and make you suffer. I'm not sure how, but I will. You believe me, right?" I nodded. "And you know I can help!"

I nodded, raised a hand in surrender. "Get your stuff. We'll wait." I did know she could help. She was a crack shot, could track pretty well, and didn't seem to mind the cold. Of course, she had grown up in it. I didn't know if I'd ever get to not minding this cold. I certainly hadn't yet.

As soon as he got back, I told Andy about Evie. "Just leave her," he said.

"I think we need somebody else." He nodded. "How about I call Vic?" I asked, setting him up. I knew he liked him around town, but didn't have much confidence in Vic's trail skills. He shook his head emphatically, making a face. "Nah. Let's wait for Evie."

She was back in about fifteen minutes... cold weather gear, pack with bedroll, Winchester .30-30, a little newer than mine, and a pair of the longer, Yukon-style snowshoes.

"I packed some food, too," she said, smiling in Andy's direction. "Pilot bread and peanut butter." Andy brightened.

"Okay, you can come." Even though he'd adapted his Alaskan palate to appreciate Italian cuisine, he'd never lost his taste for the Alaskan version of hard tack: round hard crackers that seemed to store forever. All three of us liked them with peanut butter, and they traveled well that way. You could just stick them together face to face, and never have a mess. Some of the old-timers still liked theirs with lard. I hadn't tried it and didn't want to.

"I got some too," he said, "but you can't have too many!"

We did a last gear check, just in case, and I added extra kibbles and chunks of dried salmon for Jack. Just about sunrise, midmorning, we headed out the door, opting to

217

leave the Ford where it was plugged in, rather than parking it at the trailhead and letting it get too cold to start later.

The sun comes up fast in a valley so flat. At this time of year it rises in the southeast, bathing all in a warm, summer-like yellow glow that, at this temperature—in spite of how it looked—shone absolutely heatless.

We found the trail not much used, badly drifted in places, and were soon snowshoeing. Andy wore an olive drab balaclava, left over from his army days. Evie and I were muffler wrapped, with sunglasses, almost no skin showing. We had an unusual amount of snow this year, maybe a record, and of course none of it melted, ever. Well, none melted until spring, until breakup. So, we tramped south, Andy in the lead, me next, and Evie behind, with Jack running and jumping through the drifts, often lowering his head to drive through them in torpedo fashion. That is, when he wasn't running up behind me to stand on the backs of my snowshoes, tripping me and throwing me down on my face in a snowdrift.

After about the third time, as I was picking myself up, Andy said, "Do you think you can train him to not do that?"

"Dunno," I told him. "It might be easier to train him to jump on yours."

"Swell." He turned to push on.

At noon we stopped, tramped out a snow ring, and Andy quickly built a tiny smokeless fire from small dry birch and spruce limbs, to melt water and make tea. He mixed in honey, at this temperature, caramel thick, for extra trail calories, and we used it to wash down our pilot bread and peanut butter, enjoying raisins for dessert.

Andy looked around. "Nice thing about all this snow—at least while there's no wind—it's darn near impossible to cover your tracks. If William, or if anybody is out here, we'll soon know." That said, he twisted his head around, looking back over each shoulder.

"What?" I asked him.

"Ever feel like somebody's standin' behind you, watchin' you?"

"What? You mean like God?"

"I mean in addition to God. Somebody right here on earth watching."

"And that's how you feel now?"

"Well, yeah... sorta."

We pushed on uneventfully, in spite of Andy's 'feeling,' neither seeing nor hearing any sign that humans were about. At about two thirty, the sun—now low in the southwest—winked out behind the distant mountains of the Alaska Range, Denali among them. Planets appeared as the sun sank, then stars, and—in an hour or so—the moon. Starlight on snow showed the slight trail depression as a faint gray line Andy could follow and so we pushed on.

About suppertime, with the moon rising nearly full, we stopped in the shelter of a spruce thicket, taking pains to stomp a fire pit well down and out of sight in the snow. Again, the three of us broke brittle birch and spruce limbs off small trees to get fuel for another of Andy's small hot fires. Again, we made tea, and heated cans of soup right in the flames. If anything, the temperature had dropped since we started, probably now approaching minus fifty—still fortunately windless—and we needed the hot liquids.

The tea, soup, pilot bread, and strips of moose jerky finished, Andy looked across the campfire at Evie and me, his eyes deep in his parka hood, just tiny pinpricks of reflected firelight. "We could stop. Head back."

Evie looked at him then me. "William?"

"Yeah," said Andy, "been thinking about that. We don't even really know he's out here."

"But we know he's not any of the places he's supposed to be," I said.

"Yeah," he said again. "We know that."

"Is there enough light to keep going? Can you stay on the trail?"

"Oh, yeah. It's an easy one. And the moon is about to make it a lot easier. The good thing... anybody out here probably ain't keeping much of a watch at night. It's too darn cold!"

Evie looked at me, looked at Andy. "So, let's keep going." Andy nodded and she rose, we all rose, and Andy kicked snow over our fire, darkness and starlight stealing in.

Back in our snowshoes and packs, ready to head out, Andy hesitated and turned to look back over his shoulder.

"Still feel like there's somebody out there?"

He shrugged. "Yeah!"

Together we stared off into the darkness. "If somebody is out there," I said, "he's good."

"Yeah, that's part of what troubles me." He leaned down to adjust his snowshoe strap. "Wish we knew what we're looking for."

"It's got to be shelter," I said. "Whoever they are, they've been out here since last summer. There's no way they'd still be camping. But we know it can't be seen from the air. In the summer, it's too wet out here to be a cave or something underground. But with all this snow..."

"And not likely to be showing a light," he added, and turning his snowshoes, one at a time, trod on.

220

We passed a moose, a tall cow, pawing at snow to nip off tender willow shoots. She peered at us in the gloom, hunger trumping curiosity or fear.

One hour became two, a minute at a time, and the dull murmur I get in my low back from dragging snowshoes through deep snow became a full-on aching version of something like the Mormon Tabernacle Choir. So, when Andy abruptly signaled a stop, I was more than ready—Jack too—the thrill pretty much worn off, and him now close at my side. Only Evie, distracted and weary wasn't paying attention and walked up on the backs of my snowshoes with hers.

Two trees stood in front of us, birch or willow, just a little more than sled width apart. Andy beckoned me alongside and Evie up close.

He pulled his Mauser off his shoulder, slowly and softly working the bolt to chamber a cartridge. "Almost missed this." He pointed. I saw it, a silver glimmer that might have been ice or moonlit diamonds in snow, but was neither. Softly glinting, a length of braided steel wire—like for a rabbit snare, very fine—had been stretched tight across the trail. Originally, right at the surface level, the snow had since drifted or settled and there it was. I wouldn't have seen it, but Andy did.

He chanced a small light, showing where someone had used a spruce bough to sweep away snowshoe tracks. Then the light followed the wire off to our right, to where it looped the trigger of a small revolver tied to a tree, fortunately pointed the other way.

"Wouldn't have shot us," he said, "but woulda made a helluva of a noise."

Evie said it. "It's an alarm! Somebody's out here."

"And close," I added.

CHAPTER 24

"They probably unhook this thing during the day," was Andy's assessment. "This is a public trail. You need to get a sled along this trail in daylight but anybody sneakin' around out here at night is probably looking for them." He swiveled his head. "Betcha there's more of these rigs around, so watch your step. They're easy to build. You can find this wire anywhere. And a little pistol like this in Fairbanks might run you twenty-five bucks. It's a pretty good setup for cheap."

Andy turned away from the booby trap. "Time to turn in?" It was. We'd been on the trail a long time. Worse, we'd been snowshoeing a long time. We kick-turned our snowshoes around on the trail and headed back just about a hundred feet, finding a little hummock and a cluster of small trees to settle behind, both a wind and vision screen.

As if in response, a small breeze started up, shifting and smoothing the dry snow and making us feel even colder. I shed only my mukluks, otherwise squeezing into my mummy bag wearing everything. Once I got warm—if I got warm—I could shed the parka but keep it in the bag. I did change out damp socks for a dry pair, sleeping with the damp pair on my chest to dry out. And yes, I tucked in my .38, its hammer on the empty chamber. Once in, not yet warm, but hopeful, I pulled the drawstring tight leaving only a small opening to breathe out of. In the morning, first thing, I'd break off the frost around that opening, formed by my moist breath freezing.

It felt good to be stretched out on soft snow, finished with walking, and especially finished with snowshoeing. I did warm up before too long, and should have slept. I was tired enough. I could tell that both Evie and Andy, close on either side, had gone to sleep almost immediately, and I envied them. But the activity of being on the move had kept me from thinking about William, about what kind of danger he might be in and how we might find him. Whoever this was, they'd shot the geologist dead. So why not shoot William if they found him? What if William were already dead? A vision of him frosty blue and stiff flashed under my eyelids and I put it aside. I prayed for his safety, something that often reassures me, enabling sleep. But I still lay awake.

The breeze increased gradually to a soft low moan. Though we were out of the thrust of it, I could hear the rattle of icy particles on my sleeping bag and feel weight of a drift that began forming around my feet. Just before I finally drifted off, a nearby tree cracked sharply. A long way off, a wolf howled, lonely and awake like me.

In the morning—if you could call it that—Andy had another of his magic fires already going, with coffee water near to a boil before I woke. It was still dark, would be dark for hours yet, stars still out. I had to pee fairly desperately, and frankly, it was cold enough to freeze my nuts off. I pitied Evie who had to expose a lot more skin than Andy and me, to get the job done.

Once you get up to pee, it's all done. You're up, even though you still hear the siren song of a warmish sleeping bag. Even out of the wind, our camp had drifted, filling in, rounding out, topping off—all our gear and us half buried—with yesterday's snowshoe trails obliterated.

I gratefully accepted a tin coffee mug that first tried to burn my lips and then cooled so quickly I had to gulp the coffee to get the warmth. I went to feed Jack, who in typical husky fashion, had curled himself up to sleep. Now he looked like a half-drifted doggy donut in the snow, comfortable and disinclined to climb out of a warm snowdrift for anything I had to offer, except maybe the salmon. I left him there for the time being.

Huddled in our snow pit, mostly out of the wind, we ate a bit of breakfast. This was the most comfortable spot that I knew of for about twenty miles, and I could have stayed there longer, except that we didn't have much fuel to begin with and were quickly down to coals.

Andy crunched off a piece of his peanut-butter pilot bread and chewed contentedly. "We ain't found him. But we still get to choose whether to go ahead or go back. Going back is probably safer," he added, "but I think we knew that."

Evie turned to him, her face muffler-wrapped and her eyes just glints deep in her parka hood. "We can't go back. We've got to find him. We came this far. She glanced at me. *I'm* not going back without him. Andy looked at me.

"If she's not going back, I'm not going back," I said.

"I saw that look she gave you. Lightweight!"

Jack woofed, low and urgent. He shifted, in a heartbeat from lazy dog sleeping to alert watchdog, head up, nose working, ears tilted forward.

Almost immediately, from back by the trap, a branch snapped. I stepped to get a hand on Jack while Andy tumbled through deep snow to get to a place he could look out.

"Got one!" he whispered back, holding up one gloved finger. "Maybe clearing the trap."

With the breeze in our faces, this guy wasn't likely to smell campfire smoke. No tracks left to find, and the moon setting, meant he would be unlikely to see or sense us. I thought of trying to follow him back to his lair, actually wondering how we could do that without being spotted, before I remembered he'd be leaving us a clear trail. 'You're slow but good, Hardy,' Evie sometimes says. Part of that is true.

"Clear! He's gone." Andy spoke softly but no longer whispered. "That was a piece of luck, thanks to our guard dog."

We quickly broke camp, repacked, and then stashed our carry beneath a low fan of spruce boughs. We knew we were close, and would be better able to sneak around, and possibly dodge, without wearing packs and bedrolls. Sure enough, the snare wire trigger had been undone, the wire neatly coiled and hung from the pistol, out of sight, a tiny, cheap-looking European semiautomatic.

"What is that?" I asked.

"A twenty-two. Probably shoots .22-short ammo." He checked. "Yep. Not good for much. Except this." He gestured around us. He unwired it from its tree, wiped off its dusting of frost and snow and tucked it at the back of his parka hood, first setting the safety. I must have given him an odd look. He shrugged.

By starlight—and maybe a bit of braille—we followed the faint snowshoe trail through a thickening of woods, down and up a frozen streambed and through several layers of camouflage netting. No wonder the marshal couldn't spot this place from the air. Ahead, a single square of lantern light flickered, diffused and pale through one small frosted windowpane.

"Bingo," whispered Andy.

It was an old cabin, built low with the eaves at about my eye level, likely dug out inside for extra headroom. The logs had been large ones, too large to have grown here in the flats, probably rafted down the river then hand-squared

225

to fit tight. Now snow-bundled, it would have been easy to walk right past, only the tiniest flicker of light revealing it.

Through the gloom, I saw Andy wave us to huddle up. "Nobody's gettin' out that window. Unless there's a bigger one on the other side, we'll all dig in facing the door. Less chance of shooting each other that way." We nodded and he led off, each of us taking care not to *clank* our snowshoes on the frozen trees.

He was right, just the one way out, so Andy and I dug in facing the door and another small window on the east side. Andy sent Evie wide, to shelter behind a stacked-up stone cairn, an old claim corner about forty feet farther on and impervious to flying bullets. "Anything goes wrong," he told her, "take off. Get help. You hear?"

"I hear," she said in a way that made it clear she *had* heard and had no intention of doing the thing his way.

We were in good shape, behind a stack of firewood, at least sixteen feet long, four feet high and more than four feet thick. It paralleled the door and made the only decent close cover. We moved in behind it, taking a position at either end, tramping down the snow and taking off our snowshoes, the better to duck and dodge and try to not get shot.

"Damn," Andy said, and twisted to look behind him.

"Still feel it?"

He didn't answer, just shook his head back in his parka hood, then turned to peer around the wood pile at the cabin.

So, we were all set up, still not knowing if William was here. And if he wasn't, not knowing who actually was or how many we might be up against. We also didn't know what we'd do if one of them came out the door. Shoot him? Booby traps aside, what if we were in the total wrong place? What if this was just a particularly paranoid beaver trapper, trying to exist unmolested out here in the wilderness, and now we've showed up to surround him? I could imagine myself explaining that to Marshal Jacobs, and the bishop. If we surprised him, armed, he was bound to shoot at us, just as we—in that situation—were likely to shoot back.

The whole thing had 'out on thin ice' written all over it. To make matters worse, I caught Andy hitching around again to look behind us.

"We're set," I told him. "If you think someone's out there, why don't you put on your snowshoes and go check? Or I can. If you go back a bit along the trail, then cut over, his trail will be obvious in the snow."

"If there is one."

"Well, yeah, there's that."

"I think I will." Andy reached for his snowshoes.

A shot fired behind us, on our left, where Evie hid. It wasn't loud as shots went, but loud enough. "Damn!" said Evie with feeling, loud enough for us to hear. She'd stumbled on a tripwire.

The effect was almost instantaneous. The lamp in the cabin went out.

CHAPTER 25

We waited. We waited so long we got cold, just standing or crouching, guns ready, and it began to get light. It wasn't the sun coming up, but the pale glow that begins as the sun lingers in its shallow winter arc, an hour or more before dawn.

All the while, there wasn't a sound in the woods. Well, we did hear the occasional tree crack, but no birds, not even wind. Certainly no distant voices or chainsaws. The perfect quiet only added to the sense of deadly.

Sometime between eight and nine, the cabin door cracked open. "Who's out there?" called a voice.

"We're looking for our friend, William Stoltz," I called back.

"Okay," the voice answered, "here he is." They shoved William out the door on a tether, with his hands tied behind him, his chest bare, feet bare, wearing only his wool long john bottoms.

"He'll be a 'Williamsicle' in about ten minutes, unless you put down your weapons and come forward with your hands in the air."

Andy and I looked at each other. "Got no choice." He set down the Mauser. Evie had already propped her gun and started forward. I set down my rifle and stuffed the .38 into a void in the firewood, hopeful that if I came running back and needed it in a hurry, I'd be able to find the spot.

I looked at Jack. If this had been Rinty, I could have told him to sit, or go for help, or maybe to make himself a sandwich. But Jack wasn't Rinty and he wouldn't stay in one place long enough to be helpful. So, when we without snowshoes came stumbling forward through nearly thigh-deep snow, Jack came bounding along at my side. As we reached William and formed a rough half circle around him, Jack sat and I got a hand on his collar. William stood with his head down slightly, not looking any particular way, not even looking particularly cold. He shook his head.

"I would have told you not to come!"

"We would have come anyway," said Evie. Then she turned to the cabin door, still open about six inches. "We're here, with no guns. Take him back inside!"

For what seemed like a long time—probably two or three minutes—nothing happened and no one answered. Finally, the door creaked open a few more inches, a face looked at us, and someone pulled the rope that drew William back into the unlit cabin. "You too," said the voice. We filed in behind William who had to duck under the low door frame. It wasn't a problem for Andy, Evie, or me. I managed to push Jack aside at the last second, closing him on the outside of the door.

Evie went first into the darkness, stumbling, nearly falling, apparently being caught by someone inside. "There's a step down," she called back.

There was. The cabin's dirt floor, hard packed by now, had been dug down about a foot to create headroom. I heard a match scratching, saw the flame start up and head for a kerosene lamp. The cabin had three windows in all, each an approximate one-foot square of glass set into the logs, at this hour still admitting only a lightless gray glow. The lantern showed us one room with the requisite curtained honey-bucket in the back corner. There were two handmade bunk bed sets with no mattresses, four bedrolls, a small wood-fired cook stove, a stack of wooden Blazo boxes for shelves, and an old pine table with four rickety chairs.

There were three men, all tall, having to duck under crossbeams as they moved around the cabin. Although I'd seen them all before, the only one I actually recognized was the man I'd come to know as Big Ears. The other two each held weapons on us, one a shotgun. As I pushed back my hood, Big Ears looked at me and tipped his head. "I've seen you before."

"At the store."

"Oh." His brow furrowed. "That's not it! You're the guy with the dog." He aimed a fist at my chin, which I mostly avoided by turning my head and falling back. He seemed to think he had scored. "Ha!" he said, pleased with himself, likely performing for his friends. Evie grabbed my arm.

"It's okay," I mumbled, ducking, trying to look like not much of a threat.

"Cut him loose," directed Big Ears, waving toward William, and one of the others cut the cord binding William's hands. "Get dressed."

"You three, over here." The one with the rifle gestured us toward a bunk. By now I was tired of holding my hands up and slowly eased them down. I noticed the others did too. No one objected. They hadn't even searched us. I could have kept the .38.

It was clearly William they considered dangerous. As he dressed, Big Ears stood watch, a large-bore pistol in his hand.

With a fire in the stove and the door closed, the cabin warmed rapidly. When I couldn't stand it anymore, I unzipped and opened my parka, also unbuttoning the vest I wore beneath. I noticed Evie and Andy do the same, Andy kind of giving himself a shake as he opened the parka, and I faintly heard the clunk of the small pistol as it slid down his back, landing on the edge of a sleeping bag.

Evie stood up. "I hope you're thinking about letting us all go." None of them answered and the one with the rifle pressed the muzzle against her chest until she had to sit back down.

"No." Big Ears came to stand in front of us, directing William to take a seat on the bunk next to me. "The fact is, you won't be going anywhere. You might as well know you're going to die out here tomorrow with your President. "I like Ike," he said, laughing, parroting the popular Eisenhower campaign button. "I'll like him better dead."

Andy looked up. "That's your plan? To blow us all up?"

"Oh," said Big Ears, "you won't blow up. You'll be irradiated. You'll still die almost instantly, but in one piece... if that matters to you. And without bullet holes." He glanced around significantly at his companions.

I wasn't comforted, and neither was Andy by the look of it. We exchanged a glance, punctuated by a little head bob, which I took to mean... *now!*

He pulled the .22, switched off the safety mid swing, aimed it at the man with the rifle and pulled the trigger three times. *Pop, pop, pop!* It filled the air with a surprising amount of smoke while sounding like nothing more than target shooting at tin ducks on the midway. All it lacked was a calliope playing and the smell of deep-fried elephant ears.

The first bullet hit the rifle stock, ricocheting against a log where it fell to the floor and rattled. The second and third hit the man in his well-padded chest, not producing the desired effect.

231

"Ow!" he shouted. "Ow!" He doubled over, not dropping the rifle, clutching his chest. "*Damn*, that hurts," he shouted, pointedly refusing to bleed, drop the rifle, or fall down.

With the first shot, I jumped to my feet, arm drawn back, fist ready for contact with the front of Big Ear's face... only to find myself staring down the tunnel-like muzzle of what must have been a .44 Magnum. I raised my hands, watching the gun barrel draw back then quickly arc to a spot on the side of my head. And that was it. Lights out.

* * *

I woke up, tied up and stretched out on one of the hard bunks. The sleeping bag under me smelled of cigarettes and sweat. It figured. They wouldn't see many showers out here in the Bush. Across the room on the other bottom bunk, I could just see Andy, visible by looking under the table and between chairs. He was also tied up, bleeding from a cut above his eye. It looked like they popped him, too. Someone put a hand on my bound ankle, almost like petting me. I hoped it was Evie, and it was. She was sitting, not tied, just on the bunk at my feet. And then I noticed William sitting at the end of Andy's bunk, but not petting him.

Legs walked through my field of view.

"When is he due?"

"Soon." The voice came from over by the stove. I heard a skillet hit the stovetop, and soon meat sizzled, probably Spam by the smell of it—and I didn't even like the stuff. It made me instantly hungry, even with my blinding headache, but I doubted they were cooking any for us.

I heard William's voice. "Why are you doing this?"

I recognized Big Ear's voice. "We are doing it for Mother Russia."

"You're not Russian."

Big Ears laughed. "No, but you are. Don't you get it? This will all be blamed on you, the disaffected turncoat. You'll be famous back in the Motherland."

He laughed again, but I heard something else in his voice. He sounded nervous. I wondered why. He had all of us accounted for, especially William. He had a good hideout, almost impossible to find, and had to be pretty sure nobody was looking for him, anyway. For certain, no one was out flying around in this weather. Presumably he had the Davy Crockett, and tomorrow, Ike would be delivered to him. The only way it could be any better was if someone would also deliver a hot lunch, or maybe a shower.

"Why don't we shoot them now?"

"I would," said Big Ears. "I would have shot them already. It's still looking like a pretty good idea. But the big guy wants the radiation to kill them. No bullet holes. I'm not sure why it makes a difference."

For what seemed a long time, the three puttered and nattered around the cabin, fixing and eating food, washing up, frittering with their weapons. It felt like nothing so much as killing time.

I felt Evie's hand on my ankle and heard her anxious, whispered question. "You awake?" I shifted my leg. "Good," she said.

The sun had risen, more light finding its way through windowpanes, but never enough to turn off the lantern. After a long time pretending to be still knocked out, I sat up, making my head throb. Big Ears glanced at me but said nothing. None of them seemed to care. Andy sat up as well

233

with the same effect. The three were going about their business, one cleaning the skillet, one still cleaning his rifle, and Big Ears, paging through a thick, technical-looking manual. And they were all listening, palpably waiting for something.

Finally, soft but clear from the outside, they were rewarded. I heard Jack woof, just once. The two others didn't move, but Big Ears rose from his seat at the table, not moving, not pulling out his pistol, just standing.

"Glad I waited to shoot the dog," he said. One of the others laughed without humor.

We heard thunks and thuds at the door, like someone climbing out of snowshoes and leaning them up on the cabin. Then the frosty latch lifted and with a creak, the door swung in. He had arrived, whoever he was.

I wondered if he got to be leader by virtue of being the biggest. He was. He ducked through the low doorway, filling it. For the first time, the cabin felt too small, and like there might not even be enough oxygen for all.

The newcomer dressed all in white, like the U.S. Army's 10th Mountain Division in the war, the ones who attacked the Germans from the mountains. This one wore a white parka, white canvas over-pants, white boots, not mukluks. *He's skiing!* Even a white balaclava.

As if reading my thoughts, he reached his arm out the door to bring in a pair of very long skis and poles, and tucked them high in the cabin rafters. Then he began to peel. First, the parka, the pants, the boots, and finally removing the balaclava. From behind he appeared clean-shaven, short-haired, broad-shouldered, and very fit. Something about him seemed familiar. I wondered if, as with Big Ears, I would recognize him from around town, though I think I'd remember someone that large.

234

When he turned, I shouldn't have been surprised, but I was. We all were, except maybe William. Stunned, I heard Evie suck in a shocked breath. The man laughed, a short, sharp bark, completely unlike himself—at least unlike the 'self' I thought I knew. He smiled as he greeted me.

"Father," and at Evie, Andy, and finally at William. "Brother," he said, laughing again, clapping William on the shoulder.

So, my prayers had been answered. Somehow, he *had* made it back alive.

Vadim.

CHAPTER 26

Vadim knew exactly where we'd left our packs, and sent the two junior men out to fetch them. He looked at Andy. "Thought you were on to me out there. How do you do that?"

Andy shrugged, raised his eyebrows, shook his head. "Dunno."

Vadim looked thoughtful. "It must be a *Native* thing."

"Could be the bad smell," said Andy. Vadim laughed his barky laugh and punched Andy in the stomach so hard it folded him over the fist.

"There is no need for that," William said, as though he didn't know or care that Vadim could easily do the same thing to him.

"Shut up," said Vadim, but didn't bother to punch his brother. I guessed whatever old wrong still separating them would evaporate in tomorrow's shower of lethal radiation, so potent it would firestorm neurons in our bodies. Slamming cellular division to a halt, it would kill us almost instantly. According to U.S. Army films I'd been made to watch, we'd vomit uncontrollably, defecate uncontrollably—with a blinding headache—and die in minutes. I admit I had imagined my death a number of different ways, and how my body might be found later. I'd never imagined it like this.

Evie made eye contact with Vadim. "You don't have to do this. This isn't you. You can still let us go."

"I am afraid, my dear, this *is* me and I am not going to be letting you go. You got yourself into this. If you'd just stayed home, minded your own business—according to the weather service—Chandalar won't get more than trace amounts of radiation. But no, you had to come out here searching for my brother, to be a hero. Now, it's going to kill you." He turned away, then turned back. "We have months invested in this, getting ready, camping in this godforsaken bog. You can't think we're going to walk away now, just because you ask nicely. We're going to kill your President with his own weapon! You *must* see the irony in that!"

We passed a long, agonizingly slow day. We took turns at the honey bucket, dozed, paged through their collection of well-worn *Life, Look,* and *Time magazines,* avoiding the girly magazines. But I found it hard to lose myself in an article or a story knowing that I, and everyone I cared about, would die horribly—not quickly enough—in less than twenty-four hours. Now and again we'd hear an airplane drift over. They didn't see us, couldn't see us, and the engine note remained constant as they passed. Was it Frank Jacobs, somehow alerted, out searching for us? Probably not. He'd told us what to do, or what to not do, and we'd chosen to ignore him, as we often did. So, apparently, this was what we got.

After an eternity, it grew dark again. Vadim went outside to feed Jack, which surprised me. At first I thought he was going out to lure and to shoot him. In fact, Big Ears asked him. "Time to shoot the dog?"

"Shoot him? No. The dog will tell us much more certainly if someone else should approach. We don't have to wait for intruders—hope for them—to trip the wire. No, we'll leave him alive until the end."

At dinnertime they fed us, Spam again, chopped into fried potatoes and onions, with a mug of surprisingly hearty coffee. Andy sipped.

"Good coffee," he said, probably an involuntary reaction.

Vadim sipped his own, made happy tasting mouths and agreed. "South American, from the Andes, roasted in New York, of all places."

I could see he'd impressed Andy.

We slept in our own sleeping bags—a relief. Mine smelled a lot better than the one I'd been sitting and laying on. It's true we slept on the packed-dirt floor, and also true that we weren't less comfortable than our captors, sleeping on unpadded board bunks. Unlike last night, tonight I had every reason to believe I would not sleep, but did, all night. I didn't wake until someone used the coiled steel handle to lift the heavy burner plate on the woodstove, to begin building up the morning's fire.

So, this was it—the day we'd die? Not if we could help it.

With the fire built up, the next order of business became fishing a tall pole out of the attic rafters, with a metal antenna at the top and a long loop of wire coiled at the bottom. One of the men, Anatoly—the other answered to Herb—handed the connection end to Big Ears, slid into his parka and outdoor gear, and carried the pole outside.

Big Ears pulled out a short-wave radio, black, complicated with knobs and dials, and about the size of a breadbox. He wired it up to a pair of cardboard-tubed batteries and to the antenna, and switched it on. Slowly a hum expanded in the cabin, interspersed with static, the occasional fragment of voice as the frequency tuned, then a rapid sequence of beeping tones. It was a code that had Big Ears listening hard and copying. Fortunately, it repeated, and finally he looked up, nodded, and dropped his notepaper into the woodstove. Then he opened the door to call Anatoly back with the antenna.

Vadim simply watched him, waiting. "It's all a green light," Big Ears confirmed. "The President will arrive as scheduled, at ten hundred hours. We move our prisoners up by eleven hundred and meet the others, then we clear the area and fire the missile by twelve hundred. They suspect nothing and there is no reason it should not all go as planned."

Vadim smiled at him and nodded. "It will be so very nice to finish up here and go somewhere warm, preferably a tropical beach." That got them all started fantasizing about where they'd go and how they'd spend the vast wealth they were being paid for this job. But it felt false. I wondered how many, if any, would leave here alive.

"Why did you kill the geologist?" I asked. Since we were doomed anyway, I thought Vadim might answer. Of course, he might also punch me, like he had Andy. But he didn't. He shrugged when Big Ears looked his way, as if to say, 'Go ahead, tell him.'

"We were a man short. Our cover was jumping gold claims, so we recruited a big sturdy man to help us carry gear. Who better than a geologist? The nuclear missile alone weighs fifty pounds. He carried it in by himself. Finally, he asked me what it was. Of course, he was outraged when I told him, and said he'd report us to the authorities. By then..." he shrugged and held up both hands, as if the thing was obvious. "we didn't need him anymore."

Vadim looked at him. An expression flashed on his face, just a quick twist at the side of his mouth. "It would have been better to not leave his body beside the main road."

Big Ears waved him off. "As if it has become a problem." Vadim smiled by lifting his cheeks in a mechanical kind of way. There was no humor in it. It almost felt threatening. If Big Ears noticed, he didn't let on.

"And the other man, out on the trail when you ambushed us, what about him?"

Big Ears pointed at Andy. "He shot him, right through the pumper." I saw Andy grimace. Big Ears waved him off. "You saved me the trouble."

When Vadim consulted his watch, I looked at mine. Nine a.m. "We will move the prisoners into the target area now," he announced. "We will be meeting the others. Please do not shoot them. And do not shoot the dog. Father, here, will catch him and tie him up. We want no bullet holes."

Again, I wondered why. As if hearing my thought, he said, "Everyone—all of you—must appear to have been in on the plan, which won't work if any of you—okay, too many of you—are found with bullet holes."

Big Ears grinned at me. "Later, when this is all done, people will think it was *your* idea, that you were the mastermind, with your friends."

I must have looked incredulous. "Who would believe that?"

"They'll believe the evidence... that we hide in your cabin on our way out of town. It will all be very convincing. People will say, 'He seemed so friendly, so normal.' You know, the kinds of things people always say when someone they thought they knew does something terrible."

"Swell." Thinking dark thoughts, I put on my mukluks, dry and warm from hanging by the stove, then my parka. I got the harness for my heavy mitts on and

240

arranged, pulled my muffler out and got it wrapped around my face.

Before he opened the door, Vadim turned to his men for one last caution. "Nothing must happen before we reach the site and the others arrive." Though he appeared to be talking to his three cohorts, he also made careful eye contact with Andy and with me. "While we may not shoot you, we have ways to make you wish you've been shot."

Yeah, I'll just bet you do.

We'd have to get our snowshoes. Andy's and mine were still behind the woodpile. The snow lay too deep and too drifted to walk to wherever without them. They'd removed our rifles, but if I could quickly find the place I'd stuffed the .38, that would be our last chance. So, we trudged through the snow out around the woodpile, and I gathered myself to make the big leap for the gun. It was gone, the cranny empty! And gone with it, our last hope.

As we were bent over strapping on snowshoes, frantic for a plan, Vadim called out, "Oh, hope you don't mind. I moved your little pistol." He *had* been watching us closely. The others laughed. That rankled, too.

Vadim directed Big Ears to lead. "We have about five miles to travel, and no need to hurry." He laughed. "The party can't start without us."

As we tramped down the trail single file, I found myself imagining the Eisenhower party on a parallel course, the President, probably his wife, along with his aides and security people. They'd land in Fairbanks and then helicopter down to Clear in one of the big, olive-drab Army helicopters, to their destruction.

Eisenhower wasn't the first President to visit the territory. Warren Harding had come through Nenana in 1921 to hammer down the symbolic golden spike, signifying completion of the Nenana railroad bridge. FDR had visited the territory also, much farther south, and had done some fishing. But neither of them had died here. Eisenhower would be a first.

But why would Russians come here to America to commit a deliberate act of aggression? To start a war? I turned slightly to speak to William, tramping just behind me. "I don't get it. It will be war... maybe the last war." He didn't answer for a time.

"There has been coming, for several years, a power struggle in the Soviet Union. Malenkov, heir to Stalin, is in power, but weak. Now, a brutal thug named Krushchev wants to be in power, and is not above provoking a skirmish with the United States to make it happen."

"He'd kill the President? The world will be outraged."

William nearly chuckled. That is the beauty of it. If the world is outraged, Krushchev will be also outraged, will oust Malenkov, and be contrite.

"But if the world is not outraged?"

"Krushchev will claim credit for the attack, denounce Malenkov's weakness, and push him aside."

"So Krushchev can't lose," I said, but William didn't answer. The answer was obvious.

America hadn't had a President assassinated since McKinley in 1901. Assassination wasn't who we were as a country. We didn't murder our own. In fact, in these modern times, I couldn't even imagine an assassinated President. I even thought—no, believed—America would never murder another of its own leaders. These were modern times. We wouldn't do it and we certainly wouldn't take kindly to another country doing it.

Russia interfering in this way, murdering our President, would mean war, possibly a nuclear war, since we both had the bombs and appeared ready to use them. It might turn out to be the end of the world. I guess I had a hard time believing it might start right here, with Andy, William, Evie, and me at ground zero.

In the meantime, here we all were, back on snowshoes, marching into the rising golden sun on another glorious, frigid Alaska morning, soon to perish.

I had to admire Vadim on the long skis. Even with his rifle slung over his shoulder he moved like he'd been born on skis, like they'd always been attached to his feet. What must William be thinking? Double-crossed. Betrayed by his brother—again. This was the same brother who had done his utmost to seduce Alice, even kissing and fondling her on the riverbank. Did William know this part of it then? Or when Vadim disappeared, apparently killed in the mine cave-in, William hadn't wanted to hold the memorial. Did he know *then*?

We startled a bull moose ahead on the trail, and our column stopped. Vadim slipped the rifle off his shoulder, bolted a shell into the chamber and waited. We all waited. Moose were short-sighted and could be cantankerous. The irony wasn't lost on us, that Vadim who was prepared to protect us from this creature, also led the march to our doom. We stood that way, stock still, for several moments. I knew Vadim wouldn't want to risk the shot but also knew he had to. He needed to get us *there*, wherever that was, on time and in one piece. The moose pawed away snow, finding more willow shoots to crunch off, then turned abruptly and ambled away. We all began to breathe again and I noticed Vadim finger the live shell from the chamber.

"What are we going to do?" I muttered to William.

"Wait."

Wait? The closer we got to wherever we were headed, the smaller the chance we'd be able to do anything, like save our own lives.

"You sure?"

"Yes," he said, "wait." Since I didn't seem to have a choice, I waited, marching along compliantly.

The temperature had risen, but not a lot. It felt like the mid-minus thirties. It helped that we were dressed for it. We heard the occasional airplane, but none flew near. Each time I pondered what I would do if one did. I could get myself shot for a big, daring attempt to signal, and have them fly on past, not even noticing.

We walked for an hour. The sun came up and shone in our eyes. I found sunglasses in my parka pocket and put them on, immediately noticing the Clear RADAR station towers off in the haze of distance, about two miles.

Within minutes we made a turn. Big Ears led us west, off the main dogsled trail. I knew we were present as 'ghosts' on the big RADAR and wondered fleetingly if William's moose-hunting buddy would notice us, maybe think us suspicious and call out security. More likely, he'd plan to hunt here soon, which wouldn't happen. In less than two hours, he'd be dead, too.

Our captors must have known about the RADAR ghosts. Within minutes, we dropped into a frozen streambed, out of sight and surely off radar, still moving steadily west. From time to time, Evie would turn to look at me, her eyes large and brown and worried. In my imagination, she expected me to save us, hardly a surprise since *I* expected me to save us. I just wasn't sure how. *It might not happen this time.*

If any of this were true, we were snowshoeing to our certain deaths. Much to my surprise, my single regret as I trudged, was having not married Evie. Why? We had a good life together, loved each other. We both knew we *would* get married, but hadn't yet, because other things kept happening. As it seemed to me now, in this moment of clarity, 'things' of much less consequence.

Christians—and many others—believe that two people who commit to each other in that formal way, become more than themselves. Like one plus one somehow equals three. I believe it, but I hadn't done it. And in this moment, possibly one of my last, it gnawed at me.

We walked most of another mile before rising out of the stream bed and immediately under a good-sized shelter. What had started out as several overlapping layers of camo cover, now sagged and—in some places—had collapsed under several feet of powdery snow. It had become absolutely invisible from the air.

Beneath the shelter, a second tarp lightly dusted with snow, covered what had to be the missing weapon. Anatoly and Herb each grabbed the tarp like a bedspread and stretched it tight then carried it aside.

The Davy Crockett stood on three rather spidery legs that seemed far too light for something so deadly. The weapon wasn't tied in place or braced. Being recoilless, I supposed it wouldn't have to be. I remembered William saying it could conceivably be fired from the shoulder, just not aimed well, but the shooter would have to be a brute.

The gun was a four-inch tube flared at the back, five or six feet long. The missile itself looked like a steel balloon, bulbous—larger at the nose—not sleek and pointed like most missiles. About a two- or-three-gallon size, the only thing that made it look like it might fly was four fins at its base. It wasn't terribly aerodynamic and didn't look like it would fly too far, but then it didn't have to.

With its small size and clunky shape, it almost looked cartoonish. There was nothing about it that made it look like a weapon so deadly that soon it would kill a thousand people, including our President. And we wouldn't be killed by the blast, but *snuffed* by an atomic reaction so pervasive our cells would simply stop.

"Tie up the dog," ordered Vadim, and I did. Though, if I had a way to *shoo* him to safety, I would have. Why should a faithful dog die for human sins?

I couldn't help thinking about Rinty. What would he do? He'd take a note to the cavalry and then cook breakfast. I looked at Jack, expectantly, and he looked at me, his tongue hanging out.

In the shelter, little snow had fallen. We all removed snowshoes.

Herb looked at his boss. "What now?"

"We wait," said Vadim, and I began to do that, reaching out for Evie's mitted hand that, as it turned out, came reaching for mine.

CHAPTER 27

Something beeped, muffled, then beeped again. Big Ears looked up at Vadim. "It's them!"

Vadim unzipped the top of his parka, dug for a pocket inside, and extracted a metal object the size of a paperback novel. He pushed a button and held the object to his ear. "Yes," he shouted then pushed the button again and put it away. He saw me watching and smiled proudly. "Is new Russian radio-telephone!" So excited about the invention, he forgot his English. I was unable to share his excitement.

Within about fifteen minutes, they arrived, the ones we'd been waiting for. There were eight of them, six men and two women, most likely inside workers from Clear. They came down the streambed, awkward and almost comical on snowshoes.

In new parkas and store-bought boots, they looked like city people, office people, a little puffy, not used to snow and the outdoors. Only about fifteen minutes away from their desks, they already looked uncomfortable in the cold. Traitors, turncoats, spies, working to foment the downfall of my country—their country?

"There's no shelter," said a man, the first in line.

Big Ears gave him a reassuring smile. "It's not far."

"Good," said the man. "I'm cold. We're all cold."

If anything, Big Ears widened his smile. "You won't be cold for long." The man smiled like this was a good thing. To me, it sounded like a dark, dangerous promise. But maybe that's just me faced with death.

In the meantime, Vadim had produced a black box about the size of both his fists, sprouting wires, which he now wing-nutted to the Davy Crockett. He saw me watching. "Latest thing. Adapted for a timer. Nobody has to stand here and push the button."

"So, you'll be gone," I said.

"Oh, yes." He smiled, a disarmingly friendly smile. "It's almost over."

"And that's a good thing?"

"Oh, yes," he said again. "You'll see." And he started the timer.

I wondered how much 'seeing' I'd be doing when my cells stopped dividing and I began to defecate uncontrollably. As if sensing my thoughts, Evie came to stand in my arms, her head down, as if weeping. "Got a plan?" she whispered.

"Not yet. You?"

"Not yet. There's something weird about this. Something hinky."

"*I'll* say! Whatever '*hinky*' means..."

"You know what I mean." She was right, I did. Something was off. As if in answer to my question, Big Ears, Anatoly, and Herb began to collect snowshoes from the new arrivals. They seemed glad to hand them over, not considering they couldn't get to anywhere from here without them.

"Look at that," I said. Evie turned and stepped aside to look. Almost immediately, Vadim, who had been fussing with the timer, turned without looking, took a step and crashed right into me, knocking me aside.

"Get out of my way," he barked, shoving me. For some reason, this odd bit of nastiness when we were going to die anyway was the last straw. But when I stepped up to face him, he simply turned and walked away leaving me dumbfounded. And that's when I found the pistol in my pocket—mine, my .38—where he'd slipped it.

I looked at my watch. Eleven forty. I knew the blast was scheduled for twelve. Big Ears, Anatoly, and Herb looked increasingly nervous and anxious. They wanted to be out of here and knew they should be. They kept looking at the Davy Crockett then at the trail they expected to be taking soon. Only Vadim looked calm.

"It's a suicide mission," I whispered to Evie, and to Andy who had moved close. "I'm betting only Vadim gets out alive."

"And us!" Andy did a head flick at his pocket. I looked. Now he had a pistol, too. It looked like one of William's Colt semiautomatics. We weren't the only ones who knew the time. As the clock ticked down, the eight spies who had come out from Clear, shivering from cold or adrenalin, began to mill and actually make moaning sounds, a bit like cattle. They kept looking at the Davy Crockett, like it might swing around or jump at them, doing something they needed to watch out for.

Big Ears approached Vadim, who watched it all like a stage play. Big Ears looked tense. He lowered his head to speak quietly. "We need to go. We're too close."

"We're not going." Vadim pulled an automatic from his parka pocket and jammed it into Big Ear's midsection.

BLAM! Anatoly had yanked a pocket gun and shot Vadim in the chest. It had been a setup, a mutiny. As Vadim crumpled, Herb and Big Ears bolted for snowshoes. Anatoly swung his pistol at me, but Evie blocked his shot. William and Andy both shot him. The two shots rang as one, hanging and vibrating in the icy air as Anatoly collapsed. Panicked, snowshoes half on, Big Ears and Herb stumbled down the trail as Andy assumed his shooting stance and drew a bead. Only William's hand on his arm stopped him.

"Let them go."

Thoroughly confused, panicked, and ready to run, only the lack of snowshoes kept the Clear spies from streaming off into the brush to get away from ground zero. William pointed.

"Watch them," he said to Andy, as he went to attend to Vadim, and I went to say last rites over Anatoly.

To my surprise—everyone's, actually—Vadim climbed to his feet, unaided, smiling and grimacing as he rubbed his chest and reached into his parka to retrieve the radio, now out of service. "I'm afraid my radio is shot." It definitely was.

Just like there wasn't a nuclear weapon counting down to zero, William lined up the spies, methodically frisking them, apparently finding no weapons. Finally, forgotten, but now demanding proper attention, the missile timer buzzed. Everyone froze except William, who— revolver in hand—calmly finished frisking the last one.

As if in slow motion, a turning number clicked to zero, a mechanical arm moved, the trigger on the Davy Crockett clicked, and the nuclear missile... just fell off the end of the rocket tube into the snow. We all watched like it might do a trick but it didn't. It didn't hiss, sizzle, or smoke. It just lay there, clearly a dud.

About then I realized I'd been holding my breath, and remembered to take one. I think we all did. For a long moment we just stood there, happy to be alive and to feel the chilly air moving in and out of our lungs... certainly glad not to be vomiting, defecating out of control, and breathing our last.

"Ears!" warned William, and we covered ours as he fired three quick shots into the snow. Almost immediately we heard three whistle blasts in response, and within about

250

sixty seconds, military skiers in white winter gear converged on us.

William spoke to one, the apparent leader. "Did you get them?"

"Oh, yeah, without a shot. They fingered Vadim, right away, said he threatened their wives and children."

"They both said that?"

"Yep!"

"That would be more convincing if either of them *had* wives and children."

I turned to William. "So, you have all of them for espionage."

"Yes. We knew they were in there. We even knew who some of them were. We just needed a way to bring them out."

"Do we get to meet Ike?"

He showed me his rueful face. "An actor."

"Darn," I said.

* * *

"Why..." asked Frank Jacobs, pausing to sip his coffee, "do you never listen to what I tell you? Why does me saying 'stay out of this,' sound like an invitation to get involved?" He looked around my kitchen, now stuffed to capacity. "You did exactly what William said you'd do, by the way."

The three of us, Andy, Evie, and me, turned on William and Vadim sitting on tippy stools with Alice in the middle. William ducked his head. "You told him that?" I asked.

"I am guilty," he said, affecting meekness.

Evie looked at Andy then at me. "Yeah," she said, nodding, "I think that's pretty much right."

"Pretty much," agreed Andy.

251

Jacobs turned to me. "But you're not surprised by much of this, are you?"

"Some."

"Come on, Sherlock, tell me."

"Well, I didn't think Vadim was really dead."

Jacobs looked surprised. "You didn't? I told William you'd probably want to get in there and dig him out. What gave it away?"

I jerked my head at William and Alice. "It was them... well, mostly Alice."

Alice shot me a look. "Hey... we were perfect!"

"You were very good, Alice, except..."

William looked up from his coffee. "You are guessing now. She *was* very good."

"When we came to tell her, she might have said... is he dead? Did he fall into the river and drown? Did he accidentally shoot himself? Did little green men come down from Mars to carry him away? No, none of those.

"Instead she looked at us both and said, 'Oh no, a cave in?' So, I suspected that she knew. I just didn't know why."

Jacobs toasted me with his coffee mug. "You *are* good," he said.

Evie turned to William. "Those people who came out? They were all spies? Russians?"

"They were spies. Big Ears is Russian but Anatoly and Herb are Americans, on the Soviet payroll. The rest were American too, in it for their various reasons... mostly a *lot* of money."

Evie looked at William then at the marshal. "So, everybody gets charged with espionage?"

William nodded as the marshal answered. "And one count homicide, for the murdered geologist."

"And one more," I said. Everybody in the room froze and they all looked at me.

The marshal held up one finger like he was ticking it off then put up a second finger and raised both his eyebrows in my direction. "Who?"

"Arnold Gustafson. I'm pretty sure Big Ears killed him, and that's why Jack wanted to go after him. Neighbors said Jack kept barking at night. He was barking because they were carrying gear past the cabin, but Arnold couldn't hear any of the commotion. The night he died, Arnold put in his hearing aid, heard Jack barking and followed them across the tracks to find out what they were up to. He may have confronted them, or they may have just spotted him and clubbed him. Either way, I'll bet there's traces of blood and hair on something—probably a rifle stock."

Evie nodded. "It was Arnold... and Jack... who tipped us off." She held up her coffee mug. "To Arnold and Whisky Jack," she toasted. "What is it the Irish say... 'may you be in heaven a half hour before the devil knows you're dead!'"

"Hear, hear," we all said, and drank an Irish toast to an American man and his dog, with really good Italian-roasted coffee.

I remember thinking, *Now life can get back to normal.*

CHAPTER 28

The news had it that Eisenhower *did* make a quick visit to Clear. We heard on KFAR that the helicopter landed and that the President and his wife made a quick tour with the top brass. After that, they choppered back to Fairbanks to catch the jet to wherever the real Ike and Mamie were vacationing.

Vadim, an agent loyal to Malenkov, defected to the United States. As he said it, "The handwriting is no longer on the wall, it's on the middle of my forehead." Although he'd managed to save the day for Malenkov, both their days were numbered, and he would be unlikely to survive the Khrushchev power shift. With his brother at his side, he surrendered himself to Federal agents in Fairbanks and then, from one day to the next, simply disappeared.

And life did get back to normal. For one thing, the weather finally warmed—a little—to a balmy minus twenty.

Out at Clear, they quit seeing ghosts around the edges of their screens and boogeymen behind the trees, which made William's life less hectic. The spies who had revealed themselves in the hope of not being 'nuked' also disappeared. Instead of their anticipated day in court, it was like they all just fell off the planet.

I asked William what happened to them. "I do not know, and better not to," he said. I couldn't even imagine what that actually meant. It didn't sound good.

We kept the 'prowler patrol' going, a little short-handed with Vic and one or two of the other teachers stateside for Christmas vacation. But we neither saw anyone suspicious, nor heard of any new prowler activity. As Christmas approached, life settled and smoothed and we got to remember what normal life in an Alaskan small town felt like.

Most of us got involved in the town Christmas party. It was a big deal in Chandalar. On December twenty-third, every family in town would gather at the Civic Center for hot cocoa, Christmas cookies, carol singing, and good cheer. At the magic hour, Santa appeared—this year sounding a lot like Oliver—with a big sack over his shoulder. He would call the name of every child in town— this year, one hundred thirty-nine—presenting each with a wrapped present, candy cane, and an orange. There were extra presents, too, just in case we missed a name or had a visitor, but we usually didn't. At the end, happy children clutched their gifts and bundled back up for the starlit walk home. They seemed amazed that Santa remembered *them*, even the littlest ones. For some, it would be their only boughten present, and their only brush with Santa. "Merry Christmas," they all called back, like they meant it.

Evie and I walked home close, her arm through mine. Above us, stars climbed endlessly, arcing up and up into a pure black sky, as a fingernail moon lifted in the southeast to begin its low winter arc.

"I love you," Evie said out of the blue.

"Why now?"

She hesitated. "Because you're here on my arm, and because you're brave and good—the best man I know— the best I've ever met, and I feel so lucky."

"You need to get out more," I told her.

"Oh, Hardy!"

"I feel the same about you," I told her, to not completely squander the moment. "This all feels... perfect!" And it did... except for the one thing—the prowler.

We had decorated a tree at my house. On Christmas morning we sat by it, drinking coffee—the good stuff—made with the new French press. We were eating one of our Christmas gifts from Andy, a dozen donuts from the bakery in Fairbanks. Actually we ate two each and agreed to freeze the rest for 'special,' later.

We opened gifts, a small pile of needful things. My main gift to Evie was a goose-down bathrobe, ordered out of the catalog from Eddie Bauer in Seattle. Although it made her look a little like a Campfire marshmallow with legs, she put it on, wrapped it around herself, sat back in her chair and just smiled. "Heaven," she said.

When I thought we were finished opening gifts, she told me to close my eyes. Opening them, I discovered a Winchester Model 70 hunting rifle, with scope, nearly the twin of William's new rifle, well blessed by Andy. This one featured a wide red ribbon tied in a bow at the top of the long barrel. I'd probably have to take that off for actual hunting. Like William's rifle, my Winchester was chambered as a .30-06 and featured the American-made 8x Unertl sniper scope.

The stock, she informed me, wasn't run-of-the-mill hardwood, but special-order, hand-carved from Oregon-grown Claro walnut, with a distinctive figured grain. "It's fabulous," was all I could say. Really, it was the finest hunting rifle I'd ever had my hands on and one of the nicest I'd seen. I felt lucky!

"Now I'll have to learn to really shoot!" I told her, and she kissed me.

As was our custom... well, sort of... we went to the New Year's Eve dance at the Civic Center. Last year, with Evie out of town and us sort of broken up—or so I thought—I had allowed myself to be Rosie's date, 'to cheer me up,' she said. It did cheer me up. We had a good time, and when midnight struck, we kissed each other there on the dance floor among all the other dancers and kissers. It was a good kiss and I was properly fond of Rosie, but this was better, and wouldn't come back to haunt me later.

It didn't get any better than dancing with my own girl to The Platters' *My Prayer* as midnight rang in and we shared a proper, lingering New Year's kiss. When the dance broke up, we walked back to her place down snowy streets, both wanting very much to be married and walking back together to *our* place.

There's a saying about New Year's Eve, that what you do then you'll do all year. Having danced, having kissed, having spent time with the one I loved most in the world, and now walking home at peace with everything, all felt good and right. I could easily spend a year like this.

As if in agreement, an owl hooted nearby, a dog barked, and farther out, one wolf howled and then more. I'd heard them before on nights like this one, and they sounded lonely. Tonight, they sounded 'with friends,' maybe feeling as satisfied and contented as I felt. I wished them well.

Evie had left her light on, and that's how we saw him, back along the side of her cabin in the snow. First, we saw tracks leaving the main trail then the dark shape of a tall man in a parka crouched under one of Evie's side windows.

Was I armed? You bet! After all we'd been through, I didn't even go out dancing without the .38 in my parka pocket. In the end, it was easy. We crept around to the side. I pulled the weapon and cocked it, shouting, "Hands up and freeze!"

He stood up, hands up, and in the window light we both saw him clearly: Stinky Ray, the trapper. Which was

Lucky we recognized him because in the next second, he bolted.

I lowered the hammer and let him go. Evie said it. "After all this time, Stinky Ray! He's been right here among us. No wonder he knew what we were doing, probably sitting on his stool taking notes."

I shook my head. I had no trouble believing he was a peeper. He probably hadn't seen a real naked woman in decades, if ever. He'd be lonely and near-terminally sexually frustrated. But murder?

* * *

The next morning, Andy showed up early for coffee, and to examine my new rifle. He hadn't seen it yet, said Evie wouldn't let him see or handle it until I'd seen it. We told him about discovering and not apprehending the prowler while he fussed and exclaimed over the gun, adjusting, setting, and checking things I didn't even know about on the scope and sights.

"Hard to figure Stinky Ray for a murderer," said Andy.

I called Frank Jacobs to fill him in on what we'd found.

"Damn!" he said, expansively. "We'll find him. Good work. I'll be down tomorrow." And that was it, mystery solved, danger averted. Maybe.

In the meantime, Andy, with my new rifle was like a kid with a Christmas toy. He had helped Evie select it, of course, and even filled out the order for it, apparently way back last summer. He'd been waiting all this time to get his hands on it, and especially to see the walnut stock. "I gotta get me one of these."

With Evie sleeping in, William arrived next, also examining the new rifle. He particularly liked the expressively grained Claro walnut. His was plenty serviceable but the stock showed no grain at all. "Low-cost alder," pronounced Andy, "stained to look like walnut."

"Now you are telling me? How can I expect to hit anything with only an alder stock?"

Andy smiled at him. "I've seen you shoot. You'll manage."

William had already heard about Stinky Ray from Frank Jacobs. Good news travels fast, and bad news faster. He made a face—one that I took as 'not convinced'—and shook his head.

"The prowler? It would be nice..." was all he said.

* * *

Frank Jacobs flew in the next morning. He and William, with Andy and me trailing, all armed, went out looking for Stinky Ray.

We'd heard about an abandoned cabin out near the railroad tracks on the north side of town. It was left over from building the railroad way back in the '30s. It wasn't much, and I'd walked past it many times without thinking about who might be sleeping there.

We found the door unlocked, the stove cold, the cabin almost completely empty except for a well-thumbed stack of hard-core 'stag' magazines: *Playboy, Hustler, Photo-Rama, Men's World, Knots and Pain*—a particularly graphic bondage magazine—and even old 1940s copies of *Sun Coast Nudist Magazine,* with entire families standing around, or barbecuing, or playing volleyball naked.

But we neither found a sign of Stinky Ray, nor would we, except a note he left for Alice. "I'm sorry," it read. One more reason I didn't think it was him.

The first half of January kicked off with bright, warm days—up into the minus teens—with people out and about, doing what they did.

Molly Joseph and young Henry came by to model his new parka. I particularly admired the fine recycled Wolverine around both his face ruff and his cuffs. She was a fine seamstress and didn't have a bit of trouble working around the bullet hole to turn one large surplus parka into most of a warm garment for each of them.

There were kids ice skating now, on frozen ponds, yard rinks, glazed roads, and even on windswept river ice. Dogsleds were also out, and they didn't make much noise, so I had to look both ways before stepping out into 'traffic.' There seemed a frenzy of them, back and forth, up and down the streets headed for the river. This was the time mushers exercised their dogs, their last chance to prepare for a variety of upcoming dog-sled races held through the remainder of winter and into spring.

First up would be the local races, like the Tortella Classic, followed by the North American Championships, attracting mushers from as far away as Vermont, though so far, only Alaska mushers had won.

My favorite musher, Teddy Moses, considered a good bet for this year, hailed from right here in Chandalar. But I also followed Horace 'Holy' Smoke, of Steven's Village—an excellent racer—mostly because I liked his name. Young George Attla, already known as the 'Huslia Hustler,' also looked promising.

About midmonth, the train hit a moose, not one that bounced off and flew into the woods, but one that stuck on the engine front, on top of the snowplow. We could hear the train whistle blowing repeatedly from across the river as it neared town, the usual signal that they were bringing in meat. With the heavy snowfall, moose would take to the roads or rail bed for easier walking, just like the rest of us. There hadn't been a moose yet that bested a diesel locomotive for the right-of-way.

When I heard the whistle, Jack and I turned out with my pickup truck and a length of heavy chain. If typical, the moose would be frozen solid after its ride on the snowplow. The railroad liked to get them removed from the front of the engine as quickly as possible, to not make the train any later than usual. Sometimes the truck wouldn't do the job if the moose was too badly wedged behind the big snowplow. Then we'd have to call for a backhoe, sometimes from as far away as the airport, a full mile out of town. I was right. The cow moose had frozen rock hard on the front of the diesel.

She yanked off easily, and Jack gave a cautious sniff. The brakeman thanked us, all smiles, and signaled the train away, only about twenty minutes off the timetable, which wasn't bad for winter around here.

Grandma Susie, who made my mukluks, would be very happy to have the hide intact. Rather than trying to skin it frozen, which often created holes, we skidded the moose behind the pickup, down the ice-skimmed road to the firehouse which was kept above freezing, but not much.

There we used a come-along to hoist the animal into the air to begin to thaw evenly—enough to skin—usually in a day or two.

That accomplished, I left Jack by his furnace grate and went out on my rounds with Butch. We snow-shoveled full paths to elderly and shut-in members of my congregation, finishing in late-afternoon twilight. It had been a good and strenuous day.

261

I cooked a moose roast for dinner, with our own garden potatoes and canned peas. Evie came and brought a small head of lettuce and a sort-of-fresh tomato from the general store. We marveled at it, even though it looked like it wanted to shrivel. Neither of us had seen a tomato, let alone smelled or tasted one since last summer. She held it up as if to the light.

"Where do tomatoes come from in the middle of winter?"

"I don't know—California?"

We agreed we'd probably been living in a remote Alaska town too long.

It was Vic's night to patrol, according to the calendar. Yes, we had voted to keep at it, at least until Ray was apprehended. But Vic called me after eight.

"I've got a sore throat," he croaked. "Can you cover?"

"Sure." About ten o'clock I walked Evie back to her place then came home to nap a little until midnight. I didn't. I lay there not napping, thinking about the prowler—whether he was or wasn't Ray—where he'd come from and now where he'd gone. It had been two weeks without anything odd in the night. It was okay with me. I didn't miss the excitement and was ready for life to settle down.

About midnight, I bundled up, dropped the .38 in my pocket, and headed out for two hours of walking around in the dark with my dog.

It was an odd night. Not clear, not starlit. The town lay blanketed and muffled with heavy ice fog. Smoke from chimneys rose then cooled and fell to creep along the ground, at times stinging my eyes, adding to the haze. Above it all the full moon rose, making the fog appear luminous, yet with only about fifty feet of poor visibility.

262

I couldn't see anything, couldn't hear anything, but started out anyway. After the heavy snowfall, patrolling was easier. The prowler used to walk all the way around his victim's cabins, crunching brush underfoot and generally making scary noises. Now, to get all the way around a cabin he'd need to snowshoe. So, all I had to do was approach each place, on the path, and look for footprints outside the path. At first I found none.

The last house on my patrol, the house farthest out— also the one without a phone—belonged to Molly Joseph. There were no lights on when I got there. At nearly one o'clock, I didn't expect any. I stood on the snow-packed street, the streetlight at my back. I could barely see the hard edge of her cabin jutting from the shift and swirl of fog, the air heavy, tangy with smoke from her well-banked fire. Several head-high evergreen trees grew in her yard, ghostly figures in the shifting mist. I kept seeing them out of the corners of my eyes, and startling.

It was Jack who ran up her shoveled path to sniff at something—tracks—heading off across her yard! It was one set, only one pass by the look of it. I chanced a quick look with the flashlight held low. The tracks were fresh, a man-sized boot tread—way too big for Molly—and not mukluks. The tracks were still a clear imprint, with no sift of snow settled in. Of course, the flashlight wrecked my night vision.

I saw the muzzle flashes before I heard them. And I heard the shots before I felt them—the first, a biting pain on the inside of my right thigh, like I'd deeply snagged a wire barb while crossing a fence. It takes longer to tell than it took to shoot me. *Bam! Bam! Bam! Bam!* More shots hit my chest, stinging and hurting like bare-knuckle body blows, hard sharp raps that stepped me backward until I tripped, off balance in the snow. Then I was falling, falling, falling like slow motion, into deep snow and out of the shooter's sight, though bullets still *popped* and *zipped* above me.

He finished one clip and I thought he might go. But in three or four seconds he replaced the magazine and started shooting again. I easily recognized the sound of the gun, the same .22 semiautomatic the prowler had emptied at me before, but more insistent. He'd never reloaded before, which seemed a bad sign. Worse, I realized too late, that the popping sound of the gun was coming my way. Ignoring the pain in my chest, I pulled off my mitt and went for my .38 but had waited too long. I looked up to see him closing on me, pistol held out on a straight arm, firing as he came. I squeezed off one shot, missed—the downside of hurrying with a two-inch barrel.

I heard Jack's snarling attack and saw the big husky bound into my frame of vision, launching himself at the shooter—who turned and squeezed off another shot. Jack yelped and deflected to one side. I fired again, watching a puff of goose down explode from a bullet-sliced sleeve. The shooter, now nearly above me, turned the pistol in my direction, aimed at my face from about six feet. A kill shot. Even this close I couldn't recognize him! A deep hood kept his face shadowed and features concealed, a blacker shade of deadly.

I pulled the trigger again, but without aim. All I wanted to do now was to get out from in front of that gun barrel, spitting flame. But I knew it wasn't going to happen. Shot four times by my count, I lay floundering, trying to move, to roll, to find traction where there simply wasn't any. In the final second, I forced myself to stop. I wasn't going anywhere. I vowed to take the shot straight on. *I'm not afraid to die*, I told myself in that last second, but I would regret leaving Evie and Andy... Jack. It's funny, the last thoughts.

Something boomed above me. Not just a shot, but a roar like a cannon. The top of one of the small evergreens, just by the shooter's head, exploded and disappeared. A shotgun blast! The shots had wakened Molly who swung the door open, its small squeak masked in the racket of small-arms fire from her yard. I suspect she hadn't wanted to shoot a human, even the prowler, so did the next best thing, fired an unmistakable warning shot across his bow—actually very close across the bridge of his nose. It got his attention. At this range, only scant inches stood between the prowler and losing most of his face.

He ducked, turned and snapped off a shot in Molly's direction. I heard the click of the breech breaking—hers was a single shot—she had to reload. Fortunately, the shooter didn't know that, didn't know what gun she was shooting, only knew he had to get away. She fired another shot behind him and reloaded. Then she pulled on her parka and mukluks to come see about me.

I was relieved to see Jack on his feet. He came limping through the deep snow to find me and to lick my face. I tried to get up, thinking I would just roll over and climb out of the deep powdery snow. But no, I couldn't roll, couldn't get traction. The pain in my chest made me pant like there was a fat man jumping on me. I tried again to roll as Molly reached me and knelt by my side. She tried to help with one hand, the other supporting the shotgun.

She put her face close. "You are hit. Stay down. Help is coming. I hear them, and see lights. They heard the shots. I won't leave you."

I won't leave you. I remember thinking that those were kind words to say, maybe the kindest. But I tried again anyway. As soon as my head raised, the world began spinning and I felt sick. Then... nothing.

CHAPTER 29

A second later I opened my eyes back in my own cabin, in my own room, and in my own bed. It all happened so quickly, I briefly thought it was all just a nasty dream. But when I drew a breath, it hurt like hell. So, not a dream.

It was dark outside and felt late, like the middle of the night, and Evie sat on a chair next to my bed in the cone of warm light cast by my bedside lamp. She leaned over me, close, hand over her eyes. She might have been crying or sleeping.

"I could slide over," I said, gasping a little. Turns out it hurt to talk, too.

She uncovered her eyes. "Oh, Hardy!"

"I told you he'd recover." Someone moved, out on the dark edges of the room. I knew the voice without looking. Nurse Maxine. I felt myself blush in semidarkness.

"You here, too?" It all seemed a little unreal. "Did I really get shot?"

"Oh, yeah." Maxine stepped into the light. "Four, maybe five times. I can tell it hurts you now and it will likely hurt worse, especially if you try to do anything." She was fiddling with something that turned out to be a silver syringe she upended into a small vial. "In fact, back in nursing school, I learned the technical term for how bad it's going to hurt." She flicked the syringe with her middle finger. "That's why I'm about to give you some morphine."

I did my best to ignore the syringe. It looked too big, like something left over from veterinary medicine, maybe horse care. "A technical term?" I asked her.

"It's going to hurt... like a son-of-a-bitch," she said. "But this should help." She was right, it did hurt that bad.

She prepped a vein in my arm, neatly injected me, and I could feel the wonderful stuff flowing through my body, melting and dissipating pain.

The next time, it was daylight that woke me. Maxine was gone but Evie hadn't moved. This time though, I could tell she was sleeping. I hated to wake her.

"I've got to get up and pee."

She opened her eyes. "It's gonna hurt, even with the morphine. I've got a jar here if you want to try that."

I thought about it. "No, I want to get up. Will you help me?"

"You know I will."

She was right. Even with the morphine, it hurt. I never knew crawling out from under bedcovers could be so difficult and painful. It took both of us. It wasn't until I was finally standing that I realized I didn't have many clothes on, in fact, just underwear briefs and a t-shirt. I looked at me, then looked at Evie looking at me. It was the closest to undressed I had ever been with her.

"Nice." She took my arm and helped me ease out of my bedroom and down the short hall and into the bathroom. When she had me in place, she went out and closed the door.

"I feel kind of silly," I called out to her.

"Why?"

"Because I'm shot four or five times and I'm standing here in my underwear."

"Concentrate on what matters." Finished and flushed I opened the door, meeting her eyes. "You're alive. We're here together. I get to see you in your underwear." She giggled. She was right, of course, though not necessarily about seeing me in my underwear.

It wasn't until I was on my way back from the bathroom, moving a little better but still appreciating the help, when I realized I didn't have any bandages. Well, okay, I had a wrap of taped gauze around my right thigh, but nothing on my chest, which hurt the worst, by far.

Standing in front of my dresser mirror, I pulled up my t-shirt. There was no trouble telling I'd been shot at least four times, with distinct bruising already forming up purple and overlapping, each about the size of a dessert plate.

"No bullet holes!"

"You were lucky." Evie eased my t-shirt back down and took my arm. "Let's get you back flat. Andy thinks you were shot with a .22 firing a 'short' cartridge, like target shooters use. The bullets aren't meant to go too far and so don't do much damage, especially through all the layers of winter clothing you had on. She listed: t-shirt, waffle shirt, flannel shirt, wool vest, parka. Did I miss anything? I think one of them hit your belt, too, so that bruise is smaller and kind of mixed in with the others. You were *so* lucky."

"It wasn't luck. Molly saved me. The prowler was closing in on me, still shooting, when she let go with that .410 of hers."

"Gutsy," said Evie. "He might have turned on her."

"How can I repay something like that?"

"No one expects you to. She was just doing the right thing, as you were." Off in the distance, I heard a knock and someone coming in.

Evie looked up and smiled. "You made it."

"Took off as soon as the fog cleared." It was Frank Jacobs. He stepped into the room and over by my bedside

269

to peer down at me, a concerned look on his face. "You still alive?"

"Just barely."

He shook his head gravely. "We need to figure out how to keep you that way." He began peeling out of his outerwear.

Evie looked at him. "Did you bring Andy?"

"Oh, yeah. You know him. Do you really think I could keep him from coming? He went straight to the site to dig for shell casings. We're pretty sure this is the same perp as shot at Hardy before. It would be nice to know for certain."

"Perp?" said Evie. "I love it when you talk cop."

"You like that?" He smiled at her, then assumed a hopeful look. "Got any coffee?"

"For you," she said.

"For me, too?" I asked.

"Especially for you." She leaned over to kiss my forehead then headed off to the kitchen.

Jacobs dropped onto Evie's vacated chair. He pulled a small pad and a ballpoint pen out of his uniform shirt pocket.

"Tell me something," he said. When I hesitated, he said, "Tell me everything."

So, I told him about the night, the fog, Jack finding the tracks, looking at the tracks with the flashlight—trying to be cautious—then seeing the gunshot flashes. I don't remember much after that, but I vividly remember Molly shooting the top off the evergreen, and the way the blast from her shotgun stopped the advancing shooter in his tracks. "She saved my life."

"Yeah," he agreed, "I'm afraid a face shot could have finished you. Those shorts will bounce off thick clothing or a skull, but not an eye or a nasal passage." He shook his head and stared away at nothing.

"That creep has been playing with you until now. This is serious. This is... something different. He's decided you're the enemy. You'd be dead if the fool had a real gun." He turned to look me in the eyes. "You do know that... right?"

"If I didn't yesterday, I do today," I told him.

"See that you remember."

"This isn't Ray," I said.

"You certain?"

"No."

When Evie brought us coffee, she set mine down and came to prop me up with pillows. I heard another quick knock and my front door opening.

"Hello?" It was Andy's voice. He came into the house and then followed our voices, certifiably crowding the small bedroom. He arrived with his nose working. "Coffee, I'm just in time."

The marshal looked up from sipping his. "Find any brass?"

"Oh, yeah, a ton. He was shooting all the way across the yard and these little shorts don't have enough weight to get lost in snow. He opened his hand and I saw the dull sheen of brass. "I got..." He counted. "sixteen. Almost two full clips. This guy was serious. Changed magazines half way. But he's still a crummy shot."

Evie brought his coffee. He smiled at her. "Thanks," and she leaned her cheek over for a kiss, which he provided.

Andy turned to the marshal. "What we gonna do about this guy?"

271

Jacobs made a glum face. "You're already doing it. Armed patrols, locked doors... I was beginning to think he'd moved on. It's been quiet so long. Now this."

"Us, too," I added.

"I'll put a guy here," Jacobs said, "for a week or so, or until I need him worse somewhere else. Sometimes having a uniform around makes a difference. But we all know, and the prowler will know, that it can't be permanent. So, he'll just lay low until we leave, and start up again."

"I've got a theory," said Andy, looking in my direction. "All of a sudden this guy seems to have it in for you. Why you? Why now? We all been patrolling but you're the only one gets shot at. Repeatedly. I used to think he was tryin' to miss you. Now it's pretty clear he's tryin' to hit you."

I didn't think so, and shook my head. "I know it seems that way. But last night wasn't even my night. It was supposed to be Vic patrolling. He called last minute to ask if I could fill in. He had a sore throat. If it had been him out... and he'd seen the tracks... we'd all be sitting around his bed looking at him."

Jacobs looked at Andy. "That shoots the heck out of your theory."

"Yeah," said Andy. "Seems like." But he didn't look convinced.

Jacobs stood. "I'm going back out to talk to Molly."

"Talked to her," said Andy. "She woke up hearing shots. Looked out... it was dark, couldn't see much but recognized Hardy... mostly because of the dog. Saw the tall guy coming across her yard shooting. She opened the door and pumped out a blast from the .410. By the time she reloaded, the guy had disappeared. One thing, though."

I could feel the marshal's interest quicken. "What's that?"

"The guy wasn't too good on snowshoes. She said he kept stepping on his own edges and nearly fell."

"Well," said the marshal, "that's something."

* * *

It was a week before I could begin to forget I'd been shot. Any movement—sitting, standing, turning—hurt. I mean a lot. Enough to make my breath catch. Chopping wood was out. Heck, tying my own mukluks was out. So, I managed by doing what any tough old sourdough would do. I moped, caught up on letters, sermons, books I'd promised myself, and eating lunch daily at the Coffee Cup, where I could count on Rosie to fuss over me.

Vic and Linda came to see me, him still croaky and snotty with his cold. "I'm sorry it was you out there getting shot at."

"Me too. But if it hadn't been me, then it could have been—would have been—you."

"Oh, yeah," he said. "In that case, it's probably just as well it was you."

"Victor!" exclaimed Linda, and gave him a faux swat. "He didn't mean it," she told me earnestly.

"Sure, he did," I told her. They went out laughing, him blowing his nose.

In the meantime, everything settled back. Andy and Marshal Jacobs went back to Fairbanks, Evie went back to teaching, and Maxine found others who needed care. There was nothing more to be done with or for me, but to watch my extensive pattern of bruises change color, from purple to brown to a sick shade of yellow-green, and finally to begin to fade. By then, I had begun being able to move again.

One of the first items on my list was to take my new Winchester out to sight-in the Unertl scope. It was said Unertl only made these scopes for the Marine Corps, though mine didn't have the Marine Corps stamp, which would most likely indicate it had been stolen. Except that William's scope, which *did* have the stamp hadn't been stolen—at least according to him. He said his was the gift of a grateful nation.

I'd heard, mostly from Andy, that the Unertl was the scope of choice for modern snipers. About two feet long and three-quarters of an inch thick, widening at the front, it took up most of the top of my rifle. It certainly looked snazzy.

So, on a sunny day, with the temperature a balmy minus ten, I fixed a moose meat sandwich and a couple of Pilot Breads with peanut butter. Then I successfully tied my own mukluks, gingerly donned all my layers and my parka—lifting my arms still hurt—called my dog, and shouldered my new hunting rifle. We'd been inactive for a couple of weeks, leaving Jack at first reluctant to abandon his favored spot by the heat register. But as we stepped off the porch and it finally penetrated his doggy brain that we were really headed out on an adventure, he tucked his tail, splayed his feet and began to do his puppy run around me in circles, barking and generally carrying on.

Directly across the river from town stood the only real hill for miles. A bit of hillside there, once closed and fenced as railroad property, formed a reliable backstop for bullets and, as most of the fence had fallen down, had become the town's unofficial shooting range.

I set out on snowshoes across the river in that direction, almost due north. A short hike up from river ice and just over the railroad tracks, brought me to the spot, a natural cutout. It was protected for several hundred feet by mounds of old shale and gravel that had sloughed off the main hillside, enclosing three sides and forming the perfect shooting gallery. Much used locally in all seasons, it would be littered with spent brass when the snow melted.

I took along a couple of fresh, steel, Olympia beer empties for targets, rescued from the trash bin behind the Bide-A-While. Every couple of years someone built or rebuilt a target stand with a backdrop for tacking paper targets and a shelf for objects like cans or bottles. To be sure, there would be target cans at the site that I could dig in the snow to find, but they would be already riddled and lacey from previous shooters.

By the time we got there and I stamped out a shooting path of about fifty yards and set up my targets, the sun had moved around to full south, at a low winter altitude directly behind me. With an almost cloudless sky, on an almost windless day, I had perfect conditions for shooting. My first out-of-doors glance through the Unertl was literally an eye opener. I could darn near read the writing on the Oly can!

Andy had roughly adjusted the scope back in my kitchen, but it would still require a bit of fine tuning, according to the instruction manual I'd been studying. I missed with the first shot and the second, then paused to recheck the instructions and make several minute adjustments with the silver, knurled knobs. Shot number three winged one of the cans, catching it low, blasting it high and back, spinning like a center field pop fly. With a bit more adjustment, number four hit the beer logo dead on, as did shot five, leaving me—I admit—very pleased with myself, and out of targets.

I carefully leaned the Winchester next to my snowshoes, against a standing remnant of old wire fencing, and slogged laboriously up to re-set my targets. Jack, who pointedly stayed at my side as I shot, now danced circles around me, diving and driving through snowdrifts like a torpedo, then leaping straight up out of the snow, propelled by the sheer joy of it.

I retrieved the Oly cans and got them set up. As I turned to head back, I heard a quick *zip*, then the *whack* of a bullet hitting the target backdrop, and finally the *KA-BLAM* of a heavy gun as the sound caught up and echoed off the hill.

I didn't drop to the ground and scramble for cover. Although the bullet hit in my vicinity, it was nothing like a 'near' miss, though certainly near enough. In the time it took to turn around, to see who was shooting my way, I made up a narrative about some anxious shooter coming up the hill and over the tracks, just blasting one off at the backdrop, without even thinking there might be someone else up here using the range.

"Hey!" I shouted. "Watch out! I'm over here." I waved my arms, already imagining the embarrassed look on the shooter's face when he realized. Then he shot again. Again, I heard the *zip* and the *whack*, and saw an eye wink open in the plywood as the bullet passed through.

I flat out dove into the snow to get out of the line of fire. The only embarrassment for this shooter? That he'd already missed me twice.

CHAPTER 30

I was trapped like a rat. I'd been right about this spot as the perfect shooting gallery, and now I'd become the yellow tin duck.

Whether he thought we were playing or thought he'd better get the heck out of sight, Jack came on the run from somewhere to throw himself down in the snow alongside me. I got an arm over him, relieved I didn't have to worry about the shooter targeting him because he couldn't see me.

The snow was still soft and deep enough to make us a poor target, for this moment, at least. I shucked my right mitt and dug in my parka pocket for the .38, trying to remember if I'd grabbed any extra shells. I thought I had. I rolled around in the snow, checking pockets, finally finding six more bullets tucked in my wool vest pocket. Eleven possible shots with a two-inch barrel. There were people who could hit a man-size target at more than a hundred feet with one of these, but so far I hadn't been one of them.

"We're in deep trouble," I said to Jack, who smiled at me, rolling out his long pink tongue, and thumping his tail. "Well *I'm* worried," I told him, even if he wasn't.

I raised my head to risk a look. The shooter popped off another one and I heard it hit, but not close. He either wasn't trying to hit me at all or he was a terrible shot. But he had me where he wanted me, and at only about two hundred feet. There was almost no way he *couldn't* hit me, sooner or later. The shooter had positioned himself low, just on the other side of the railroad tracks, backed by full sun. I squinted in his direction, then ducked my head, closing my eyes. Opening them, I saw only a residual purple ball in my field of vision where the orb of sun had been. I dug in my other pocket for sunglasses.

I felt my heart thumping in my chest, and throwing up wasn't out of the question. I did a quick inventory of who might be able to help me out of this predicament. Evie and Vic were still in school and Andy, all the way in Fairbanks. I didn't know where William or Oliver might be. But from here, the chance of any of them just happening along to help turn the tide looked pretty slim. And no, I hadn't remembered to tell anyone where I was going, or to leave a note. *Dumb, dumb, dumb!* They wouldn't even know where to look for the body.

On the other hand, in less than an hour, the sun would start down. Having it fall behind the raised railroad embankment would make it harder for the shooter to see and easier for me.

I risked another look, just as the shooter rose, carelessly, visible from about the waist up. I admired his leisure as he positioned his rifle, aimed and squeezed off another round in my direction. It hit one of the target posts behind me about twelve feet, and when I looked, saw it had blasted away a big chunk of weathered wood.

The shooter left himself exposed. With my rifle leaning closer to him than to me, it was clear he felt safe. It would be nice to put a hole in at least his confidence. I cocked the .38 and aiming carefully, squeezed off a round in his direction. I didn't get anything like a near miss, but the bullet hit one of the steel rails, making an echoing *thwack*, and then a noisy and dangerous-sounding ricochet *ping* and its echoes. He dove for cover! It was hard not to smile. Even though I still might die, I could die with a measure of satisfaction. This wasn't turning out to be the turkey shoot he had imagined, not when the turkey could shoot back. I started crawling.

If he wasn't reloading right now, hunkered down and safe, then he was probably about empty. He'd fired five rounds, which would empty a good many of the local guns. Unless he was using a magazine of some kind. He didn't seem like the magazine type. In fact, he didn't even seem like the rifle type. He wasn't good at it.

Sure enough, I saw his head raise, saw the rifle come over. I wanted to duck, but by now was willing to bet he couldn't hit me even if he could see me, and I held still. I didn't have to find out. He squeezed the trigger. Nothing! I heard the trigger mechanism snap from here. Empty. I got up and ran for my rifle.

I wasn't fast. The snow lay too deep and too soft for fast footwork. I made it about two-thirds of the way when I saw him come up over the rails again, aim, and fire. Again, I dove, my dog at my side. I don't know where the bullet hit. I checked Jack. He was fine, still smiling. He seemed to think whatever we were doing was a whole lot of fun. I ruffled his ears.

This much closer at a lower angle, I didn't get the sun in my eyes as badly, though I still saw the shooter—when he hiked up—outlined in gold. Even though he seemed intent on killing me, in that instant he looked like an angel. *Maybe the angel of death!* Who knew the angel of death would come carrying a .30-06?

I fired again, this time hitting on the near side of the rails, spattering my assailant with tiny stinging missiles of pulverized rock, propelling him down and out of sight. *Hah!* But I got a better look at him. He wore a full-face black military balaclava. Unless he got a chip in one of his

279

eyes, the fragments were unlikely to hurt him. But I felt good about seeing him throw himself down.

As if to keep my high spirits in check, he rose and fired off three rounds, as quickly as he could bolt them, hitting nothing, ducking back behind the rails.

The 'wrong thing' about this was that I kept running closer to the man who apparently wanted me dead. But with only a box canyon at my back, what other choice did I have? Trying to climb out, up the hill, would make me the easiest possible target. This kind of predicament happened to TV cowboy Roy Rogers on an almost weekly basis. What did Roy do? Tried to not get shot and called his magic horse. That was my problem. I forgot to bring my magic horse.

The next time I chanced a look, I saw the intensity of the sunlight ratchet back, the lens of the day closing down. I felt the worst of the intense light finally stop stabbing at my eyes. It helped.

I was now only about forty feet from the Winchester. My problem? I'd nearly halved my distance to the shooter. Even a lousy shooter could get lucky if I kept running closer.

Then I heard something distant, so faint I might have missed it—except for desperation. A train whistle. I knew where it was, knew exactly where it was. The train always blew for the crossing at North Chandalar, just about a mile from here. It would be here, shooting right past me, in a little more than a minute. Not that I had a minute to spare.

Feeling confident, and apparently not hearing the train, the shooter rose, stood looking in my direction, fired off a shot that missed widely, and then took a step over the far rail. I snapped off a round with the .38 and he ducked, but took another step and fired again.

I fired back, three quick shots, in the hope of keeping him in place. If he'd just keep standing there on the sleepers, I wouldn't have to shoot him. In about a minute he'd be train fodder. If only he didn't make shooting me his last act on earth. He stepped to the near rail, put his foot up on it, steadied himself and shot again. He was now only about sixty feet from me, the misses a lot closer, the last one *zipping* just over my head. Jack was the sensible one, he wanted to get out of there, to run. It took all I had to hold the big husky tight to the ground. I still hoped to get both of us out of there alive.

It was his foot on the rail that warned him. Wearing a parka hood and a balaclava—probably with ears ringing from all the rifle shots—he didn't hear the low rumble of the train approaching. But he did feel the vibrations. I saw his gaze fall abruptly to his foot on the rail, and then off to his left to see what must have appeared a huge, blue and gold diesel locomotive filling his field of vision.

I heard the panic squeal of brakes, the scream of steel sliding on steel. The engineer's frantic blast on the whistle, hanging, echoing, shivering the very air, assaulting our ears. Magnified as it was by the steep hill and the rock, the sonic blast nearly lifted the shooter off the ground. He had seconds to move or become a moose-like ornament on the snowplow. That would be my vote.

At the last second, he whirled and dashed away, the train suddenly sweeping into—filling—my view, bored passengers in the windows looking out to see what was the fracas. I could imagine one bored traveler saying to another, 'Look, there's a man about to be murdered,' and the equally bored spouse, without looking up from her potboiler replies, 'That's nice, dear.'

I ran for my rifle. I knew he could still nail me by ducking low and timing his fire between the rumbling, rolling, wheel trucks. By running, I was betting he wouldn't or couldn't. He hadn't hit anything he actually aimed at yet. I knew these trains, their length and duration. I had but six or seven cars' time to get to my Winchester, snatch it up, and bolt a shell into the chamber. I checked that the safety was off and, dropping to one knee, drew a careful bead on where my assailant had last been, waiting only for the last of the train to flow by.

When it did, he was gone, completely gone. It was nearly startling, like a magic trick. Now you see him, now you don't.

As the rumble and vibration faded, I cautiously stepped up on the embankment, half expecting him to rise and snap off what had better, at this distance, be his 'kill' shot. But he didn't. He wasn't here. He had left the party. Then from the slight rise of the rails, I caught sight of him down the grade. He struggled desperately to bound through deep snow, back down toward the river. At two-or-three-hundred feet he was nothing but an easy shot for me with the scope. I raised the rifle, centered the crosshairs on the middle of his back and in that second, wanted desperately to squeeze the trigger. He had become a target I wanted to hit. Not a living human being whose murder while running away I'd have to explain or cover up, neither choice being 'right' with my day job and the man I claimed to be.

So, I did something immature and immensely satisfying. My would-be assassin, half falling down the hill through deep snow with only one hand free, had to reach out to catch tree branches to keep from overbalancing, rolling and tumbling down. I began to shoot off the branches, one by one. Each time he grabbed one, I shot it loose. By the third branch, he lost it completely, going into free fall, rolling, flailing, completely losing his snowshoes. Between the near miss with the train and the careening, shooting-gallery tumble down the hill, if he hadn't soiled himself by now, I didn't know why.

I called Jack, who came running, bounding joyfully through the snow. We were finished shooting for the day. The rifle worked, we hadn't been murdered, and were heading home with a hair-raising story for Andy. All in all, it had gone pretty well.

CHAPTER 31

"You shot off the tree limbs! Sorry I missed it." Andy laughed, but not much. "He could have killed you."

I stirred canned milk into my coffee, the spoon tinkling against the side of the ceramic mug. "He gave it his all. He was just a plain shitty shot."

"I hope that's not a complaint."

We were in my kitchen before sunup on a Saturday in January, safe, warm, no one shooting at us, with Evie expected after she'd had time to sleep in.

Andy fixed me with a steely gaze. "But *was* it the prowler?"

"He was wearing a mask." I couldn't help the shrug. "But yes, it's how I'd bet. He was tall, thin..."

"Shooting at you," Andy added.

"... and missing. A really poor shot."

Andy took a sip. "Yep, it was him."

For a couple of minutes, we sat without speaking, something friends can do without effort. I knew what we were both thinking, that there had to be some way to trap this guy, close him down, make Chandalar safe again.

Truth, I'd never thought of our town as a particularly safe place. A big part of my 'business' was death. Death by gunshot, drowning, freezing, collisions with car, train, or moose, and all forms of alcohol. But until recently, homes and vehicles had always been unlocked, people would open their cabin doors, unreservedly, at any hour of the day or night, and willingly rush to help anyone who needed it. In the summer, kids played outside around the clock, without any sense of danger from other humans. So, it had been a safe place and needed to be again.

At about ten, Vic and Linda showed up, then William, and closer to eleven, Evie finally arrived. She came around behind, wrapped her arms around my neck and leaned over to kiss me. "Oh, get a room," said Andy, predictably.

"Or get married," said Linda, making what was supposed to be an excited-looking face, like she might be the first one to voice a really good idea we hadn't thought of. Evie just smiled and raised her eyebrows, like she agreed, but said nothing. Then she let go of me to go pour her coffee.

"We need to set a trap." That was Vic's idea.

"For the marriage?" That was Andy. Evie gave him a mock hard look and he pretended to wilt.

"For the prowler," said Vic.

Andy straightened on his stool. "We did that already." He waved a hand dismissively. "You were there. The prowler knew. Somehow he knew."

"Someone told someone," added William. "It is a small town and word travels quickly." He looked around. "We all know we can trust each other, but one of us is talking to someone else, someone we can't trust." He looked around and leaned in a bit, confidentially. I think the rest of us did too. "But I do have an idea.

"We have been walking about, patrolling. We are easy to see and easy to avoid. When we head off to one end of town, the other end is wide open."

Andy looked at him. "Yeah!" He said it with several syllables, like 'Okay, that's obvious.'

"So, what do we do different?" I asked.

William turned to look at my new Winchester and scope. I'd been cleaning it and left it leaning in the corner next to the refrigerator. He reached to pick it up and nodded his head at the scope.

285

"We patrol the whole town at once. Andy, you, me... we all have exceptional scopes that allow us to take a position and survey the whole street to its end. With one or two streetlights operating in each direction, and any kind of moon at all, we will know who is out walking about. And they won't know we are watching." He put the rifle back in its corner. "But we must tell no one."

We did that for a week, stood out in the cold from eleven to three, scoping three different streets. We saw moose, wolves, owls, known drunks staggering home, but no prowler, no mysterious stranger, no one to suspect.

We decided to give it up, and told the group the next Saturday. "We tried," said Vic, who hadn't tried at all. Without a scope, he'd been snug and warm, sleeping, while we'd been out standing around with our rifles. "It was a good effort," he said as he went out.

When the others had gone, William fixed Andy and me with one of his sneaky looks.

"Let us," he said, "give it another week or two without proclamation."

"You mean secret," said Andy.

William nodded and I heard him sigh. "If that's possible."

We spent nights, for most of the next two weeks, standing out in the cold with rifles and scopes. I saw several moose and William saw a bear. Andy reported seeing lynx and a good number of wolves prowling town, but nothing more.

Finally, very early on Thursday morning, January 23, I saw a movement in my scope all the way down at the end of Setsoo. It turned out to be a small wild creature that at first I couldn't recognize. But then I did and started running. In the crosshairs, I had made out the figure of a small child, bundled in parka, mitts and mukluks, out alone in darkness on a minus-thirty-degree night.

I didn't run right up to the child, which might be scary, but stopped about thirty feet away and walked closer. It was young Henry Joseph, Molly's boy. His words chilled me more than the cold temperature.

"Mama gone," he sobbed.

CHAPTER 32

Warning Henry to cover his ears, aiming at the dark, steep hill across the river, I fired three shots. The noise left my ears ringing and a cloud of gun smoke hanging around us, reluctant to dissipate in the chill night air. I saw a couple of lights snap on in nearby cabins, doors opening, men stepping out as they bundled into parkas, carrying long guns. Soon I saw Andy and William as they jogged in, rifles held ready.

In short order, there were six of us, armed and alarmed. I turned to the men. "It sounds like the prowler has Molly."

"Mama gone," added Henry.

"Oh, shit," said Andy.

I scooped up Henry. "We need to check the cabin first." The group turned as one and we hurried up one block and over one block to where her cabin sat. We found lights on, the door closed, a fire in the stove, no sign of a struggle, and no sign of Molly.

Andy looked at the door, and looked at Henry. "I don't get it. He's not big enough to get himself completely dressed and out the door." We pondered that.

William turned to the group. "The prowler probably dressed him, let him out the door and aimed him for town."

"Why?" I asked. "Why would he do that?"

He looked grim. "Because Henry's mother is not coming back and, left by himself, he would most likely freeze to death before anyone found him. Oddly, an act of kindness."

"Hah!" said Andy. "Maybe. But it was also a message, a taunt. The cocky bastard wants to make sure we know he has her. And now we do." He looked around at the group.

"We need more searchers with more guns. Everybody go wake up one or two and get them to do the same." He quickly divided the group into four quadrants. "Don't shoot each other," he cautioned. He and I would head out together among those who searched south. He looked at me. "We need to drop Henry with Evie."

"You sure?" I asked. He nodded. "Okay," I said, but knowing how it would go. When we got there, I let Andy tell her.

She answered the door looking sweet but rummy. I admit I had forgotten it was after three. She had wrapped up in her pink bathrobe, her revolver half hidden behind her thigh. She immediately recognized Henry and put her hand to her mouth.

"Oh, no!"

Andy nodded. "Molly's been taken. We're going to search and need you to stay here and watch Henry."

She looked at him, turned to make a sweet baby face at Henry and tickled him under the chin, then looked at me. It wasn't an I-want-to-tickle-you look.

"Your idea?" I shook my head, raising both hands in a shrug. So, she turned on Andy. "Hell, no," she said. "I'm *not* staying here. In fact, *I'm* going to get dressed and load my rifle while *you* get Henry over to Maxine, who *is* set up for children and would rather not join the search." She leaned in. "You got it?"

Andy ducked his head and flung up an arm for cover. "Okay, okay... I get it... I'm on my way," and he handed me his rifle, taking Henry, holding him close, and hurrying away up the snowy trail. "We'll go to Auntie Maxine's," I heard him say.

Evie turned to me. "Come in where it's warm," she said in a lighter tone. She turned away, then turned back,

289

taking me by my parka lapels, kissing me. "You're learning," she said.

* * *

We picked up—woke up—Vic and then Oliver. Oliver got up quickly enough but waking Vic took a lot of banging on his door. I knew Linda had gone to Anchorage for a week, and had begun to think he went along. When he finally answered, he looked rough and dull, drugged almost, so much that when we told him Molly had been taken, his first reaction was to shake his head like we were going too fast for him, mumbling, "Molly who?" We suggested coffee, told him to hurry up, and ultimately had to go on without him.

We continued door-to-door through the town, checking cabins, checking for chimney smoke at unoccupied cabins, talking to sleepy, startled people. Most of the men nodded knowingly, and without being asked, slid into their heavy-weather gear and loaded up a rifle. Of the three hundred fifty people in town this time of year, we had at least seventy-five searching, mostly men. It didn't help. There was simply no sign.

To make matters worse, we were heading back for breakfast when Andy stopped in the middle of the snowy street and looked around. "Warming up," he said. "Hope it don't snow." Within minutes, snow began, a few small flakes at first. I didn't see them in the darkness, just felt my nose start to tickle. Then sure enough, snow.

Within about an hour, we had larger flakes, coming down heavy on an insistent wind. It moaned and muttered while driven snow filled tracks and trails, smoothing and erasing any possible signs we might have found and followed. It felt like the world had given up on Molly,

290

throwing a heavy blanket over us, over her and over any chance we might have had of finding her alive.

Back at the rectory, Evie, Andy, and I chewed our untasted breakfast. Sipping our coffee, not saying much, we glanced out the window as the sun rose, the light grown thick and flickery with falling snow.

I had called the marshal as soon as we got back. "Oh, no," he said. Then, "Guess we knew this was going to happen." I agreed.

"Snowing heavy here," he said.

"Here, too."

"No flying out of here today," he said. I admit I thought he was telling me he wouldn't be coming. It felt like one more heavy anvil of discouragement dropping into our pockets.

"I'll catch the train," he said. And I felt better. "But it won't be a quick ride. See you, probably early afternoon."

Breakfast finished, dishes done, Andy dropped into an easy chair closed his eyes and began to snore. No surprise. We'd been up and moving all night. I felt lost. Evie went to stand by my sofa, looking lost, too, then turned to me and opened her arms. I walked into them and we held each other for a long time. "C'mon," she said, lying down, stretching out and pulling me next to her, nesting like spoons in the too-narrow space. I tossed a 'throw' over us, colorfully crocheted in brown, yellow, and orange, by a kind lady in Alabama. Feeling the warmth of her along my back, resting my head on a sofa pillow, I remember thinking, *I won't sleep.*

We woke when the marshal came in just a little after two. He quickly knocked, then stepped in propelled by wind and driving snow. He walked into the living room without taking off his parka or even setting down his rifle, seeing us waking. "Oops," he said. "Bet you people were sleeping. Probably had a long night."

"We *were* sleeping." Andy climbed out of his chair. Yawning and stretching he headed for the kitchen where I heard him put on water to boil. We'd have coffee soon. I needed it.

"Train couldn't make any time in the snow." The marshal began to peel. "I heard we averaged about twenty-five miles an hour coming down. Couldn't see anything out the side windows, either. It was like a tunnel of moving snow."

I got up so Evie could get up. She went over to the marshal on her way to the bathroom, patting him on the arm without saying anything. He smiled at her. "She sure is cute," he said when she'd gone.

"I heard that," came her distant voice.

"Sure is," I agreed.

"That, too!"

"Nothing wrong with her hearing," said the marshal.

Having us all ready and in place didn't help. The wind kept blowing and the snow kept falling. The weatherman in Fairbanks wouldn't even guess how long this could go on.

"Had it snow for a solid week once," said Andy, pushing down the French press piston, leaning down to breathe the coffee aroma, and smiling. "Hope to never have *that* happen again." He looked around like there might be someone listening who had influence with the weather gods. Shrugging, he poured.

Yawning, selecting mugs, filling them, doctoring or not doctoring our coffee, we nearly staggered to the tippy stools. Andy, Evie, and I settled on our elbows, and tried to fight our way out of the fog.

The marshal looked at us. "Buck up, people."

Andy raised his eyes. "Hard to buck up when we know this creep is somewhere, doing something horrible to someone we care about."

The marshal took a sip of his coffee and set down the mug.

"Unless he's not."

Andy sat up straighter. "Whaddya mean?"

"Let's think about it. When he grabbed Alice, he didn't take her out of town because he wanted us to find her. I think he was playing with us on that one. Marjorie, he took out of town. I'm sorry to say, but guys like this enjoy hearing their victims scream. You can't fart in a town like this without everybody knowing it. So, you can't have a woman screaming. He's got to take her away."

Evie woke up. "Ugh. I don't like hearing that." She thought about it a minute. "And with the storm, he didn't have time to take her away?"

The marshal shrugged. "Maybe not. Is anybody away... unaccounted for?"

We all thought about that, revulsed anew by the idea that someone we know is not around because he's out torturing and killing Molly."

Evie shuddered. "It *can't* be someone we know, can it?"

"It's a small town," Andy said. "Is there anyone here we *don't* know at least a little?"

"I don't think you can count on knowing everybody," Jacobs said. "But know him or not, the bad weather hit without much warning, just about the time he took her. So maybe—*maybe*—this prowler is just as delayed as we are."

"Boy," said Andy. "Boy! That almost seems like too much to hope for."

Jacobs took another sip. "Might as well hope for something."

Just before five, Evie switched on the radio for weather. We had shifted to trying to figure out what to fix for dinner for people who felt like they were too upset to eat. "Got to keep your strength up," said Jacobs.

The radio tubes warmed up to a man singing about his chainsaw. 'You're in luck when you got a McCulloch chain saw,' and then the news.

A Chandalar woman, Molly Joseph, was missing, presumed kidnapped. The territorial highway patrol had set up roadblocks north and south, and authorities were watching train stations down the line, as well as what they now called the Fairbanks International Airport, even though it was only a couple of buildings and a windsock. There'd been no sight of her.

Elsewhere, a ferry sank off an island in Japan, killing one hundred sixty-seven. It was horrible, I knew it was horrible, and briefly imagined their last minutes. But it was somewhere else, a long way away.

Sputnik, the Soviet's ultimate space triumph, fell out of orbit after traveling some seventy million miles. They immediately launched another. The U.S. was planning a launch soon, something they were calling Explorer 1. If the Soviets could go into space, we certainly could.

The weather? No end in sight. The weather service predicted an accumulation of at least twenty-four inches. Andy looked up from water he was boiling in a big pot, for pasta.

"How can you tell how much snow accumulates if you don't know how long the snowstorm will last? That's just

294

crazy." He shook his head and eyeballed a measure of brittle spaghetti noodles. I envied him his cooking prowess. I felt the same about accumulations of pasta noodles as about snow. I just never knew how much I'd get.

It turned out, faced with pasta, tasty sauce, and moose meatballs, we managed to find our appetites. Later, all of us full and feeling better, drinking more coffee, Andy looked up from his mug.

"I got an idea."

"Had to happen," said the marshal, "sooner or later."

"Yeah, laugh it up. Listen. As soon as the snow quits, we go out and snowshoe the town perimeter."

"Looking for?" I asked him.

"Tracks! Nobody, or almost nobody, been out since yesterday. This prowler guy, he's gonna need to get out of town quick. He's either carrying Molly—so leaving *deep* snowshoe tracks—or more likely, he's dragging her on a deep-snow sled, like a toboggan, something that slides along the top."

Evie looked at him. "What if he just throws her in the trunk and drives her out?"

"Can't risk it," said Jacobs. "The highway patrol will be checking cars immediately north and south. And even if they aren't, would you risk being stopped with a woman in your trunk? I don't think so."

Evie made a face at him. "But it has to be dark. He's not going to make it out of town in daylight. He's going as soon as it begins to slack off, in the dark. He has to."

Andy looked around the table at us, nodding, a determined look on his face. "Then so will we."

CHAPTER 33

Rosie showed up at five, gung ho, wearing bright red lipstick and the black-framed glasses with her caribou-skin parka. She carried a .30-30 lever action and wore her pistol in a holster at her waist. She looked like a *Life* magazine photo with the caption, 'Glamour on the last frontier.' Andy had called her after dinner and told her the plan. Tired of not being able to do a single useful thing for Molly, she brought in someone to work her morning shift, 'gunned up,' and hurried over.

"Snow's done," she announced. "It'll be light in an hour or so. Let's get going."

There had been a good bit of debate around the dinner table about who would be in the search party. "Nobody else!" had been Andy's declaration, seconded by Frank Jacobs.

"There's a leak somewhere," he said. So, we had agreed to keep the circle small, calling William, of course, and Oliver.

Phone in hand, Evie looked over at me and raised her eyebrows. "Vic?"

"You know he doesn't get up very well. Early morning is not his friend. Let's let him sleep." We ended up in groups of two or three, nobody searching alone, which seemed needlessly risky.

The next twenty minutes or so saw the others arrive already on snowshoes since nothing had been plowed yet, everybody armed and determined looking.

Evie and I—Jack prancing and carrying on—along with Andy and Rosie, headed out the south trail. Just about a half-mile beyond the railroad tracks we split up. They turned east as we headed west.

The predawn glow revealed a landscape as white, untracked, and full of fresh promise as an artist's canvas. Sure enough, the last few flakes came straggling down and the wind settled, just about the time we headed out. We snowshoed down drifted city streets with no car tracks, and down trails with no human, sled, or dog tracks.

On the other hand, we found moose tracks in my driveway, wolf tracks in the near streets, and bear tracks before we made it out of town. Also snowshoe hare, lynx, possibly a wolverine, all in town as well.

With me in the lead and Evie right behind, we started west through a snow-softened and drifted silent world. There were no birdcalls, no distant dog barks and it was too early to hear vehicles from town or a train. The silence made us not want to say much, or if we did speak, to speak quietly, like we were in a library or church.

The day eventually dawned, somber, brooding, like it knew what we were up against and didn't hold out much hope. Whatever kind of winter-wonderland feeling we might have started with was gone, darkened and compressed until the very silence had weight.

We weren't fast on snowshoes, not like Andy who could actually run. But we were competent, plodding steadily along. I was happy to not trip, happy neither Evie nor Jack walked on the backs of my snowshoes, throwing me on my face in deep snow. After about an hour, we stopped for pilot bread with peanut butter, and hot coffee from a Thermos, and dried salmon bits for the dog. To my relief, Evie looked okay. I'd been worried about wearing her out.

She looked at me from out of her fur-ruffed parka hood, across her steaming Thermos cup. "Do you think we have this wrong? Should we be doing something else?"

297

"What?"

She shook her head. "I don't know."

I thought about it for a minute. "If the prowler walked out—dragged Molly out—last night, through the storm, then it's already over. If that happened, she's probably already dead. But it was pretty nasty last night. If Andy's right, if..."

She picked up my thought. "If he was stuck in town like the rest of us, then we should find tracks." She looked around like she might see some. "So far, nothing," she said. "I think we missed him." She twisted the Thermos lid tight and I turned to let her lift the canvas flap and stuff it in my daypack.

"Maybe we did, but he's got to come out somewhere. Someone will see tracks."

"I'm just feeling kind of hopeless," she said.

We started off again, grim and depressed. Within a hundred yards we came to a slight rise of stream bank, followed by a ramp down to snow-covered ice before rising again on the other side. By walking along the ice down in the creek bottom, a person—especially pulling a toboggan—would remain almost completely concealed. The way would be flat, smooth, and easy with no willow shoots or buried trees to catch a snowshoe or hook a sled.

That's where we found them. The tracks were here just like Andy predicted and described, the snowshoe tracks overlaid with a smooth sled print about sixteen inches wide.

We stopped, examined the tracks, then met each other's eyes. Evie looked tense, frightened.

"Look!" I pointed at the snowshoe tracks, where the one on the right frequently overlaid the one on the left.

"This is the guy who shot at me across the river. See how he steps on his snowshoe!"

She examined the tracks. "Yeah," she said. "It's him. What now?"

I pulled the Winchester off my shoulder, bolted a shell into the chamber and set the safety. Then I dropped my right mitt on its cord to pull the .38 out of my parka pocket, checking the load again, shells in all six chambers. I hoped I wouldn't trip and blow a hole in my leg.

"Did you set the safety?"

"There is no safety on a revolver."

She smiled. "I know. Just checking. Are you ready?"

"Ready as I'm gonna be." I started to turn, to follow the tracks, but Evie caught my arm, not ready to move.

"We need Andy."

She was right. That would be smarter and safer, but Andy wasn't here and as far as I knew, wasn't close.

"But we can't wait."

"No, I know that."

I wanted to send her to find Andy but didn't think she'd go. The trip would be easy but time consuming. All she had to do was follow our tracks back to Andy and Rosie's tracks and then keep going. It would be impossible to not catch up to them.

She chewed her lower lip. "You go on," she said, "follow the tracks. I'll take Jack and backtrack until I find Andy. If you get to where they are, and fire signal shots, at least the prowler will have to stop—whatever he's doing—won't he?"

I nodded.

"And if you do find them, you'll wait until Andy gets there, to close in. *Promise* me!"

"I do promise." I admit I was thinking, *If I can.*

"Okay, then." She kissed me. "Be safe." Then she whistled softly for Jack, smoothly kick-turned her snowshoes and made off back down the trail at a seemingly effortless near jog. So much for wearing her out.

I watched her power away, then turned. I had my own set of tracks to follow. I wondered how much farther out he would go. It would have to be to a cabin, someplace he could heat up. I didn't know this area, had never been out here before. But the prowler, caught up in some kind of mental state and dragging his victim, wasn't likely to go too far. At least that's how I saw it.

I couldn't help thinking of Molly as I walked, replaying scenes from my two-plus years here. Like all the times she and I and young Henry had rummaged for clothing in the mission barrel. Seeing her in church most Sundays, and how the two had showed up to join the party and eat moose ribs. She was so small, she almost seemed like a girl. Yet she had a child of her own, had the shape and bearing of a woman, had the steely courage of an Alaskan, and was known for being a good shot and an excellent hunter. My mind kept superimposing her likeness on my last memory of Marjorie. It made me angry and afraid. It also made me feel like I might need to stop and throw up.

I saw smoke before I smelled it, wood smoke, still showing white with moisture from the new fire. The trail had just led me up and out of the streambed when smoke came drifting toward me on a breeze out of the south. Hot in the stove and up the chimney, it quickly cooled in the frigid air, sinking, drifting along the ground.

In another moment or two I saw the cabin, nearly drifted in on one side to its eaves and several more feet of snow on the steeply-pitched roof. Built of logs, the footprint would measure about fifteen by twenty feet, probably one room, with a rusted tin stovepipe. It had two small windows in front, panes still in, with a pair of snowshoes and a toboggan leaned next to a planked door with a rope latch.

Still about one hundred feet distant, I walked far enough away from his tracks that he wouldn't see mine if he looked out. Circling in a loop to find cover behind a cluster of small swamp spruce, I set up just about fifty feet directly in front of the cabin door. Any closer and I'd be fully exposed.

My heart rate accelerated, thudding in my chest and in my ears. A burst of adrenalin jolted me, tightening already tight muscles until they quivered. Distantly, in the absolute dead silence, I heard an iron stove door squeak, and saw fresh, white smoke surge from the chimney as he fed up the fire. It had to be cold in there. Even if the prowler had come out here before the storm to prepare, and to build up a fire, that heat would be long gone. Before building the fire, the temperature inside would have been the same as outdoors, somewhere in the minus twenties. Any crime that involved exposing skin required heat and heat requires time, a blessing now that I was in place, waiting for Andy.

An hour went by, minute by minute. Nothing changed. With my body set for fight or flight, and nowhere to go, I rigged a seat on my snowshoes and settled down to wait. And twitch. For a long time, I just sat there, checking the front door, checking the trail. Nothing. That's when I decided to get closer. Looping out into the brush to conceal my tracks, I approached from the cabin's left side, around the corner from the door.

This close, I could easily hear a low voice, sometimes questioning, sometimes demanding. But I heard no answers.

In a few more minutes, I heard cloth rip, followed shortly by a hard *smack*, like a leather belt on bare flesh, and a cry, bitten off. I'd settled myself low, half sitting and half leaning on the wall. I jumped to my feet, clutching the .38, wanting desperately to do something, feeling torn. I looked north on the trail, hoping to see Andy come loping along and again saw nothing, though with most of the trail in the creek bottom, I wouldn't see him until he was here. Another smack, another brief cry. I clenched my teeth until my jaw muscle knotted and I had to open my mouth and finally force a yawn to stretch it loose.

Sneaking a look at the cabin front, I could see ice on the top window panes growing translucent and knew the cabin was warming. The prowler was on the clock here, and would know it. He had to do whatever he was going to do and get back to town before he was missed, or before searchers found him. Except for his own snowshoe trail, he could hide out here for a week without much danger. Now, as it happened, his own tracks led me directly here. Which got me thinking. *He has to be a greenhorn.* Who else would try to sneak out after a storm, leaving *the only* tracks to be seen on the landscape, and think no one would notice... that he would get away with it. *Who?*

I heard another sharp smack, then a series of smaller cries as something happened, something I couldn't hear. I had seen his handiwork before. Likely, he'd be tying her, stretching her in painful, vulnerable ways, doing a veritable macramé across her body, around her breasts, wrists, and ankles.

I found myself fearing the man inside. His very viciousness making him too big, too tough, and too mean to take on. What if I went running in there and couldn't beat him, couldn't save Molly? What if he knocked me down? Shot me? Would Andy arrive in time to make the difference?

From there I began to imagine shooting him, though I knew, or at least believed, I never would. It's against my calling, my upbringing, against everything I believe and against everything I've ever said to anybody. Love your neighbor, turn the other cheek, leave judgment to God. Just the same, I sat there in the snow, seeing myself lift the .38, aim it—not center mass—as instructed, but right between this stranger's angry, malevolent eyes. I knew him to be big and tall and I imagined him to be rough and hairy— heavy bearded, demonic. I began to hate—and fear—a face I didn't even know.

I heard more of the small cries, then a long, heart-rending near scream. A sound that had to be forced out of a person as quiet as Molly. I remember looking at the sky. Did I expect an angel with a flaming sword? There wasn't one. I stretched up as tall as I could to look down the trail for someone coming. Andy. Anybody. I saw no one. In that moment, I started around the corner. I gave up on secrecy, wading, punching footsteps through deep snow, knowing, finally, surely, that for better or for worse help was on the way. Not an angel with a flaming sword.

Me.

CHAPTER 34

I kicked the heavy door and it shuddered in, slamming wide, crashing into something as I drove through. Ducking forward, I had my gun out and up, ready to fire. What—*who*—I saw stopped me in my tracks, stunned me.

The prowler stood naked, but for the protection of snow boots on the icy floor. Tall and thin with a body completely unlike the monster I'd imagined. For one thing, pale and nearly hairless.

I saw Molly, completely naked on a table. She'd been tied intricately, painfully, with knees bound wide, and struck with a heavy leather belt. Dried blood on her nostrils and one side of her mouth showed she'd been hit on her face, too, probably when attacked at her cabin. I glimpsed her grimace of pain and fear, the whites of her eyes showing all around.

The prowler's right hand clutched the belt, and with the left hand, snatched up a .22 caliber semiautomatic, blasting off a shot. The shooter, clearly not left-handed, yanked the trigger, missing widely. Before the next shot, I stepped forward with the .38 stiff-armed at forehead height, and thumbed back the hammer. The prowler's gun barrel angled toward the ceiling and froze.

I saw the eyes shift from wild and frenzied back to the usual pleasant, harmless look. It was like knowing the devil had peeked out at you through the eyes of someone you thought was your friend.

After Alice's comment, I couldn't help glancing at the penis. She'd been right. It was the smallest I'd ever seen. As Alice said, smaller than *anyone*. And limp. For a sexual predator, this should have been the finest moment, completely aroused. But even this wasn't working.

Instead, caught in a terrible confusion of sexual pain, domination, and cruelty, the penis flopped uselessly, less than half erect, not likely to penetrate anything.

In stark contrast, the straight-stem pipe jutted proudly, clenched in the teeth. It looked like nothing so much as General Douglas MacArthur conquering something, or promising to return.

The prowler looked almost embarrassed, half smiling, shrugging. "This isn't what it looks like."

"Shut up," I said.

There was a noise behind me, Andy arriving. "I'm here," he said, knowing I wouldn't want to take my eyes off Linda. As if I could.

She had full breasts like a woman, but a tiny penis and scrotum and, right below, I thought I could see a small vaginal opening. No wonder she and Vic had little sex.

"Better close the door and cut Molly loose," I told him. "It's freezing in here." He closed the door and set to with his hunting knife, quickly slicing through the knotted handiwork. I could see Linda wince as the cords were cut carelessly away. She thought she'd really created something here.

Linda tried again. "You're making a big mistake."

I just shook my head at her. "Put the gun down slowly." I thought of all the time we spent together, work, laughs, coffee, Sundays she and Vic came to church. I thought of confiding our plans with them, for catching this prowler—her—and all the hours Vic patrolled... or pretended to patrol.

In that moment, looking back, the prowler had always, *obviously* been at least one of them. And yet I'd never seen it. None of us had ever seen it. None of us had ever wanted to.

"Gun. Down. Now," I said.

"Or what?"

"Or I'll shoot you in place."

"I don't think you'll shoot me." She looked a little crafty, testing, like she was figuring out how this could work, how far she could go. "You wouldn't shoot a woman."

I heard Andy's revolver hammer click back. "Do you think that about me, too?" Linda immediately set the .22 down on the floor.

I waved the .38 at her. "Drop the belt, too." She did.

By now, Andy had Molly freed and was helping her off the table. "My feet are numb," she said. Linda couldn't take her eyes off Molly's naked body.

"Outside," I told her. When she didn't start moving, I got around to the side and jabbed her with my gun barrel.

"Ouch! Alright, I'm going!" She took the pipe out of her mouth like she was about to launch into a story or tell a joke. I'd never seen a woman with a pipe before, but it looked so natural on her. Of course, I'd seen Vic do it a hundred times. "You do know it's minus thirty-something, and I'm only wearing boots?"

"Whose idea was that?" I poked her again. She pulled the door open and started out, me following.

"Let's get some clothes on you," I heard Andy say to Molly. Good luck. Everything she'd been wearing, Linda had sliced to pieces.

Outside, mounded, drifted snow lay still and silent. There was no wind, but for a naked woman, it was very, very cold. She wrapped her breasts in her skinny arms, which didn't help. "Are you going to leave me out here? Is that your plan, to let me freeze to death? Is that what God wants? That would make *you* a murderer." She unwrapped

306

one arm to emphasize with her pipe, as though lecturing, teaching me something important, something I hadn't thought of. The image would have been laughable except for the horror of it.

"You know," she said, her teeth starting to chatter, and I could see the wheels turning again. "You *could* let me go. I'd be out of here, out of your hair in a couple of hours. I could move to the East Coast maybe, or the Gulf. I'd never bother any more of your... women." She almost sneered when she said it, her familiar features twisting into a cruel stranger's face. "You like these brown ones, don't you?"

I shook my head to clear it. More than anything else in that moment, I wanted to shoot her. And even more than that, I wanted to keep shooting until the gun was empty. But then I started to think about Marjorie. And about Evie—what I'd tell her—and Molly, even though horribly abused by another woman, how I'd explain it to any of them, and of course I couldn't. So, slowly I began to settle back into myself.

The door opened with a groan, and Andy came out. "I'm glad you didn't shoot her."

"I am... was tempted."

"I know. Me, too."

"She thinks we should let her go. Says she'll leave town, we'll never see her again. What do you think?" Linda gave him a hopeful look.

"I think what you think," said Andy. He turned to Linda, who was now beginning to seriously shiver. "Not a snowball's chance in hell. You're going to jail, with creeps just like you, who won't treat you very well. In fact, you'll get a taste of some of this action," he gestured at the cabin, "for yourself."

Linda leaned forward, nearly animated, shivering, jabbing at the air with her pipe stem. "You know what? I'll never see jail. I'm an attractive white woman and she's just an Indian. Nobody cares about her. Nobody cares about any of these little brown women. I'll tell them how she was a pervert and came on to me... how I was horrified and it made me snap. Nobody will blame me. And if that *doesn't* work, I'll just make them think I'm crazy and they won't put me in prison. They'll put me in a hospital. Sure, I'll be locked up, but safe in a clean, warm room. I'll have nurses in white uniforms, not guards. In a couple of years, I'll let them see that I'm actually sane. They'll turn me loose, and chalk me up in their win column. I'll be *cured,* one of their successes. They'll *brag* about me!" By then she had put the pipe back in her mouth, and finished up her little fantasy by swiping her hands together, like 'job well done.'

She was right. In a heartbeat, I knew she was right. She might spend a little time inside but mostly she'd get off. She was bright, pretty, articulate, a jury would eat her up. And I could tell by the look on Andy's face that he knew it, too. Marjorie, and God knows how many other women were dead. Molly would be lucky not to have nightmares her whole life, and this woman was already looking forward to how she'd get off and get back at it.

"Except you're not sane," I said. "No sane person would do these things you do. If this works out, if they send you to some hospital somewhere, I'm going to dedicate myself to making sure you spend the rest of your life there."

She looked at me. "Ha!"

I wondered where God was in all this, how he could allow such an evil creature to walk among us and

308

seemingly thrive. Standing there staring at Linda, I knew I'd have to let her back into the cabin, let her get some clothes on, get her back to town. But then I saw a strange expression darken Linda's face, like a shifting cloud quickly blocks the sun. I saw it like it happened slowly, which it didn't.

She jerked her head to look at something behind me, blond hair swinging. Her eyes widened as her expression changed from surprise to... fear. She started to step back just as I heard a *zip*. A small black hole appeared in her forehead, with a spray of red out behind, catching the light. Her eyes closed, her head rolled, and she tipped back, falling full length toward the snow before I fully heard the sharp crack of the rifle. She hit the snow all loose-limbed, dead already, and sank. From a few yards back, invisible.

As I turned, Molly, only half dressed, set down the rifle. She shook her head. "No hospital." She pulled on Linda's t-shirt, visibly shuddering as she did, having to smell Linda's body scent, deodorant and cologne on herself. I saw her begin to retch, then fight it back. Linda had shredded Molly's clothing, and now Molly would have to walk back to town in hers. Linda's final abuse. It was that or freeze. Andy and I left Linda where she'd fallen, went into the cabin and closed the door, and—when Molly had gotten herself dressed—the two of us put our arms around her, holding her as she finally let herself cry.

* * *

Jacobs shook his head. I had hoped he'd see it sensibly. He didn't. I'd imagined his reassuring 'No problem.' Instead he said, "Not good."

I'd been awake too much of the night, sitting up drinking coffee and talking with Evie, worrying, imagining what might happen, what could happen, and what would happen. In my heart, I thought it would probably all turn out okay. Evie thought it wouldn't and she had an idea. Luckily, I listened to her.

As expected, Jacobs flew in with his assistant at first light, to snowshoe with Andy, Molly, Evie, and me, back out to the cabin. We found it very chilly and mostly undisturbed.

I had blessed the body, not wanting to, and then we dragged her inside, leaving a vivid trail of red blood in the snow. During the night, animals—probably wolves—had come to lick the blood away. As we had moved the body, it was Molly who saw Linda's straight-stemmed pipe in the snow and picked it up. Holding it away from herself, pinching it between index finger and thumb like it had been soiled, she carried it in and set it on one corner of the table.

We returned to find Linda as we left her, except now frozen rigid, covered with the tarp from the toboggan. It was the same tarp she used to conceal Molly on the sled that early morning. She lay stretched out neatly on the rough planked floor, legs straight and arms at her sides, easy to pick up and load into the body bag. The very first body I'd had to move in Chandalar had been frozen spread-eagled, very awkward and difficult to bring home by dogsled. Linda, we'd bring back easily on her own toboggan.

Jacobs looked around, inside and out. He collected and examined the guns, as well as examining the dead-woman's wound, all the while shaking his head and clucking. Finally, he turned to us. "This isn't good." Evie put a protective arm around Molly's shoulders.

I met his eyes. "How so? She tortured Molly and would have killed her."

310

"Molly didn't kill Linda until you'd subdued her. That won't pass for self-defense. Molly no longer had to fear for her life." He waved a hand in the direction of the frozen corpse. "Just for a minute, imagine the trial. It will be a jury of Linda's peers, not Molly's. They will be mostly men from within fifteen miles of Fairbanks—not here—maybe a woman or two and no Indians. Prosecutor will say Molly came on to Linda... or Vic... lured her... wanted sex, just like Marjorie. They'll make it sound like Linda, a decent white woman, just snapped. Went temporarily insane at such perversion. Then they'll suggest that Linda's life as an upstanding white professional was worth a whole bunch more than *any* of her victims, or all her victims, including Molly. And you know what? I hear the Territorial Legislature is about to do away with capital punishment. Otherwise—being Native—there's a good chance Molly would hang."

I stepped back without meaning to, and must have changed expression. He held up his hands.

"Don't look at me like that. I'm just telling you what they'll say... what they've said before. That jury might have given *Linda* insanity, or a little prison time. But the same jury will give *Molly* at least murder two and lock her up for a long time, and put little Henry out for adoption."

There was a long minute of silence in the icy room. I looked at Andy who looked back at me.

"I killed her." Andy and I both said it, nearly as one.

The marshal blinked and took a step back. "Oh, swell." He looked from Andy to me. "You guys are just killin' me here."

Molly pushed herself out from under Evie's protective arm and came to stand in front of Jacobs. She pointed at her own chest with her moose hide mitt. "I killed her. No

311

one else. I shot her because she hurt me, did terrible things to me, and would have killed me. I shot her and I'm not sorry. I'm glad. She deserved to die." She turned to look at Andy then at me, to make sure we all understood. "*I* killed her. You can't take this away from me."

Before we went out, Jacobs turned to us. "You did the best you could here. Look, I know this woman was a monster. The town... everybody... is better off for it. But, you know me. I've got to do it right, follow the evidence." He shrugged.

"I know," I said, and Andy patted him on the shoulder. His was a hard place to be.

Jacobs didn't arrest Molly. "We know where you are," he told her, "and who you're with," with an eye to me. "I'll catch heck about this from the judge, but better for you to be here with Henry. If I arrest you, then we all got to worry about how to care for him." He took Linda's body in its black, rubberized-canvas body bag, with all the evidence and flew back to Fairbanks to set the wheels of justice—or injustice—turning. The last thing he said, "See that she's here when we need her."

"Sure," I promised, "she'll be here." But I didn't mean it.

As we left the cabin, Andy looked around to where Linda's pipe lay on the table. He looked at the pipe then at me and didn't say anything. But I knew he was wondering. We had both seen Molly set it there yesterday, intact.

Overnight, someone had smashed it flat.

CHAPTER 35

Vic had been surprised to see me that night, no doubt expecting Linda. He even peered around me into the yard to see if she might be standing there. Or coming along behind, as though we were both coming home late from choir practice. After a moment's hesitation, he let me in and watched as I climbed out of my parka, mitts, and muffler, grabbing a prayer book from my pocket to hold in my hand, and sat in the armchair Vic offered.

We were in their teacherage apartment at nearly midnight. He sat humped over in an easy chair, under a brass lamp with a green glass shade. Uncharacteristically disheveled, he wore a plaid flannel robe over rumpled clothes and fiddled with a cold corncob pipe.

"Uh..." he said, "Linda had to make a run to Fairbanks."

I shook my head. "No." I saw something shift behind his eyes. "I know where Linda is and what she's been doing. And it's over." He didn't say anything, didn't protest—didn't look surprised—just sat there looking at his feet. I let him.

He looked up. "So, you know." I nodded. He looked at me with his earnest expression in place. "I didn't know it was her. Really."

He sniffed, seeming near tears. "But after a while I began to suspect. One reason we left Seattle was the murders, not too far from our neighborhood. The victims were mostly Indian or Negro women, sometimes prostitutes but sometimes just women on the way home from low-paying jobs, found tortured, molested, and dead." He looked up. "It was Linda who suggested we move. Then after we found Marjorie, I remember thinking how odd it was, that here were these killings again. We *hadn't* left them behind. I even said it to her, "'Isn't it odd?' And she agreed. And then after a while..."

"You put it all together."

"I didn't want to. I tried not to."

"What gave her away?"

He made a glum face. "A couple of things. One day when she was gone, I found a little bottle with an eyedropper, stuffed behind books on a shelf. One of those little brown medicine bottles? The label was hand-written... it said KO drops.

"Knock out?"

"That's what I thought. I walked around wondering about it until I realized that every time one of these prowler things happened, I slept through it. She was always making cocoa for me in the evening." He considered. "It was always one of the things I thought I loved about her, that she was so considerate. Then stupid me would wake up the next morning feeling sick and awful, to find that something terrible had happened.

"At first I thought she might just be having an affair, doping me and sneaking out to meet someone. I think she might have wanted me to think that. She made a big deal about Myles Conway down at the bar, like she might have something going on with him—or want to—but I knew that wasn't happening. I knew she couldn't risk revealing what she really was. Conway would have had a field day with her."

"What else?"

"Well, I... one night I came home and found her reading one of those bondage magazines. I'd never even seen one before. Women get tied up, beaten, raped, tortured... I found her reading one in bed, naked, fully aroused... erect. She has..." he said with difficulty, "a penis."

"Yes," I said, "I know." That bothered him. He shook it off.

"I didn't know she even could be aroused... like a man. That made it all pretty clear. We never even tried to have sex again." His voice faded off. "I used to really love her... didn't mind that her *equipment* was scrambled. But of course, that wasn't all. Turns out she was a monster, like a sphinx, one of those half-animal creatures that tears a human to pieces. I know I feel torn to pieces, so it must be true."

I looked at him. "So that's going to be your story?" I asked. He shrugged and looked pathetic. Successfully.

"What do you mean?"

"You're going to be explaining all this to Frank Jacobs in the morning. You need to work out details, like... when she called *me* over because of the prowler, it was *you* in the bushes, shooting. And it was you that night, outside of Evie's, shooting and running. It was you across the river at the shooting range. You've been involved in this right along, right up to your eyeballs."

He smiled sadly. Didn't say anything, just smiled. It made me shiver.

"Prove it."

"Let's start with this. Linda isn't your wife, she's your sister."

"She's my wife."

"So, you married your sister. Probably your twin."

He shrugged. "Fraternal." As if it somehow made a difference. "No harm if you don't have kids. If you really did see her, you know that's not happening."

I couldn't help shaking my head. "I can accept that she was crazy, but what about you?"

He leaned forward, posing, gripping his pipe. "These women... brown women, black women, they're not like us." His voice had an earnest quality, like he might be able to explain or somehow convince me. "If more people knew what we were doing, they might even thank us."

I couldn't keep the disbelief from my face. "Cruelty isn't a democratic process. It doesn't become right just because more cruel people agree with you."

His face darkened and attitude changed. He sat back. "It's just you and me here. I don't suppose you could just let me walk away?"

"She said that, too."

He looked around again as if he might see her, even rose a little to look out the window into the night. "Where is she, by the way, where are you keeping her? I need to see her."

I just looked at him, a bit of my own cruelty stirring. "She's still out at your cabin... naked and dead on the floor, covered with a tarp... by now..." I looked at my watch, "probably mostly frozen."

He grimaced, shocked, horrified. "Dead! You *killed* her?" His expression changed. "You're joking, right?" He squeezed his eyes shut but one tear escaped from each.

I shook my head. "The last time I saw her she had a little bullet hole, right here." I touched a point between my eyes.

"You shot her?"

"I didn't, but she's dead, just the same. This is all over. She's gone, and you're left to pay the tab... all by yourself."

His shoulders began to shake with real crying. "I know it was wrong."

"But...?"

"But I loved her," he sobbed. "I always loved her. She was born three minutes before me. I always thought of her as my big sister. She always knew what to do. Always made things safe."

"She was insane, you must have known, and yet you helped. You were... a team."

"What could I do? Would you turn in Evie if you found out she was doing... something... wrong?"

"In a heartbeat."

"But, I thought you loved her."

"I do. And I'd have some bad nights. Cruel is still cruel. Wrong is still wrong. Torture and murder are still those things."

He wiped his eyes on his sleeve and sat up straighter.

"So... what is it you think you're going to do with me?" I heard the implicit threat.

But I shook my head. "Not a thing. I'm going to leave you here to think about your life. To wait for the marshal. To consider whether they'll hang you. I'm betting *yes*. It's tough being the one that gets left behind."

He stood and, in the reflection of a buffet mirror, I could see the hunting knife in its sheath at the center of his back. He nodded at my prayer book. "You honestly think that book will stop me from finishing you, taking your truck, driving away?"

I looked up at him. "I *don't* think you'll finish me because... we've been friends. I think we've really been friends. I don't think you've had that many friends in your life.

"And now you're on your own. Now finally, you only have to answer to yourself. *You* get to choose. You and Linda have been making bad choices together since childhood. With her gone, you have the opportunity to choose to do the right thing, instead."

He smiled faintly. "You're so *you*," he said.

"No. The truth is, you're down to the last hours and minutes of life as you've known it. You have the opportunity to do the decent thing... to hand me that knife—handle first—and then to sit here like a man and wait for Frank Jacobs to show up in the morning."

He bent his face into what was supposed to be a smile. "I'm standing here with a knife and," he nodded again at the prayer book, "you're going to hold me off with what? A prayer?"

"Probably seems crazy," I told him, "but it's what I do... what I'm good at." He stared at me then reached back to grab the knife from its sheath. The thing was huge, a Bowie-style knife with a bone handle, heavy brass finger guard, and about eight inches of gleaming steel blade, looking even longer from where I sat. It was a real carving tool and he held it firmly, his wrist twisting and hand shifting as light played across the blade.

I felt my breath catch and struggled to appear unmoved. Evie told me not to come alone, to bring someone. To bring her with a gun. But I'd turned her down. Now, I felt sweat break on the surface of my skin in one instant, though the room still felt cool. I made myself take a deep, steadying breath.

"Make the right choice," I told him. "You can do this."

He took a step forward and I resisted flinching with difficulty. I could see by his eyes he'd made his choice. Here it came.

He reversed the handle, handing the knife to me, and I began to breathe again. Unbuckling his belt, he slid the sheath loose, handing it to me. "You'll need this, too. Wouldn't want you to cut yourself on the way home.

"You're right about friends," he said, as I stood to grab my parka. "You and Andy are the first real friends of my life. No sense making that end badly."

He followed me to the door and didn't offer to shake hands, which was a relief. I didn't want to shake hands with a man I now knew to be a monster, even if we had been friends. And I didn't want to have to fumble with the .38 I held under the prayer book.

* * *

I drove home in a funk. Not surprisingly, Evie was waiting. Yes, we'd found the killer... *killers*. We'd also lost people we'd come to think of as friends and helpers. Both Vic and Linda had always been active, seemingly good-spirited, willing to help out at the church, willing to build and do. I thought of him hunting with us and helping to fix the mimeograph.

"Remember when they both helped with cleanup, and construction of Marjorie's wall?"

Evie looked up from a magazine she'd been not reading. "Yes, I remember that. But Linda had already killed her, hadn't she? After Vic made her feel safe and lured her home."

"Most likely."

"Poor little Marjorie."

Evie looked up, meeting my eyes. "I'm glad Linda's dead. Honestly, I wish they both were and this was really over."

I agreed. "I think we're mostly *relieved*. This dark thing that's been hanging over us is finally finished." And it was.

In the morning, the school janitor drove over with news. When Vic didn't show up for school, they went to check his place, forced the door, and found him hanging.

* * *

Although there was pressure from Fairbanks to arrest Molly, the marshal resisted. *The Daily News Miner* lamented the Territory's loss of a "professional educator," but balanced it off with the fear of local women and the alleged connection to a high-profile Stateside case.

According to Frank Jacobs, we had at least a month to wait before reports came back from the Federal crime lab in Seattle, and he would be ready to charge Molly, or not. It seemed we all made preparation for the outcome in our own unique ways.

Evie began researching similar criminal cases, their findings and outcomes. She went to Fairbanks on the train, just to use the University law library. Meals with her became legal briefing sessions, some quite passionate and hard on the digestion.

For my purposes, I called the bishop and asked him to find a defense attorney. A good one. He said he would, and I was confident. He knew an amazing range of highly-qualified professional people, both in Alaska and elsewhere. People who would contribute their time. In short order, he called back. "I have one. One of the best. But he's in Boston."

Even so, I went ahead and told Molly she would be well represented, but found that she was making her own preparations. She asked me to come back by and bring Evie, which I did, midmorning on a Saturday.

I knocked on her sturdy door, the one Andy and I had installed, and heard her slide the bolt and shift the bar. After her ordeal, she was taking no chances. But she opened it readily, so I knew she had seen us approach. She still kept the .410 handy.

There were only two chairs in the cabin. She sat us in those at the table, served us tea, then pulled up a proper-sized wooden keg to sit with us. I sensed this was business. She didn't smile, and as she looked up from her tea, a tear streaked down each cheek.

"When they send me away, they will take Henry."

Evie shook her head and reached across the table to cover Molly's hand. "They're not going to send you away." I knew she was trying to be encouraging, but a prison term seemed likely.

Molly smiled slightly. "I know you two love each other. Everybody knows. It is like a light that shines between you."

I felt embarrassed and like I should say something, but didn't know what to say. She went on. "I want you two to raise Henry. I know you'll keep him safe, and save him for me, if I... when I come back."

Evie looked at me, but not much. "Of course, we will." It wasn't enough. Molly turned her serious gaze on me.

"You, too?"

I looked at Evie then back to Molly. "Of course, we will. But..." Molly waved me off, shaking her head.

"I need a plan."

"Yes," I agreed. "Of course. We'll keep him safe."

She had begun boxing his things, two smallish boxes, and she showed us where they were. We each hugged her as we left, small as a child, but now with eyes old and sad looking.

"This can't happen," I said to Evie as we walked up the trail.

"Sure, it can. And it probably will. That's why it's all so upsetting."

That night, I told Andy about agreeing to take Henry. He wasn't surprised. "So now you're a dad."

"Maybe."

"Scared?"

"Not for myself. Although I haven't had much chance to think about it. I've always thought being a dad would happen, wanted to have kids, and thought it would be a good thing. I'm just worried about Molly."

That's when he told us about *his* plan. He'd already contacted our old friend, Captain Simon Nicholai, west of here out along the Yukon. Simon had readily agreed to take Molly on, hide her, keep her safe, and at some point, get someone to guide her over the border into northern Canada. "It isn't the best plan, isn't the best life, but it's better than prison or a rope. It'll go easier if you and Evie keep Henry 'til she gets settled."

I didn't think it was such a great idea, to make her a permanent fugitive, but wasn't prepared to argue against it. The idea of someone like Molly locked up, almost permanently kept indoors, far from here, would be hell right here on earth. She didn't deserve it. I wasn't sure she could survive it.

"I can't blame him for thinking of it," I said to Evie.

We were standing in my kitchen when she stepped close—almost too close for me to focus—and looked into my eyes. "Did you tell him what we did?"

I shook my head. "I didn't. I thought the fewer who know, the better."

She nodded. "Good."

* * *

The report came back a month to the day from when the evidence had shipped. Jacobs called me. "I've got it—the lab report. I'm flying down. Be there in about an hour. You get everybody together. I don't want to have to go over this twice."

And that was it, no hints, no clues. Evie volunteered to drive over to get Molly and Henry and to stop by Andy's cabin to let him know. I called William and Rosie, who had asked to be here. Then I went out into my kitchen and set up for coffee, watching through the kitchen window as the day brightened or darkened with passing clouds—much like life—and listened to my Krazy Kat Klock tick.

We were all in place before Jacobs arrived, including Molly and Henry with his cardboard boxes. In fact, we heard the Cessna circle then bank into the wind and swoop down for a landing on river ice. It took about twenty minutes for Jacobs to tie down the airplane, plug in the oil heater, and trudge up the riverbank and across the tracks.

I greeted him as he walked in with a quick knock. He sniffed the air and smiled a bit. "Ahh, coffee," then shrugged out of his heavy gear and walked into the living room, not surprised to see us all in place.

He dropped into his favorite chair and accepted a coffee mug from Evie. "Just the way I like it." It was a joke. We all knew how he liked it: hot, wet, and dark. Or any way he could get it. But we smiled.

He looked around, nodded, then climbed out of the chair and crossed the room to go down on one knee to take Molly's hands in his. "I'm so sorry for all you've been

323

through." She nodded at him with a serious look but didn't say anything. When he got settled back in his chair he held up several pages of typewritten document and looked around the room, meeting all eyes.

"No surprises here. Suspect Linda Huxton died instantly as the result of a .22 caliber projectile fired deliberately, point-blank range into the center of her forehead. Her own rifle. Open and shut." He looked around again, as if daring objection.

"You all know what my job requires. But I want to be very clear about this. And I want *you* to be very clear."

None of that sounded encouraging.

"I don't get to play this my way. It doesn't matter how I feel about Molly, or Vic, or anybody. I collect the evidence, send it to the lab, and ultimately, I take it to the inquest or the trial, and present what I found. That's it. Does everybody understand that?"

We did. There were nods, no smiles. We knew him to be thorough and fair, a good guy. But I could see him setting this up. There could be no discussion, no argument.

"So, here's how it went. First..." he looked from Andy to me, "I know you guys are not lawmen, and you're usually not careless. But you let this one get away from you. You could have prevented this."

That stung. I wanted to protest. We did *everything* we could. I could see Andy felt the same, but we kept our mouths shut. This wasn't about us.

"You apprehended suspect Linda Huxton in the middle of a vicious attack on Miss Molly Joseph," he went on, partly reading. It was the last in a series of more than twenty attacks on women, culminating in eighteen separate first-degree murder charges, here and in Washington State. Two more victims suspected, but bodies never recovered." Jacobs looked up from his papers. "She may have had one or two good qualities, but she was a vicious, stone-cold killer. Vic, too."

He let the information settle, then took a deep breath and let it out slowly. This would be it. I felt my heart rate tick up and reached out to take Evie's extended hand.

Jacobs cleared his throat and read on. "The afternoon of January 24th, near the town of Chandalar, Territory of Alaska, suspect Linda Huxton did viciously kidnap and attack Miss Molly Joseph with murderous intent. She was interrupted and apprehended by two local men, Chandalar Episcopal priest, Father Hardy, and Mr. Andrew Silas. Without a doubt, they saved the life of Molly Joseph.

"Evidence will show that while the two men were distracted, caring for the victim, Huxton picked up a loaded .22 caliber rifle and managed to fatally wound herself. The fingerprint evidence on the suspect rifle is incontrovertible. Incontrovertible." He said it again, as if making certain we understood. Then he looked up, looked straight into my eyes.

"You guys dropped the ball on this one. You took your eyes off her and she killed herself." And then he added, "End of discussion."

CHAPTER 36

George Attla, the Huslia Hustler, won his first Anchorage Fur Rendezvous dogsled championship in March. I told Teddy Moses, our local musher—who hadn't done so well—that maybe he'd do better if he had a nickname.

"Tenth-Place Teddy?" he suggested, clearly still blue about the results.

On that Saturday afternoon, Evie and I drove to Nenana, walking down to the river to watch them build and set the big log tripod for the Ice Classic. Each log was painted alternating black and white, to enhance visibility on ice from the shore. Four angled posts, their bases frozen into river ice, supported a center post standing about sixteen feet tall. From the top of that center post, a cable would soon be attached to a clock on the shore. When Breakup began and the ice traveled at least twenty feet, the clock would stop. Whoever guessed the day, hour, and minute the clock stopped, would go home several hundred thousand dollars richer. Evie and I each bought a ticket. The average, since it all started in 1909, was May 7, so I chose that date.

She waved her ticket. "I feel really good about this one. Maybe we should buy airplane tickets for Hawaii, pay ourselves back with our winnings!"

"That sounds good." I began to imagine the two of us together on a warm beach, her wearing a two-piece yellow swimsuit. "That sounds really good." I must have sounded too enthusiastic. She gave me a suspicious look. "But I think we should hold off on spending our winnings until they are winnings."

"Killjoy!"

Back in Chandalar, we found Andy waiting in my kitchen. Confident we'd show, he'd been reading a magazine article about how to tell if you're sensitive enough for a relationship. He'd even taken the quiz. "I'm definitely ready," he told us, having scored the full ten points for sensitivity. He'd brought more of the Italian roast and when he heard us come through the door, he lit the burner to boil water.

We hadn't seen him since the marshal's visit. He looked happy and prosperous and said the restaurant continued well. He'd be seeing Rosie later, but wanted to "pop over," to see us first. His face wore an intent look I recognized.

But it wasn't until we had coffee made and poured, and were seated across from him at my kitchen table, that he spoke up.

Skipping the preamble, he looked at me across his coffee mug. "I think I finally got this figured out. You went back out there that night, didn't you." It wasn't really a question.

"Not me," I told him, sliding my arm through Evie's. "We. It was all Evie's idea."

"Ahhh," he said, as if that explained something.

All the way back into town that afternoon, I remember trying to soothe Evie. "It will all work out. Jacobs will handle it."

"I don't know," she kept saying.

Just over the railroad tracks, back in town, we had pulled off our snowshoes and were walking the freshly plowed street back toward my place. I was hungry after all that trouble, all that snowshoeing, rambling dully on about what to fix for dinner, when she grabbed my arm, stopping and turning me.

"But, what if Jacobs doesn't handle it? What if he can't? What happens to Molly and to Henry? By then it will be too late."

I shook my head. After an absurdly long and genuinely terrible day, in addition to hungry, I felt upset and even a little cranky. What I wanted to do was get home and be done with this. Worse, I still had to visit the new widower and confront him.

Turning to Evie, I said, "So, what's *your* idea? What do *you* want to do?" And she told me.

About an hour later, after a quick snack, we found ourselves back on snowshoes and back on the trail headed south. We'd started out that morning before sunrise, and then started out all over again after sunset. It made for a long day.

The night was cool, mid-minus thirties, and the sky as clear and black as a sky can be, glittered with stars. Behind us to the north, Polaris blazed at the pole of the Big Dipper. Evie pointed a mitt skyward.

"You know you can tell time by the rotation of the Dipper?"

I turned to follow her point. "I didn't. So, what time is it?"

"I don't know," she said. "I didn't say *I* could do it. Let's see, early March, I guess the dipper is vertical at about midnight and spins counter clockwise." She looked around and smiled at me, just visible in the glow. "Right now is definitely sometime before midnight."

"Glad we got that worked out." We pressed on.

I couldn't help thinking—worrying, really—about what we were doing: conspiring to conceal a killing from the marshal and the justice system. We both felt strongly that Linda had deserved to die and that Molly didn't—after all she'd been through—deserve to sacrifice a part of her life for it.

But behind all that, I didn't want to go out there again, to the death scene. I didn't want to have to look at the frozen naked body of someone we'd considered a friend. Didn't want to have to handle the body—and we would—didn't want to deceive a friend, Frank Jacobs. And of course, I didn't want us to get caught. I could imagine myself trying to explain it all to the bishop. Actually that would be easy. I had a hunch, in the same situation, he'd be doing the same thing.

So, by starlight we followed the dim gray line of our snowshoe tracks back south across the flats. How far? I'm still not sure. Not more than five miles, really. The 'dread factor' made it all harder and feel farther.

We found the cabin as we'd left it, snow shrouded, dark and silent. The door remained shut tight and pinned by a bit of branch stuck in the rusty padlock hasp. And we found the earthly remains of Linda Huxton waiting to help us protect Molly. It was the one thing left she could do to help make amends for the living hell she'd made of her own life and tried to make of Molly's.

Her thinner parts, hands in particular, that lay frozen and rigid, could be thawed, we reasoned. We knew her to be right-handed, so took turns warming that palm with our own hands, trying to get her skin surface to soften enough to leave an imprint. Because that's what we were about: making sure when they dusted the rifle for fingerprints, they found hers.

Working by flashlight, wearing light-weight gloves, Evie wiped down the .22, making sure to include the trigger. Then, as carefully as we could, we pressed the dead woman's icy hand against the stock, and her finger on the trigger and on the trigger guard. Yes, it was a long shot, but it was also our only shot.

Finally, glad to be finished, we covered the body, taking a last look around at the torture scene, with the braided, knotted rope ends still hanging where Andy had cut them. Standing by the table with the rifle in her mitted hands, Evie looked down at the straight-stemmed pipe Linda had been smoking, even as she tortured her victim.

"Damn you!" she shouted suddenly, her voice hard as a hammer. She drove the rifle butt down on the pipe, smashing it to pieces. Then more softly, she leaned the rifle in a corner, and we went out, repinning the hasp, snowshoeing back down the trail to town.

Our spirits lightened on the way home and we became, for the first time that day, a bit hopeful. Would it fool the lab or the marshal? Would it come back on us? In that moment, we didn't know, and didn't care. We'd done it for Molly and it seemed a chance well worth taking.

* * *

"I thought so." Andy took a sip from his coffee cup, which turned out to be empty. He'd already taken the last sip while we were telling our story. He did a double take at the empty mug then got up for a refill. Still standing, he toasted us with his filled mug. "Good job. Here's to you!"

We couldn't help smiling and feeling good about it, and mostly feeling good that it was now in our past.

"But what about this?" asked Andy. "How did Vic manage to smash his own forehead with a board, and leave a mark?"

"You don't know?" I asked.

"No. Do you?"

"I didn't for a while," I confessed. "In its way, it was a lucky break for him."

Andy took a sip of his hot coffee, pausing to taste it before swallowing. "Well, yeah, when I saw how hard he got walloped, it never occurred to me to not believe him. But how?"

"Here's what I think," I said. "Both Vic and Linda were out there that night. When Molly blasted off a shot at Linda, right through her door, he went running around that shed of hers, trying to get out of sight and out of the line of fire."

"Yeah?"

"So, Vic was what—six or seven inches taller than you or me. *We* never need to duck under anything, but with his height, plus running on snow buildup, he smashed his forehead full force into one of the shed's rafter ends. Darn near gave himself a concussion. Then all he had to do was stagger back out to collapse under the streetlight where we could find him. As I say, lucky."

Evie had been listening, head down. "As long as you're clearing things up, tell me this. He had so many opportunities to shoot you, but—for a long time—never did. How could he miss shooting you that many times?"

"In his heart of hearts, I don't think he really wanted to shoot me. Truth is, he liked me. He even said so later. I just kept getting in his, and Linda's way."

Andy said it, and we all agreed. "She was one sick, sick sucker."

Our eyes met. "They both were."

CHAPTER 37

With all the trouble done, and life comfortably back to predictable and normal, I did something I'd never done before. I threw a party.

I didn't let Evie help me, or Andy, or Rosie, though any of them would have. I'd been thinking about this party for a long time and felt it was important to do it all myself.

Andy and Rosie showed up early, just in case. Then Evie. She came in, looked around at the way I'd cleaned up and fixed up, sniffed the air, dinner cooking. "Mmm, good smells!" Then she kissed me warmly, fondly.

Oliver arrived, Butch and Adele, William and Alice, and finally, Molly with Henry. I presented Henry with a wooden train, one of a pair of things I'd ordered from Sears, especially for tonight. His eyes grew round, he put his hands over his mouth and looked, as if to verify, at his mother. She nodded. He couldn't believe his good fortune and didn't need any more encouragement to get down on the floor and drive it around through legs and furniture, making train noises. I'd seen his two small boxes and knew he didn't have many toys.

I had fixed a big moose roast, with potatoes and peas on the side, used my Betty Crocker cookbook to make gravy. It worked! For dessert, I baked a cake from scratch, and made Crocker's seven-minute frosting.

I did get help moving a table and extra chairs over from the parish hall, that we set up in my living room, big enough to seat everybody.

Dinner was delicious. Cooking-wise, my finest hour. Then Andy presided over coffee-making, and when it came time, I carried in the cake. There were plenty of *oohs* and *aahs*, and I felt so... competent.

Andy fetched me a long knife from the kitchen. "Time to cut the cake?"

"Not yet." Surprised, he made a face, his eyebrows raising the question.

I'd been practicing for this moment, anticipating and dreading. It felt more public than I like to be, but...somehow these people had become my family.

I tapped on my water glass with my butter knife, and everybody quieted. Nervous, I stood.

"You all are my friends. Knowing you, I feel so... lucky." Then I turned to Evie, who cocked her head and looked up at me, curious.

"Knowing you," I said to Evie, "my *best* friend, I feel enriched, transformed, truly blessed. I took her hand and, holding it, dropped to one knee. I took a breath. "Evie, will you marry me?"

Clearly surprised, she smiled. "That's easy. Sure! I will be so happy to marry you." She looked around, as if to say, "That's done."

I pulled out the ring box, *Sears* embossed on the lid, opened it and slid a silver ring with a small, raised diamond onto her left ring finger. It went smoothly, fitting perfectly, and she looked stunned. She held it out and up, admiring the way her hand looked wearing it. As I stood, she smiled up at me, the lovely smile that, I'm sure would both launch ships and stop traffic. Everyone clapped and cheered.

I held up a hand. "One more thing," and I couldn't help a quick glance at Molly before I smiled at Evie. "I've *decided* to ask the bishop if he can be available Sunday, June twelfth... if you are."

Her eyes glistened. "Oh Hardy," she said softly.

333

ABOUT THE AUTHOR

Photo by V. Judy

A NOTE FROM THE AUTHOR

Dear Reader,
If you enjoyed this book, would you please go to Amazon.com or Goodreads under 'Jonathan Thomas Stratman' and write a quick review? I'd appreciate it very much!

You can also check out my Facebook page:
Jonathan Thomas Stratman, Author. A "Like" would be very helpful, too.

Thanks!

Jonathan

P.S. *Without a Prayer*—**Book 5** in the Father Hardy Mystery Series will be available in 2018.